THE STONE OF EBENEZER

THE
STONE OF
EBENEZER

BOOK I: TRILOGY OF KINGS SAGA

SUSAN VAN VOLKENBURGH

Creek Bluff Digital books may be ordered through booksellers or by contacting:

Creek Bluff Digital
9005 County Road 302
Kaufman, TX 75142
www.creekbluff.com
1 (817) 427-8755

Second Edition – Revised by the Author
Cover design – Susan Van Volkenburgh & Ron Van Volkenburgh
Map illustration – BMR Williams

ISBN: 978-0-9600755-3-9
ISBN: 978-0-9600755-4-6
ISBN: 978-0-9600755-5-3

Library of Congress Control Number: 2026932997

CREEK BLUFF DIGITAL REV. DATE: 2/10/2026

To all who have fought the good fight.

2 TIMOTHY 4:7

Then Samuel took a stone and set it up
between Mizpah and Shen,
and called its name EBENEZER, saying,
"Thus far the Lord has helped us."

1 SAMUEL 7:12

SIDONIANS
ARAM
N
W E
S
Sidon
Zarephath
Mt. Herman
Tyre
Iyyon
Abel-beth Macaah
Dan
The Great Sea
Hazor
Gennesaret
Sea of
Chinnereth
Mt. Carmel
Kishon R.
Mt. Tabor
Dor
Yarmuk R.
Ramoth-Gilead
Megiddo
En Dor
Jordan R.
Jazreel
Tishbe
AMMON
Taanach
Beth-shan
CANAAN
Mt. Gilboa
Penuel
Mt. Ebal
Zarethan
Pirathon
Shechem
Succoth
Mt. Gerizim
Yarkon R.
Eben-Ezer
Arumah
Jabbok R.
Aphek
Tappuah
Joppa
Shiloh
Lod
Aijalon R.
Jabneel
Aijalon
Bethel
Rabbah
Gezer
Mizpah
Sorek R.
Kirjath-Jearim
Ashdod
Gibeon
Ramah
Jericho
Heshbon
Ekron
Jebus
Mt. Nebo
Beth Shemesh
Elah R.
Askelon
Zephathah R.
Sochoh
Gath
Mareshah
Hebron
Salt Sea
PHILISTINES
En Gedi
Arnon R.
Gaza
Ziklag
MOAB
Beersheba
Zered River
EDOM
Tamar

CONTENTS

PART THE THIRD

FOREWORD

REV. JUDITH WEIGMAN

As I begin this Foreword, I am reminded of the call from Susan when she completed her manuscript, "The Stone of Ebenezer." Months before, she had contacted me to pray about writing the Foreword; a request that aroused a feeling of deep responsibility. I am a pastor, author, and faith writer columnist, but this was more than a writing assignment, more than a column for the newspaper, it was a call from Susan's heart to mine; one I accepted with feelings of immense humility.

Susan and I met when as a children's pastor, I taught her three children in a Dallas area church. Our mutual love for prayer, music, and writing bound our hearts and minds together as kindred spirits. One summer I learned of Susan's love for biblical, historical accuracy when she created booths for a children's vacation Bible school. The children were intrigued to step back in time and experience life in the little village of Nazareth where Jesus grew in *"wisdom, and stature and in favor with God and men."*[1]

I agonized with Susan and her family upon learning how deeply they were all wounded two years prior to our meeting in the powerful tragedy of September 11, 2001. They were forced to travel a journey, not of their choice, but theirs just the same. One of the passengers aboard American Airlines Flight 77 that hit the Pentagon was her

---

[1] Luke 2:52

father, Stanley R. Hall. I prayed diligently for her as she struggled to publish her first book, *Silent Resolve and the God Who Let Me Down*. I share her grief each time I pick up the book and re-read any portion.

During our times together, Susan would share about another "book" gathering momentum in her heart and head. As an author I could certainly relate and was not surprised when she completed her second work, *The Stone of Ebenezer*. Susan sent this message: "*I am sending the manuscript certified mail. It is always a frightening thing to put your manuscript in the mail. It is like sending your child away unsupervised.*" Her choice of words struck a memory in my thoughts as they wandered to an Old Testament mother who placed her child in a basket made of bulrushes and "sent him away" unsupervised. As the mother gave the basket a small push, she trusted God to provide a person who would receive the child and care for him.[2]

I could picture Susan as the manuscript left her hands in Texas headed for mine in Pennsylvania. It arrived! Overwhelmed by excitement, I signed for the treasured box. I held it in my hands, called immediately to announce its safe arrival and curled up in a sunny spot to begin an incredible journey that began long ago in Ancient Israel. A journey traveled by Old Testament characters, re-born in Susan's heart, now ready for anxious readers such as myself.

As I began to read, I envisioned the daunting task Susan faced as the overwhelming "I must write" feeling flooded her mind repeatedly in the early dawn. I marveled at the countless hours of research she logged in on this work. Her dedication allowed her to portray the events found in 1 Samuel chapters 4–7. Its amazing, vivid account of biblical events is historically accurate. The Bible states "*So the Philistines fought, and the Israelites were defeated and every man fled to his tent. The slaughter was very great; Israel lost thirty thousand foot soldiers. The ark of God was captured and Eli's two sons Hophni and Phinehas died.*"[3] God's judgments, treacherous journeys, blood battles and even romance come alive to the reader in this skillfully written epic story.

Portrayed in her book are characters brought forward from Old Testament antiquity and presented face to face for the reader to experience. This novel draws the reader to "be at home" in the

---

[2] Exodus 1:22–2:10

[3] 1 Samuel 4:10–11

Old Testament setting. Woven throughout its pages, the reader will readily see the hand of God as it moved in times past to protect the ark of God and the chosen children, Israel. It will allow the reader to grasp the fact that God's faithfulness to His Word in both blessing and judgment has not changed and can be claimed by us today.

I am honored to introduce this work by Susan Van Volkenburgh and to encourage her to pursue the completion of the series, *Trilogy of Kings Saga.*

PROLOGUE

Time was, when the world was young, that *El-Elohim*, the Creator, whose name is Yahweh, gathered together a people to call His own. A promise He gave to Abraham, the father of these children of men, chosen to be a race for His possession, a people begotten by faith. To this tribal band, the pledge was given to become a great nation, a multitude to prosper in a land endowed. Twelve tribes arose, emerging as descendants from this troth, an espoused lineage bound by the blood oath to their God. The children of Israel, as they came to be called, made a covenant, a sacred vow to walk always in the ways of their Creator.

But the deceitful hand of the Enemy was laid heavy upon the people; for he sought to cause the Chosen to stumble, and by works of darkness he led them astray. Disregarding the oath, the tribes rebelled against the dominion of Yahweh and turned from the path appointed of old. Soon they forgot the works of their Creator, pledging themselves to foreign deities. Dismissed by His people, Yahweh, banished, turned His face. A mighty nation arose, overpowering the Israelites and carrying them off into bondage, slaves in a distant land. Four hundred years passed. Hope withered. Time itself seemed to forget this chosen race, buried in the pits of despair. Egypt, it seemed, would be their doom.

Yet in the fullness of time, God beheld His people, and He heard their cries. His heart melted toward them; pity overtook His wrath, and He looked upon them once more. The Creator raised up a deliverer to lead His people out of Egypt. Moses guided the tribes of Israel through the wilderness of Paran and brought them into the land promised to them, a land flowing with milk and honey, the land of Canaan. Indeed, the word of the Creator proved true, for this people, restored to Yahweh's favor, became a mighty host and drove out the inhabitants of Canaan, establishing for themselves an ordained dwelling, and so they became a great nation.

As time wore on, this chosen band again turned from the ways of the Lord and followed after the Dark One. The pledge broken, the Enemy rose against them, casting a blight upon the people. The Chosen of Yahweh fell, torn from their Creator. Great was the sorrow of the Lord at the loss of His people's fidelity.

And in mercy, *El-Elohim* moved to redeem them, seeking to purchase His children back from their fall. He raised up judges to guide the Hebrew nation in His ways and to restore them to His favor.

For a time, the people returned, drawing close to their Deliverer, walking in His prescribed ways. But the Enemy lingered in the shadows, and by his cunning, he tempted the Israelites with the images of other gods. The chosen race turned away their face, finding delight in strange deities. In time, they succumbed, withdrawn from the One True God, and bowed down before the carved images, as the nations they had conquered had done. They took wives from among these heathen peoples.

It seemed all bonds of fellowship with their Creator were severed, and the God of Israel, rejected, would be forgotten by those He had lovingly formed and faithfully preserved.

Yet just as hope seemed to fade, a judge, Samuel, rose to lead Israel's children. Under his hand, the pagan images were torn down, and the Chosen cleansed themselves of their apostasy, returning to the favor of God.

But peace would not endure. A shadow and a threat were growing in the west. A Philistine host, like none before it, advanced upon the Promised Land. The scattered tribes of Israel grew unsettled, and terror overwhelmed them. And in this moment of fear, they took upon themselves that which should not have been taken.

PART THE FIRST

And the cherubim shall stretch out their wings above, covering the mercy seat with their wings, and they shall face one another; the faces of the cherubim shall be toward the mercy seat. You shall put the mercy seat on top of the ark, and in the ark you shall put the Testimony that I will give you. And there I will meet with you, and I will speak with you from above the mercy seat, from between the two cherubim which are on the ark of the Testimony, about everything which I will give you in commandment to the children of Israel.

EXODUS 25:20–22

CHAPTER 1

A DIRE NEED

The sun stood at its full height over the once lush valley, laid to ruin by the ravages of war, now a barren wasteland, littered with corpses and blood-soaked earth. It was early spring. Still, the heat bore down upon them. The reek of slaughter rose with the sweat of men, fouling the air with the breath of death.

Nagad's blade tore through flesh and bone. Warm spray struck his face. He staggered back. Before him, soldiers fled, bodies crumpled, smoke climbed heavenward.

Amid the tempest he stood, caught in a tide that threatened to swallow all. The air rang shrill with the sounds of battle: swords clashing, spears splintering, cries of the dying.

Overcome, Nagad retched.

From behind came the creak of leather and the scrape of metal. He spun round. A glint of iron flashed as a sword struck toward him. The young conscript raised his shield and caught the blow from the towering Philistine. The thrust glanced wide, yet the tip bit into his shoulder. Down his bare arm, warm blood trickled.

"Ha! Well, played, Hebrew," scoffed the enemy. "But you have been marked by my blade."

Nagad had no voice.

The Philistine lunged again. Nagad sidestepped and struck across the left flank.

The enemy recoiled, wrenching free of the blow. But his armor was thick, the sword turned aside, marring the breastplate, yet found no flesh. With a growl he swung down upon the young Hebrew. Nagad raised his shield to meet the blade, but his footing failed beneath the fury.

The Philistine pressed forward, driving him back. Size and experience served the enemy well. Nagad struggled to hold his ground. Their swords rang, the young conscript grunting with each desperate effort.

A heavy clout to the head sent him sprawling. He fell hard upon his side.

"It is enough," spat the enemy.

As he lifted his shield, Nagad pushed with his heels against the hard earth, scrambling backward.

The Philistine advanced upon his prey. Looming over the youth, he raised his sword.

"Away with you, dog!"

Lunging upward with all his strength, Nagad thrust his blade forward. The sword met its mark, its tip driving deep into the gut of his enemy.

The Philistine's eyes widened in surprise as he reached out, seizing Nagad by the arm. Slowly, the foe slumped to the ground, clinging to him.

Hate burned in the young Hebrew's blood, a rage not born in this moment. Nagad held the adversary's gaze as he drew his final breath.

"Nay—it is you who must be away."

Pushing the Philistine carcass aside, Nagad turned his gaze to the battle at hand. With shield and sword, he entered the fray. Clash for clash, the opposing lines meted out blows of equal valor, though one force held sway over the other.

The Philistine machine was vast, trained solely for war, its soldiers armed and arrayed for the fight. Even so, both sides wearied, for the battle grew long. Where the Hebrews lacked in skill and iron, they bore the weight of stubborn resolve.

So on the battle issued forth in endless contention, as the tide of men ebbed and flowed over the tarnished field.

Nagad struggled in the thick of battle, overwhelmed by the unbounded flood of enemies. As he struck one down, another rose to take the fallen's place. The young conscript wondered how much more he could endure. His breath came short. His sides ached from unbroken strife. Too long had the war waged for one so new and untried.

The protracted barrage covered a broad swath of earth astride the ruined valley—two hosts vying for the same land, the bitter dispute of fathers afore, passed down from timeworn days.

Wiping the back of his hand across his brow, Nagad turned, his eyes taking in the surge of battle that lay before him. Overhead, several ossifrages circled. Bone-breakers they were called, bearded vultures, biding their time to feast upon the flesh of the slain.

Below, winged shadows danced across the dying embers of smoldering fields and the umbral mounds of fallen men, a pirouette in silent song, toying with the cast down, waiting to descend.

Closing his eyes, the young soldier drew a long breath. In his heart, he knew he would never return to the man he had been. Nothing would ever be as it was ere the sights and sounds of death laid claim to his soul.

As he looked again across the field, a sharp breath seized him. Fear swept over him. In the fading light he beheld his captain kneeling, head bowed as in desperate prayer, leaning hard upon his sword. Hurrying to the weary warrior, Nagad laid a hand upon his shoulder.

"Tiphcar, my captain, are you injured?"

"Nay—the wind taken from me, only. The battle goes ill, my son."

Tiphcar rose with difficulty, defeat heavy in his eyes as he looked upon Nagad. A rivulet of blood trickled down the left side of his face.

Braced against the conscript, Tiphcar called over his shoulder, "Sound the retreat."

And so, the trumpet resounded, and the call went forth:

"Retreat! Retreat!"

Terror and confusion mounted as the Israelites flew from the field of battle. The Philistines pursued, driving the Chosen of God back toward their camp. But as the weary host neared Eben-Ezer, the enemy gave off the chase, for the day waned, and night grew heavy over the eastern hills.

Slowing at last, the Israelites entered the encampment and took refuge behind the barricade. With sullen faces the warriors gathered their wounded and reckoned the cost.

Nagad assisted Tiphcar to his tent. Within, he espied a chair and guided his captain to it, easing him down.

The shelter was held by two central poles, bearing a wide roof of black goat hair. At the center stood a table spread with maps. A simple oil lamp hung from one of the poles, casting its light across the room.

As Nagad stood gazing about the tent, the elders of the camp entered quietly, their heads bowed.

Tiphcar lifted his face. "What are our losses?"

"*Sar,* our best count is near four thousand dead and many more wounded."

Tiphcar released a weary sigh and lowered his head, shaking it in disbelief.

"*Sar* Tiphcar, what are we to do?" inquired one of the elders.

"Why has the Lord defeated us today before the Philistines?" asked another.

Silence settled over the room, the sorrow of the day sinking deep into the souls of the men. Slowly and with deliberation, one began to speak. Gadowl it was. There was cunning in his voice, and all met his words with uplifted eye.

"Was it not, in the day of Joshua, that the children of Israel fought many battles with the Ark of God going before them? And is it not so, that in every such battle, they prevailed?"

The elders nodded in agreement, murmuring among themselves.

"What is it that you propose, Gadowl?"

At the sound of the captain's voice, all murmuring ceased, for even after the wear of battle, Tiphcar's voice held strength enough to still them all.

Gadowl, the elder, bent his head slightly toward Tiphcar.

"Let us bring the Ark of the Covenant of the Lord from Shiloh to Eben-Ezer, that when it comes among us, it may save us from the hand of our enemies."

"This cannot be," spoke another elder. "The Ark of God has not left its seat in the Tent of Meeting since Joshua placed it there. This must never be."

Gadowl turned toward the one who had spoken.

"Zaqen, my brother, it is our only hope. Their numbers are too great, and their weapons too strong. There is no other way."

The debate continued for some time in like manner.

Forgotten, Nagad stood quietly by his captain, listening to all that was said. Without stirring, Tiphcar regarded the elders as they spoke among themselves with growing fervor.

Nagad knew not what to make of the scene before him, for never had he witnessed the council of elders in deliberation. As he watched Gadowl striving to persuade the others, a quiet unease rose within him.

There is something about this man that troubles my spirit.

Into his tunic he reached and drew forth an iron spearhead. Gazing into the palm of his hand, he ran his thumb along its edge, still sharp after these many years.

The clangor of arguing men faded, overtaken by the sound of a little girl's laughter. Sunlight gleamed upon her chestnut hair as she twirled through the golden wheat. She was a beautiful child, full of life and joy.

A raven cawed. The vision vanished. Nagad took in a sharp breath and closed his hand tightly over the spearhead.

"What do you say, Tiphcar?"

Nagad was pulled from his reverie, becoming aware of the address made to his captain. All eyes had turned to Tiphcar, awaiting his reply.

Slowly, Tiphcar, regarding Gadowl as he spoke, asked, "Are you certain this will work?"

"I am sure that with the Ark before us, the battle will be ours."

"Nagad."

Startled at the call of his name, Nagad stood straight and returned the spearhead to the folds of his tunic, slipping it into the little pocket sewn within the garment.

"Yes, *Sar* Tiphcar."

"You are swift of foot." It was a statement more than a question.

"Yes, *Sar.*"

"Tend to your wound, then run swift as you can to Shiloh. There, find the priests, Hophni and Phinehas. Tell them all that has transpired, of our urgent necessity. Tell them we require the Ark of the Covenant, or else all is lost. Go now."

"As you wish, *Sar* Tiphcar."

With that, Nagad took leave of the tent and left his captain behind. He had forgotten the wound dealt to his arm by the Philistine's sword. His left arm hung heavy, cloaked in a thick coat of blood, still flowing from the open gash.

Uncertain, Nagad stood surveying the camp, seeking the healer's tent. Never before had he occasion to seek it. Rows of tents stretched in ordered lines, too many to count, though he knew well that the Philistines' camp at Aphek stood far greater.

Impatience rose within him, burdened by the urgency of his charge. At length, he espied the tent of *Refu'ah*, the place of healing. He hastened toward it, passing rows of mats where wounded men lay. Many bore the signs of their trials: bandages marked with crimson stains. One moved among them, tending their needs, offering water to the thirsty and comfort to the dying.

Time pressed upon him, and the need for deliverance grew ever more dire. This would be the fate of all Israel, should he fail to retrieve the Ark—or if, having succeeded, he arrived too late. Then all would be as these men were, wounded and bleeding. The Philistines would show no mercy; all would perish, even to the last child.

Entering the tent, Nagad waited while a healer dressed the wound of a large soldier seated upon a table at the center of the room. Blood-soaked cloth and torn garments lay strewn across the floor.

When the soldier departed, Nagad stepped forward as the *rofe* cleaned the table.

Without looking up, the healer said, "Come. Up on the table."

Nagad obeyed.

Silently, the *rofe* worked. The young conscript watched the healer's skilled hands examine the injured arm. Silence grew long, and uncertainty stirred within him. He opened his mouth to speak, then stayed his speech, not wishing to disturb the careful tending.

Nagad returned his gaze to the healer's hands. The gash he washed with a mixture of wine and olive oil, infused with choice herbs. At first it stung, and Nagad flinched, but soon the pulsing pain abated, and a coolness spread over the wound.

An aromatic balm of Gilead he laid upon the torn flesh, then bound it with clean linen. Relief came as the discomfort in his arm eased. The healer's hands were gentle, and in his silence, there dwelt an empathy deeper than words.

"Finished."

Nagad was startled by the sudden intrusion, having grown accustomed to the stillness. He slid off the table, cradling his wounded arm.

"Thank you."

For the first time, the healer's eyes met Nagad's gaze. Smiling, he inclined his head and said, "You are welcome, soldier."

The *rofe* returned to his labor, clearing the treatment table in preparation for the next wounded man who might require tending. Nagad left him to his task. He did not wait until first light; his mission was far too urgent.

Before leaving camp, Nagad seized a wooden torch, its tip wrapped in oil-soaked cloth.

He paused, gazing westward beyond the Great Sea, where the sun hung low over the water. A heaviness stirred within him, an unshakable sense that the world should have ceased its turning after the horrors of the day. *So many lost...*

At a nearby fire he lit the torch. Turning his countenance eastward, Nagad set forth on his journey to Shiloh, trotting at a steady pace so as not to expend too much strength at the start.

A long night's trek lay before him, through the peaks and dales that marked the hill country of Ephraim. The valleys were fertile, studded with lush orchards and marshy plains.

In contrast to these plenteous hollows, the peaks stood bald, sparsely clothed in straggled shrubbery. Near the Vale of Shechem yawned a great hollow that cleft the mountain range in two. Mount Gerizim rose to the south, Mount Ebal to the north, each giving rise to a ridge that ran the length of the land, tracing the coast of the Great Sea to the west.

The main thoroughfare through the mountains stretched within this central vale, but it lay a great distance to the north.

Pausing to consider, Nagad chose to forgo the main path, fearing it would cost him precious time. Instead, he turned toward the narrow passage over the mountains, a more difficult way, yet the swifter course east to Shiloh.

With great effort, he kept his pace as darkness overtook the last light of day. A chill of foreboding stole over him, a sense of being alone in a world much larger than he. It was unwise, even for a soldier, to travel unguarded at night, for bandits oft lay in wait for those who walked alone.

Nagad quickened his pace.

Weariness threatened to claim him as the long night wore on. The climb did prove difficult, at times, even treacherous, in the dark of the nocturnal realm. Sounds of unseen beasts filled his ears, and a shiver of dread crept down his spine. The early spring night was cold despite his exertion. His armor hung heavy upon his body as stiffness settled into his limbs. Blisters had formed where his sandals rubbed against his feet.

Still, Nagad pressed on, for need drove him. *I must reach Shiloh in time. I will not disappoint Tiphcar, nor my people.*

As the pale light of dawn alighted upon the hills before him, Nagad slowed to a brisk walk. He had journeyed through the night, never once pausing to rest.

Drawing forth his water jar, he drank deeply; the clear liquid spilled down his neck in frigid rivulets. The morning's breath brushed his face, chill and clean beneath the waking sky. A fine dew blanketed the earth, and his garments clung cold and wet against his skin. His thoughts were troubled as he quickened his pace once more. With every step, he knew Israel's need grew more dire.

Upon cresting yet another rise, Nagad entered into the Vale of Shiloh.

Within this valley it was, that in an age long past, the men of Benjamin had lain in wait, hiding in the vineyard for the daughters of Shiloh. The Benjaminites had been decimated by civil war with the other tribes of Israel; there no longer remained enough women to ensure their survival.

And so, when the maidens came forth to dance in the autumn festival, the Benjaminites sprang upon them and stole away the daughters of Shiloh to be their wives.

Upon a height in the valley floor, a fortress domain rose through the morning mist like a celestial city upon the clouds. The metropolis lay lush and tranquil, hemmed in on all sides by hills, save the southwest, the only entry point into or out of the valley. A spring, *Ein Seilun*, ran adjacent to the city, providing water for the inhabitants and irrigation for the surrounding fields.

The shadow of the tower gate, strong and silent, loomed on the horizon. The city, a mighty bastion of old, bore still the fortifications of a lost polestar, discernible in its massive stone walls twelve cubits in height. Yet now it lay in disrepair. The once grand earthen glacis, raised to shield the walls from assault, stood cloven by buildings underpinned from its slopes with pillars.

Nagad looked upon the city and thought, *This valley will not be easily defended.*

CHAPTER 2

THE SEAT OF GOD

Hophni laid his hand upon the horn of the goat and raised its head. With practiced ease, he drew the blade across the exposed throat, and life spilled from the flawless creature. Blood streamed into the channel carved along the table's edge, trickling down into a basin of burnished brass. When the vessel was filled, the priest sprinkled the crimson dower, the bride-price of covenant, along the edges of the altar. Each drop fell in accordance with the law.

Returning to the carcass, he set to work with swift precision. The knife parted flesh from bone, unveiling the inward parts. He drew forth the fat and entrails, laying them aside for the offering of thanksgiving. Then, taking the portion appointed, he lowered the meat into the boiling pot, that it might be readied for the altar, an oblation by fire, a fragrance meant to please the Almighty.

The priest's servant reached for a three-pronged fleshhook and thrust it into the cauldron. What he drew forth was meat yet uncooked, the fat still clinging to the flesh.

"Give meat for roasting to the priest," the servant said. "He will not take boiled meat from you, but raw."

But the worshiper who brought the goat as a peace offering replied, "The fat must first be burned upon the altar; then you may take as much as your heart desires, for it is written: *All the fat is the Lord's.*"[4]

---

[4] Leviticus 3:16

The servant answered him, saying, "Nay, but you must give it now. And if not—I will take it by force."

Drawing out the meat, the servant delivered it to Hophni, who received it with eager hands. The priest then blessed the offering and sent the astonished supplicant away.

"Come, prepare us a meal," Hophni proclaimed. "For we shall feast this day."

The servant gathered the meat, along with the unleavened cakes bequeathed for an offering, and set about preparing the meal as he had been instructed. While Hophni washed away the stains left by the sacrifice, his brother Phinehas entered the courtyard of the sanctuary.

Phinehas was clothed in his priestly attire, even as was his brother. Their cassocks were of fine white linen, woven in a diamond pattern, seamless garments falling nearly to the heel. An intricately embroidered girdle bound the vesture about the waist. Upon their heads rested bonnets of choice linen. And ever, while ministering within the sanctuary, their feet were bare, for where they trod was holy ground.

"*Boker tov*, good morning," Phinehas spoke, his voice bright. "You have begun your priestly duties early, my brother."

Hophni regarded him. "*Boker tov* to you, good brother. How fares your lovely Esha?"

"She fares well, *todah*, thanks to God. Though she longs for the child's birth." He glanced at the meal being prepared. "I see you have gathered a choice portion from the offering. It seems many must partake, if the meal is to be consumed before the sun sets."

"Yes, brother, we shall have a feast tonight." A sly grin stole across Hophni's face. "We do not want to displease the Lord and leave any part remaining.[5] Come, let us see to the preparations."

Phinehas placed an arm around his brother's shoulder as they began their trek across the court. Looking up, he beheld their father as he entered the sanctuary yard, walking with heavy steps, his head bowed, muttering to himself.

Eli, who had judged Israel forty years, was very old. He had succeeded to the office of *Shofet* and *Kohen Gadol*, Judge and High Priest of Israel, upon the death of Phinehas, son of Eleazar, Ithamar's elder

---

[5] Leviticus 7:15

brother. He was arrayed in the garments of the High Priest, the sacred vestments ordained by the Lord Himself: layers of cloth in heavenly accord, dyed in hues of blue, gold, purple, and scarlet, each bearing its own holy significance.

The *ephod* was fashioned in two parts, fastened at the shoulders with great onyx clasps and bound at the waist by a woven girdle. Upon the stones were inscribed the names of the tribes: six upon one and six upon the other.

Beneath the *ephod* was the *me'il techelet*, a robe of seamless blue linen that flowed to the ground. Along its hem were alternating pomegranates and golden bells, their sound marking the progress of the High Priest as he entered the Holy of Holies.

The most costly of the garments was the breastplate, adorned with twelve precious stones, one for each tribe of Israel, worn upon the heart of the priest as a memorial before the Lord, that he might carry their names into the Holy Place. The breastplate doubled over to form a pouch into which were placed the judgment stones, *Urim* and *Thummim*.

A linen mitre lay wrapped upon Eli's head, and upon it a plate of gold bore the inscription: *Holiness to the Lord*. A solemn reminder of man's imperfection.

The grievance just received from a troubled supplicant stirred within Eli the memory of a warning long ago, a message spoken by a prophet of God. His heart grew heavy as he recalled the seer's words concerning all that his sons had done.

> Your sons have forsaken their priestly heritage,
> passed down from the house of Aaron.
>
> And you, Eli, why do you trample
> My sacrifice and My offering,
> which I commanded in My dwelling place?
>
> You have honored your sons above Me,
> fattening yourselves with the choicest portions
> of all the offerings of Israel, My people.

> Did not the Lord promise that your house
> and the house of your father
> would walk before Him forever?
>
> But now, all has changed.
>
> For those who honor God, He will honor;
> but those who despise Him shall be lightly esteemed.[6]

Then the prophet of God looked deep into Eli's failing eyes and proclaimed a message of warning:

> Behold, a shadow is falling;
> The days of the curse are at hand.
> The old in your house, they shall perish;
> The young in their youth shall not stand.
>
> Forever the shadow shall linger,
> The end of your line drawing near.
> The house of your father is failing,
> Undone by the sword and the spear.
>
> The good God has done is forsaken;
> An enemy within His house dwells.
> The shadow of judgment has taken;
> The tide against you now swells.
>
> Those not cut off at God's altar,
> A blight to your eye to consume,
> A grief to your heart shall awaken,
> No agèd shall ever resume.

The prophet of God continued, saying, "Now this shall be a sign to you that will come upon your two sons, on Hophni and Phinehas: in one day they shall die, both of them. Then the Lord will raise up for

---

[6] 1 Samuel 2:30

Himself a faithful priest, who shall do according to what is in His heart and in His mind. He will build him a sure house, and he shall walk before the Lord's anointed forever.

"And it shall come to pass that everyone who is left in your house will come and bow down to him for a piece of silver and a morsel of bread, and say, 'Please, put me in one of the priestly positions, that I may eat a piece of bread.'"[7]

"*Avi*, my father, *boker tov*," said Phinehas, smiling.

Eli was startled out of his troubled thoughts. The curse now weighed heavily upon him. With trembling restraint, he once more relayed the warning to his sons.

"Why do you do such things? This is not the first I have heard of your debauchery, for I hear of your evil dealings from all the people, how you lie with the women who assemble at the door of the Tabernacle, and how you defile the offerings of God, requiring the first and best portions for yourselves.

"My sons, this wickedness is not of God. Why do you continue in these ways?"

Phinehas opened his mouth to protest, but Eli silenced him with a shake of his head and an uplifted hand.

"No, my sons! For it is not a good report that I hear. You make the Lord's people transgress. If one man sins against another, God will judge him; but if a man sins against the Lord, who will intercede for him?"[8]

"You are old. Your time is nearly over. What do you know of our needs? Our position affords us certain privileges," Hophni returned.

"Please, my sons, your office as priest is not one of privilege, but of sacred obligation. You are to be the spiritual shepherds of this people, not their oppressors."

"There are certain rights and provisions afforded to us by our station. We are only ensuring that our needs are satisfied," answered Phinehas.

"Do you not recall the warning the prophet of God gave me? Why do you not heed these tidings?"

---

[7] 1 Samuel 2:34–36
[8] 1 Samuel 2:25

Eli knew his sons' fate hung upon his appeal. Yet there was nothing more he could do, for their hearts had grown hard.

Their sin is very great before the Lord, brooded Eli.

"My sons, it is not too late—"

But even as he spoke, a great clamor erupted outside the court. Voices rose beyond the sanctuary wall.

"What is the meaning of this interruption?" demanded Hophni as he threw open the gate.

"Forgive me, *kohen,*" said a temple servant, his hands wringing one another. "This young conscript says he must speak with both of you."

Before them stood a soldier clad in armor, looking as though he had just left the field of battle: breath came hard, sweat was upon his brow. Chestnut hair lay in disarray about his shoulders. A beard, yet scarcely grown, a shadow of what was to come, whispered of his youth.

Under his left arm, he carried a helm of leather. A breastplate of scaled hide was worn over a plain woven tunic that reached to the knees. Sheathed at his side, the soldier bore a straight sword. His left arm was wounded, blood still fresh upon the dressing.

Phinehas stepped forward. "What is your name, young man?"

"*Calach*—forgive me, *kohen,*" the soldier replied, bowing his head. "I am Nagad of Benjamin. I come to you in great need."

Nagad had entered Shiloh just as the city gates were pressed ajar. The purple rays lingered as the eyelids of morning opened, cresting the hills to the east. The streets stirred with the day's early labors. Nagad knew where to go; he had been there before.

After the Conquest of the Promised Land, Shiloh had become the religious center of Israel. At Shiloh, Joshua had set up the Tent of Meeting after casting lots to divide the land among the seven tribes who had not yet received their inheritance.

Since that time, year after year, all would go up from their home villages to worship and sacrifice to *El Shaddai,* the Lord Almighty, at Shiloh.

It was here that Hannah, wife of Elkanah, barren and in great distress, vowed that if God would grant her a son, she would return him for service to the Lord.

God regarded her affliction and gave her the desire of her heart. She named the boy Samuel, *God has heard*, and returned him to Shiloh to become the ward of Eli, the High Priest.

Nagad had walked quickly to the hill at the edge of town where the Tabernacle stood. A single gate pierced the wall that enclosed the temple court. Now within, Nagad recalled the layout of the sacred grounds.

The Tabernacle rose before him, cast in shadow by the rising sun. Upon the walls of the Tent of Meeting, a canvas roof was fastened with cords, tied to pegs driven into the earth. Several steps ascended to five brazen pillars, marking the entrance of the sanctuary.

Before the doorpost lay a level platform, where a stool had been placed, a seat upon which the priest might rest. In front of the Tabernacle stood an altar of bronze, bearing four horns. A large brazen pot sat upon the fire; the aroma of the morning's offering yet lingered in the air.

Drawing a deep breath, Nagad continued, "The Philistines have encamped at Aphek and again arrayed themselves for battle against Israel. The army of Israel went out to meet them, only to be defeated and driven back, with great loss of life."

His voice caught in his throat.

After a moment's pause, he went on, "When despair was at its greatest, the elders of Israel recalled how, in the days of Joshua, all battles were won when the Ark of God went before them. So it was that they sent me to Shiloh to request the Ark of the Covenant of the Lord of hosts, who dwells between the cherubim, be brought to where they are encamped beside Eben-Ezer.

"I ran through the night, and I humbly ask you…"

Nagad lowered his head as he placed his hand upon his heart.

"*Kohen*, to come with the Ark of God."

A wave of astonishment swept over all who heard these tragic words.

"How can this be? We have had no word of a battle," spoke Phinehas, his voice strained.

"Ebed," called Hophni.

"Yes, *adon*, my lord," the servant replied.

"Go. Gather four Levitical priests, for ever has it been entrusted to them to care for the Ark of God. Bring them here. We must prepare the Ark for battle." Hophni spoke with forceful resolve. "We leave in one hour's time."

"My *adon*, no one may enter the Holy of Holies save the High Priest, and then only on the Day of Atonement. It is forbidden. How shall we retrieve the Ark?"

"It will be without injury, for the Lord of hosts will not forsake us in our great need," answered Hophni. "Now go, without delay."

The servant departed in haste.

When the Levitical priests heard what they had been commanded to do, their hearts failed within them. Nevertheless, with fear and trembling, they followed the servant to Hophni and Phinehas.

"My *adon*, we are at your service," said Kamar as they drew near the waiting assembly.

"Hophni," said Eli sternly, "what the servant spoke is true. They may not enter the Holy of Holies, save under pain of death. The Lord will surely strike them down if they do this."

The priests looked to Hophni, their faces marked by fear.

"I promise, no harm will come to you, my priests," Hophni replied. "The Lord will make an exception, just this once, for we are in great need. But first, you must consecrate yourselves. Then nothing will befall you. You will see; all will be well."

The four priests: Kamar, Polchan, Sharath, and Qatan, prepared themselves as instructed. With water from the brazen laver, they bathed and clothed themselves in pure white linen robes. Phinehas prayed over them and anointed their heads with oil.

Hophni brought forward a fine young bull. Placing the hands of the priests upon its head, he sacrificed it as a sin offering to God. Its blood was applied to the horns and base of the altar, to make atonement.

Thus the priests consecrated themselves before the Lord.

With solemn faces, the priests entered the Tabernacle of the Lord. The Holy Place, the first chamber within the sanctuary, was sparsely furnished. To their right stood the Table of Showbread, upon which perpetually rested twelve loaves. On the left, the Golden Candlestick bore seven lights.

No chair was found within that sacred room where a priest might sit, for the work of his office was never complete—not until the One foretold should come. Then would the work be finished, for He, the perfect Lamb, would sit at the right hand of Yahweh, and all would be fulfilled.

No windows were cut into the walls of the chamber; no other light entered, save that which issued from the lampstand. Shadows danced eerily within the confines of the room; light reflecting from the golden furnishings called out a warning as a foreboding settled upon the hearts of the priests.

A stillness overspread the Holy Place. Fear threatened to overwhelm the priests as they perceived the mighty power within the sanctuary. The desire to turn and flee rose within them as they looked about the room.

Yet each drew a deep breath, and gazing upon one another, they gave a solemn nod.

Before them stood the Altar of Incense, overlaid in pure gold. A gilded crown encircled its top, each corner adorned with a horn of gold.

They took incense of sweet spices: stacte, onycha, galbanum, and frankincense, blended in equal measure, compounded by the sacred art of the perfumer, salted and beaten very fine. This fragrant offering they laid upon the altar, set before the Testimony of the Lord.

The poles that bore the Ark of the Covenant extended outward, touching the veil that separated the first chamber from the inner sanctuary, the Holy of Holies, wherein it resided. With two priests upon each pole, they carefully withdrew the Sacred Coffer from its place beyond the veil, taking great care not to gaze upon it, for it was forbidden for any but the High Priest.

The veil, they took down, covering the Ark with it, mindful not to touch this most holy object, for this too was forbidden under pain of death. Over the veil, the priests placed a covering of badger skin, then overspread it with a cloth entirely of blue.

The priests worked without a sound, in silent reverence, lest the holy be violated.

Each priest placed the end of a pole upon his shoulder, Kamar and Polchan before the Ark, Qatan and Sharath behind. With one accord, the Ark of the Lord was lifted from the ground. The weight of the Golden Coffer bore heavily upon their shoulders as they harbored the Ark between them.

With trepidation, the four priests moved as one, carrying the Ark of the Covenant from the Holy Place and down the steps into the courtyard, where the assembly waited in anxious silence.

Hophni and Phinehas exchanged a glance, a smile upon their lips and a sigh of relief upon their breath, as the priests emerged from the chamber.

For three hundred and sixty-nine years, the Ark of the Covenant had sojourned within the sanctuary at Shiloh, now stirred from its long abiding, now the hope of Israel's host.

All marked the moment in watchful stillness as the Holy Shrine was conveyed down the temple steps. Then the priests lowered the Ark to the ground.

This is a momentous hour, thought Nagad, as in wonder he bore witness.

"Phinehas!"

The voice of a woman broke the silence that had enveloped the assembly. Phinehas looked up to see his wife, Esha, great with child, drawing near, her eyes shadowed with concern.

"Phinehas, my husband, what has happened? I was awakened by a dread that threatened to steal the very breath from me."

Her gaze fell to the Ark of the Lord resting upon the ground in their midst.

"What have you done?" Her words came in a whisper as fear and grief tore at her.

"Esha, you should not be here. This is no concern of yours," Phinehas replied, his jaw set.

"Kamar, let us gather the Ark of the Lord and make haste to Eben-Ezer, and our men. Time is of the essence," Hophni interrupted.

"My *adon*," spoke Ebed as he entered the court, "all is prepared for our departure. We await your command."

Once more, the four Levitical priests lifted the Ark, to bear it upon their shoulders as though the sins of all Israel rested upon them.

"We will muster the people to battle as we proceed. Send word to all mighty men. Tell them we march to defend Israel against invasion. Now is the hour to make good every oath," Hophni declared with fierce resolve.

A sense of pride and duty rose within Nagad's chest. *At last, hope has come.*

Eli watched with growing impatience.

"This is no mere trinket that you carry before you. It is the very seat of God!"

"You are an old man," Hophni retorted. "Circumstances are not as they once were. You do not understand the workings of our time."

"At the least, let me consult *Urim* and *Thummim*, to discern the will of the Lord in this matter."

"We cannot delay," Phinehas answered. "We know all we need to know. Without the Ark, our people are lost. We cannot leave them in their great need."

"Phinehas, husband, please listen to your father, Eli. He is very wise," pleaded Esha, her hand fast upon his arm.

Aware that all eyes rested upon him, Phinehas frowned and unclasped Esha's hold.

"Out of my way, woman. Who are you to question the ways of a priest of God?"

"This act is not sanctioned by the Lord!" Eli cried, his voice harsh, contrary to his nature. "No good will come of it. Only the High Priest may blow the trumpet of war. God will not be in this deed."

Phinehas' mind wavered with a fleeting doubt. *He is old. His mind grows dim.*

Shaking off the thought, Phinehas turned from his uncertainty, and cast it aside.

Hophni's voice pierced his reverie, drawing him again to the matter at hand.

"You forget, my father—I shall soon be High Priest. You are too old to go to war. I will go in your stead."

"And it will be your doom!" Eli turned and walked away, his steps sharp against the stones.

"Ebed," Phinehas called, his voice strained with feeling.

"Yes, *adon.*"

"You will remain behind. Tend to my father while we are away. He may need you."

"My *adon*—" Ebed faltered.

"Do not fear," assured Phinehas. "We will return shortly, and we will be victorious."

"It is time. We cannot delay," said Hophni.

"Then let us proceed," answered Phinehas.

Slowly, the procession made its way through the narrow streets that led from the temple mount to the heart of town. A single chord of awe stirred the gathering throng as word of the Ark's departure spread. All who beheld it bowed low as the Ark passed by. Those prepared for battle formed ranks behind it, the host growing ever larger as the cavalcade advanced through the city.

A voice rose from the crowd—clear and bold:

> Rise up, O Lord!
> Let Your enemies be scattered,
> And let those who hate You flee before You.[9]

Soon others joined the Song of the Ark, and the people fell in step with the marching column as it moved toward the outskirts of the town.

Eli watched from a distance, given over to despair, remembering the prophecy delivered when the Lord spoke to his young ward, Samuel:

> Behold, I will do a thing in Israel
> at which both ears of everyone who hears it shall tingle.
> In that day, I will perform against Eli
> all that I have spoken concerning his house,
> from beginning to end.
>
> For I have told him that I will judge his house forever,
> for the iniquity he knows,
> because his sons made themselves vile,
> and he did not restrain them.

---

[9] Numbers 10:35

And therefore, I have sworn to the house of Eli
that the iniquity of his house
shall not be atoned for by sacrifice or offering forever.[10]

And now, what hope remained for his sons? Eli, watching as the column reached the city gates, softly spoke:
"He is the Lord. Let Him do what seems good to Him."

---

[10] 1 Samuel 3:11–14

CHAPTER 3

RAGING WATER

Casting shadows to their left, the sun advanced in its course across the azure sky, drawing the dew from the fields. Hills crowned with peaks rose about the host as they moved in solemn array along the Great North Road, which led toward Shechem. Lebonah, set upon the slope of a mount, lay to the northwest, three miles from the place where their journey began. Shiloh had faded quickly from view, swallowed by the surrounding mounds and earthen swells.

Prickly weeds choked the expanse, bleak and straggled, their dismal grasp a curse upon the land. Yet here and there, mountain tulips lifted their fragrant heads through the tangle of barbed intruders. Occasionally, chamois, small, goat-like antelope scarcely a cubit in height, were seen dotting the hillsides, their brown coats marked by white faces and black stripes beneath the eyes.

The contingent progressed slowly over the mountains of Ephraim, accommodating the burden carried upon the priests' shoulders. The path Nagad had taken the night before could not be retraced, for it was too arduous for those bearing the Ark of God. Messengers had been dispatched to muster troops from the surrounding countryside, for stronger forces would be needed to face the great numbers of the enemy.

Though weary, Nagad was glad to be moving, for urgency had settled upon him, making him restless in the hours of waiting. Time hastened, and he knew that delay could bring defeat upon the regiment that awaited his return.

As they journeyed through the mountain pass, the cavalcade crested yet another hill. Below lay a lush valley full of orchards. The sweet fragrance of apple blossoms rose to meet them, carried on a gentle breeze. Pale pink petals danced into the air, swirling about the company, teasing the men until they showered down like snow upon the mountain.

Now that is a pretty sight, thought Nagad, drawing in a deep breath, savoring the fragrance of peace and beauty. And he marveled at the contrast between such loveliness and the horror of battle. *How could the two dwell in the same realm? Truly, Yahweh had fashioned the world in beauty. Man, it was who marred the land with war, rending the very foundation of the earth with the rampage of contention and rage.* Yet the march toward battle pressed ever onward, set against the backdrop of God's creation.

Ahead, the valley of Tappuah lay. The town had been given to the tribe of Manasseh long ago, after Joshua slew the Canaanite king, though the land surrounding this royal city belonged to the tribe of Ephraim.

To the north of the valley ran the Kanah Ravine, a cleft through the mountains that reached to the Great Sea. The city was heavily fortified with high walls, gates, and bars. *En-Tappuah*, the fountain of an apple, flowed just beyond the fortifications. It was here, at the spring of cool water, that the growing regiment took its rest during the heat of the day.

It seemed to Nagad that he had been marching for days. He took repose beneath a tree, his back resting against the trunk, its sturdy bole cracked and flaking. Removing his sandals, the young conscript examined his painful feet. The skin had worn away over the blisters, exposing raw flesh. Taking a clean cloth, he bound them to guard against further injury.

"A soldier's feet are worth more than his weight in gold. You had best take better care of them, *Na'ar.*"

Nagad lifted his gaze to find a stout soldier with a full beard smiling down at him.

The man extended a hand to Nagad, saying, "Orach is my name, *Na'ar.*"

"Nagad, I am called." The young conscript offered his hand, grasping in friendship the one reaching down to him.

Lowering himself to the ground, Orach said, "I am pleased to know you, *Na'ar.* Looks like you have seen some action already." As he spoke, he gestured toward Nagad's left arm.

Orach had a pleasing face that seemed older than his eyes, which still held a spark of youthful vitality. His frame, though substantial, was not tall, yet he imbued a strength and magnitude that caused one to sense an assembly of greatness in his stature. In addition to the sword sheathed at his side, he carried a thrusting spear, favored by the northern tribe of Naphtali.

"By your tongue, I reckon you hail from the hills of Ephraim," spoke Orach.

"I am a Benjaminite."

Shaking his head gently, Orach replied, "Your people have seen much conflict over the years, suffered much at the hands of these Philistines."

Nagad lowered his head, working the muscles in his jaw. Unbidden, his hand lifted to his tunic and fingered the object hidden beneath the fabric. He nodded.

"I never thought I would see the day when the Ark of the Lord would once more join us in battle. It will be quite a sight," spoke Orach, a gleam in his dark eyes.

"Oft have I fought against the Ammonites to the north, yet I have not had the pleasure of contending with these interlopers. Tell me of the Philistines. What are they like in battle? Oh, how I long to sink my spear deep into their pretty sides."

Nagad's voice was low with memory. "They are a fierce race, great in number and savage upon the battlefield. Their armor is thick, and their swords are of iron. Our bronze weapons cannot contend with theirs, unyielding as they are. It is nothing for their spears to run a man through, or their blades to shear our swords. Horses. Many horses, they have, to trample our lines and scatter our troops. It is a dreadful thing, to face the Philistines in battle."

His stomach turned as he recalled the contest of the previous day.

"These Philistines have been allowed to trouble us far too long. It is about time we cut them down to size," said Orach, elbowing Nagad in the side. "And now, with the Ark before us, well, victory will be forthcoming."

Nagad noticed the swell of Orach's chest as he spoke.

Looking down, Nagad, heavy with doubt, felt a darkness come over him. From the folds of his tunic, he drew the spearhead and ran his fingers along its edge. All around him, the men brimmed with confidence, yet a shadow lingered within. *Is victory assured because the Ark goes before them? Does it truly possess power to overcome the enemy by its very presence?*

Nagad's thoughts faded into memory. The soft laughter of the fair child rang sweetly in his ears. Sighing, he reached deeper, closing his eyes. He saw the little girl with chestnut hair, twirling in the summer breeze. He saw the golden wheat field waving.

Then came the harsh, grating caw of a raven, perched upon the fence post, stark and dark against the gilded grain. The feathered harbinger took to flight.

The vision shifted. Gravel underfoot blurred beneath running, sandaled feet. The world around was silent, save the sound of his own breath, drawn in deep, hurried waves. He saw a door slightly ajar. It was dark inside.

A boy's hand reached up and slowly pushed it open. Nagad looked into the blackness, his breath held. As he stepped into the sable-cloaked entrance, a thrill of fear ran through him.

The sound of the trumpet roused him, so that his heart skipped a beat.

"Well, it is time. We are off," spoke Orach, his voice loud after the stillness of the vision. "Come, I will walk with you, *Na'ar.*"

Orach had risen swiftly, extending his hand to help the stiffened youth to his sore feet. Nagad placed the spearhead securely within his tunic, then accepted the proffered hand. Involuntarily, he groaned. It seemed every muscle in his body ached with the effort of rising.

"Shechem is our next destination, a quaint little town with much history. Jacob's Well lies just outside the city. It is said he paid one hundred *Kesitahs* for the land near Shechem."

Orach spoke with animation as he continued, "They had a king once: Abimelech, son of Gideon. His rule lasted but three years, yet in that time he utterly destroyed the city. It has since been rebuilt."

"I have seen the city once before," Nagad offered.

Shechem was anything but quaint. It was a flourishing metropolis at the crossroads of the Great North Road, which followed the watershed fifty miles south of Hebron, and the western route that passed between Mount Gerizim and Mount Ebal, descending through the Plain of Sharon to meet the Way of the Sea at Sochoh. The land was rich in grapes, olives, and wheat. Lush pastures spread across the valley, sustaining a variety of livestock. The road ran high through the Hill Country: the Jordan Valley lay to the east, the Great Sea to the west.

The company of men trudged on in loosely ordered rank and file. Many spoke openly to one another, ambling rather than marching, as though on a journey of leisure and not an excursion toward war. For most, the battle remained a distant thought, not yet a realization, but a far-off figment, intangible and dim.

The afternoon sun bore down, heating the soldiers as they passed through the wooded country. Peaks and valleys rose and fell, revealing themselves, then vanishing again. Nagad licked his parched lips, wishing for water.

On the road north of Tappuah, half-way to Shechem, just west of Arumah, in the place where the mountains press together forming a watershed in winter, the progression stalled.

For on the ground, a trickle of water flowed down the wadi, running from the western mountains to the Jordan Valley in the east. Overjoyed, the men crowded around to partake of the cool, clear draught.

Nagad looked on, unknowingly moving toward the bent forms of his comrades. Many pressed forward, eager to reach the transitory stream, laughing at their good fortune.

Orach pushed past Nagad, breaking the spell. "No!" he shouted. "Get away! Run!"

Startled, the young conscript followed after him as Orach rushed toward the men, trying to get them to listen.

Confused, Nagad called, "What is it?"

He stood watching as Orach grabbed hold of several men, dragging them aside, all the while crying out for the others to abandon their frenzy and flee. Yet, as so often happens when danger arises, none would heed the warning. Deaf they were to the voice of doom.

Nagad's eyes were drawn down. Beneath his feet, the earth began to tremble.

A sound rose like a mighty rushing river, a driving stream, living water, cascading from the mountains. The torrent struck, seizing several soldiers and dragging them into the flood, a deluge that engulfed all in its path.

Panic erupted. Men shoved and stumbled, scrambling to escape the sudden rush. Nagad stood wide-eyed as the stampede of frightened soldiers collided with him, entangling him in their retreat.

Knocked to the ground, he struggled to rise, fearing he would be trampled. Too slow he was. In that moment, the rushing flood reached out its hands, and with unrelenting grasp hurled Nagad into the raging stream.

All the world changed.

White, frothy water filled his vision. Groping for a handhold, Nagad lashed out in panicked frenzy. Though he thrashed to stay the pull, the torrent bore him down the valley.

His head broke above the water, and he gasped for air. For a fleeting moment, he glimpsed Orach running along the edge of the flood, chasing after him. But just as swiftly, he was plunged once more beneath the raging tide.

The struggle began to take its toll. His armor weighed heavily upon him, dragging him deeper below the surface. Weariness seeped into his limbs, and he sensed the end was near, the last shred of his strength slipping away.

Everything grew quiet. The world slowed. Nagad fought to keep struggling. The rhythmic beat of his labored heart kept time.

His vision turned white. He perceived sandaled feet running on gravel. Panting, it was he rushing toward the door. His forward momentum suddenly suspended as he saw feet lying before the threshold, motionless.

Blood flowed freely from the body, spilling over graveled walkway, filling cracks in sun-baked earth. He stepped back in horror, wanting to scream, yet no voice came from his gaping mouth.

The door stood slightly ajar. Placing a hand upon the hinged barrier, he slowly pushed it open. His heart pounded. He could not breathe.

Inside, the room was dark. Smoke filled the air. His lungs felt as though they would burst.

Slowly, as he stood frozen in place, his eyes began to adjust. Two forms emerged from the shadows against the far wall, one smaller than the other. He could not bear to look further.

At his feet, he struck something with his sandal, sending a sharp scrape across the wooden floor. Looking down, he saw an iron spear, the bloody point broken from the shaft.

Reaching down, he picked it up. The blood, still fresh, stained his hands crimson. He stood gazing at the spearhead resting upon his bloodied palm.

His throat closed. His lungs screamed for air. A shadow fell over his eyes. Nagad felt his body go limp as he succumbed to the darkness.

Time rested as emptiness enfolded him. Peaceful nothingness caressed his senses as the numbing quiet of the void opened around him. And he surrendered. Free from struggle, free from the past, just blissful floating.

Something disturbed the water, plunging down, grasping, tearing at him. For a moment, panic seized him. Then came anger. He sensed a hand reaching from above, firmly gripping his own, drawing him from the grasp of the raging flood.

He felt his body exhumed from the watery grave as the silent shield was torn away and the fight resumed. Gasping, he filled his lungs as life returned to him.

His limp and waterlogged carcass was dragged to the shore, where he lay spent upon the sand, each breath a labored grasp. Beside him, the bulky form of Orach reclined, drenched and winded.

Looking over at his rescuer, Nagad spoke with a raspy voice, "Orach?"

"Aye, *Na'ar*, it is I. You gave me quite a chase. I thought I lost you."

Orach was visibly shaken, his stout heart trembling from the ordeal. Nagad looked upon him; fear still lingered in the depths of his eyes.

A wave of emotion swept over him, for there was something familiar in Orach's look: a quiet comfort that stirred Nagad's soul.

He studied Orach's face as his own breath grew steady. Then it came to him. It was his father's eyes, that paternal bond, ancient and unspoken, which ties a son to the one who shields and holds.

Orach was his need's answer, and Nagad's heart melded to his, the void of the past filled with a father's love. And, like a sheltering tree, Orach's heart reached out to the young conscript.

In that moment, something spiritual passed between them, an all-knowing vision shared by the inner orb that sees all things. Marked forever by the crossing of their paths, Nagad's destiny henceforth intertwined with Orach's.

Nagad lay back upon the solid ground, his eyes fixed on the clear azure sky. The sound of his breath entering, then leaving his chest, filled his ears with its calming rhythm.

Memory returned. He sat up quickly. The world tilted, and his vision swam for a moment. The landscape looked strange, unfamiliar.

A few soldiers wandered nearby, gathering the unfortunate who had been caught yet spared from death's grasp. Others retrieved the bodies of those who could not be rescued in time.

"Where are we?" asked Nagad, turning his head to see the lay of the land.

"Half-way to Arumah by the looks of these hills," answered Orach. "Come, let us rejoin our men."

Orach grasped the young conscript by the forearm and pulled him to his feet. Nagad's legs wobbled, still weak from the struggle. Yet slowly, strength returned, and his feet found firm ground beneath them.

As they reunited with those transported, one called out in astonishment, "Where did that come from?"

"It is a warning!" cried another, lifting the lifeless body of his comrade onto his back.

"No," spoke Orach, shaking his head. "It is but rain in the mountains that brought the torrent upon us. I have seen it before. Though I grant you, such a flood is late in the season."

Traveling back over the rolling terrain, the soldiers rejoined the rest of the contingent. Nagad and Orach, along with a few other men, had ended up on the north side of the raging river where the main host waited, while others had been left to the south.

The men stood looking at one another, the army now divided, the rushing torrent between them, a third of the force cut off from the larger body.

Hophni cast his eyes across the waters and called to those on the far side, "You men will have to find another way. We will meet at Eben-Ezer. Make haste; do not delay."

Nagad watched as a third of the army turned and marched slowly away, their backs to their destination. Another path would have to be forged through the wilderness, another trek over the mountains. Their journey would be more difficult, their fate a different path than the remaining host.

But the priests, bearing their sacred burden, had passed beyond the flood before the torrent struck. The seat of God would continue on as planned. And the host of men would follow: a holy battalion on its way to its own destiny, unknowing the distant course that would be their doom.

Nagad glanced over at Orach. "Will the others make it in time?"

"They will find their own path, and they will come when they come."

"Those hills are difficult. It will be a challenge for so many to travel the mountain path. I am glad we are on this side of the stream. I do not envy their journey. I will not feel at ease 'til we get to Eben-Ezer. I fear our delay will have dire consequences."

Orach nodded slowly. "It is the journey, *Na'ar*, that is important. For with each step, we are a little closer to finding ourselves. When we arrive, it is over, and self-discovery is at an end. Yes, *Na'ar*, it is the journey that is important. Which path we are given is up to God."

CHAPTER 4

MOUNTAIN OF PROMISE

The shadows lengthened as the company came upon the slender shoulder of land nestled between Mount Ebal and Mount Gerizim. Shechem lay vulnerable on the southeastern edge of the narrow pass, cleft between the mountains, at the foot of Gerizim, whose slopes abounded with springs and fruitful groves.

Encircled by fortified walls, the city was well-defended, its gate reinforced with three piers and flanked by two chambers. Large and teeming with life, Shechem stood ancient and proud, a city carved by time.

Within the gathering shadows, the company made their camp beneath the rise of Mount Ebal, whose name means bald stone.

Looking up at the barren summit, Nagad was drawn to its height. *The mountain of promise. Abraham's mountain.*

Though weariness pulled at his limbs, he began to climb. What drew him there, he did not know. Was it a sense of something great, an awareness of a higher presence?

If the earth is the work of the Lord, then surely the mountains are the pillars of the sky upon which the heavens rest. With their faces lifted toward the world's outer stage, the mountains are the bridge between heaven and earth. Upon the mount is the place of spiritual truth, a place of revelation.

And he must go. Go to the summit. To reach up and see. To know. So he climbed, climbed to the place of the One True God. Each step he took with great care, each foothold with deliberate intent.

It is the journey that is important, Orach had said, the journey up the mountain toward understanding. I must go and see for myself what Abraham saw, what he knew to be true.

Nagad reached the crown of Mount Ebal and looked out upon the land, even as Abraham had done so long ago. It was here that God made His covenant with the Patriarch, promising that if he followed the Lord, the land would belong to his descendants, and they would become a mighty nation.

Years later, after the long season of wandering, Joshua brought the twelve tribes atop this very mountain to renew their commitment to the Lord. He set up a great stone as a witness to the covenant, inscribing upon it a copy of the law. From the bald face of Mount Ebal, half the tribes proclaimed the curses that would befall them should they turn away. The other half, standing upon the fruitful dome of Mount Gerizim, shouted back the blessings granted to those who obey. In this way, Joshua reestablished Israel's covenant with their God.

Nagad could not help but feel the sanctity of this mountaintop. Before him, a sweeping view of the Promised Land stretched out across the distant countryside, wrapped in hues of purple and gold. This was a land steeped in history, and blood, both Israelite and Philistine.

His gaze wandered over the hills and valleys below, and he was moved by its beauty. *This is truly a land of promise. And yet... why the harboring doubt? Why can I not trust?*

As the young conscript turned his eyes toward the horizon, the sun took his vision. In the whiteness that followed, Nagad heard the caw of a lone raven. He was just a boy raising his head to the sound of the dark messenger. Again, the harsh, grating voice of the sable scavenger rang against the stillness. His eyes found the raven perched upon a fence post, stark and dark against the gilded grain. Then the bird took flight. Something was strange. Not right. The world had gone quiet.

Confused, Nagad stood still, not making a sound, waiting to see. His throat grew tight as fear took a stranglehold on him. Then he saw it. Smoke rising.

Where there is smoke there is fire. Is that not so? Fire. Death. Destruction. The world spun out of control. His breath caught in his throat. *Breathe. Run. Run for home... Ima, Abba, sister. Run.*

Gravel blurred beneath his racing sandaled feet. No sound reached his ears save the rhythmic draw and release of labored breath. Worlds were colliding as the enemy and neighbors clashed, red-feathered headdresses vying with turbaned, draped pates. Ducking around the raging conflict, Nagad ran toward shattered lives and ruined homes.

Too late. All burned. Broken. Lost. I am too late.

Panting, he reached the door of his home. Mid-gait, he halted; his hide-clad soles slid through graveled walkway. There—feet lying before the threshold.

The leather sandals were well worn, and the flesh beneath, flesh that had always been in motion, never resting, now lay so still. Blood flowed freely, spilling over pebbled-path, filling cracks in sun-baked earth.

Abba, Nagad mouthed, yet no voice came. In horror, he stepped back. His mind reeled. Then his thoughts returned to him—*Ima, Sister.*

Looking up, he saw the door to his family's modest home standing slightly ajar. He saw his hand, as if moving of its own accord, reach up and slowly push the door open. He could hear his heart race. He could not breathe. Stunned, terror-filled, Nagad stepped over his lifeless father and entered the darkness.

Smoke choked the air. His lungs burned. He could not get any air. Whether it was smoke or fear that stayed his breath, he could not tell.

As he stood motionless with his blinded eyes wide open, his vision adjusted to the pitch of the room. Yet as his eyes regained sight, he longed for the darkness to remain. He did not wish to see what he already knew. But his eyes opened to the horror before him: two forms against the far wall: one smaller than the other, mother clasping daughter, crumpled on the floor.

Death had entered the room before him. No more mother. No more sister. No more family. The world tilted out of joint.

He could bear it no longer. As he turned away, his foot struck something that scraped against the wooden floor. His eyes dropped toward the sound. An iron spear lay before him, the bloody point broken from the shaft.

There was no conscious thought that drew his hand or called his fingers to close over its sharp edge. The blood, still fresh, stained his hands crimson.

Nagad stood looking at the spearhead resting upon his bloodied palm. His throat closed. His lungs burned. He needed air. A shadow fell over his eyes. Clasping his hand tightly over the iron blade, he fell limp upon the floor.

In anguish, Nagad, now grown, collapsed to his knees. Leaning forward, he gripped handfuls of wild grass, clinging beneath the God-throned sky. His voice broke free, and he cried out his pain. The burn of revenge flared within him, and again he shouted as the horror of the past raged through him.

"God, what do You want of me?"

He heard the soft, sweet voice of his mother, resonating from somewhere deep within. He was a boy again. As he entered the room, his mother raised her face toward the sound of his quiet sobbing.

"Nagad," she spoke gently, "what is it?"

He ran to her and fell into her waiting arms. Gently, she lifted his face and brushed away the tender tears of a boy's wounded heart.

"Tell me, child, what has caused you this distress?"

Through tears and broken sobs, Nagad spoke his heart. "Joseph and the others… they… they… Joseph tripped me while we played, and… and the others, they all laughed at me, *Ima*. They called me names."

Nagad broke into whimpering wails and buried his head in the folds of her lap.

"My child," she whispered, stroking his chestnut hair, "it is a sorrowful thing when those to whom we are close wound us."

"*Ima*," spoke Nagad as he raised his tear-streaked face, "why are they so mean?"

"They are afraid, my son. They are afraid."

"Afraid?" he repeated. "Afraid of what?"

Smiling, his mother placed a hand upon his damp cheek. "Of their own weakness. They fear they will never become who they are meant to be. They fear what might be."

"*Ima*, I do not understand." Nagad stood and shook his head. "What does that have to do with how they treated me? It makes no sense."

His face crumpled with anger. Clenching his boy-fists at his sides, Nagad cried through gritted teeth, "I will get them back for what they have done! All of them will pay!"

Calmly, his mother gathered him into her arms. Her warmth softened the stiffness in his body. She drew a tender hand along the back of his head.

"Do not hold a vengeful heart, Nagad. Yahweh forgives, so also we must forgive. It is the only way to be free. Do not carry the hurt with you; it will only weigh you down and steal your joy."

She felt her son shudder and release a ragged breath. Drawing him back, she looked into his eyes.

"Nagad, my sweet, put your trust in God. Then there is no need to fear, and no need for vengeance."

Coming to himself, Nagad looked once more into the heights of heaven.

"Forgive the Philistines? The ones who murdered my family? Who decimated our ranks? Is that what You ask of me? That is the one thing I cannot do. Do not ask me to let go of this hurt!"

Yet doubt clung to him, heavy as a millstone upon his soul.

The sun lowered in the sky, casting orange streaks across the horizon of the Great Sea. It was an ill wind that rose out of the west and struck Nagad in the face, whispering in his ear the very word of doom, and fear took his heart.

Was the old priest Eli right? Are we marching to our ruin? The cause is just, is it not? I must trust those above me. Who am I but a lowly foot soldier? What do I know of such things?

Yet unease settled upon the young conscript, a shadow he could not cast off. Nagad wondered what the morrow would bring: victory, or utter defeat.

Standing there upon the rise, gazing out at the sea glittering in the west, the thought came to him, not all that is done in the name of the Lord is right.

Lifting his eyes to the heavens, Nagad cried out in great distress, "O Lord, my fate is in Your hands. Let not my heart be vengeful. Teach me to trust, to see as You see. I do not know if this battle is just, but I go forth for Your name's sake. Do not forsake me in this struggle. Grant me strength to do what I must."

Words came to Nagad's mind. Whence they came, he did not know, but the sound of them was of power and authority:

> Behold, God will not cast away the blameless,
> nor will He uphold the evildoer;
> For the hand of our God is upon all those
> for good who seek Him,
> But His power and His wrath are
> against all those who forsake Him.[11]

Peace settled upon him. For good or for ill, his path was set before him, and he could not look back. Duty and honor ruled his fate; all else was not his to decide.

The sun was sinking fast into the west when Nagad began his journey back down the mountain.

I should not have lingered so long.

The way grew ever more perilous as the light faded. When at last he stepped from the mountain's base, Nagad loosed a breath of relief. Glancing about the camp, he saw Orach seated by the fire, a morsel of food in hand.

He looked up as Nagad approached.

"Ah, where have you been off to, *Na'ar*?" Not waiting for an answer, he continued, "Come. Eat. Renew your strength, for you will need it on the morrow."

Nagad settled beside Orach, before the balmy glow of the fire. The night air had grown chill, but the warmth of the flames was a comfort. Orach handed him a strip of roasted meat, which Nagad received gladly. Hunger had grown to ferocity unawares. With great fervor, Nagad tore into the portion, then downed a jar of cool water. As his appetite waned, a quiet satisfaction settled upon him.

For some time, the two sat in silence, listening to the crackle of the fire, each deep in his own thoughts. A jackal howled somewhere high in the mountains, breaking through the night and sending a shudder down Nagad's spine.

Orach began to sing in a soft baritone voice:

---

[11] Job 8:20 / Ezra 8:22

> Kings came, they fought;
>> the kings of Canaan fought
>> at Taanach by the waters of Megiddo,
>> but they carried off no silver, no plunder.
> From the heavens the stars fought,
>> from their courses they fought against Sisera.
> The river Kishon swept them away,
>> the age-old river, the river Kishon.
> March on, my soul; be strong!
> Then thundered the horses' hoofs—
>> galloping, galloping go his mighty steeds.
> So may all Your enemies perish, O Lord!
> But may they who love You be like the sun
>> when it rises in its strength.[12]

Nagad listened intently, stirred by the words. "What is this that you sing of, Orach? It brings to mind a story I have heard long ago but cannot recall."

"It is the song of the battle between Barak, commander under the prophetess Deborah, and Sisera, the captain of Jabin's host. Ten thousand of my tribesmen were summoned to fight beneath the shadow of Mount Tabor.

"Sisera gathered together his nine hundred chariots of iron and all the men with him, from Harosheth Haggoyim to the Kishon River. At Barak's advance, the Lord routed Sisera, all his chariots, and his mighty company by the sword.

"Abandoning his chariot, Sisera fled on foot. But Barak pursued the main force as far as Harosheth Haggoyim. Every warrior of Sisera was struck down; not a man remained, save Sisera, who escaped."

"What became of him?" asked Nagad.

"Who?"

"Sisera."

"Ah," Orach replied, "he died at the hands of a woman, Jael. As he lay sleeping, she drove a tent peg through his temple."

Nagad cringed at the thought, praying he would not meet an end so dishonorable.

---

[12] Judges 5:19–22, 31 (NIV)

Together they sat in the glow of the fire. With solvent affection, unspoken yet unmistakable, the space between them gave way, and in the stillness bloomed a fellowship beyond words, the quiet knowing of brotherhood.

Two souls lingering in the hush of time, enwrapped upon a pilgrimage of understanding, each fulfilling in the other the need that gaped within his heart.

And as the quiet expanse of shared solitude deepened, Orach stirred.

"So, you be from the tribe of Benjamin. Tell me of your family, *Na'ar*. What brings you to this place?"

"When I was but a boy, we lived in a small village nestled in the mountains of Ephraim, not far from here." Nagad motioned toward the shadowed ridges to the southwest. "It was a meager life, growing grain in the valley, herding sheep upon the hills. But we were content... happy."

A smile softened the young conscript's face. With a quiet sigh, he continued, "My sister's hair glistened chestnut in the sun. I remember her laughter. She was a joyful child, kind and sweet. She would follow me everywhere, always just a few steps behind. I used to get so annoyed with her."

Nagad lifted his tear-brimmed eyes to meet Orach's. "She was taken from me, Orach. They were all taken. It is all gone now, the village, the people. All destroyed at the hands of the Philistines. My entire family. I was not there when they came. They burned everything. They killed everyone. I should have been there to help them. I should have died with them."

He looked down at his left hand. Without thinking, he ran his right hand slowly across the open palm, as though touching something no longer there. "But that was long ago."

"Hmm," Orach grunted softly. "How did you escape?"

"I saw the smoke. I ran as fast as I could. But I was too late. The house was burning. Smoke filled the air. I could not breathe. I blacked out. All I remember is the feeling of being lifted, carried away. Another family in a neighboring village took me in, until I was conscripted into the army."

He paused, voice low. "I am alone, Orach. Alone in this world."

"No, *Na'ar*. Not alone anymore. You are not in this fight unaided. These Philistines—*bah*—they shall not go unpunished. Cursed are they for what they have done. And we shall see the end of their days. You will see, *Na'ar*; we are all brothers in this war."

Orach nodded, firm in his own words. His face was fierce, resolute, etched with the firelight of conviction.

Nagad looked in earnest at this bold friend. He felt himself grow lighter, as if the burden he held so long had been eased from his shoulders, if only but a fraction. And as he gazed at the face before him, as the flame of the fire caused Orach's countenance to glow, some unspoken bond grew between them, forged by the common hatred of the shared foe.

The depth of the bond not fully understood until that which was between them was severed.

CHAPTER 5

A JUST CAUSE

The night was long; rest came in short bouts, broken by restless thoughts and troubled dreams. Nagad was relieved when the first rays of light crested over the eastern hills. The company roused early to begin the final leg of their journey, a journey that would alter the course of a nation.

The trumpet sounded, and the regiment, grown in number over the advance of night, set out on its trek southwest, past Mount Ebal and toward the Great Sea.

The western waters looked as an empty expanse of nothingness, caressing the edge of the coastal plain, for the glimmer of day had not yet adorned the crystal sea. The somber bleak of the unlit roof retreated as the ascending orb glowed golden before the forward thrust of the forging troops. In the hush of morning, the procession marched in censored quiet.

Content to be together, the bond indelibly etched upon the tablets of their hearts, Nagad and Orach ventured on in double file. The young conscript's thoughts weighed heavily upon him; doubts lingered within the confines of an anxious mind. After a time, Nagad broke the silence.

"Orach, what do you think will happen? Is our battle just?"

Orach walked on as though he had not heard. Nagad grew impatient, but feared to speak again.

At length, Orach said, "Do you know what the name *Naphtali* means, *Na'ar*?"

"No, I do not."

Silence lingered. Then Nagad asked, "Why do you ask, Orach?"

A smile touched Orach's face. "The name means *My struggle*. And do you know whose struggle it is?"

"No, *Sar*, I do not."

"It is the very struggle of God after which my tribe was named. We have always fought for the Lord in these pagan lands. Our struggle has long been His struggle. We are as a hind let loose, which yields goodly words."[13]

Again, silence ruled the air. Nagad was not certain what Orach was trying to tell him.

At last, Orach halted and laid a hand upon the young conscript's shoulder. Pity shone in his dark eyes as he looked long into Nagad's searching gaze.

Smiling, Orach said, "*Na'ar*, you are a good boy. This day we fight for our land, for our people. The very Ark of God goes before us. Who can stand against us? We are God's chosen."

Straightening, Orach released Nagad's shoulder and strode ahead, his pace swift and sure, as though his own words had lent him courage.

"God will not desert us, *Na'ar*, so long as we fight for the right reasons."

"Are we fighting for the right reasons, Orach?"

"That, my *Na'ar*, is between you and God."

It was not yet midday when they reached the summit of Pirathon, ten miles southwest of Shechem. Once an Amalekite stronghold, the town crowned the hilltop, overlooking the plain below. Within its bounds lay the tomb of Abdon, the tenth judge of Israel.

Nagad wished he had listened more closely to the tales of the elders. Images of forgotten stories stirred within him, shadowy recollections of a city now passed into legend. Yet the details eluded him, like voices carried away on the wind.

The cavalcade rested only briefly, for all felt the press of urgency. Time moved swiftly, and still they had far to go.

---

[13] Genesis 49:21 (KJV)

Continuing westward, the Hebrew battalion marched on as the sun centered over the Great Sea, a golden reflection shimmering across the expanse.

The company grew ever more silent as they advanced toward the camp at Eben-Ezer. Dark storm clouds gathered in the west, blotting out the golden rays of the sinking sun, as thunder doled out its warning.

"That may wet more than our cloaks," Orach said, nodding toward the ominous clouds rising above the Great Sea.

Nagad dipped his head as a shadow settled over him.

The camp at Eben-Ezer stood upon a hill, its tents stretched across the height overlooking the valley where Israel had suffered bitter defeat. Looming across the plain, the well-fortified Philistine stronghold of Aphek guarded the Way of the Sea, the main trade route running north and south through the coastal plain. This fortress was the first to meet the eyes of the weary regiment as they travailed southward. The company hastened their steps, fearing they would arrive too late.

Relief stirred as the camp came into view. A barricade of wagons encircled the hilltop, forming a makeshift rampart. Family ensigns and tribal standards snapped upon the breeze, rising like tongues of flame above the spread of tents.

The garrison looked much as it had when Nagad departed for Shiloh. *Had only two days passed since the terrible defeat?* he wondered. It seemed an age had fallen between that day and this. Time itself felt sundered since last he stood at Eben-Ezer.

The noise of their coming filled the ears of those who waited. Men lined the way, forming an alley through which the regiment advanced. Then they saw it—the Shrine of Yahweh, the seat of God.

As the Ark entered the camp, the courage of Israel returned. A mighty shout rose, a cry so great the earth itself trembled with adulation.

Tiphcar, upon hearing the great commotion, emerged from his tent. His heart was uplifted as he espied the regiment drawing near, the Ark of God before it. Nagad hurried to his captain, relieved to find him restored.

"Nagad, you have been long looked for. I am pleased to see your charge has been successful," spoke Tiphcar, a warm smile upon his face. "And you have brought more men than I had hoped."

"*Sar* Tiphcar, many have left hearth and home to fight beside you. They bring light to break through the darkness that yet lingers before us."

"Who is this who follows you so mindfully?" asked Tiphcar, noting the soldier beside the young conscript.

"Orach, of the tribe of Naphtali. He has been with me since Tappuah."

Tiphcar dipped his head in acknowledgment. "I know of the good repute of your tribe. You are most welcome in this conflict."

Turning to Nagad, he said, "Come. The elders await. Much remains to be decided."

A quiet awe settled over him, honored, yet uncertain, as though he had stepped into the company of kings.

"I will await your return." Orach lowered his head and took his leave.

Within the tent, the Council of Elders had assembled, deep in debate over the course that might yet deliver them. Nagad stood behind Tiphcar's chair, uneasy, for he knew not what was expected of him. Reaching into his tunic, he drew out the spearhead, as was his wont, tracing the sharp edge beneath his fingers.

Tiphcar rose and addressed them.

"As you have heard, the Ark of God has come to us from Shiloh, and with it, many men, ready to stand and fight. Yet even so, our number remains few beside the great host of the Philistines. As we all have seen, our defenses fall short."

"We must press our advantage before the Philistines can react," Gadowl spoke, excitement growing in his voice. "We must strike at first light. How say you?"

"It is in God we must trust, not in the Ark," said Zaqen, his concern mounting. "Only God can send us to battle and secure our victory. I fear we have taken matters into our own hands and forgotten our place before Him. Give ear to reason. This campaign is folly."

"Do not heed this harbinger of doom," retorted Gadowl. "To have the Ark before us is to have God before us. We cannot allow these uncircumcised pagans to come and take our lands. We must fight. Fight for what is right. Our cause is just; we have no reason to fear."

With fervor, he continued, his words ablaze. "It is too late to turn back. Our course is set. To yield now would only embolden the Philistines to press farther into our land, for they will see us as fearful beasts, fit only to be driven aside. We must stand and fight!"

Most of the council gave assent with a nod, their faces set with resolve. Yet all were ready to face the enemy.

"Since it is the will of the council to fight," declared Tiphcar, "our only hope lies in swift action. Before daybreak, we must set out. By now the enemy will have surmised our intent and begun preparing their defense. The sooner we strike, the greater our chances of victory."

"On this we are agreed. Make whatever preparations you must. Tomorrow then, our fate will be decided," spoke Gadowl, triumph alight in his eyes.

The council dispersed, each man taking his leave.

Tiphcar turned to Nagad. "You have done well. Tell your men to rest now, for weariness has overtaken them. We attack at first light."

Nagad and Orach sat in silence, gazing into the fire. All had been prepared; nothing remained but to wait for dawn. Yet a heaviness lingered in Nagad's heart, a quiet doubt he could not shake. Something in him whispered that this battle was not as it should be.

"Have you ever been north? Have you seen the beauty of the land about the Sea of Chinnereth?" Orach spoke, longing in his voice, his eyes still fixed upon the flame.

Drawn from his thoughts by the sound of Orach's voice, Nagad looked up, the question etched across his face. "No, I have not been that far north, but I have heard of its beauty."

"Ah, *Na'ar*, you have missed a wondrous sight, a wondrous sight indeed. You must go there in time, before this life takes you. You will be glad to behold it. The plain of Gennesaret is the very *ambition of nature*,[14] an earthly paradise."

Orach smiled faintly and began to recite, the words like an old song upon his tongue.

> O Naphtali, satisfied with favor,
> And full of the blessing of the Lord,
>
> Blessed of the Lord is his land,
> With the precious things of heaven, with the dew,
> And the deep lying beneath,
>
> With the precious fruits of the sun,
> With the precious produce of the months,
>
> With the best things of the ancient mountains,
> With the precious things of the everlasting hills,
>
> With the precious things of the earth and its fullness,
> And the favor of Him who dwelt in the bush.[15]

"I long to see my land once more, to hear the shores of the Sea bid me home."

Orach shook his head. "Ah, but this is the reminiscing of an old fool. Never mind. We must rest, for tomorrow we will need our strength."

Lying down upon his mat, Orach said, "*Laylah Tov*, good night, *Na'ar*. May blessings come to you this night."

Seren, captain of the Philistine regiment, watched the sun sink behind dark clouds into the Great Sea. From the watchtower at Aphek,

---

[14] (Josephus 1930)
[15] Deuteronomy 33:23, 13–16

he beheld a sweeping view of the land: southward over the plains of Philistia, east to the hills of Ephraim, and north across the valley that lay between the Hebrew camp at Eben-Ezer and the Philistine fortress. This stronghold guarded the headwaters of the Yarkon River, at the place where the road narrows between the swamp and the western slopes of the Hill Country.

In their effort to expand their northern reach, the Philistines had taken this strategic city from Israel. Ever pressing outward, they extended their dominion over much of the coastal plain west of the mountains.

If not for these stubborn Hebrews, the entire coastal plain, with its rich harbors, would already be under Philistine rule, thought Seren.

No movement had been seen in the enemy's camp since the massacre dealt them several days earlier. Seren turned northward, scanning the horizon, though the camp at Eben-Ezer was fading into the gathering dusk.

They are planning something—of that I am certain. They do not yield so easily, never learning their place in this world.

Eyeing the valley, Seren recalled the bloody slaughter. The lowland had been littered with the hewn corpses of Hebrew soldiers. Now, it lay barren, almost serene, with no trace of the carnage, save the scars still etched upon the earth.

"Seren, *Sar*," said a soldier clad in a leather kilt and polished breastplate. "Reinforcements have just arrived from the south."

"Ah, Moloch, this is good news. How many?"

"The regiment is ten thousand strong, heavily armored, with many horses."

"This is good, indeed," Seren replied, eyeing the shadowed horizon. "Good, indeed."

A great tumult arose, jarring the two men from their contemplation. So great was this uproar that the very stones beneath their feet began to quake.

"What is the cause of this agitation?" asked Seren, shaken.

A shout sprang from below the watchtower. "*Sar* Seren! It comes from the Hebrew encampment!"

When the Philistines heard the noise from Eben-Ezer, they grew fearful. A great cry rose from the garrison: "Woe to us! For such a thing has never happened before. Woe to us!"

"What is this that I hear from my men? They cry out with the voices of women," Seren chided.

"It is the Hebrews," came the reply. "The Ark of God has been brought into their camp."

"Woe to us!" cried a soldier from below.

"What are we to do?" called another from the rabble beneath the tower.

"Who shall deliver us from the hand of these mighty gods? These are the gods who struck the Egyptians with many plagues!"

A multitude of voices lifted in like manner, as fear spread through the ranks of the Philistine camp.

Seren knew something must be done, and swiftly, before order was lost.

"They will try to seize their advantage and strike while our ranks are disheartened," he said to Moloch, his voice hard with resolve. "We must be prepared for battle by first light."

Seren took leave of the watchtower and stood upon the outer wall, gazing down at the ranks below. A shadowed form, he loomed above them as though he were a figure removed from the mortal realm. His very presence stirred the hearts of the troops.

"Be strong, and conduct yourselves like men, you Philistines, that you do not become servants of the Hebrews, as they once were to you! These are the same Hebrews who served under your yoke. They will not stand against our might. We have strength and numbers to our advantage."

A cheer rose from the ranks as the men raised their arms, rallying themselves to courage.

"Yes—we will fight, and we will have victory," Seren declared. "These Hebrews are a ragged band of tribal herdsmen. They have no king, no single banner, no common purpose. But we fight for the five lords of Philistia! We fight for our nation! One will, one command. In unity, there is victory. We shall teach these shepherd dogs a lesson they will not soon forget."

CHAPTER 6

A STORM APPROACHES

Out of the dark came the crack of a whip, the echo of snorting steeds driven to fury. A thunder of wheels and galloping hooves shattered the silence of the unseeing night, swelling ever greater, until the very ground beneath him began to quake with the storm's approach.

Nagad turned and ran, every stride driven by the will to survive. He did not need to look back; he could sense it gaining upon him. The sound swelled behind, the tremor in the earth growing stronger. Its presence pressed ever nearer, until at last he felt it—the very breath of the horses upon his neck, like a warm blast from a fire stoked too high.

There was no escape. He wheeled about to meet what hunted him.

Twin beasts reared before him, eyes ablaze with fire, their nostrils flaring with putrid breath.

Then came the glint of a spear.

It lunged.

He opened his mouth to cry out—

Nagad bolted upright, panting, sweat pouring down his brow.

A horn pierced the darkness, the call of a *shofar* rising through the camp.

Only a dream.

But it left him winded, and deeply unsettled.

Orach looked at Nagad with concern.

"You look as though you have seen a ghost, *Na'ar*. What is it that haunts you?"

Still shaken, Nagad replied, "A nightmare only. It is nothing." Yet even as he girded himself for battle, a shadow lingered within him.

"To arms! To arms! Fall in!"

Nagad and Orach took their places among the ranks. As the faint light of morning began to stir upon the mountains, Nagad cast his gaze across the field. Though the dawn lay cloaked beneath a veil of dark clouds, a great host stood before him, line upon line of men, set for war.

It was a sight the likes of which he had never seen. Magnificent. Terrible.

They came, tribe by tribe, as in the days of old, each man beneath his banner, each lineage in its place.

The host was drawn up in three divisions, arranged by house and clan: in tens and fifties, in hundreds and thousands, each man clad in armor of his own making.

At the forefront stood a tight rank and file of foot soldiers, long thrusting spears jutting from behind broad, rectangular shields. They guarded the van beneath the banner of Judah

the dark eyes of Judah, the lion's whelp.

To their left and right, two regiments of Naphtali held the flanks, formed in like manner, steady, silent, resolute.

And behind them, the sons of Israel:

Simeon and Levi
the flaming sword, swift and fierce.

Gad and Manasseh
raiders of valor,
banners lifted high,
bows strung and javelins ready,
light shields upon their arms.

Zebulun
a safe harbor,
his slingers and axemen
stationed where need may bid.

Issachar
the beast of burden,
with shield and spear,
his banner rising in the breeze.

Ephraim
the ox,
unshaken and strong.

Reuben
the mandrake,
eldest of the tribes,
holding the second rank
on the right flank.

Benjamin
the ravenous wolf,
mighty men of sling and stone,
left and right handed,
who never miss their mark.

Asher and Dan
Dan the viper,
striking the heel of the enemy,
Asher guarding the rear,
to shield those who may fall behind.

Weapons of wood and stone and bronze
filled the ranks behind
swords to cleave,
maces to crush,
axes to hew the enemy down.

Nagad drew his gaze across the field. Before the fortress of Aphek, the Philistine host was gathering in strength. The enemy presented a spectacle of unrivaled might. Stationed in ranks of four, each soldier bore a round shield, a long sword, and two spears.

Upon their heads, they wore distinctive headbands that held their hair stiff and upright. Now and again, a red-feathered headdress of similar design appeared among the ranks. The armor about their breasts gleamed, polished and ribbed. Each man was wrapped in a tasseled kilt bound with a girdle about the waist.

Weapons and armor were uniform, rendering the multitude as one. A singular machine of war.

Trembling, Nagad remembered the blessing given to the house of Benjamin long ago, and spoke it softly under his breath:

> The beloved of the Lord shall dwell in safety by Him,
> Who shelters him all the day long;
> And he shall dwell between His shoulders.[16]

With the battle lines drawn and all set in their place, the Ark of God was borne through the host, coming to rest among the innermost forces.

Hophni lifted his voice before the Ark and cried aloud:

> "There is no one like the God of Jeshurun,
> who rides on the heavens to help you,
> and on the clouds in His majesty.[17]
> Yahweh will kneel before you, presenting gifts,
> and will guard you with a hedge of protection.
> *Y'hi ratzon mil'fanekha Adonai Eloheinu vei'lohei avoteinu,*
> may it be Your will, Lord,
> our God and God of our ancestors."[18]

Gripping his spear with two hands, a ravenous grin spread across Orach's face as he said, "I am swift as a hind's feet, and as belligerent as an ass."

---

[16] Deuteronomy 33:12

[17] Deuteronomy 33:26 (NIV)

[18] (Benner, Numbers 6:24-27 1999-2012)

Tiphcar paced to and fro before the line of fighting men, encouraging and spurring them on, speaking loudly so that all could hear.

> Long have we fought for this land,
> the land promised to our father Abraham.
> With the Ark before us, there is no fear of defeat.
> Your sandals shall be of iron and bronze;
> as your days, so shall your strength be.
> Strike the loins of those who rise against you,
> and of those who hate you, that they rise not again.
> God is your refuge;
> He will drive out your enemy before you, saying,
> '*Destroy him!*'
> Now go—to honor and to victory! Destroy![19]

As he spoke these words, Tiphcar raised his sword and turned to face the enemy.

A mighty shout rose from the waiting throng. With sword and spear lifted to heaven, they cried out as one:

> Destroy!
> Destroy!
> Destroy!

Hophni sounded the *shofar*, blown to keep God in remembrance, that Israel might gain the victory.[20]

Swords were drawn from the sheath, shields borne high. A wall of shield and spear pressed forward, advancing toward the enemy's line. With quivers rattling and javelins flashing, the Israelites raised their battle cry—shaking the hearts of the Philistines with dread.

---

[19] Deuteronomy 33:11,27,35
[20] Numbers 10:9

Seren looked over at Moloch, then turned his face toward the gathering armies of Israel. In a loud voice, he called out, "Take no survivors. We will rout this rabble of jackals once and for all. No longer will they stand in our way. Now conduct yourselves like men—and fight!"

"Fight!

"Fight!" came the mighty cry as the Philistines rallied for battle.

With shaking rage, the forces raced over the ground; not a one stood still at the voice of the trumpet. The opposing columns met with a clash of arms. The roar of captains and the war cries of men filled the air, even as the heavens opened and a spring squall thundered down upon the ensuing battle.

Nagad ever held his ground, lashing out with sword and shield, striking the foe with violent force. Orach, steadfast in his staunch fidelity, stood at his flank, his spear sweeping wide, splintering ranks with his heavy hand.

Through the distemper of the storm, the forces fought on, each side striving to gain the upper hand.

Swift, the battle issued forth. Soldiers, soaked in blood, slipped upon the ruin of their enemies. Screams and agonized cries of the wounded rose across the field. Thunder rumbled as though voices echoed down from the mountains. They fought on through the fullness of day.

There was power behind the Hebrew lines, unnatural fortitude, unwavering. With confidence overreaching by the presence of the Holy Shrine, the men of Yahweh, in full trust, struck out against the foe, for the Ark of God went with them into battle. The Israelite forces were likened to a conflagration bursting upon the enemy, until they had driven back their foe to the very hem of Aphek.

"Withdraw! Withdraw!"

The shout arose from the ranks of the Philistines. The enemy fled toward the safety of Aphek and her strong tower. The Israelites gave chase, cutting down all who lagged behind, as a mighty shout rose from the Chosen of God:

"Victory! We have defeated the enemy!"

At the sound of neighing, the very earth trembled. The long-resounding cries of battle were swallowed by the gathering murmur of hooves thundering over the ridge. The Philistine ranks broke, for horse and rider, numbering in the hundreds, bore down upon the Israelites.

"Pull back! Pull back!" came the cry from Tiphcar.

All fighting ceased as the forces parted and the Israelites withdrew. Terror-stricken, the bands of Hebrew fighters fled back toward Eben-Ezer, dismayed at the turn the battle had taken.

The trumpet sounded, reclaiming the courage of the men, as Tiphcar bellowed in his strong voice:

"Reform the line! Reform the line!"

The horde of horses loomed on the horizon, filling the wind with snorting and the pawing of hooves upon the mud-laden earth.

Regrouping, the phalanx of foot soldiers pressed their spear-bolstered shield wall into action. Shields locked, spears angled upward—they waited for the undulating wave of hoof and rider to break over their line.

"Archers, arrows on my command. *Reggah*, wait."

Tiphcar raised his arm, steadying the bowmen.

"Now this is getting interesting!" Orach's voice rang out above the clamor as he gripped his spear tighter.

The horses bore down, ever closer to the rocky shore of shields. Riders lifted sword and spear above heads as they pressed forward, soon to overtake their mark.

"*Attah*! Now!" Tiphcar shouted, lowering his arm toward the onslaught of charging horsemen.

A volley of arrows loosed with the twang of the bowstring. So great was their number that they darkened the very sky. Horse and rider were brought down, pierced through by barbed shafts. Many foes fell, yet where one left off, another swiftly took his place, so that the wave of horse and rider seemed to have no end.

The front line braced for impact, heels dug into rain-soaked earth, heads ducked behind bulwarks, shoulders pressed firm against shield-wall.

Upon them broke the galloping host, like water over stone. Spears pierced horse, horse trampled man. Riders jabbed and hacked, slicing through the line, sending the Hebrew ranks into a swell of agonized confusion.

"The horses! Kill the horses!"

"Come to me, my pretty, I will knock thee down to size," shouted Orach, elated with the frenzy of battle.

With a mighty thrust of his spear, he sent a rider flailing to the ground, his point piercing the breast of the bolting beast.

In uncanny haste, Orach unsheathed his sword and plunged it deep into the belly of the Philistine as he struggled to rise.

"Ah-ha!" growled Orach, raising his blood-stained blade above his head.

Nagad fought at Orach's side, holding his own at every turn. Together, the mighty duo brought terror to the enemy, as they gasped their last breath upon this earth. Nothing could touch them. Yet valor draws opposition. Taking note of the two warriors' deeds, the mounted Philistines wheeled about their steeds. At full gallop, several horsemen charged headlong toward Orach and Nagad.

Seeing the line of beasts pressing near, Nagad froze, gaping in dismay at the approaching torrent.

"Quick, *Na'ar*—to the swamp!"

Racing with great haste, the pair led the chase over the field, the sea rising before them. Knee deep, they sank into the leaching loam of a peat marsh.

Unsure of the wisdom of this move, Nagad glanced at Orach, struggling beside him through the mire.

"Keep moving," Orach instructed.

The pounding beasts raced into the swamp. Horse and rider sank into the quagmire, deeper and deeper, as the animals flailed for footing. Nagad watched as two horses, along with their burdens, sank beneath the surface of the soft earth, never to rise again.

"*Na'ar*, quickly—come, or you will meet the same fate." Orach spoke softly, yet with urgent breath into Nagad's ear.

Veering north, they struggled through the bog. A black smoke began to sully the air, and an acrid stench overtook them. Orach looked back, eyes narrowing.

"They have set fire to the swamp! Hurry, *Na'ar*, or we shall be baked where we stand!"

With great effort, under cover of smoke, they journeyed to the far side of the marsh. Once free of the muck and mire, they turned south, back into the fray. Before them, the onslaught raged: the flash of the sword, the glitter of the spear. Many were the slain; a mass of bodies, and no end to the carcasses. Soldiers stumbled, vying for ground amid the tainted field.[21]

The glory of battle had given way to the horror of war.

How much more the Israelite forces could endure, Nagad did not know. All around, the enemy unleashed its terrible barrage. Together, Nagad and Orach raised their swords, pressing forward through the thick of battle until they had pushed beyond the Israelite lines and plunged into the heart of the enemy.

The clash of arms revealed Tiphcar locked in combat with many foes, unaided, for he, too, had broken into the adversary's ranks ere his men could reach him. Orach and Nagad hastened to his relief, hope unlooked for. Beneath their fury, Tiphcar's fate was decided, as the swarming swordsmen melted away, driven back by the might of the three Hebrews.

"Well-timed, my friends."

Wiping his forehead with the back of his bloodied hand, Tiphcar turned toward the Ark. Seeing the horses of the Philistine contingent racing across the field toward the Holy Shrine, he shouted:

"To the Ark! To the Ark!"

Nagad and Orach beheld the scene in horror, for the priests stood defenseless as the cavalry bore down upon them. As many as were able ran to assist, but the holy men were cut down where they stood, struck with vicious intent.

Hophni lay slain at his brother's feet. Phinehas stood transfixed, frozen before the oncoming horsemen. With a single thrust, horse and rider burst upon him, plunging a spear deep into his belly. He dropped to his knees, clutching the shaft now buried in his body.

Looking up from his doom, Phinehas, son of Eli, cried out, "Esha!"—then fell forward, and death took him.

Orach, Nagad, and Tiphcar hastened to the priests, but to no avail. All were lost to the point of the Philistine spear.

The terrible trio crossed the field, bloodlust overtaking them so that all caution was lost. None could withstand the tremor of their might, as they threw down all foes in their path.

---

[21] Nahum 3:3

Yet the charge of the indomitable beasts would not yield to their thirst. The enemy drove the Hebrews from the Holy Coffer. And reaching forth, the Philistines seized the Ark to carry it away, back to the fortress at Aphek.

Orach roared in heated wrath. Spear gripped tight, he hurled it across the distance, the point driving deep into a Philistine who stood before the Ark. With sword drawn, Orach surged forward to reclaim his spear. Tiphcar and Nagad followed, springing into action.

But before they could reach their quarry, a sound rose in the distance, low and growing.

It was a fell force that bore down upon them: the noise of the rumbling wheel and the galloping horse, the jolting chariot and the rearing horsemen,[22] wreaking havoc in their midst.

Bounding chariots, each drawn by two horses, stormed across the field. All were manned by a crew of three, each bearing two long spears.

The icy fingers of fear gripped the hearts of Yahweh's Chosen. Unable to advance, the Hebrew forces withdrew, watching in dismay as the Ark of God was carried away in the hands of the enemy. The Israelites stood transfixed—undone.

A mournful wail rose from the Hebrew lines; so haunting was this cry of woe that for a moment all fighting ceased. Even the Philistine forces recoiled at the wound they had inflicted upon the tribes.

"All is lost," went up the cry.

The sky grew dark with a crack of thunder that shuddered through the ranks. The clouds burst open, releasing a torrent of rain that veiled their sight. Then, out of the gloom, Nagad heard the crack of the whip, the echo of horses snorting. A shiver coursed down his spine.

Not a dream.

The earth trembled beneath his feet as the sound bore down upon them. From the dismal shroud, the shadowy figure of a chariot emerged.

Nagad's courage faltered. He turned to flee.

Just as the breath of the horse was upon his neck, Orach, having reclaimed his spear from the felled foe, thrust it through the spokes of the chariot's wheel.

---

[22] Nahum 3:2

With all his mighty power, he dug his heels into the mire and halted the chariot with such great force that the Philistine warriors were hurled into the air as the horses fell to their knees.

The fight raged on, but doom settled in the heart of Israel. Nagad and Orach, side by side, fought with sword and spear. Out of the conflict, the iron-tipped shaft of a Philistine spear sailed into the mass of soldiered bodies. Orach, caught mid-motion, drew a sharp breath as the point struck his side, wounding him gravely.

Yet on he fought, by the might of his will, this stout son of Naphtali. Many foes surrounded them, pressing from all sides, yet the companions would not yield. With a strength beyond their own, the two laid waste to every foe within reach.

Nagad looked into Orach's eyes and saw them flutter—then Orach fell, wounded. Kneeling at his side, Nagad trembled with emotion.

"Orach," he cried.

"Do not fret, *Na'ar*. Do not fear."

"All is lost," Nagad whispered.

"No," spoke Orach, a smile ever upon his face. "This battle is over, but the fate of Israel is not yet decided. Flee, flee for now. Another day will come to fight. But now, *Na'ar*, you must run. Tell the old priest what has happened. He will—"

Orach winced and shifted, seeking relief from the stabbing pain.

"He will tell you what to do."

Closing his eyes, he drew in a ragged breath.

"Orach," cried Nagad, "leave me not alone."

With effort, he reached and laid a strong hand upon Nagad's shoulder.

"I must go. All is well, *Na'ar*. It is the will of God. I see now, the battle was wrong. Go now. Flee, for the battle is over. Go—"

He let out a shudder and breathed his last, going the way of Sheol, for every man must give forth his bond.

It was said of Orach, that he laughed at fear and was not dismayed; that whenever the trumpet sounded, he turned not back from the sword.[23]

Overmuch with grief, Nagad grasped the blood-drenched soil. The world began to spin. Then slowed.

---

[23] Job 39:22

All around him rose the cries of the dying. Mayhem erupted; men fled in confusion, trampled under hoof and wheel as chariots ran them down in sport. A noxious cloud rose from the earth like a black mist, encircling the horror around him. The stench of burnt flesh seared his nostrils.

With both hands, he clawed at the ground. Blood pooled beneath him—Orach's blood. Gathering with his hands the sanguine earth, Nagad smeared it over his hair, dragging his muddied hands down his tear-streaked face.

A mighty groan stirred deep within his soul. Rising to his feet, he threw back his head as the cry broke forth, a savage roar of anguish.

Gripping the collar of his garment, he rent it in two with the strength that only grief could beget.

He could no longer see; he could no longer hear. Nagad ran as he had never run before. To camp he raced, swift as a hind.

Tiphcar, he thought.

Looking about, all he saw was ruin. Tents burnt and trampled. Bodies beyond number. Elders cut down where they had stood—but no sign of Tiphcar.

Flee. That was what Orach had said. Flee to Shiloh.

Nagad turned east and ran. Sensing the enemy behind him, he sped over the very pass he had crossed to plead for the Ark. This time, he ran for his very life.

He did not look back. He flew as one pursued by death.

Tears streaked his soot-smeared face, mingling with the grime of battle. Calamity had struck; doom had come, just as Eli had foretold.

Treacherous was the path, for the storm-shroud had overtaken the day. The earth, muddied by the rain, was slick, causing Nagad to slip and slide up the side of the ridge.

The delay over the mountains alarmed him. The enemy could be just behind him, tracking his steps as he struggled to keep his footing. He was wet and cold and covered in mud.

Rain unrelenting beat down, blinding his path. Loose rocks and rivulets of muddy water betrayed his steps. His limbs grew heavy, unwilling to trudge through the muck and mire.

It took all his will to force himself forward.

Ragged breaths tore from his chest, each one more labored than the last, pulling on the thinning threads of his strength.

After hours of hard and bitter labor, Nagad's will gave way. Falling to the path, the shadow of despair rolled over him. He lay still, gazing up at the veiled sky. Rain spattered his pallid face, his eyes blinking against its sting.

Turning his face from the merciless downpour, Nagad heaved a heavy sigh.

Nothing. I see nothing to hold on to. The Lord has deserted us for our great sin. And now the hope of all Israel is lost, the Ark of God, in the hands of the enemy.

As he rolled over to rise, to forge ahead in urgent need, he noticed a single flower, a cyclamen, white, with petals reaching toward heaven, clinging to a crack upon a barren rock.

He reached out and touched the delicate bloom, the pale-petaled hope that stood defiant against the storm.

This small flower grew in the young conscript a glimmer of renewal, of stubborn resistance, that brought him to his feet.

KOHEN GADOL

It was the tenth day of *Iyyar,* in the year 2871[24], when Eli, a descendant of Ithamar, the youngest son of Aaron the *Kohen Gadol,* the High Priest, sat upon a stool by the wayside, waiting for word of his sons. The mournful bale of a turtle-dove, calling to its lost mate, broke the silence of the still air, as storm clouds gathered over the western hills. Word had not come since the Ark of God was removed from the Tabernacle, and another day was swiftly waning.

So Eli waited as the sun dipped low, and the shadow of night crept upward from the east. He was anxious for his sons, yet it was for the Ark of God that dread pressed deepest upon his soul. The aged priest ran a trembling hand across his face, as if to wipe away the burden of his thoughts. His mind was about to turn over another reflection, when he was interrupted by a great tumult coming from the direction of the city gate.

In the waning light, a man of Benjamin came running up the narrow road, garments rent, his head crowned with earth, a sign of deep mourning.

Eli was ninety-eight years old, and his eyes were so dim that he could see but images faded and blurred.

Hearing the outcry, Eli spoke, reaching out with both hands as he sensed a presence before him. "What is the meaning of this noise of unrest?"

---

24 Reckoning of the Hebrew calendar

The Benjaminite came near to where the old priest sat. He was tall and comely, though weariness darkened his eyes. And though Eli could not see clearly, he knew the tale they told.

"I have come from the battle this very day," gasped the young man. "The war has gone ill."

Eli knew the voice; he had heard it before. "Nagad," he said, "tell me, what has happened, my son? What has befallen the Ark of God since it was taken from the Tent of Meeting?"

As Eli spoke, he grasped the young man's ragged tunic, drawing him near, that he might better hear his words.

Nagad leaned down and took hold of Eli's shoulders, resting gently upon the old priest. Composing himself, for emotion threatened to spill over, he spoke, though his voice wavered with grief.

"When the Ark entered the camp, the courage of all Israel was restored. A mighty shout rose from the people as they beheld the Ark of God, a shout so great the earth shook beneath them. Upon hearing the noise, the Philistines grew fearful, perceiving that the Ark of God had come into our midst. A great cry broke forth from their encampment."

Nagad released his hold on the priest. Straightening, he turned his face away from Eli.

"At their outcry, we grew confident the battle would turn in our favor. We outfitted ourselves for war and drew upon the enemy, the Ark of God standing ever before us. We fought with renewed vigor."

Once more, Nagad leaned toward the old priest and clasped his shoulders.

"We thought the power of the Ark would deliver us from the hand of our enemies. But we were wrong."

With pleading eyes, Nagad looked into the clouded gaze of the High Priest.

"And though we fought with desperate courage, it was to no avail. There was a great slaughter; many thousands of our kinsmen were butchered. The rest fled in confusion."

He paused, lowering his eyes in shame and sorrow as the horrors of the day returned to him.

The old priest pulled Nagad closer. "And my sons—what of them?" asked Eli, grief raking through his chest.

"Also, your two sons…" Nagad's voice caught. "Your sons, Hophni and Phinehas, they too have fallen. Killed. And the Ark of God has been taken."

At Nagad's words, when he spoke of what had befallen the Ark of God, Eli, overcome by grief, released his hold upon the young conscript. Throwing up his arms in shock, he fell backward from his seat.

Nagad, in horror, looked upon the lifeless body of Eli. Stooping down, he touched him, and saw that the old priest's neck was broken.

"He is dead," spoke Nagad solemnly, lowering his head in sorrow.

A great cry arose from the crowd that had gathered, for Eli had been greatly loved. The old priest possessed a kind heart, and many had looked to him for spiritual guidance.

Especially fond of him was Eli's young ward, who followed faithfully in all the priest's counsel and preparation. In Samuel, Eli had found a foster-son worthy of praise.

Mourning fell upon the city of Shiloh. In one day, they had lost not only their High Priest, but the Ark of God, the very Seat of Yahweh. Word spread swiftly through the streets until it reached Eli's daughter-in-law, Esha, the wife of Phinehas, who was great with child.

When tidings came that the Ark was taken, and that her father-in-law and her husband were dead, Esha was stricken. Her pangs were upon her, and with great travail she brought forth a son. Yet her cries were not her own, for they mingled with the lament of the nation, her labor the sorrow of Israel, her travail the birth-throes of a people undone.

The midwife who attended her said, "Do not fear, for you have borne a son."

But Esha, too grieved to respond, would not look upon the child. "I will call him Ichabod, for the glory has departed from Israel! The glory has departed, for the Ark of God has been taken."

Having spoken thus, she turned her face away and sighed. All desire to live had left her, and death took her to join her husband in Sheol.

So it was, on that day, the prophecy long spoken concerning the house of Eli was fulfilled. All perished, save the little babe born in the midst of sorrow, for Israel had lost more than she dared fear.

As the veiled light of the next day broke upon Shiloh, the holy city became a city of sorrow. The dawn brought no comfort. Storm clouds threatened overhead. Sounds of mourning filled the streets as word of the losses spread. All Israel seemed forfeit. God had deserted them.

No family remained to prepare the bodies of Eli and Esha for burial. Others in the community came, lovingly washing and wrapping the bodies in fine linen, anointing their remains with oil and spices.

Nagad waited as the preparations were completed. Sitting against the wall of the city, the young conscript drew forth his spearhead and laid it in his open palm. So much had been lost. So many now knew the way of grief.

He saw it clearly in his mind, Orach's body lying there on the war-torn plain, forsaken on the field of battle, left for the sport of foul carrion. All the dead of Israel lay abandoned. No loved ones would attend their bodies. No sacred rites would mark their passage.

They would be left for the enemy to collect and cast aside, consigned to a common grave without name or stone. Unknown would be their final rest. And oh, how he grieved. Grieved that he had not Orach's body to bury.

A loud wail swelled as the people of Shiloh, clothed in sackcloth, gathered behind the funeral procession. The dead were carried upon a pallet through the city gates. A flute sang its sorrowful note, keeping time with the marching throng. The weeping rose with great volume as the company of mourners followed, just beyond the city walls, to the tombs hewn from the rocky hillside.

Families had been buried in these chambers for generations. Now the tomb waited, gaping wide, ready to receive two more within the pallid vault.

The temple priest stood clad in white linen, his countenance lifted toward heaven. His clear voice rang out in solemn modulation.

"Barukh ata Adonai Eloheinu melekh ha'olam, Dayan ha'emet. Blessed are You, Lord our God, King of the universe, the True Judge."

Lowering his face, the priest looked upon the earth. "He rests now with his fathers."

As if in answer to the lamentation of the people, the heavens gave way. Rain came, falling on the mourners, wetting their cheeks with cloud-tears.

Nagad looked on with sorrow as Eli and Esha were laid to rest within the tomb. Yet even as he stood among the mourners, he felt apart—alone. There was no comfort for him, for Orach was dead, Tiphcar missing. All whom he had loved were gone. And now, Eli, the High Priest, was dead, and the Lord, *El-Elohim*, had forsaken them.

I am alone. Then it came to Nagad that the cost of love is grief. *I will guard my heart with more care from this day onward.*

He wondered if Orach had a family. He regretted never asking. They had known each other only a few days, yet the loss Nagad felt was profound, as though Orach had been a friend of many years. The hopes he had allowed himself to form, the friendship that might have been, were stolen from him. When he considered all the loss he had lately witnessed, it was as though a great weight lay crushing his chest.

Tears, he would not shed, but bore his grief with stern face uplifted, and shoulders thrown back. Yet, his soul was restless within him. Those who looked upon him feared him, for they perceived a dark hollowness behind his eyes that they were loath to see.

After returning within the walls of Shiloh, Nagad was approached by Ebed, the priest's servant.

"*Sar* Nagad, come, eat and rest. It is what my *adon* would have wanted."

"*Todah*, thank you, but food would be of no use to me. I have no stomach for it. I am too anguished of spirit."

Nagad wandered the narrow streets of the city, through the maze of shops and homes, restless and lost. *What happens now? What should I do?* A weariness settled upon him. *I am worn, and I have no heart for life.*

Finding a place apart, along the outer wall, Nagad sat and leaned his head against the cold stone of the battlements. Taking out the spearhead, his fingers again traced its sharp edge.

It was an instrument of doom that rested in his open palm. Flashes of memory invaded his waking thoughts, of home and family, and of Orach.

Clenching his hand tightly over the iron point, Nagad closed his eyes, but sleep would not come. The horror of the past days played out in his mind as the darkness of night overtook the day.

At Aphek, Seren surveyed his troops, satisfied with the numbers before him. Moloch approached, battle-weary, but in good spirits.

"Your orders, *Sar*?"

Seren nodded. "Send a small garrison to Ashdod. Let them deliver the Hebrews' Ark to our lord. The rest—rally them. We are not yet finished with the Israelites."

A smile touched his lips. "We will march on Shiloh and deliver the final blow. We will destroy their sacred city. And all who dwell within."

CHAPTER 8

IN THE PRESENCE OF THE ENEMY

The peal of a trumpet cut through the air, startling Nagad from his weary vigil. All through the night, he had sat beneath the shadow of the wall, eyes fixed upon the darkness, the cold iron of the spear-point clutched to his chest.

Daylight now laid open morning, fresh and new, with the promise that life carries on. The black clouds of yesterday had scattered. The storm had passed.

Nagad jumped to his feet. The iron trinket slipped from his hand as he unsheathed his sword, ready for battle.

"Open the gates! Friends approach!" came the cry from the wall.

Returning his sword to its sleeve, Nagad stooped to retrieve the spearhead. Tucking the point into the fold of his tunic, he hastened toward the gate, anxious to see who was drawing near.

His heart leapt when he caught sight of them, the company of soldiers returning from Eben-Ezer. At their lead was Tiphcar, battle-worn, but alive. Beside him walked Gadowl, the elder.

With renewed spirit, Nagad rushed to meet them.

Falling to one knee, he said, "Tiphcar, *Sar*, I rejoice at seeing you."

Tiphcar looked at Nagad with compassion, for he saw the shadow that had settled across his face, and he was sorry for the grief the young man carried, his youth clouded in the shroud of loss. Taking him by the shoulders, Tiphcar lifted him to his feet.

"I have gathered all I could find. We must meet with the elders who remain, for trouble brews. The Philistines have assembled and march toward Shiloh. They will be upon us by nightfall."

Ebed entered through the gate and into the chamber where the elders and leaders of Israel had assembled. In his hands, he carried well-needed refreshments.

The room was bare, save for a few wooden benches lining the stone-masoned walls. Few there were that remained alive, or unmarked by blade, to sit upon these council seats.

"There has been a very great slaughter," Gadowl began, his voice slow and heavy. "There fell of Israel a great host of foot soldiers. Also, the Ark of God is taken. And now we learn that not only have the two sons of Eli, Hophni and Phinehas, been slain, but Eli, the High Priest, has died as well. Too great have been our losses, and more will follow, for the armies of Philistia march. We cannot withstand an assault on this city."

Nagad looked upon him with disdain; his dislike for the elder rekindled.

One among them, Haddabar it was, wounded on the head, stepped forward. With finger raised toward Gadowl, he cried out with passion, "It is your fault this calamity has befallen us! You were the one who urged us to take the Ark of God into battle. And now look what has happened. The Ark rests in the very hands of the enemy!"

Several men moved to restrain him, but few disagreed with his rebuke.

"Nay," spoke Tiphcar softly. Rising to his feet, he continued, "I alone must bear this guilt upon my shoulders."

"No, *Sar*," Nagad cried, rising to come to his captain's side.

But with a gesture, Tiphcar bade him remain seated. "It was I who gave command to retrieve the Ark. I gave the order. The guilt is mine alone to carry."

He looked weary, his shoulders sagging beneath the weight.

"All that aside, what are we to do? You say the enemy is approaching. We have not the time to place blame. What is done is done. The question remains: what shall we do now?" So spoke Etsah the wise, an elder who had seen many days.

With measured intonation, he continued. "By our count, we have lost some thirty thousand men to death, and thousands more lie wounded or missing. We have already seen what the forces of the enemy can do. The walls of this city are old and crumbling. They will not withstand the onslaught of the Philistines.

"We grope for the wall like the blind, as if we had no eyes; we stumble at noonday as at twilight; we are as dead men in desolate places. We all growl like bears, and moan sadly like doves; we look for justice, but there is none, for salvation, but it is far from us."[25]

Tiphcar lowered himself slowly onto the bench. He sat in silence for some time, thoughtfully running his hand down the length of his beard.

Nagad grew restless as the stillness lingered. Nervously, he raked his fingers through his disheveled hair, catching in its tangles. He could feel the weight of the spearhead within the fold of his tunic. Drawn by habit more than thought, he laid his palm over it.

Rising slowly to his feet, Tiphcar spoke, his voice strained and hoarse.

"Gather all in the city who can bear arms. Send the women and children to Lebonah. Make sure the gates, and mend what you can of the outer wall. Here we make our stand. If Shiloh falls... then all is lost. We shall be as brambles trodden underfoot by the Philistines. The enemy will show no mercy. They will destroy all who stand in their way."

"And what of the Ark?" asked Haddabar, somewhat subdued.

"There is nothing we can do at this time," Tiphcar replied. "All focus must be placed on defending this holy city. Despite our great trespass, I do not believe God will forsake us forever. He will not leave the enemy unpunished for their molestation. For now, we must leave the fate of the Ark in the Lord's hands."

Then, turning to Nagad, his now-trusted aide, Tiphcar said, "Make ready the city. We have but small time to prepare."

---

[25] Isaiah 59:10–11

"As you wish, *Sar* Tiphcar. All will be accomplished as you have instructed."

At that, the council dispersed, and every person set to work, clearing the city and making ready for battle. A great wailing rose from the streets as the old and infirm, and the women and children, gave their farewells and prepared for the exodus to Lebonah. Every cistern, jar, and bowl was filled with water drawn from *Ein Seilun*, the spring beyond the gate, then carried into the city. Stores of food were gathered, livestock and grain, enough to endure for months, if need be.

The evacuation complete, efforts turned once more to restoring the walls, old and in disrepair. Once a mighty defense, the fortifications stood weakened, beyond full repair before the onslaught of battle. Those within the city, strong and old enough to fight, gathered their farm implements and hammered them into weapons: their ploughshares into swords, their pruning hooks into spears.[26]

"Scorch the earth. Lay fire to the crops," came the order from Tiphcar, laboring alongside the people. "Our enemy will hunger before the defenders even pang for food."

A mighty blaze rose from the surrounding fields of barley, white-headed and ready for harvest. Smoke-laden air swept through the narrow streets, curling above the rooftops and rising into the valley, hemmed in by the encircling hills.

The captain and his conscript stood upon the wall, watching the flames devour the fields that filled the pass between the mountains.

Nagad leaned forward, a frown etched upon his brow.

He spoke low. "One way in, one way out. There will be no retreat from defending this city. We fight here—or we die."

Tiphcar had been resting his arm upon the wall, thoughtfully stroking his beard. He stood, his gaze fixed on something far away.

"We will fight. But it is not the Philistines alone against whom we contend. Our true battle is against our own wickedness, our own vanity."

Turning to Nagad, he added,

"This is the true enemy of Israel."

There was sorrow in Tiphcar's voice. Nagad looked closely at his captain, studying his features, sensing the burden he bore.

---

[26] Joel 3:10

Work continued even as the sun hung heavy in the western sky.

As darkness settled upon the city, soldiers took their stations along the walls, gazing out across the abysmal depths of the vale. Night soon fell, but no rest was given to those who labored.

Tiphcar and Nagad turned their attention to the outer fortification, where the masonry had been undercut in the city's haste to expand, pushing the township beyond the old wall. Shiloh was far from ready. Too long had her people dwelt in ease, trusting the fear of their God to keep the enemy away. They had let their defenses crumble, and now they were unprepared to stand.

"*Sar!*" came a cry from the wall. "Fire arrows!"

All eyes turned to the heavens. Arrows ablaze tore through the night sky, swift and searing. A molten rain fell upon the city, setting rooftops and scattered debris aflame.

"Give them a volley—light the arrows!" Tiphcar shouted above the rising roar, as he and Nagad made their way to the outer wall.

Arrows pierced the darkness like fire from heaven, torch-lit missiles streaking across the sky. Though falling short of their mark, the arrows told their tale nonetheless. Under cover of night, the enemy had stolen through the mountain gate and now camped within the vale.

A great host lay between the city and the only means of escape: the Gap of Shiloh.

Response came swift, the twang of bowstrings rising like a solemn chorus. All looked skyward. But the heavens, veiled in shadow, were empty.

Confused, the Chosen of God turned one to another.

"Night arrows!"

Out of the darkness, shafts disrupted the sky, visible only as they neared their quarry. No flame betrayed the place from which these bolts of doom had sprung. Shields rose above bowed heads to ward off the storm of death, as arrows fell like hail upon rooftops in spring. Many were struck before they could raise their defense.

"Answer their request. Send these heathens to their gods!" Tiphcar cried.

Arrows voiced their reply as bowstrings sang in unison. Missiles unseen flew into the night and vanished into shadow. Then came the sound, arrows striking shield and armor, and the cries of the wounded rising from the vale.

A great roar rose from the Philistine ranks as their trick was repaid.

Splitting the night came the cadence of the drum and the footfall of many soldiers. The valley trembled beneath the pulsing beat. 'Twas the voice of doom, echoing off the mountains, reverberating through the valley, even unto the very stones upon which they trod.

Death was at their gate.

"To the wall—everyone, defend the wall! Fire at will!"

Arrows rained down upon the Philistines as they closed in around the city. Out of the darkness, ladders were carried forward, an unstoppable force narrowing the gap between the enemy and the Israelite fortifications.

As the lines drew near the wall, the men of Israel hurled down stones, bricks, pots, whatever could be found, upon the encroaching foe, but to no avail. Too many there were that swarmed the outer defenses.

Ladders rose against the stone barrier, bearing many foes upon the waiting Hebrews. Fierce fighting, hand to hand, began in earnest as the defenders strove to turn back the tide that crashed against the bulwark.

Nagad, rungs of wood rising before his place on the wall, kicked out with a mighty force, thrusting the ladder, laden with men, down upon the growing throng below. Sword drawn, he hewed his way through the enemy until he reached another ladder. Again, with fierce discharge, the timbered frame was repelled and cast below.

Yet for every ladder that was thrown down, two were raised in its place. Quickly, the outer defenses were heavy with the adversary.

Below the tower gate, the lines of the enemy parted as a battering ram rolled forward on wheels, bearing down upon the barred entrance. The metal-tipped menace struck the wooden gate with a mighty concussion.

"The gate! Brace the gate!"

The defenders on the wall flung millstones down upon the advancing army as it approached the threshold.

Even so, the city gates broke open.

Oil and pitch, fired and ablaze, were poured into the inner corridor as the onrushing enemy siphoned through the narrow passage of the tower gate. Agonized cries rose as men were battered and burned, yet soon, the enemy overwhelmed those Hebrew warriors who held the entrance.

The foe turned its battering rams and axes against the eastern wall. Undetected, others climbed the once-grand glacis, sabotaging the pillars underpinning a structure, causing it to collapse and the building to topple. A great breach opened in the outer wall.

The enemy poured in through the ruined gate and the breaches cleaved in the failing battlements. Slaughter and mayhem ensued as the Israelites were pressed on every side.

Nagad fought on. This time without Orach beside him, alone amid the crush of foes. Grief rose like a tide within him, grief for his family, for his friend now fallen. Vengeance pierced his soul, and with burning wrath he met the enemy's blade. Many fell at his feet, yet more advanced, as though summoned from the depths, an unbroken host sent forth to devour.

Weariness crept into his limbs, the fire within fading. As his blood cooled, fear took hold.

The outer walls crumbled, and the enemy, unnumbered, rushed in over the rubble left in their wake. Their shields were colored red, and the warriors were dressed in scarlet, painted by the slaughter wreaked upon the Israelites. Blood ran as rivulets through the street, crimson streams over cobbled pathway.

Then came fire.

The city was set ablaze, flame raging, smoke rising. As scorching sparks weakened the masonry, the enemy brought down the tower with a mighty crash.

Dust and debris choked the air, mingling with the bitter brume that swallowed the holy city.

Enveloped in flashing iron, chariots, brandishing their cypress spears, raged madly in the streets, rushing wildly in the square. Their appearance shone like torches. They dashed to and fro like lightning.[27]

The battle had become but a fight to survive.

Little hope remained that any would live to see the morning.

The city was lost. The enemy too great. Shiloh was overrun.

"Fall back! Fall back to the temple court!" cried Tiphcar.

---

[27] Nahum 2:4 (NASB)

Few warriors remained. The Hebrews took refuge within the courtyard of the sanctuary, the inner gate braced and barred. Ebed, eyes wide with terror, hurried to Nagad and Tiphcar as they secured the last barrier between them and death.

"*Adon*! What shall we do? There is no hope! We are surely going to die!"

"Still your tongue and meet your doom with honor," rebuked Tiphcar, his voice resolute. "We will defend this city until there is none left to defend her."

Bitterly rang the sound of wood upon wood, while the cries of the enemy rose beyond the temple gate. The last of Israel's warriors, blades drawn, stood ready for what must come.

With wringing hands, Ebed implored, "*Adon*, might we not surrender? Perhaps the enemy will take pity and spare our lives."

"We will not yield. This is our fate."

"*Sar*—" Nagad's voice broke through, strained with urgency. "No, we cannot lose heart. Shiloh may be lost, but hope is not gone. We must find a way through the wall and escape. We must survive, to make this right. We must take back the Ark of God."

While they debated, the temple court was breached, and the gate cast down. The enemy rushed in to meet the broken lines of Hebrew warriors. The fight renewed with greater fervor, for there was no place left to withdraw.

Nagad resolved, the sacrifice of Orach, and all the fallen of Israel, would not be in vain. *The memory of the slain must not be forgotten by the living.*

"For Orach," spoke Nagad with fierce defiance as he plunged into the waiting throng.

Fire lapped at the walls of the temple, sending sparks and smoke curling into the air. Amid the chaos, Ebed ran toward the Tabernacle. He overturned the sacred laver, pouring out the Holy Sea upon the house of Yahweh in a desperate bid to quench the flames. Yet it was to no avail, the sacred tent, the temple of Yahweh, stood engulfed.

A terrible popping, then a loud crack rent the air as stone from the temple court gave way. Ebed stood near the Tabernacle, watching in horror as the outer walls collapsed and debris rained down upon him. The sound of the ruin turned all eyes toward the holy place.

"Surely, the glory of the Lord has departed from us," murmured a battered soldier at Nagad's side.

Nagad turned, sorrow piercing his gaze as he beheld the devastation. He ran to the ruin, and there, amid the scattered wreckage, found yet another loss. Ebed lay among the fallen timbers, his eyes fixed toward heaven, the light gone from them.

Grief rose upon grief; loss mounted upon loss. All was laid waste. The city was reduced to smoldering ruin. The sacking of Shiloh was complete, its sanctuary's destruction the final blow. The heart of Israel beat its last.

"Abandon the city! Flee! The city is lost!" cried Nagad.

Tiphcar, wounded in the belly, stood transfixed by the carnage. No strength remained in him, nor will to endure. His choices had left Israel broken. With guilt heavy upon him, Tiphcar fell to his knees.

Nagad saw him go down and rushed to him. Grasping his arm, he pulled Tiphcar to his feet.

"I will not let you give up. I will not lose you as well."

Together they fled, drawn forward by the strength of Nagad's will. They passed over the ruined walls of Shiloh, once beautiful and full of life, now laid waste. Under cover of night, the two warriors scaled the hills behind the city. Tiphcar, walking with difficulty, let Nagad lead him, for he had no will left to resist. And Nagad, with one arm around his captain's waist, half-carried him beyond the vale and into the wilderness that lay before them.

"Come, *Sar*—we go to Ramah."

PART THE SECOND

To you it was shown, that you might know that the Lord Himself is God; there is none other besides Him. Therefore know this day, and consider it in your heart, that the Lord Himself is God in heaven above and on the earth beneath; there is no other.

Deuteronomy 4:35, 39

CHAPTER 9

A HOLY PRIZE

Laden with the spoils of war: armor and weaponry stripped from fallen heroes, and prized above all, the Hebrews' Ark of God, the Philistine forces marched from the fortress city of Aphek down the coastal plain toward Ashdod. The day was fair as the procession of victors descended through the Vale of Aijalon, the storm having passed soon after the downfall of the Israelite contingent. The air bore the scent of salt and fish, but beneath it there lingered a foulness of burning and death. Carrion birds, their circling ceased, were about the feast upon the field below.

The Judean Hills lay to the east, the Great Sea to the west, as the Philistine captors made their way south through the lush pastureland along the road that led toward the Aijalon River. Just south of the Plain of Sharon, the Aijalon Valley marked the northernmost reach of the Shephelah. From the foothills it stretched east to west, rising at last into the heart of the central mountains. This had long been the chief route of armies and merchants, from Joppa and the Way of the Sea into the hill country of Judah. Yet this same passage stood ever as a breach in the land's defense, a corridor through which empires moved and kingdoms fell.

Aijalon was given to the tribe of Dan, yet the Philistines, pressing hard to seize the valleys of the Shephelah, drove them westward, until at last the tribe forsook its inheritance.

It was in this valley that Joshua spoke unto the Lord, in the day when Yahweh delivered the Amorites into the hand of Israel. And before all the children of Jacob, he cried, "Sun, stand thou still upon Gibeon; and Moon, in the Valley of Aijalon."

So the sun stood still in the midst of heaven, and the moon did not hasten to go down for a whole day, until the people had avenged themselves upon their enemies. There was no day like it, before or after, when the Lord hearkened to the voice of a man, for on that day, the Lord fought for Israel.[28]

The Lord had not fought for Israel at Eben-Ezer, for the slaughter was terrible and the defeat complete, and now the Ark of God was in the hands of the enemy. Word of its capture spread swiftly through the region, and crowds gathered to behold the Philistine host as they passed by cities and through vales, brandishing their prize before the ranks of soldiers.

Elated was the company with their sacred spoil, for it seemed to them that not only had they vanquished the Hebrews, but their gods had prevailed over the God of Israel. Truly, the presence of the Ark in their midst was counted a sign of divine supremacy.

Yet no voice rose above the cadence of marching feet. The Philistines were disciplined. They advanced in perfect order, row by row, column by column, with stern faces and straight backs, ever with eyes facing forward.

And so it was, after a day's march, that the company of soldiers came to rest north of the Aijalon River, across from the city of Lod. Having advanced from the coastal plain into the Shephelah at the root of the mountains, the Philistines had secured control of that city not long after it was founded by Shemed, son of Elpaal, of the tribe of Benjamin.

Well-fortified and set at a crossroads of empire, Lod had long been sought after, for both its wealth and its walls. It lay astride two great trade routes: one stretching from Egypt in the south to Babylon in the northeast, the other running west from Joppa to Jebus in the east. Along these roads passed caravans and kings, merchants and armies, for Lod was a gate to nations.

Lodgings were plentiful for those who came bearing goods and coin. But it was not traders who waited on the outskirts of Lod this

---

[28] Joshua 10:12-14

day. It was a conquering host—heroes of Philistia, brandishing their sacred prize.

Smoke rose from the Philistine camp as fires kindled across the plain. A cool breeze drifted in from the sea, bearing fog upon its breath, while the weary soldiers gathered near the warmth, firelight dancing upon their grim faces. Shadows moved about them, strange and flickering, cast long upon the ground.

After a good meal and a long draught, contentment settled upon the men, grateful for a brief respite from their footslog. Silence reigned, broken only by the crackling of flame, each man lost in his own thoughts.

Armor and weapons, polished and bright, lay at each man's side, ready should the call to arms be sounded. All were arrayed in like manner: leather kilts and ribbed breastplates, smooth-cheeked soldiers with dark hair banded and spiked, unified in form, alike in every detail, save one whose stature surpassed them all.

With a resonating sigh, Lukka, ruddy and indelible, broke the quiet. "It was a hard-fought battle, yet in the end, one we overcame. Valiantly we fought, and victoriously, we have prevailed."

"Yes, and what a prize lies here before us; what a victory it was," declared Ekwesh, whose eyes were sharp and wit keen. "It was as though the very gods fought beside us. Baal, father of thunder, clapped out his wrath upon the Hebrews; Dagon, father of rain, poured forth his vengeance. Truly, it is we the gods favor."

"There is a shadow upon my mind, a lurking malice that grips the heart," Phicol spoke with care. Though his face was hard and battle-scarred, his eyes were warm and gentle. "I do not trust that all is as well as you say."

"The storm was fierce, as if the gods themselves warred alongside us," echoed Lukka.

"Baal-Hadad, son of Dagon, god of thunder, fought with us," Ekwesh insisted. "The thunder spoke as we struck down the Hebrew dogs; it was the voice of favor."

"And yet I wonder," mused Phicol, "if we should tempt the gods—whether ours or another's. What know we of the power of the Hebrew God? Does He lie in wait, seeking to strike us another way? Will He have His vengeance still?"

"Ah," replied Ekwesh, impatience in his voice, "this Hebrew God has lost His power, or else He has abandoned His people. For truly I tell you, He did not fight on the day of battle."

"Even so, I wonder what awaits us in payment for this deed." Phicol paused, then added, "I have heard tales of the terrible cost of crossing the God of the Israelites, how He troubled the Egyptians of old. I do not think we should treat this matter so lightly."

"Ah, those are but fair-tales and legends, hearth-whispers by mothers meant to frighten the young in the night. You are a child, or a woman!" scoffed Ekwesh.

"Aye!" laughed Lukka, ever quick to jest. "You scare too easily; you are not fit to wear a soldier's armor!"

Raising his cup to the sky, Lukka bellowed, "Let us drink again, for the victory is ours!"

"To victory!" cried Ekwesh.

"To drinking!" guffawed Lukka.

"I'll even drink to your Hebrew God—for delivering His people into our hands!" Ekwesh jeered.

Three cups met with a dull thud, earthen vessels lifted in salute to their triumph: three, for Phicol's joined as well, though with less fervor, for dark thoughts weighed heavy upon his heart.

"Rash deeds oft lead to sorrowful ends," Phicol spoke at last, his eyes fixed on the fire.

The three sat quietly, caught upon the tail of his words.

An owl screeched in the distance, its cry echoing in the dark as it passed over the camp. Shaking his head, Ekwesh sat upright and emptied his cup into the fire. The flames hissed in reply, sending up a scatter of sparks.

"Ah, go to sleep and dream of sorrow. I shall dream of Ashdod, and of what awaits us there: conquering heroes, returning in triumph!" Ekwesh spoke with relish. "And I know well what awaits this soldier."

The night faded as morning crested over a grove of palm trees, rousing the company of soldiers, calling them to return to their journey.

With the Ark borne upon the shoulders of four men, the Philistine forces marched on by rank and file, over the Aijalon River and south along the highway.

At noontide, as the sun stood high and the shadows grew small, the well-ordered lines began to slow. Confusion crept through the columns as their pace faltered, until at last the battalion, impeded, could go no farther.

Caphtor struck his heels against the sides of his horse and trotted through the ranks, indignant at the unlooked-for delay. Well-seated upon his saddle, horse and rider stood dignified, looking down upon the bowed bearer who knelt beneath the burden of the Ark. To those below, the dread commander ascended like a high tower, casting a shadow over the stricken soldier.

With feathered helm raised high and glaring eyes cast down upon the hapless warrior, Caphtor spoke in a voice deep and resounding: "What is this? What ill befalls? Why do you halt from your marching?"

"It is the Ark, *Sar*, it grows heavy," answered the burdened soldier, as the others in tandem struggled to keep the sacred chest from toppling.

"Nonsense. The Ark appears as it did from the first. It is unchanged to my eyes. How can it grow heavier? It is unaltered. It does not change."

"*Sar*, it is more than I can bear."

"*Sar*, he speaks the truth. I know not how, but the Ark grows heavier with each step we take," the soldier to the right, struggling to stand, spoke hesitantly to his commander. "I myself can scarce go on."

"Put the Ark down—before you, too, are stricken!" Caphtor snapped.

With great difficulty, the four men unburdened themselves and laid the Ark upon the ground. Relief washed over their pallid faces, damp with perspiration.

"You four—take up the Ark. Quickly! I will suffer no more delay," Caphtor bellowed, pointing to a line of onlooking soldiers.

Ekwesh, Lukka, Phicol, and Teresh they were, chosen by the commander to bear the Holy Coffer. Without hesitation, the four stepped forward, fell into line, and, in one accord, raised the Hebrew shrine upon their shoulders.

Yet the Ark, heavier than they had reckoned, bore down upon them so that they leaned inward to keep the sacred chest aloft.

As the day wore on, Lukka could not be sure but that the Ark indeed seemed to grow heavier. *It must be my weariness, or imagination playing tricks.* But the feeling would not leave his thoughts. *Perhaps Phicol is right; perhaps this God is to be feared.*

Then came a sound: a voice upon the breeze, softly whispered, barely audible, yet calling, speaking his name: "Lukka."

Was that my imagination? A chill ran down his spine.

By evening, the troops came to the city of Jabneel, the building of God, it was called, established upon the Sorek River, eleven miles south of Joppa. Jabneel stood strong atop a small hill along the road south to Askelon. Just inland of *Jabneh-Yam*, the harbor on the western sea, the city was girded by a rampart and wall, three-fifths of a mile in length. Outside the city, wheat fields, their heads heavy and ripe, spread wide across the plain.

Near the shore of the river Sorek, among cattle unnumbered that grazed lazily within the peaceful land, night settled upon the camp of the Philistine battalion, weary from their toil.

This night, Teresh joined the trio, a brother now in their journey, fellow bearer of the Ark. Younger than the others, he was eager to win respect from the older soldiers of the company. Eben-Ezer had been his first battle, yet he had fought well and turned not from the sword. Now, sitting about the fire, each visage illumined by the flame, Teresh looked upon their weary faces, wondering what thoughts stirred within his comrades.

Lukka, ever quick to engage, spoke first: "I imagine it was my weariness, but—did not the Ark grow heavier toward the end of our march this day?"

"Yes, I felt it too," agreed Teresh timidly, relieved that another had voiced the thought.

"I do not think it truly grew heavier; we only grew more tired as the day wore on. It seemed more burdensome only because of our weariness," spoke Ekwesh. "Let not fear take hold of your heart, Lukka."

After some silence passed between them, Lukka could not help but speak again. "I know this will sound foolish—I—but—thought I did hear something speak."

"Something speak? What mean you by 'something speak'?" questioned Ekwesh.

"I thought I heard it whisper my name upon the breeze," blurted Lukka.

"Heard what whisper your name? You speak in riddles, man! Speak plainly," Ekwesh snapped, impatience in his voice.

"Lukka, what is it you would tell us? Fear not our ridicule," encouraged Phicol.

"It was the Ark itself that whispered my name, soft upon the breeze. I heard it say: 'Lukka.'"

"You are daft!" rebuked Ekwesh. "The Ark is but an object, not a god. How can an object speak?"

"I cannot say how, only that it did speak my name. The Hebrew God knew my name. How is that so?"

"I heard something also," spoke Teresh, his words uneasy. "But it was my name that came to me upon the breeze."

"Oh! Not you too!" Ekwesh exclaimed with growing irritation, shaking his head in disbelief.

"I hear that the Ark is the very seat of their God, His throne. He dwells there invisible, yet ever present," Teresh said, gaining confidence.

"We are caught in an immortal struggle," murmured Phicol aloud.

"What can mortal man do against the will of the gods?" questioned Lukka, fear darkening his eyes.

"We are delving into matters yet unknown to us. We should not meddle in affairs beyond our understanding," warned Phicol. "It is not unlike the eternal struggle between Mot, god of the dead and all barren places, and Baal, god of life and fertility. Mot has ever strove against the good forces of Baal, bringing death and barrenness to our land with each passing season. Mark my words, only grief shall come of this."

His words fell like a shadow upon them, heavy with resignation, for there was naught any could do to alter the course that lay ahead.

"I agree," spoke Teresh, "for this is the God of Samson—"

"Yah, the same God who deserted Samson and delivered him into our hands!" interrupted Ekwesh, unable to grasp the talk he heard. "You are all unbelievable! This God of the Hebrews is a fickle god who turns His back on those He calls His own."

"I do not think so. If you remember, Samson pulled down the temple and slew many Philistines with him. Not just any man could do that without the help of a god," Teresh replied.

"I fear we have not yet seen the end of this God's wrath," warned Phicol.

"Enough of this talk!" bellowed Ekwesh. "You are all old women, the lot of you. Go to sleep; we have an early start tomorrow, carrying your God's Ark!"

Though the four men laid their heads down, sleep escaped them, their minds heavy with apprehension.

I do not relish bearing this Ark once more, thought Lukka. *At least we have but one day's journey remaining until we reach Ashdod.*

Yet Phicol's warning hung in the night as a prophecy foretold.

CHAPTER 10

ASHDOD

Once more, the regiment rallied as dawn lifted her rosy head above the mountains to the east. Ekwesh, Lukka, Phicol, and Teresh again took up their burden, the Ark pressing down upon their shoulders.

It does not seem as heavy today, thought Lukka. *Perhaps it was as Ekwesh spoke.*

Amid shadows long, the soldiers broke camp and, with weary limbs, marched on.

Yet another day's journey brought the company through the ravine to the north of Mareshah, across the Zephathah River. But as the Ark-bearers entered that valley, fear clutched their hearts, for the burden grew heavier upon each man's frame. Ekwesh, Lukka, Phicol, and Teresh all strained beneath it, their breath drawn with effort, their steps slow and faltering.

This cannot be only imagined, thought Lukka, *for surely, the Ark's weight is greater even than yesterday.*

It was here, in the Valley of Zephathah, the watchtower, that Judah went with Simeon his brother, and they slew the Canaanites who dwelt in Zephath and utterly destroyed them. To the city of palms, he gave the name *Hormah,* broken rock. The Lord had been with Judah, for he drove out the inhabitants of the mountains, and of Gaza along the coast, Askelon with its harbors, and also Ekron. But of the valley of Zephathah, Judah could not cast them out, for they possessed chariots of iron. Thus was Judah unable to claim his allotted inheritance, and that which he possessed was soon stripped from him, as the Philistines pressed ever northward in their quest for dominion.[29]

And so, the regiment of weary soldiers pressed on to Ashdod, their journey now nearly complete.

By midday, they beheld the city, a stronghold rising upon the horizon, tall and imposing.

None too soon, thought Lukka, for with each step, the Ark bore down ever heavier upon their shoulders, until their knees threatened to give way beneath the load.

Halting the regiment, Caphtor came before the anguished Ark bearers. "Why do you slow our pace, soldiers?"

"*Sar*, we falter under the weight of the Ark," gasped Phicol. "It is a grievous burden, a millstone about our necks."

"What is this I hear?" Caphtor growled. "Do I command an army of women? Put down the Ark! We shall not enter the city looking vanquished by an object. You four—" he pointed to a line of nearby soldiers, "take up the Ark and show these nebbish milksops how men carry spoils from war! Look alive, men. Now we receive our glory, for the victory is ours!"

A mighty cheer rose from the contingent as the weary four returned to their ranks, shame and exhaustion etched upon their faces. With renewed fervor, the company of exalted soldiers hastened toward the gates of Ashdod—and to their journey's end.

Midway between Gaza and Joppa, Ashdod lay three miles east of the Great Sea, situated along the high road that stretched from Egypt to the northern lands. Its position upon the Way of the Sea and at the juncture of the east–west trade route, which connected the coastal settlements with those farther inland, made Ashdod a vital center of commerce. Tidal rivers strengthened the region's economic power, linking *Ashdod-Yam*, Ashdod-on-the-Sea, with other ports and providing anchorage for ships trading upon the Great Sea.

Strongly fortified, the city, once allotted to the tribe of Judah, had since become one of the capital cities of the Philistine pentapolis. Though the land was divided after the Israelite conquest, Judah failed to drive out the Philistines who dwelt there. It was said the Anakim, a

---

[29] Judges 1:3–19

people of towering stature beyond all measure, giants, they were called, were numbered among the Canaanite tribes of Ashdod. Fear stayed Judah's hand from pressing further to claim his inheritance.

Now, with the Hebrew conquest long forgotten, the inhabitants of Ashdod lined the streets to welcome home their victors.

The Ark of God was lifted high upon the shoulders of its captors, the army of Philistia, who, in perfect order, passed through the high city gates with pomp and ceremony. The crowd that gathered to witness the spectacle cheered with delight as the sacred burden was paraded before them.

Beyond the strong ramparts encircling the city, they ascended the steeply sloped main street of Ashdod, passing through the lower city, an expanse of densely peopled districts enclosed by thick stone walls. Well-planned and ordered, the stronghold held separate sections for living and working, and a designated quarter for public buildings, temples, and palaces, each area set apart by high walls, some as thick as thirteen feet. A network of straight, intersecting roads formed a precise lattice of streets and evenly laid city blocks.

The lower city, home to the working class, now swelled with rejoicing. Brandishing palm leaves and banners, the people waved their arms high, exalting their returning victors.

Unhindered, the procession of the captured shrine moved through the growing throng of onlookers, beyond the inner barrier into the upper city, ringed with massive walls. Large houses lined the cobbled street, elaborate structures with many rooms and courtyards, paved and commodious. These were the homes of the elite: wealthy and powerful citizens who reaped the benefits of the laboring class.

Still, the cheering crowd pressed in along the roadway as the company of soldiers advanced toward the palace, a great hall of sun-baked brick, looming white and bright above the city. Strong pillars bounded the entrance to the imposing structure, where twin hearths, framed in brick, stood on either side of the threshold.

As the regiment neared the lofty estate, an imposing figure descended the steps, flanked by two well-armed, ornately fitted sentries. Caphtor bid the contingent halt with an uplifted hand, his eyes never leaving the figure before him. With perfect precision, the battalion of trained soldiers ceased moving. Then, with surprising grace, Caphtor, the commander of Philistia, dismounted and bowed low before the resplendent nobleman.

"You are late in coming, commander," spoke the figure, his voice rich and melodious. Lavishly arrayed in fine cloth, his bearing was erect and assured, confident in his authority.

"We were delayed, my lord Seranim," Caphtor replied humbly, rising before his ruler.

"Word of your victory has reached our ears. Well pleased are we that you have brought us honor," spoke Seranim, lord of Ashdod, and one of the five lords of Philistia. "But surely this is not all that endures of our army?"

"No, my lord," answered Caphtor. "Many troops remain. More than half of your lordship's regiment has gone east over the mountains in pursuit of the Hebrews, to Shiloh, to destroy the enemy's capital, with Seren leading them."

"Exquisite! And what have you brought us here?"

"*Sar*, we have captured the very shrine of the Hebrews' God, and we present it now before you."

As Caphtor spoke, he motioned the bearers of the Ark to come forward. "Also, we have recovered much armor from the Hebrew fallen, and many treasures from their abandoned camp."

Delight filled Seranim's eyes as he gazed upon the veiled Ark set before him. "You have done well, commander. We shall place these trophies at the feet of Dagon, lord of Ashdod, father of life and light. Tonight, we celebrate our triumph in royal fashion. Go now to the temple and deliver our offering!"

Caphtor bowed low once more, then mounted his horse. With a single motion of his hand, he led the army of Philistia toward the temple complex.

Women, their long hair bound beneath headscarves, danced along the streets to the sound of flute, cymbal, and drum, lifting their garments, long and straight, in the frenzy. Children, unclothed, ran after the procession waving reeds and banners, their laughter piercing the noise like birdsong.

The company halted before the sacred precinct. Caphtor dismounted and stepped toward the entrance of the holy place. Then, with measured tread, the dread commander, followed by those laden with the spoils of war, and the four who bore the Ark, passed beneath the temple gates.

Altars for blood sacrifice stood in the outer court, where the congregation gathered for sacramental rites. Beyond the walls of stone and across the cobbled way, the Philistines conveyed the Ark of God into the temple's most sacred chamber. Cedarwood pillars upheld the lofty ceiling above white-plastered walls, ornately adorned with red-painted lotus flowers and long-necked fowl.

As Caphtor and his men entered the inner sanctum of the temple, the image of Dagon, half-man, half-fish, rose before them, set upon a two-cubit-high dais along the rear wall of the hall.

Benches of brick, clad in plaster, lined the temple walls confronting the altar. At its base, a large hearth rested, mud-bricked and covered with fine plaster and pebbles and bits of broken pottery. Set into the floor along the fire's edge stood several great earthen jars, silent keepers of the implements of sacred rite.

Before the altar were placed various vessels of pottery bedecked with long-necked birds, special receptacles for worship: drinking cups in the shape of a lion's head, hollow clay tubes patterned into circles and adorned with little animals, and bowls crafted into the form of birds with heads, wings, and tails. Among the offerings laid upon the dais most high were Egyptian scarabs and beads of bright blue stone. A figure of a woman, fashioned into a four-legged throne and adorned with a necklace of lotus blossoms about her breast, Ashdoda, the fertility goddess she was, rested at the feet of Dagon.

The gentle strumming of the lyre entwined with the clear voices of the temple musicians. Two priests stood before the altar, each wearing the mitre of the fish-god upon his head, a staff in his left hand, and a vessel of holy water in his right. Draped across their shoulders hung cloaks of scales that shimmered in the firelight. With eyes narrowed against the flame, the holy men watched as Caphtor and his men brought forth the trophies: first the weapons, then the armor.

And at last the Ark of God, the Hebrews' hallowed shrine, and placed it upon the floor, beneath the looming shadow of Dagon's image.

A horn of conch was lifted. A single, deep note sounded, its voice rolling through the hall and down the byways, blown to summon

Dagon, father of corn and sun. A sudden hush fell over the gathered throng as in silence they waited.

"Dagon, son of El, creator of earth, father of Baal, storm god, come and receive these offerings of thanksgiving, for thou hast granted us victory in battle; Dagon, keeper of the dead and giver of life to come, lord of all fruitfulness, who hath given us the plough, come and receive our gifts," proclaimed the temple priest, his voice strong, echoing beyond the gates.

Then came the lord of Ashdod to offer a great sacrifice unto Dagon his god and to rejoice: "Our god hath delivered the Ark of our enemy into our hand."

And when the people beheld the Ark, they praised their god, saying, "Our god hath delivered into our hands our enemy, and the destroyer of our country, who slew many of us."[30]

The priest then lifted the *kernos* and into its ring poured the sacred wine, filling the vessel just beneath the fruit and birds, and the bowls set upon its outer rim. After a moment of prayer, the libation was spilt upon the altar at the feet of Dagon.

Various sacrificial and divinatory rites were enacted in the presence of the people. The clear golden flames upon the hearth leapt higher, an omen read as good, as though the gods had received the sacrament with honored approval, infusing the temple with jubilation.

Thus began the celebration, as the procession of soldiers and citizens filled the streets and palace grounds with riotous revelry. A feast was laid before the contingent, hosted by the lord of Ashdod, a fine table spread with beef and lamb, and whole roasted pigs. Beautifully crafted vessels, painted in black and red with long-necked birds, adorned the tables, bearing dates and figs, olives and chickpeas. But valued above all was the drink: clay jars brimming with beer and wine, the finest Philistia could offer.

"Now this is living!" cried Lukka with a gleam in his eye.

"Yah, Phicol, was our labor not worth it? Look about you and behold the glory that is ours!" Ekwesh declared.

But Phicol could not cast off the shadow that clung to him. The memory of what they had seen on the road still haunted his thoughts.

---

[30] Judges 16:23–24 (NASB)

Yet, not wishing to dampen the spirits of his companions, he merely shook his head and raised his cup toward Ekwesh. "To us!"

"To us!" came the chorus in reply.

Seranim, long-winded, for he never wearied of his own voice, stood before them, lifting his cup in salutation. His speech filled the court, resounding with the cadence of the ancient scrolls.

"Men, you have proved yourselves worthy this day. An eternal bond has been forged. Dagon has established it for us, together with all the divine beings, yea, the great assembly of the holy ones, through the bond of heaven and earth, forever.

"The eternal has sworn a covenant oath with us; Asherah has pledged her pact. The sons of El, the council of the holy ones, have confirmed it with oaths of heaven and ancient earth.

> *As Baal, rider of the clouds, son of Dagon, smote Yam,*
> *So has Philistia smitten the Hebrews.*
> *As the gods eat and drink, so shall we eat:*
> *With a keen knife, a slice of fatling,*
> *And drink wine from a goblet,*
> *From a cup of gold, the blood of vines.*

With a wave of his hand, Seranim pressed on, ever fond of his own voice, ever speaking to his waiting men.

"Forward we go, as Anath with Baal, as he departs for the heights of Saphon. At the feet of El we bow and fall, we prostrate ourselves in honor.

> *Lo—it is the time of his rain.*
> *Baal sets the seasons;*
> *He gives forth his voice from the clouds.*
> *He flashes lightning to the earth.*
> *Baal opens the clouds with rain;*
> *His holy voice thunders through the heavens.*

Seranim lifted his arms toward the celestial abode, his cup still in hand, yet not a drop did he spill.

"Lord Baal went on to take possession of many earthly cities."

Slowly, he lowered his arms. Then, turning to his men, the lord of Ashdod gestured broadly with his upraised cup.

> *Sixty-six, seventy-seven, towns he claimed.*
> *Eighty, ninety, such was the number of cities that fell*
> *To the might of Baal-Hadad,*
> *Thundering son of mighty Dagon.*
> *Thus Baal returned to his home, lord of all the world.*

Pausing, Seranim sighed in satisfaction, stirring hope among his men that his allocution was drawing to a close. To their dismay, he continued:

> *Of cedars is his house constructed,*
> *Of bricks is his palace raised.*
> *He journeys to Lebanon and its trees,*
> *To Syria and the choicest of its cedars.*

> *Fire is set upon the house, flame upon the palace.*

Here, his voice rose to a mighty incantation.

> *Behold—a day and a second,*
> *The fire eats into the house,*
> *The flame into the palace.*

> *A fifth, a sixth day.*
> *The fire devours the house,*
> *The flame in the midst of the palace.*

> *Behold, on the seventh day,*
> *The fire departs from the house,*
> *The flame from the palace.*

> *Silver is drawn from blocks;*
> *Gold is turned from bricks.*

With tremulous decrescendo, Seranim's voice softened, his men, as one, leaned forward to catch his words.

"And so his house has been lifted up, even as you have lifted Philistia. Thus for seven days, we shall feast to the glory of our victory."

Once more, Seranim, lord of Ashdod, raised his cup to his men, a smile spreading across his resplendent face.

> *You have made them like a lamb in your mouth,*
> *Like a kid in your jaws, they be crushed!*
>
> *The torch of the gods burns;*
> *The heavens halt on account of you.*
>
> *With a sword you cleave him,*
> *With a pitchfork you winnow him,*
> *With a fire you burn him,*
> *In the millstones you grind him,*
> *In the fields you leave him,*
> *That the birds may eat his flesh,*
> *And the fowl destroy his portion.*
>
> *Flesh calls to flesh.*

With uplifted hands, and to the dismay of the men, Seranim's speech endured without interruption.

> *Let the heavens rain oil,*
> *Let the wadis run with honey,*
> *That we may know, Dagon, lord of the furrows, is alive,*
> *That the Prince, lord of earth, exists.*
>
> *Because of thee, the Hebrews have known defeat,*
> *Scattering by the sword,*
> *Burning in the fire,*
> *Grinding in the millstones,*
> *Being forgotten in the fields,*
> *Because of thee, sown in the sea.*

In restless anticipation, the men grew uneasy in the wake of their master's voice. Many a stomach rumbled out complaint, yet all sat quietly, showing due respect to their lord.

With Anath, our hand is victory.
Knee-deep she plunges in the blood of soldiery,
Up to the neck in the gore of troops.

She gathers water and washes,
With the dew of heaven, fat of earth,
Rain of the rider of clouds.

Pitchers he takes of new autumn wine,
Ten thousand he mixes in.
Wine enough for ten thousand portions.

And while he is mixing it, one does rise,
One chants and sings,
Cymbals in hand, the minstrel lifts his voice:

Art thou hungry?
Then have a morsel!
Or art thou thirsty?
Then have a drink!
Eat!
Drink!

Again, Seranim addressed his men with the uplifted cup. His voice rose to a mighty crescendo as the men, encouraged, felt the end of his speech drawing near.

Eat bread from the tables!
Drink wine from the goblets!
From a cup of gold, the blood of vines!

If the love of El moves thee,
Yea, if the affection of the bull arouses thee,

Eat, drink, be satisfied.
For well you have earned this feast.

May the gods guard thee in Sheol.[31]

And at last, when his voice fell silent, the court seemed suddenly larger, for the weight of his words had passed, yet left behind no peace.

Lifting the lion-headed *rhyton* to his lips, Seranim saluted the troops before him. The company of soldiers returned the gesture with a shout, and a generous draught of wine. Then, with regal satisfaction, Seranim took his place at the head table, and the long-anticipated feast began.

The eating of meat and the drinking of wine consumed the men, their bellies filled with warmth, their hearts loosened by revelry. Laughter rang out. Bowls clattered. The sacred words were forgotten, and the clamor of indulgence swelled beneath the vaulted roof.

Music unfurled like smoke, slow and heavy, as seven priestesses of the temple stepped forth. Their ritual dance began: sensuous, deliberate, rising like a flame drawn toward the dark. The beat of the drum quickened. Movements once measured became wild, frenzied. The men, dulled by wine and swooning with carnal passion, burned with desire.

Their licentious mirth carried on through the waning night, many collapsing where they had cavorted, sinking into stuporous sleep. The sounds of revelry waned until, at last, as morning stirred, silence pervaded the hall. One by one, the last of the revelers succumbed to sleep, until only the sound of rhythmic breathing remained, heavy and unbroken.

But the silence did not last.

A distant cry rose, sharp and urgent, drawing near, until the drunken men were jolted from their insentient hebetude.

"Sacrilege! Sacrilege!" cried a priest as he ran into the palace court, "It is sacrilege!"

With their senses blunted by the copious quantity of strong drink consumed, the men were slow to react. Confusion rippled through the grounds as many reached for their swords, expecting the enemy had

---

[31] (Khalaf 1996)

breached the city walls. Seranim rose, gathering his wits, and cried out in a voice that cut through the din until silence once more reigned.

"Calm yourselves!" spoke Seranim. "Shekresh, priest, what is this tumult? Why do you shout and disturb our slumber?"

"Forgive me, my lord," replied the priest, his voice trembling. "The temple has been defiled!"

"Defiled?" Seranim repeated. "What do you mean, 'defiled'?"

"Please, *Sar*," said the priest, bowing low, "you must see for yourself. I cannot speak of it. I beg you—come and see."

Seranim drew a long breath and shook his head, not at all pleased by this loud intrusion. With long and measured strides, he crossed the court. Many of the revelers fell into step behind him, murmuring among themselves, uncertain of what they would find.

"Let us go," spoke Ekwesh to his companions. "Hurry, before the crowd presses us."

The convocation was led through the upper city to the holy precinct. Many had gathered, so much so, that not all could enter into the sanctuary. Ekwesh, Lukka, Phicol, and Teresh, who now kept constant company with the three, managed to force their way to the front, just behind Seranim as he passed through the temple gates.

And so it was, that when the men crossed the threshold, there was Dagon—fallen upon his face to the earth, prostrate before the Ark of the Lord.

Rage ignited within Seranim at the sight of his god bowed low before the Hebrews' shrine.

"What is the meaning of this blasphemy? Who dares desecrate the temple of Dagon, god of life and light?" Seranim cried, his whole frame trembling with wrath. "Set the image in its place, and station a guard at the gate. We shall not suffer heretics to profane our sacred grounds."

So they took Dagon and set him in his place upon the dais, lifted up once more before the Ark of the Covenant.

Looking on, the four companions stood in silent dread, recalling the weight of the Ark upon their shoulders and all that had transpired on the road to Ashdod.

"What could have caused such a thing?" spoke Teresh, concern etched upon his brow.

"It was likely an earthquake that caused the image of Dagon to fall from the dais. There is a logical explanation," said Ekwesh, unwilling to believe. "Do not allow the fear of others sway your senses."

"I felt not the earth move," answered Teresh, his voice taut with unease.

"There is nothing unearthly at play here. Too much drink made dull our senses. We must have slept through it," reasoned Ekwesh.

"Come, let us leave," urged Lukka, "I do not like being so close to the Hebrews' God."

As the four turned to go, Phicol spoke quietly, "It is our beginning woe."

Ekwesh looked hard into Phicol's eyes, unsettled by the solemn words. The cold fingers of fear gripped him. Without another word, he turned away and led the others from the temple.

Teresh paused, casting one last glance upon the image of Dagon, now standing proud in his rightful place. Then, his gaze fell upon the Ark—and a shiver ran cold along his spine.

I fear Phicol speaks the truth.

CHAPTER 11

SOOTH-SAYER

A cool breeze lingered as the morning opened fair, bearing with it the scent of the sea. Gulls wheeled across the azure sky, their cries ringing with the vibrancy of a new day. Word had already spread through the city concerning the incident at the temple of Dagon. Rumors ran rampant, even as the city stirred to life and preparations for the evening's feast began.

Ekwesh, Lukka, Phicol, and Teresh wandered the lower city, seeking distraction from their troubled thoughts.

On either side of the street, shops raised their shutters: butchers and olive dressers, tanners and carpenters. Awnings stretched wide above doorways, casting shade upon those who tended their wares. Women sat at looms, spinning and weaving, the steady rhythm echoing the cadence of labor and life.

Teresh watched as one woman knotted threads to a wooden beam, fastening their ends to clay weights that held the warp taut. With practiced rhythm, she passed the shuttle swiftly, drawing the woof through the warp, interlacing each fine strand into a splendid cloth. Down came the batten of the loom, beating the fibers firm, binding the pattern with every stroke.

As Teresh beheld the woman's skill, the agile quickness of her hands, he recalled a saying he had heard in his youth:

> My days are swifter than a weaver's shuttle,
> And are spent without hope,
> My life span is gone,
> I have cut off my life like a weaver.
> He cuts me off from the loom;
> From day until night You make an end of me.[32]

Something dark skittered past his foot, and he called out with a start.

"Ay, what is eating you?" asked Lukka.

Teresh shivered. "Foul creatures, rats are."

"What, does a little rodent cause your heart to quake?" bantered Lukka.

"There are many rats in the city; I have seen several already this morning," noted Phicol.

"Are you frightened by a few rodents?" scoffed Ekwesh. "The whole of you shrinks from your own likeness, cast by the sun. Have you no backbone?"

His voice was harsh, for his mood was dark. A shadow lay over him still, unsettled by the events at Dagon's sanctuary.

Ignoring Ekwesh's outburst, Teresh asked, "What do you think happened? What caused this? Who would defile the temple of Dagon, especially during a victory celebration?"

"Do not speak of *it*. I have had my fill of *it*," retorted Ekwesh.

"It would not have been an easy task to overturn Dagon's image, for the statue is great, and of much weight," mused Lukka. "It would have taken several men to push it over. And how would they have done this thing without being seen or heard? I do not believe mortal hands were the cause."

"Do not vex me round!" cried Ekwesh, as with his forearm he thrust Lukka by the neck against the wall. "Do not speak of it!"

Lukka pushed him aside with ease, being larger and stronger than he. Grasping tightly the neck of Ekwesh's tunic, he drew him up until their faces met, and through clenched teeth, he spoke, "Do not tempt my anger, Ekwesh."

---

[32] Job 7:6; Isaiah 38:12

Calming himself, Lukka released his hold on him. "Why do you bellow? We are your friends. What has abashed you so?"

Phicol and Teresh looked on in alarm.

Already we see the curse, thought Phicol.

"I am in need of a drink," spoke Ekwesh, trembling with emotion as he wiped the back of his hand across his opposite cheek.

"Yes, a drink would be good," remarked Teresh, shaken by the sudden outburst. "Nothing like a drink to smooth things over."

"Oh, do be quiet!" scowled Ekwesh.

Seeking a drinkery, the four companions passed by the crucibles of the metalsmiths. Overhead hung the implements of war: swords, spearheads, and daggers, each wrought of iron, sharpened to edges cruel and points unyielding, forged for hardness and strength.

The din of hammers striking iron jarred the air in rhythmic fashion, as the smith bent fire to his bidding. The heat of the furnace, fueled by charcoal, kissed their faces, as fire, that primal flame, a living inferno, used its ruinous power to transmute raw ore into weapons of wonder, paid for in earth and blood.

They walked on in silence, wary of provoking another outburst. Ekwesh's stride was wide and quick as he led the way down the sloping street.

Within minutes, they came upon a shop with a sign above the threshold that read: "Red Wine and Strong Drink."

Beer mugs and wine craters lined the shelves on the back wall. Upon the counter stood a scale, a balance it was, with small bronze pans on either side.

Ekwesh looked to the proprietor, a short, rounded man with a balding crown, who met his gaze with quiet expectation.

"Four craters of wine," bellowed Ekwesh.

The owner, put off by the manner of Ekwesh's speech, dipped a small jug into the vat of wine and poured the crimson liquid into four separate bowls. He held out an empty hand, palm up, like a beggar petitioning for alms.

Ekwesh placed two silver pieces into the proprietor's outstretched hand. The man dropped them into one bronze pan of the balance, and into the other he placed a weight in the fashion of a fish, to prove the coins' worth.

Satisfied, he surrendered the craters of wine to the thirsty companions.

Ekwesh drank from the shallow bowl, grasping its flat, horizontal handles, a *kalathos* it was, full of sweet wine, smooth to the palate and buttery upon the tongue. A warmth filled his chest as the mollifying liquid slid down his throat, soothing his nerves and dulling his unrest.

He stared across the narrow street, lost in thought, while the others sipped their wine in silence, joy upon their faces, though muted still for fear of Ekwesh's dark mood.

A potter's stall held his gaze, and regret filled his heart. His mind turned inward, drawing together fragments of unease, seeking to shape confusion and dread into some semblance of understanding.

"Look on these pots," spoke Ekwesh, startling all from their stillness as he strode toward the potter's shop. "Beautifully crafted, long enduring, glazed and sealed for patience. The making of the Philistines."

The others followed Ekwesh, taken aback by his speech; nevertheless, they played along, casting glances over the well-made pottery.

Artistically crafted, the earthen vessels displayed a skill beyond measure. There were fine tableware and storage jars, bell-shaped bowls, kraters with horizontal handles, and strainer-spout jugs, each adorned with pairs of spirals separated by triglyphs of vertical and wavy lines, alongside images of birds, fish, lotuses, and triangular forms. All were painted in black and red upon a white-slipped background.

Only the finest clay had been chosen, carefully selected, smoothed, then fired at extreme heat for exceptional hardness. Impermeable, created for long use, superior in all its qualities.

"The pottery of Israel," Ekwesh continued, "is but crudely made, coarse and unpainted. You have seen it. It is thrown into the fire, covered to hasten curing, then discarded."

Ekwesh folded his arms across his chest, looking pleased with himself, waiting for the others to see his point.

Confounded, the three watched on, expecting more speech to follow.

Exasperated, he threw down his arms.

"Do you not see?"

The others shook their heads in unison.

"I am sorry, Ekwesh, I do not read your meaning," spoke Phicol, voicing what all were thinking.

Frustration passed across Ekwesh's face.

He flung out his hand and declared:

"We are Philistines! Long enduring, well-crafted, exceptional in all we do. We are like this fine pottery!"

"You think we are pots!" spoke Lukka, bewildered.

"You are an idle-brained brute!"

Lukka looked down, hurt within his eyes, as Ekwesh's insult stung him.

"Now, now, Ekwesh, there is no need for offense," spoke Phicol softly, laying a hand upon Lukka's shoulder. "Please, go on."

"What I am trying to explain," Ekwesh continued, fixing Lukka with a cold glare, "is that we are cultivated warriors. There is naught to dread. These Hebrew are no better than their crude pottery. They may strike a heavy blow, but they will not endure. You will see—we shall cast them upon the trash heap before long. We will overcome them. Already we have crushed their army, and when Seren and his forces destroy their holy city and its temple, the very heart of Israel will be cut out."

"Perhaps Ekwesh speaks rightly," said Teresh. "We are Philistines! Have we let our emotions unman us? We must not surrender to fear."

A measure of courage returned to Teresh, and he was grateful for it.

Soon, their foreboding gave way to festal cheer, for the time of celebration drew near. The gates of the palace court were thrown open, and a multitude of eager guests poured through the threshold. The city was alive with anticipation as the four companions took their place once more within the palace court, awaiting the feast.

The meal, with care prepared, sealed within fine earthen vessels to slowly cook, filled the court with its sweet aroma. Roasted boar, beef, and best of all, dog, a delicacy esteemed by all, were served upon beautifully painted ceramic platters. And lastly, the finest cultivated wine, *yn 'dm*, freely it was passed, until all had their fill.

Music saturated the air, melodies as intoxicating as the strong drink consumed without restraint. Players took the stage, and the revelers looked on with eager delight as the tale of the Philistine sea battle with Egypt was performed, how the Sea Peoples rose to overpower that mighty empire and conquer the sea.

"The people of the North made a plot in their islands," proclaimed the lead actor, clad in full Philistine armor. "Dislodged and scattered by battle were the lands, all at one time swept away in the fray, no land could stand before their arms. From Hatti, Qode, Carchemish, Arzawa, and Alasiya, each was cut off in one blow.

"A camp was pitched in Amurru. Its people were laid waste; the land left as though it had never been. They came with fire prepared before them. Forward to Egypt, they were coming.

"Their confederation was of the Peleset, Tjeker, Shekelesh, Denyen, and Weshesh, lands united. They laid their hands upon the land as far as the circuit of the earth, their hearts confident and bold: 'Our plans will succeed!'"

Leaning forward slightly, the player continued, his voice low, rising as the tale took form.

"Whispers of their coming, soft as breath—until their wrath rumbled to a mighty roar. Loud and terrible, with swords unsheathed, their clamor echoed throughout the land. They ruled the sea. Their fury raged across the earth, reaching even to the doorsteps of Egypt."

Then came forth a second player, his garb the likeness of an Egyptian warrior.

"His majesty, Pharaoh Merneptah of Egypt, was enraged, like a lion he was enraged. He beheld Ptah handing him a sword and saying, 'Take thou it and banish thou the fearful heart of thee.' Amun was with them as a shield; the bowmen went forth."

Taking a step closer to the audience, the mock Egyptian continued, "But the heart of this god, the lord of the gods, was ready, prepared to ensnare them like birds.

"'I established my boundary in Djahi, set before them the local princes, garrison-commanders, and the Maryannu. I caused the rivermouth to be fortified like a strong wall, with warships, galleys, and skiffs.'

"They were fully equipped, both fore and aft, with brave fighters bearing their arms: infantry of all the pick of Egypt, chariotry with able warriors, and officers of renown, whose hands were sure. Their horses quivered in all their limbs, ready to crush the foreign lands beneath their hooves."

Pacing before the onlookers, the player's voice rose and fell with the weight of his words. He gestured with fervor, driving home the fury of battle as the deeds of old were summoned upon the stage.

"So this host of the Peleset, being all gathered together, once launched an assault to enslave, by one fell stroke, both their land and ours, and the whole of the territory within the Straits.

"Shall the land lie desolate while the Nine Bows plunder its borders and rebels press in each day?"

Here, the Egyptian player paused, then, with sudden force, pierced the air with a thunderous call.

"No! I shall bind the heads of the Nine Bows—I shall gather them all into my fist! My mace shall crash upon their skulls. Bring forth the weapons! Let the archers march with might, to destroy the enemies who know not Egypt!"

Shifting back to the first player, the scene changed.

"Those who came forward upon the sea, the full flame blazed before them at the rivermouths, and a stockade of lances hemmed them in upon the shore. Yet they laid their hands upon the land as far as the Circle of the Earth. Their hearts were bold and trusting. 'Our plan is accomplished!' was their cry."[33]

"The prows and sterns of their ships, painted with long-necked birds, were manned from end to end with valiant warriors bearing arms, soldiers chosen from the choicest of the Peleset, like lions roaring from the mountain-tops.

"'I am the valiant Peleset, stationed before them that they might behold the hand-to-hand fighting of my arms. I, Peleset, was made a far-striding hero, conscious of my might, valiant to lead my army in the day of battle.'"

In mock conflict, the two actors crossed swords, the war portrayed in counterfeit. On the close of several minutes, the Philistine actor threw down his enemy and, in feigned combat, smote him. The audience cheered with expectant delight.

Holding his sword aloft, one foot upon the prostrate form of the vanquished, the victor proclaimed: "After six hours, the mighty

---

[33] (Anderson 2011)

Egyptians: they were dragged, overturned, and laid low upon the beach, slain and heaped from stern to bow of their galleys, their possessions scattered upon the waters.

"'Thus I turned back the waters to remember Egypt; when they utter my name in their land, may it consume them, while I sit upon my throne. I permit not the nations to rise against us. As for the Nine Bows, I have broadened their lands and their boundaries; they are added to mine. Their chiefs and their people come to me with praise. I carried out our plans and was victorious.'"[34]

And so the tale advanced with vigor and pomp, the onlookers, entangled in the power of the telling, felt their courage renewed.

"You see, my friends, we Philistines have always been victorious," spoke Ekwesh, pleased with his own insight. "Our voices are heard throughout the ages, and we are strong. All this doubt is but superstitious nonsense."

A cheer rose from the crowd as the play came to its end and the actors took their bows. Once more, strains of music caressed the ear with pleasing melodies, stirring elation and gladness.

Raising his bowl in a gesture of toast, Ekwesh declared, "May your armor be bright, and your sword at the ready."

The salute was warmly received, as the others lifted their bowls to join his.

"This is a goodly feast," spoke Lukka as he reached for another slab of meat.

All nodded in agreement, and for a time, silence reigned as they ate and drank their fill.

The music ceased as Seranim stood with his hands outstretched to quiet the crowd.

"A contest, we shall have. To any man who can pose a riddle without answer for the span of this week's celebration, I shall grant thirty linen garments."

The court rang with mirth, laughter rising like a sudden wind upon the gathering.

"Aye, that is a princely gift," exclaimed Lukka.

"That it is," echoed Ekwesh with a nod.

"Do you know any good riddles?" asked Teresh, glancing about.

---

[34] (Breasted 2001)

All sat quietly, deep in thought.

"I have a riddle," spoke a voice in the crowd.

"Let it be spoken," said Seranim, gesturing with an open hand.

"What flies forever and rests never?"

"That one is easy," said Ekwesh with a grin. "It is the wind!"

There was a murmur of agreement as the challenger sat down.

Another man rose. "What is wingless and legless, yet flies fast and cannot be imprisoned?"

"It is the voice," answered one seated at the end of the table.

The riddle-giver sighed and returned to his place, disheartened.

"Come now," Seranim said, shaking his head with mock severity. "Is there none among you who can offer a true challenge? These are but games for children."

Teresh rose with hesitation, his voice soft, "I have a riddle to pose."

"Then speak up, and let your challenge be heard," declared Seranim.

"When one does not know what it is, then it is something; but when one knows what it is, then it is nothing."

"That is a good one, Teresh," said Lukka, clapping him on the back.

"Aye, a clever puzzle," added Ekwesh, "but not enough to win the prize. Forgive me, Teresh—but the answer is a riddle."

"You are sharp with puzzles, Ekwesh," said Phicol. "Let me test you with one of my own: I saw a woman, solitary, brooding."

"Very good, Phicol, very good," spoke Ekwesh. "That may require a little brooding."

"I know it!" cried Lukka, bright-eyed. "Is it a widow?"

"Nay, Lukka, not so," said Ekwesh. "Though a good guess, the answer lies elsewhere. It is not so sorrowful a tale. The answer, my friend, is a hen—is it not?"

"You are quite good," replied Phicol. "Few can confound you."

"A riddle I bring for you to weigh, ere ruin come to your dismay."

All eyes turned as an aged man, bent with years, made his way toward the head table, his eyes fixed upon Seranim's stern gaze.

"Who let this unbidden sooth-sayer into my court?" Seranim growled. "I put no trust in the mutterings of your kind, old man. Remove him."

"My Seranim, was it not your voice that declared any man might speak a riddle? Will you now break your word, and deny an old soul his chance to earn bread in his last days?"

A hush fell over the court as all awaited Seranim's reply.

Seranim narrowed his gaze, his lip curling. "Very well," he said, each word dripping with disdain. "Speak your riddle, and then begone. You are not welcome in my house."

"I thank you for your indulgence, my Seranim."

The seer turned to face the crowd and raised both arms high, still clutching the staff in his withered hand. Slowly, he turned his head and fixed his gaze upon Ekwesh, who grew uneasy beneath the seer's piercing stare. Visibly shaken, Ekwesh shifted in his seat as the sooth-sayer began, his eyes still locked upon him.

> Twice thrown down upon the tor,
> Twice to fall to the cold stone floor,
> The conquered first will conqueror be,
> Until all have fallen on bended knee.
> Short the time until you see,
> What my riddle's end shall be.

Silence ruled the night as the seer lowered his arms, his eyes still fast upon Ekwesh, whose face had grown pale.

"What sort of riddle do you speak?" Seranim barked, his voice heavy and hard. "That was no riddle. It sounded more a threat. Take him away. I do not care to look upon him."

The aged man regarded Ekwesh once more, his countenance deepening, and spoke again:

> Soon you will see as light of ray,
> The rhyme I speak at break of day.

"Get thee gone, withered fool!" Seranim snapped, rising partly from his seat.

To Ekwesh's relief, the sooth-sayer's gaze left him. The seer turned to Seranim and smiled faintly.

"As you wish. But heed what I have spoken."

Slowly, he hobbled across the court, leaning heavily upon his staff, and passed through the open gate.

Stillness lingered in his wake. The company sat quiet, uncertain what to do or say.

At last, Seranim waved a hand toward the musicians. "Play us a lively tune. Continue, men, with your merriment.

"The night waxes on."

CHAPTER 12

WRITHING IN THE NIGHT

The old seer departed the palace grounds, his tattered robe billowing about him. Drawing his cloak tight, he cast a glance over his shoulder at the radiant threshold of Seranim's court, inflamed against the swarthy sky. A knowing smile curved upon his lips.

"You shall see, my lord. You shall see."

Having spoken thus, he turned his back upon the rising clamor of festivity and vanished into the waiting dark.

With the intonation of the musicians' song, the celebration quickly overshadowed the seer's warning, pushing back the solemn mood, replacing the night with the sounds of melodious harmony and genial banter.

Hours passed in merriment. The wine poured freely, the scent of roasted meat thick upon the air. They ate with gladness and drank deep, laughter rising among them like incense. In the sharing of bread and tale, a bond was forged, companions drawn close in the warmth of feast and fire.

Ekwesh smiled as his gaze moved across the table to the mirthful faces of his companions.

Lukka, boisterous and loud, held aloft a half-gnawed bone, his great hand gesturing wildly as he recounted some tale. Phicol shook his head in wonder; and Teresh, his brow lowered, laughed quietly at the gentle giant's jest.

Gradually, the music faded. Time passed until Ekwesh sensed a strangeness come upon him. He turned about and found himself alone, standing in an open field.

All about him rose a queer noise, like a thousand tiny squeaks. He felt himself spinning, though he had not moved.

It is the ground that moves!

He looked down and the earth flowed like a stream: brown, writhing.

What is it?

His vision sharpened. Shapes began to form. Something seized his right arm. Turning, he beheld a pitiful face, sallow, sunken, eyes pleading. A skeletal wraith clutched him with bony fingers, reaching out with the other hand.

Revulsion gripped him. He tried to push the figure away.

But another seized his left arm.

And another.

They closed in, hollow-eyed and desperate, clawing, grasping, pulling him down.

The squeaking swelled, rising into a single, deafening cry.

"Sacrilege! Sacrilege most heinous!"

Ekwesh jolted upright, breath catching, sweat upon his brow.

"What?"

All were in motion. The company of men sprang to their feet, not waiting for the priest to enter the palace court.

"Hurry!" cried Teresh. "It is the priest again. Something has happened, once more, at the temple!"

Ekwesh gathered his senses and followed, still reeling from the dream.

Lukka took hold his arm, urging him along.

"What is with you? You look terrible."

He only shook his head and hurried on toward the temple court.

The guard stood outside the sanctuary. Confused. Afraid. Every eye turned to behold the scene within.

There lay Dagon—twice thrown down, fallen on his face before the Ark of the Lord. His head and the palms of his hands were broken off upon the threshold; only the fish-shaped trunk remained. No longer divine, but to the eyes of men, a fish only.

Therefore, neither the priests of Dagon, nor any who enter the house of the fish god, tread upon the threshold in Ashdod, to this day.

The priest stood beyond the entrance to the temple. With arms raised toward the heavens, he cried out with a loud voice:

Woe to the people of Dagon!
Woe to the multitudes of Athar-Baal!

He pours the ashes of grief on his head,
The dust of wallowing on his pate.
For clothing, he is covered with a doubled cloak.

He roams the mountain in mourning,
Yea through the forest in grief.
I shall go down into the earth and drink tears like wine
I shall weep for him and bury him.
I shall lay him in the grave of the gods of the earth.

And thou—take thy clouds,
Thy wind, thy storm, thy rains!
With thee, thy seven lads,
Thine eight swine.
With thee, Pidray, maiden of light,
With thee, Tallay, maiden of rain.

Then thy face shalt thou set toward the mountain of Kenkeny.
Lift the mountain on the hands,
The hill on top of the palms,
And go down to the nether reaches of the earth
So that thou mayest be counted among those
Who go down into the earth,
And all may know—thou art dead![35]

When at last his voice grew quiet, the priest rent his garments in two, clawing at his chest, ploughing his flesh like a garden.

---

[35] (Khalaf 1996)

Drawing a blade from within his robe, he lifted it to his face and cut his cheek and chin, scored his forearms, and, like a vale, raked furrows in his back.

He raised his voice, and cried, "Dagon is dead!"

In horror, the men watched. No word passed their lips, for their hearts had failed them. Seranim stepped forward and wrenched the knife from the priest's bloodied hand.

"Dagon is not dead!" he cried, his eyes fierce with fury. He turned sharply to the stricken throng. "Where is the guard?"

"I am here, *Sar*," the soldier answered, his voice edged with fear.

"Well? What have you to say for yourself? Were you asleep at your post?"

"*Sar*—no, *Sar*. No one passed by. I—I saw no one, *Sar*."

"How, then," Seranim hissed through his teeth, "did this thing happen?"

The soldier quaked beneath his lord's scowl. "I cannot say, *Sar*. All I know is no one came near. All was silent—until a great crash came from within. I rushed inside, and found all as you see it now."

Seranim exhaled sharply. "I am surrounded by addle-brained dregs!"

Despondent they were, all who stood witness to the scene. With heads bowed, the men considered the ruin set before them.

How could it be that Dagon, great lord of the earth, had been thrown down? And by what, or who? Ekwesh sighed in despair. *All has come undone: belief, order, meaning. What once was sure is now shattered. How is one to make reason of this?*

And then it began: the wailing.
At first, it was small.
Then it grew,
a sound gathering strength and sorrow,
until it tore at the heart.

It was the wretched shriek of loss.

The blood of each hearer waxed cold. The sound was as the tenor of many rushing waters, carving its path, cutting deep into the earth, ripping away the soil, changing the shape of the land.

And then, all went quiet.

To the men, the silence was more loathsome than the wailing. It was the sound of utter despair. They looked upon one another, uncertain what ought to be done.

"Now what!" barked Seranim, cleaving the silence like a blade through a man's chest.

Flinging the knife down at the feet of the bleeding priest, Seranim, with Caphtor in his wake, stormed from the temple court and into the streets of the upper city.

"Come on," urged Ekwesh to his three companions.

Obediently, Lukka, Phicol, and Teresh followed.

Screams rose into the air like smoke curling through mountain heights. It was from the lower city that the anguished cries ascended. And it was to the lower city that Seranim and his men made their way.

The day was shrouded behind a curtain of dark clouds, ominous and threatening. And still, the cries of the tormented souls filled the city. All around, mothers clutched the lifeless bodies of their children. Women held their men as they died in their arms. Everywhere, the grotesque appearance of the ravaged victims scorched the eye with horror.

"What is happening? What does all this mean?" asked Teresh, his agitation growing.

"We have offended the gods, and now we pay the price," spoke Phicol, his voice heavy.

"Enough of this nonsense!" Ekwesh retorted. "We are not old women trembling at tales of wrath and shadow. There is a reasonable explanation. Sickness comes to cities, and it means nothing other than what it is—sickness. It will pass. And all will be as it was."

"Still you deny, despite all that you have seen and heard these past few days." Phicol's voice was firm. "Your heart is hard my friend—but your eyes will be opened before this is done."

"Come," commanded Seranim. "We return to the temple court. It is to Baal-Zebul, lord deliverer, that we must cry out, lest this plague consume us all."

The day sank behind a veil of stars as the four companions left the temple court. They passed through the streets toward the palace, yet the cries from the city below still rose to meet them.

Baal-Zebul had not heard their pleas.

All day, sacrifice and prayer had been lifted up, yet the agonized cries continued into the night. With heavy hearts and bowed heads, the four walked on.

A screech owl cut low across the street, piercing the silence with its shrill cry as it snatched its prey in talons of iron. It was then that the men noticed the ground.

"Look!" cried Teresh.

The ground was writhing, tormented. Ekwesh, in horror, beheld a familiar scene. The earth was alive with brown, quivering waves.

"Rats!" Phicol cried out.

Something seized Ekwesh's right arm. He turned, and met a pitiful face, pale and sunken, skeletal in form. Eyes pleaded. Bony fingers clutched at him with desperate strength. Recoiling, Ekwesh struggled to break free of the clawing hands.

The squealing from the earth swelled, erupting as the owl screeched overhead, diving upon another victim.

"It is Lilith, the night hag, come to steal our children away!" ranted the woman, her claw-like hands locked tight around his arm.

At last, he broke her grip and shoved her aside.

"Come, let us get away from here," spoke Ekwesh, his voice quavering.

With great haste, the four moved silently along the upper street and entered through the gate of the palace. The feast lay spread before the assembling crowd, yet not a one felt cause to celebrate this night. Food clung to the throat, rankled the palate. No merriment rang out, no jest was shared; this was a chamber of lamentation.

Seranim stood before them. Slowly had he risen, broken, his head bowed in sorrow. At length, he lifted his face to the assembly, his visage marked with the chisel of grief.

"My friends," Seranim began, his voice low, "this is a time of great darkness. A shadow lies heavy upon us, and all has come to ruin. Hope has forsaken us, and the path ahead is lost. Something has occurred that has not happened ere this time. The gods have left us.

Over us are hands like locusts,
Like thorns, the hands of troops.
He piles up heads on His back,
He ties up hands in His bundle.

Knee-deep He plunges in the blood of men,
Up to the neck in the gore of corses
With a stick, He drives out foes,
Against the flank, He draws His bow.

Then He sets face toward El
At the sources of the Two Rivers,
In the midst of the streams of the Two Deeps.
He enters the abode of El,
Goes into the domicile of the king.

He lifts up His voice
And shouts:

'Let Asherah and her sons mourn,
The goddess and the band of her brood!
For dead is Dagon,
For perished is the prince, lord of earth!'" [36]

Seranim grew quiet. He stood gazing at the men, each one he beheld in turn, until he had looked into the eye of every man assembled. Then he sat down. His hands rested heavy upon his knees, his frame bent beneath sorrow's burden.

Not a sound was heard. No one spoke, for there was naught to say. A heaviness hung in the air, and none dared disturb it. Even the torches burned without crackle, their flames wavering in stillness.

"Begging your pardon, *Sar*—but hope is not lost. Not all goes ill this day."

All heads turned to behold the one so bold as to speak so favorably.

"It is I, Seren, just returned from battle, bearing good news. Shiloh has fallen. The temple of the Israelite God, destroyed."

---

[36] (Khalaf 1996)

"You see, my Seranim," he declared, bowing low before his lord, "all is not lost. We have vanquished our foe. The house of Israel shall soon crumble."

CHAPTER 13

RAMAH

Day approached as Nagad and Tiphcar struggled over the mountains of Ephraim, south and then west, toward the high place of Ramah. Wounded and bleeding, Tiphcar stumbled. The air was sharp with morning cold, their breath rising as vapor before them. Thirst and weariness tore at their bodies, but the heights offered no water. Dew clung to the withered grass, grasping at life upon the barren rise. Overcome, the men collapsed, pressing their mouths to the earth and lapping what little moisture the turf would yield. The dew was cool upon their tongues, a fleeting balm. Still, they yearned for more.

Tiphcar lay still upon the ground, the last of his strength slipping away. He sank into the damp earth, resigned to remain ever as he was.

This is no bitter end, he thought, *to die here, upon the cool and silent hill.*

A strange peace enfolded him. The chill of the earth dulled his wounds. Pain faded, and with it, the will to rise. But then—

A hand seized his arm.

Why do they trouble me? Can they not see I have found my rest?

"*Sar*," came the voice, urgent yet low, "we must keep moving."

Lifting Tiphcar to his feet, Nagad half-carried him down the slope of yet another mountain. Their destination was Ramah, that is, Ramathaim-Zophim, the two heights of the Zophites. Watchers, they were called, dwelling in the land of Zuph, on the eastern edge of the Benjamite Plain, opposite Gibeon.

The city stood at the junction of the Great North-South Ridge Road, an unbroken spine, the only such route in the central highlands, and the east-west way, ascending from the west through Beth Horon toward Gibeon on the plateau, then descending to Jericho, crossing the Jordan River to Heshbon and beyond.

This district, assigned to the sons of Kohath, descendants of Zuph, was Levitical land. It was the birthplace of Samuel, Eli's ward, and the seat of his authority.

Through the undulating hilltops, the two weary warriors pressed on. Uprising earth they ascended, grasping at the ground, clawing their way beyond the brow of the mountain.

At last they reached the summit, and there the land swept before them, vast and staggering, plunging from beneath their feet, tumbling into the valley below.

"Look, Tiphcar. The Plain of Benjamin," Nagad spoke with breathless relief. "And there is Ramah, upon the hill. We are almost there."

Tiphcar remained quiet and unresponsive, insensible to the world around him. Nagad could hear his captain's labored breath, feel the warmth of his ragged exhalations as he bore him upon his back.

Rising from a wide, grassy field, upon a high and solitary crest, Ramah stood, like a beacon to a ship lost at sea. Strength stirred within Nagad, and with renewed resolve, he made his way forward, Tiphcar slumped across his back. Through fresh-ploughed vine-fields he passed, and into shadowed oak groves, where tall trees reached with long arms, their heavy branches drooping with prickly leaves.

As they neared the gates, men came forth from the city to receive them. Tiphcar was eased from Nagad's shoulders, gently borne away by four. And as the burden he had carried so long was lifted, a hush settled over him, as though the very earth exhaled. His strength was finally spent. As his knees buckled beneath him, he sagged into the waiting arms of two men.

"Please," he spoke with difficulty, yielding to their hold, "I must speak with Samuel, the prophet."

"I am sorry," said one who steadied him. "Samuel is not here. He has been gone these many weeks, preaching in the villages."

At this, defeat sank into Nagad's bones. He drew a tattered breath, and all went dark, as thirst and weariness overcame him.

Light began to show through his closed eyelids, bright and warm upon his face.

How long have I lain here? he wondered. He was comfortable, content. *I have not felt this peaceful in such a long time. It would be a mercy to remain like this forever.*

And then his body stirred, and pain came upon him, jarring in his back, biting at his shoulder, drawing him out of languor, back into the world of remembrance. With a start, Nagad opened his eyes. The brightness blinded him, and he squinted until the room came into focus.

A man sat nearby, smiling gently as he looked down upon him. He was not more than a few years older than Nagad. Yet, though youthful in form, his eyes and manner were old, wise, even aged, as though he had lived many lives of men.

There was a quiet strength in his presence, and though it unnerved Nagad for a moment, it also comforted him, like waking from fever to find your father watching at the bedside.

"I must speak to Samuel," spoke Nagad, when he found his voice. His words felt distant, far off, as though outside himself.

"It is he who looks upon you," came the reply.

Nagad studied him, scrutinizing the face that gazed back at him, as though seeking the answer to some far-reaching question.

"You expected Samuel to be older, much older than I?" the man said, a knowing smile in his tone. "Do not be concerned. I have been about the Lord's work these many years. My age is of little account."

Leaning forward, Samuel continued, "Now tell me, what has passed? Your sleep was troubled. You cried out more than once. Tell me, who is this Orach?"

Hearing Orach's name spoken stung Nagad; the wound gripped his heart. He looked about the room, delaying his reply.

The chamber was sparsely furnished. The bed upon which he lay was of wood, raised a cubit and a span from the floor. A network of cords, stretched across its breadth, held a mattress. Nagad had never slept upon a bed such as this. It was a good bed, something a wealthy man might own, yet it stood in sharp contrast to the meager surroundings in which he found himself.

Limestone blocks enclosed a small square cell, its only window set high and narrow, drawn across like a slit, and barred with a crisscross lattice of wooden slats. Beside the cot stood a small table with four legs, upon which rested a single lamp. A jar of water lay open next to a clay bowl, ready to satisfy the thirst of any in need.

Samuel sat upon the room's only chair, his eyes calm with expectation, waiting for Nagad's answer.

"What day is this? How long have I been here?"

"It is the sixteenth day of Iyyar, by my reckoning. You have lain here these past two days," Samuel answered gently.

Memory returned in full force. Nagad sat up too quickly; his body cried out in painful protest, his head spinning in reply.

Lying back once more, he asked, "And Tiphcar, the captain? Where is he? Is he—" But he could not finish the thought, wincing as pain tore through his memory.

"*Al Tid' ag*, all is well. Your captain rests in the next room. His wounds are grave, but I trust he will survive. You have done well in bringing him here."

"Where are we?" Nagad's voice was low. "I remember coming to Ramah, looking for you, but you were not there."

"I returned from my circuit not long after your arrival. I have brought you here, to the Naioth, my house of instruction, or what, in time, shall be so, though its walls are yet unfinished. You are the first to rest within. When your strength returns, I will show you all. But first, you must tell me what has come to pass concerning the Ark of the Lord."

"How did you know about the Ark?"

"Ah," Samuel replied, "you speak much in your sleep, but not enough. Still, I know in my spirit that some great calamity has befallen our people. Several days past, I felt it, a stirring deep within, which I could not name. I hastened to Ramah at once, as though summoned. And behold, there you were, at my very doorstep. Now, I ask again—what has happened?"

A lifetime ago it seemed, across time, a specter of thought.

"Dead is Eli, the High Priest, and his two sons also. Shiloh is destroyed, the Tabernacle torn down, and the Ark of the Lord lies in the hands of the Philistines," Nagad spoke, his voice trembling with more emotion than he intended, for great was his distress. To speak the calamity aloud made it all the more terrible, fixing it in reality.

"When did this happen? How long since the Ark was taken?"

Nagad was quiet, eyes distant as he tried to remember. "Naught, but six days ago."

Samuel looked intently into Nagad's eyes. Leaning forward, he grasped his arm. "Tell me all. Do not leave out any detail."

Nagad recounted all, save for Orach, for that wound was too new to be spoken. He could not bear it. Samuel's expression, though grim, held steady through the telling. And when at last Nagad had finished, Samuel released a deep sigh and fell silent.

Spent, Nagad lay back and closed his eyes, pain written upon his face.

Samuel stirred, rousing Nagad from his weariness. *I must have fallen asleep*, he thought.

"So—it is done," Samuel spoke, his voice laden with sorrow. "It is as I feared. Israel has fallen into disobedience. Once more, they have put their trust in something other than God."

"What shall we do? And the Ark—what of it? We cannot leave it in the hands of our enemy."

"No, of course not," Samuel replied, rising from his chair. "But we cannot act until a change is wrought in the hearts of men. Now, sleep. When you are well-rested, I will take you to see your captain. All else can wait."

Samuel turned and left the room, leaving Nagad alone with his thoughts. He lay upon the cot, watching cloud shadows drift across the stone walls. The room was quiet. A gentle breeze passed outside the window, brushing unseen vegetation against the limestone. Leaves rustled across the courtyard beyond his cell.

His chest rose and fell in rhythmic fashion; in and out his breath came, each cycle deeper than the last. His eyelids grew heavy. And he was thankful, thankful that Samuel was there, caring for the wounds of two weary soldiers. Letting go of concern, Nagad yielded to the hush of rest, his mind clearing as sleep quietly stole over him.

CHAPTER 14

THE NAIOTH

Nagad looked upon the still face of his captain, once powerful, now pale and gaunt. To see Tiphcar lying thus, frail and exposed, stirred unease within him, a quiet reckoning with mortality and the passing of time. What he felt was loss, not of life, but of strength, of what once was. Tiphcar had ever stood tall, a soldier of renown, leading his men with unwavering hand. Now he lay silent, weariness carved deep into his brow, a dim shadow of the warrior he had been.

Bowing his head, he loosed a breath long held.

Samuel, perceiving the young man's sorrow, laid a gentle hand upon his shoulder. With calm assurance, the prophet spoke, "His fever is broken. The wound is healing."

Nagad stepped to the bedside, a cot much like the one he himself had risen from but moments before. He seated himself upon the chair beside it and extended his hand to take his captain's. He found the gesture awkward, yet he needed to feel the warmth of living flesh, to be certain that Tiphcar still breathed. Alive he was, for at the touch of Nagad's hand upon his own, Tiphcar returned the grasp.

"*Sar?*"

He watched as Tiphcar's eyes slowly opened. For a moment, he stared blankly into space—until at last his gaze found Nagad's face, and he smiled, though weakly.

"My son."

His voice was soft and rasped with strain, but to the conscript, it was as manna in the wilderness.

Tears of relief welled in Nagad's eyes, yet he did not look away. The tension he had carried washed from him as he clasped both hands over Tiphcar's, pressing them between his own.

"*Sar*... how goes it with you?" he asked, unsure what else to say.

Tiphcar stirred, a faint smile on his lips. But as he moved, a grimace of anguish passed across his face, for the motion brought pain.

"I am alive," he said, "yet strange have been my dreams."

"*Sar*?"

With eyes uplifted, Tiphcar continued. "It was as a shadowed vision. Light surrounded me, wrapping me in warmth. I could not lift my eyes to the one who stood before me, for the radiance was too great. The secrets of my heart were revealed, laid bare in his presence, and I fell upon my face and cried out: 'O wretched man that I am! Deliver me from my blood guiltiness, O God!'"

Turning his gaze to Nagad, he said, "Then I saw your face. You have done well, Nagad. I am well pleased with how you discharged your duty. You have put gladness in my heart. You are a comfort in my affliction. You have given me life, though I would that I had died upon the field of battle, with the others. For I shall not recover. I have brought this ruin to my people, or, at the very least, I did not stay its hand."

"*Sar*?" Nagad spoke, cut to the heart.

Tiphcar dropped his gaze, his eyes fixed upon a distant place. "Oh, my body will heal, but I shall never be free of this torment of grief. I shall find no cure for this loss. I am undone! All flesh is as grass, and all the glory of man as the flower, it withers and falls away."[37]

Nagad, crestfallen by Tiphcar's words, bowed his head. His captain, his friend, carried a heavy burden, one of guilt and shame.

No! He must not bear this alone. We are all a part of this calamity. This cannot be how it all ends.

With quiet resolve, Nagad lifted his head and spoke: "You have not yet passed from life to death. It is like precious oil upon the head. I do not believe all hope of recovery is lost. Though we fall, we shall

---

[37] Isaiah 40:6–7

not be utterly cast down; the Lord will uphold us with His hand.[38] The Lord is a shield to those who trust in Him."[39]

Tiphcar met his eyes with a faint smile. "You have grown in wisdom, Nagad, my son. Yet I count all as loss. There is no more strength within me."

Wearied by his speech, Tiphcar closed his eyes as though in sleep.

Nagad watched him, his chest heavy with fear. *I have stolen an honorable death from my captain. He must have a chance to redeem his good name.*

Samuel laid a hand upon Nagad's shoulder.

"Come."

With reluctance, Nagad loosed his hold on Tiphcar and rose from his side.

"Two are better than one," Samuel said as he led Nagad from the room, "because they have a good reward for their labor. For if they fall, one will lift up his companion. But woe to him who is alone when he falls, for he has no one to help him up."[40]

Turning, Samuel placed his hand once more upon Nagad's shoulder, his gaze resting with kindness upon the eyes of the troubled soldier.

"Be not anxious for your captain. He needs time to heal, for his wounds, all of them, are not beyond mending. The Lord heals the brokenhearted and binds up their wounds.[41] Come, now, let us reason together."

Leaving the building that housed Tiphcar in his recovery, Samuel and Nagad entered a courtyard, which was open to the air. A cluster of separate dwellings surrounded the inner court, some not yet complete in their construction. A slight breeze brushed past them, scattering dried leaves beyond the stone walls that had sheltered the young conscript not long hence. The branches of a young fig tree scratched softly against the masonry. Nagad's gaze lingered on the small lattice-covered windows of the rooms, one of which held Tiphcar as he slept.

"This is the Naioth, the house of instruction," Samuel spoke as he gestured with his outstretched hand. "And these are the dormitories, a

---

[38] Psalm 37:24
[39] Proverbs 30:5
[40] Ecclesiastes 4:9–10
[41] Psalm 147:3

common residence for the prophets. Or rather, they will be, for I have yet to enroll students in my academy."

Samuel led Nagad through the grounds of the Naioth, situated on the lower slope of the city of Ramah. Long-lived olive trees, their silvery-green leaves feathered upon gnarled branches, stretched across a landscape veined with springs of water. It was an idyllic scene, vastly different from the images Nagad carried in his mind from the days just past.

"This is the high place of Gibeon, the mountain of joy. It borders the lands of Benjamin and Judah. The village of Gibeon lies at its base."

Raising his arm, Samuel pointed toward the root of the hill. Then, swinging his arm in the opposite direction, he gestured to the summit of the promontory.

"Ramah, my home, is at the top."

Nagad followed Samuel's line of vision, lifting his eyes to behold the upper city. The whitewashed stone walls of the village shimmered beneath the sun's rays. He raised a hand to shield his gaze from the brightness.

"I was naught but the age of three when it was that my mother brought me from Ramah to Eli at Shiloh, and in accord with her vow, gave me to the old priest in dedication to the worship of God. As a mere child, the word of the Lord came to me. Hophni and Phinehas, the sons of Eli, could not abide my presence, for they sensed the anointing of the Lord upon me. As they meted out their full measure of iniquity, I was not idle.

"But my calling could not be fulfilled at the Tabernacle. So I returned to Ramah, my old home, and went out among the tribes, an itinerant Levite, proclaiming the will of God to my people, learning their needs, that I might turn hearts of stone back to the fear of the Lord."

Samuel took Nagad by the arm and gently guided him as the two walked slowly across the grounds of the Naioth.

"And so it is that I have established this school, to instruct the young prophets in the law and the history of Israel, our people. The seasoning of sacred music and poetry shall be cultivated here, to lift the senses toward the Spirit of God and prepare the called for their destiny.

"It is in this place that those who hunger after God shall gather for training, in spirit and in thought, that they might become a force to stir the hearts of the people, to cast off the idols of the nations, and draw near to the Lord. Here, the word of the Lord shall be proclaimed to all Israel."

Halting in his stride, Samuel turned and looked intently upon Nagad, taking hold of both the young conscript's arms as he faced him.

"I do not wait for the people to come to me, but I go to them. Year after year, to town and tribe, I go, to exhort, to instruct, to call them to godliness and the keeping of His commandments. This is of greater worth than sacrifice, for there can be no compromise where the law of God is concerned."

Samuel's gaze shifted to the unfinished dwellings. He sighed, and a quiet smile touched his face. He turned back to Nagad and met his eyes. The young conscript did not look away, speechless, awed by the man before him, youthful and yet ancient in soul.

The prophet placed a hand upon his shoulder. Again, he faced the Naioth and resumed his slow pace.

"Just twelve, I was, when the Lord revealed to me the curse set upon the house of Eli. That prophecy which the Lord entrusted to me is now fulfilled; the house of Eli is no more. And so it falls to me, Samuel, son of Elkanah of Ramathaim-Zophim, of the tribe of Levi, to serve as judge over the nation."

Nagad's eyes widened in wonder as the truth settled upon him: he stood before not only the new *Kohen Gadol*, Prophet and High Priest, but the Judge of all Israel.

Releasing his grip upon Nagad's shoulder, Samuel tipped back his head and closed his eyes. Great grief lay upon his countenance as he spoke again.

"The wrath of God has been provoked; the punishment delivered among our people, for they took the offensive and broke the truce with the Philistines without the command of God."

Samuel lowered his head and shook it slowly. "They did not seek the Lord's direction, but relied wholly upon the arm of flesh, which always fails. They have fled from God, transgressed His law, departed from Him. How is it that they, instead of turning to God for help, sought out His Ark, hoping it would save them?

"What help did they imagine the mere token of God's presence could give, when they had grievously offended Him, and delegated the Ark's care to the condemned sons of Eli?

"They had no authority to remove the Ark from its settled resting-place. Did they not understand that they were to present themselves before Yahweh, that He does not do their bidding? Alas, they bethink themselves masters of God.

"O, what shall I say when Israel turns her back before her God!"

"Then all is lost," spoke Nagad, with desolation. "There is no hope. I am in great distress; my heart is overturned within me. Outside the sword bereaves, at home it is as death."[42]

"Israel is in spiritual decline: her sacred institutions corrupted, the Ark lost to the Philistines, and the Tabernacle destroyed," continued Samuel. "The task before us is a difficult one. Though He has given His people to the sword and has become wroth with His inheritance, though fire has consumed their young men, their priests fallen by the sword, and their widows made to lament—the Lord will arise as one awakened from sleep, like a mighty man who shouts aloud. He will smite His enemies and give them over to everlasting shame."[43]

Samuel looked hard into Nagad's eyes. "Let no one deceive you with empty words, the wrath of God comes to the disobedient. In His anger, the Lord has struck us—yet Mercy remains. We are hard-pressed on every side, yet not crushed; perplexed, but not in despair; persecuted, but not forsaken. He has not utterly destroyed us. For the Lord will not cast us off forever. Though He causes grief, yet He will show compassion, for He does not afflict willingly, nor grieve the children of men.[44] He does not retain His anger forever. Be of good courage and wait on the Lord. He will strengthen you."

"Guide me with your good counsel," Nagad requested. *He instructs with right judgment, for his God teaches him*, he thought.

Samuel continued, "I will instruct you and teach you in the way you should go; I will guide you with my eye.[45] I do not speak on my own authority, but whatever I hear I speak. We must bring Israel back to God."

---

[42] Lamentations 1:20

[43] Psalm 78:62–66 (KJV)

[44] Ephesians 5:6 (NASB) / 2 Corinthians 4:8–9 / Lamentations 3:31–33

[45] Psalm 32:8

Nagad stood before him, slowly shaking his head, arms open. "But how? They will not heed me. I bear no name among them."

"We must serve in little things ere we be called to greater. One must purchase to himself a good degree, win the hearts of the people, and then speak with boldness in the faith. Let us now pursue the knowledge of the Lord, that He might deliver us from this present age. His going forth is established as the morning; He will come to us like the rain.

"When Israel turns her face toward God, then shall we speak—and the Lord will answer. In that day, the Lord will defend His people. He is not slack concerning His promise.[46]

"I believe, He may yet be at work."

---

[46] Hosea 6:3 / 2 Peter 3:9

CHAPTER 15

RIOTS AND WRATH

The hand of the Lord was heavy upon Ashdod. He ravaged the people and struck them with tumors, Ashdod and all its surrounding territory. The city lay decimated, its pride brought low in ruin. Sickness stalked the streets, tormenting all who dared dwell within its grasp. All daily labors yielded to the tending of the sick and the cries of the dying.

Soon, grim death was everywhere. The stench of decay clung to the air, acrid and sweet. Fires were kept burning both day and night, pungent herbs cast into the eternal flames in hope that the heady fragrance would cleanse the air and ward off the deadly vapors.

Fear and confusion ruled. Fathers abandoned their dying sons, children fled from stricken parents. Husband deserted wife, and wife turned from husband. Forsaken were the rites of burial as corpses mounted beyond count, until the dead lay abandoned in the streets.

Beyond the city walls, vast pits gaped beneath the sun, dug to receive the nameless dead. Within, hired men wandered the silent homes, lifting lifeless forms from where they lay. Many houses became tombs, their inhabitants perishing unnoticed until the air itself cried out. For months they suffered, until at last the cry for mercy rose from their midst.

"It is a strange thing, walking the streets of late," remarked Teresh. "When you are not overtaken by the cries of the suffering, the silence threatens to swallow you whole."

"Aye, there is nothing left in all the city but to carry out the dead for burial," said Lukka. "The shops are shut, aye, even the drinkery has barred its doors against us!"

"Yes, only the healers and priests fare well, though the people have naught left to give in return," added Phicol.

"I could do with a good meal," muttered Teresh.

"Aye, and a strong drink," Lukka returned with a half-hearted grin. Turning, he eyed their silent companion. "Ay, what gnaws at you, Ekwesh? Has your voice fled as the gods have abandoned us? You have not spoken but two words this day."

The three halted and looked upon their friend. His head hung low, eyes closed. At last, he raised his face to meet theirs, drawing in a long breath. "I am well, do not fear," he said. "It is just." He faltered, the rest unspoken. His thoughts were heavy, and his heart unsure.

Sensing Ekwesh's distress, Phicol spoke. "We know. It is how we all feel these days. So much death and suffering, it is more than any of us can bear."

Ekwesh met Phicol's gaze. *Yes, but that is not it. Something else is tearing at me, but what, I cannot tell.* "Yes," he lied. "It is as you say."

Their conversation was cut short by the sound of screams, followed by the sharp thud of a hammer echoing through the street. Teresh ran toward the disturbance, the others hurrying to keep pace.

Before them, the scene unfolded: two soldiers stood outside a house, watching as a third nailed boards across the door. From within came the cries of a woman, pleading for help, the sound of her fists pounding against the sealed frame.

"Wait!" Teresh cried, leaping in front of the soldier and catching his arm mid-swing, halting him before he could complete his dread errand. "What are you doing? They are still alive!"

"The plague is in that house," the soldier replied. "We have orders to seal any dwelling marked by sickness. None may leave, or they will carry the plague with them."

"But you surely condemn them all to death!" protested Teresh.

"They are already dead," spoke one of the soldiers standing by. "Now move." He seized the hammer from his companion and resumed the work, striking the boards into place. From within came the sound of weeping, sobs of despair muffled by wood and stone.

Teresh wedged himself between the door and the soldier, barring the man as he sought to discharge his grim duty, blocking the final act that would entomb the family within. Anger kindled across the face of the executioner, his patience fraying. It was clear this standoff would soon turn to blows.

With his hammer raised high, the soldier made to strike Teresh upon the skull.

But Lukka stepped in. With his massive hand, he seized the man's arm and twisted it until the hammer slipped from his grasp and fell with a dull thud upon the stone. The soldier stared upward, startled, into Lukka's unyielding gaze.

Still Teresh stood, arms stretched across the doorway of the condemned house, unmoved, daring any cross him.

"Now, now, men, let us not come to blows. We are all on the same side," spoke Phicol. "Tell us, who would give such an order as this?"

"I would," came a resonant voice from behind. All eyes turned toward the source, and there stood Caphtor, their commander. "I would appreciate it if you would allow these men to carry out my orders unmolested."

"But, *Sar*," spoke Teresh, "these people need our help. We cannot seal them in as though they were entombed. They still breathe. They may yet live, if we but give them a chance."

"When I require your advice, soldier, I will ask for it. Until that time, your task is to follow my orders to the letter. Do I make myself perfectly clear?"

"Yes, *Sar*."

"Men, it may seem cruel," continued Caphtor, his voice softening, "but we are facing catastrophe. The plague runs rampant. Half the populace of Ashdod has already perished. If we do not act swiftly, there will be no one left alive. Whatever measures must be taken, we shall employ, before it is too late. Now, go about your duties and let these men see to theirs."

Teresh opened his mouth to protest, arms yet stretched across the doorway, but Ekwesh stepped forward and placed a steady hand on the young conscript's shoulder, guiding him away. Inside, the sobs had quieted, soft, resigned.

Teresh lowered his arms. His head bowed. Slowly, he turned from the house and stepped aside, casting one last glance at the sealed door.

"Come, Teresh," Ekwesh said gently. "There is naught we can do here."

The four companions walked slowly away as the sound of a hammer striking wood echoed behind them. Their pace quickened, driven by a need to escape the blow of impending doom. Tears rolled down the young soldier's face, his body trembling.

"How can they do this evil thing? What have we become?" cried Teresh. "The rich flee the city, and the poor are boarded up in their houses whilst still alive! Is there no humanity left in Ashdod?"

"I fear despair has caused many to grow indifferent to the laws of gods and men," said Phicol.

"Come," Lukka added, hopeful, "let us see what meager fare awaits us. If we are fortunate, we may yet find meat."

"I do not think I have the stomach for it," murmured Teresh.

"Still, you must try," Phicol urged, "for our strength must be kept, lest we too succumb to this dread sickness."

Men gathered, taking what comfort they could in the meal shared between them. But there was no grand celebration in the palace court this night, no melodious music, no players recounting victories of old. As in the months before, they took their meal in the barracks.

The fortress comprised a central court flanked by three rows of parallel halls, each divided by a colonnade of stone pillars that served as quarters for the soldiers. Smooth and white, the plastered walls and floors bore an alabaster sheen, unsullied by the grief without. Tables lined the center of the court where men sat in silence, partaking of the sparse fare prepared for them. The mood hung heavy, unsung sorrow pressing like a weight upon the air.

"There are fewer men present tonight than when last we met," spoke Lukka.

"Aye," replied Ekwesh, noting the empty seats scattered throughout the mess. "It seems many are missing again this day."

"Many who ate breakfast with us now sup with their ancestors in paradise," spoke Phicol.

"If this keeps up, we shall not want for food," mused Lukka, "for there will be none left to attend the meals."

"I see you have found some meat this day, Lukka," observed Phicol.

Lukka smiled as he bit into a meager morsel of some unknown quarry. Nodding, he said, "Not bad—though what it is I could not say. Still, any meat is better than none. I have hungered for such a length of time."

"It would take a horse to fill you up, my friend," Ekwesh quipped.

"Forgive me," interrupted a nearby soldier, "but I could not help but overhear your conversation. I have heard one must avoid certain foods. As for me, I will no longer consume poultry or waterfowl. I shall abstain from pig, and old beef. Altogether, I will avoid any fatty meat, for this, they say, is how the sickness comes."

"No, Saph," said Azzuzath, seated beside Lukka. "It is fish that must be avoided, nothing more."

"I have heard," spoke another, "that nothing should be cooked in rainwater, for it hastens the plague's spread."

Another conscript, Rapha the Tall he was called, remarked, "I have heard that if you sleep during the day, you will get the sickness."

"Do not speak to, nor go near, any who are sick," interjected a fourth, "for this will bring on the sickness, and death will soon follow. Moreover, touch not their clothing, nor aught they have handled or worn, for this, too, shall quickly bring the plague upon you."

"Also, it is said," added Azzuzath, "that one must not bathe, nor think of death; let nothing distress you. Rather, think upon pleasant things and delicious delights, so then, let us eat, and drink, and make merry."

"Yes, for tomorrow we shall surely die!" saluted Lukka, downing his final gulp of wine.

Leaning forward across the table, a wary-looking soldier spoke low, glancing into the eyes of each man as he gave voice to his tale. "I saw them board up a house today, one within was sick, but all yet lived. And still they sealed them in, while breath remained. They will die, I wager, and soon, for no food nor water will be brought to them. It is their living tomb. I shall never forget the sound of that poor woman shrieking for mercy on her children. It made my hair stand on end."

"You lie," spoke Rapha. "Not even old Seranim himself would stoop to such a dreadful thing."

"By this foul death, I swear it true," the witness said with fervor. His gaze swept the table and came to rest upon the silent Teresh. "Hey, you were one of those who tried to stop it, were you not? Brave, if you ask me, standing up to old Caphtor. Fortunate you are, he did not seal you in along with the others."

Teresh could not meet the man's eyes, for grief pressed too near. Quiet and somber, he held his head low.

"I hear that the lords of Philistia have all been summoned for a meeting," spoke Rapha, who had slid down to sit beside Ekwesh. "A council to decide the fate of Ashdod. They will surely determine the cause of this sickness, or rather, what is to be done about it."

"It is the gods who are angry with us," said Lukka.

"Not our gods," Azzuzath added, "but the Hebrews' God. He punishes us for seizing their sacred shrine."

"The sooner we are rid of that thing, the better I shall feel," spoke Rapha.

"Aye, it would be to our advantage to cast it out, lest we all find ourselves in paradise before long," agreed Saph.

Silence settled over the men as they nodded in grim accord, each turning inward. The meal, consumed in quiet, did not last long, for scant were the portions set before each conscript. And so the days waned, their bellies unfilled, as they watched death march through the streets of Ashdod, unhindered by their presence in the city.

Realizing what a deadly disaster had come upon them, the men of Ashdod did indeed send for, and gather to themselves, all the lords of Philistia, that they might determine what must be done to drive the plague from their land.

Philistia's five principal cities: Ashdod, Askelon, Gath, Ekron, and Gaza, formed a united federation, governed by an oligarchy of five rulers. Now came these to Ashdod to convene in council.

The cavalcade of lofty rulers and royal attendants, astride magnificent steeds, careened through the streets of Ashdod with banners aloft and horns resounding, a spectacle of pomp and ceremony in stark contrast to the pallid, troubled visages of the citizens who looked on in despair. The people surged close to behold the pageant, but the soldiers held firm, lining the streets to keep them back, while the lords hastened through the city, knowing full well that the plague loitered in the quarter below.

Attendants bearing brass censers walked beside the lords, incense rising to ward off the stench of death that hung upon the air. The crowd pressed hard against the line of soldiers, crying out for aid, angry words loosed in fear and desperation. Ekwesh, Lukka, Phicol, and Teresh stood shoulder to shoulder, struggling to hold the throng at bay as unrest swelled among the multitude.

"Help us!"

"Have mercy on us!"

The mournful bale rang out through the city as many gaunt and sallow faces followed alongside the procession of splendidly adorned lords.

"Get back!" barked Caphtor, striking a man aside with the shaft of his spear.

"Clear the streets! Clear the streets!"

With force, the soldiers pushed the crowd back, driving them farther from the haughty procession. A ragged man broke through the line and ran at one of the lords, Sherden of Askelon, he was, grasping his foot where it rested in the stirrup, causing the horse to rear and wheel about.

"Please, *Sar*, you must help me!"

Sherden kicked free, casting the man to the ground. At once, several soldiers fell upon the hapless citizen, beating him with the butts of their spears until he moved no more. They dragged him to the side of the street and left him for the crowd to tend.

Anger stirred in the hearts of the people. Stones flew. The city erupted, its people lashing out in a sudden and intense frenzy of violence.

Through fist and stone, with cries and clamor, the riotous rancor raged on. A multitude of rats, roused from their slumber, joined the fray, adding shrill squeaks to the screams that split the air. Chaos burst its chains, plunder and wrath surged through the streets, consuming all restraint.

People and property alike were dragged into the street, brutalized and despoiled. The terrified cries of children echoed through the stone corridors as smoke billowed heavenward in dark, rising coils.

"The very firmament of hell has ascended upon us," spoke Phicol.

Those in authority came under mortal peril as the city unraveled. Sherden looked on in horror as several enraged citizens set upon his horse, bent on tearing him from his mount. Teresh and Ekwesh rushed to his side and, raising their shields, drove the men back.

Swept away by the encroaching crowd, Teresh found himself alone within the sea of rioters. Heavy blows battered down upon him, his shield torn from his arm. Down his face, blood coursed, veiling his sight.

Fury came, sudden, and from all sides, each strike more brutal than the last.

He staggered.

His footing gave way, and he fell at the feet of the angry mob. Like hounds, they descended, kicking, beating, their rage unspent.

Curled upon the ground, arms over his head, Teresh braced against the savage assault.

As he lay disoriented and near despair, he became dimly aware, the press above him had thinned.

Ekwesh and Lukka, seeing his plight, came to his aid, shields raised, shoving back the enraged citizens, step by step, until they reached him.

"Teresh! Can you stand?" called Ekwesh as he knelt down beside his wounded friend.

Lukka stood guard, shield and spear in hand, massive and immovable, daring any to approach.

Shaken but alive, Teresh rose, leaning upon his companion, as strength returned to his limbs. "I am all right, thanks to you."

Smoke rose, crowd pressed, and anguish gave voice. Death reigned in the midst of the people. All beheld it with fear and trembling.

Out of the shadows, a bent figure emerged, hands raised, crying aloud:

> *The enemies of Baal seize the forests,*
> *The foes of Hadad, the fringes of the mountain.*
> *And Aliyan Baal declares:*
> *'Enemies of Hadad, why do Ye invade?*
> *Why do Ye invade the arsenal of our defense?*

A chill ran down the spine of all who heard, frigid fear that gripped the heart and turned the blood cold, a hoarfrost upon the soul. The tumult halted mid-stream as the voice of the seer rose above the crowd.

Fearsome He came to rule the gods with an iron fist.
He caused them to labor and toil under His reign.
They cried unto their mother, Asherah, Lady of the Sea.
They convinced her to confront Him, to intercede.
Aliyan Baal fears Him,
The Rider of the Clouds dreads Him.

"Depart!"
'One feeble of frame shall not vie with Him,
He who wields a spear against Dagon.'

Anath turns her wrath upon the enemies of Dagon,
Upon those found fickle in his trials.
She smites in the valley between the cities,
Striking the people of the seashore,
Destroying the dwellers of the sunrise.
Beneath her feet lie heads like vultures.

'Give up, O gods, Him whom you harbor,
Him whom the multitude harbor!' [47]

It was before the palace that the seer cried out his warning.

With haste, the cavalcade crossed the threshold. Once within, the gate was barred, sealed against the devastation without.

Garrisoned inside the fortress, the lords of Philistia: Seranim of Ashdod, Nasib of Ekron, Shekelesh of Gaza, Danuna of Gath, and Sherden the Feared of Askelon, gathered for council, their countenances grave with care.

As was custom after such a journey, they were offered refreshment. Once their strength was restored, the five sovereigns took their place, each seat turned inward, forming a circle of authority.

---

[47] (Khalaf 1996)

Seranim stood before them, his gaze fixed upon the four enthroned lords. Turning to Tiglath, his adviser, he commanded, "Give us your report."

Tiglath rose slowly, uneasy before so great an assemblage, and began.

"The people sicken by the thousands, dying daily, unattended, without aid. Many there are who find death in the open street, others in their homes, made known only by the stench of their rotting corpses. Everywhere, the dead litter the city. Brother forsakes brother. Even the beasts lie dead in the street.

"Plague has reached even the inner farmlands. Though the grain stands ripe, there are none to harvest it. Cattle and livestock roam untended. Food and fresh water have grown scarce. The people chafe with unrest. Riots and looting erupt daily. It is all our forces can do to keep order from completely breaking down."

"Thank you, Tiglath, you may go," spoke Seranim.

Dismissed, Tiglath retreated slowly from the circle of lords.

"To what do you attribute this sickness?" inquired Nasib.

"Yes—what offense has stirred the gods to anger?" Danuna demanded.

"It is the God of the Hebrews whom we have provoked," spoke Seranim, his voice heavy with resignation, his head bowed and shaking slowly. "We seized His shrine and now harbor it within the temple of Dagon, who has been utterly cast down. We are undone."

"By all the gods, what you speak is madness," scoffed Sherden. "Dagon cannot be conquered, least of all by this Hebrew deity. Do not be a superstitious oaf."

"I was as you are now," answered Seranim, "doubting the wrath and power of this God. But all I have seen has proven otherwise. What else could explain the ruin that has befallen us?"

"Yet sickness visits us from time to time," reasoned Shekelesh. "How is this different? Why claim it an act of this God? Perhaps your people have grown slack in their offerings, to Dagon, or Baal, or even to Asherah."

At this, Seranim rose, ire kindling in his breast. "It is not as you say. We have done nothing to warrant such devastation, save conquer the Hebrews and capture their Ark. A curse has been upon us ever since."

Seranim paused as he sat back down, steadying himself. "The Ark of the God of Israel must not remain with us, for His hand is harsh against us, and against Dagon, our god."

"What then shall be done with the Ark?" asked Nasib.

"Let us take the Ark of the God of Israel and carry it away to Gath," proposed Danuna. "Then we shall see whether this Hebrew God is truly the cause of our wretchedness."

"If it is indeed the curse of this God," spoke Shekelesh, "will not that curse fall upon Gath as well? We cannot barter with the lives of our citizens. It may prove a costly price to pay for certainty."

Nasib considered his words, then turned to him. "What would you have us do?"

"Return the shrine to the Hebrews," replied Shekelesh. "It is not worth the welfare of our people."

"That would be seen as weakness," Danuna snapped. "We cannot bow to these Hebrew dogs. No—we shall take the Ark to Gath. In my city it shall remain, and glory *will* be ours."

"A vote must be taken," declared Seranim.

Summoned, Tiglath returned to preside over the proceedings. The ostraca were passed, one for each lord, a potsherd to serve as ballot. "Vote yea if to Gath the Ark must go; vote nay, if this be not your wish," instructed the adviser. "Please, my lords, cast your vote."

The five rulers of Philistia: Seranim, Danuna, Nasib, Shekelesh, and Sherden, each scratched their choice into the hardened clay, sealing the fate of their people. Silence fell upon the palace court as the ballots were gathered and counted.

Tiglath stood before the assembly. "The vote is cast. Our fate is set. Yea is the answer: four to one in favor. The shrine of the Hebrews shall go to the city of Gath, pride of Philistia. May the gods have mercy upon us."

Seranim rose, his voice firm. "So be it. For good or ill, the matter is decided. To Gath we send the Ark. Let us make haste—for I long to relieve my people of this burden they have borne so long."

CHAPTER 16

GATH

Rays of light pierced the veil of cloud, casting streams of splendor upon the heads and backs of the soldiers, an aurora illuminating the way, as though the gods themselves looked down upon the Philistines, warming them in the cool breath of morning. As the forenoon clouds evaporated with the warmth of the encroaching day, the sky lay serene. Summer was upon them, hot and dry, for no rain had quenched the parched earth in many months. The verdure of the fields had faded to brown, the aspect of drought and desolation steeping the once green countryside. Unyielding foliage of scattered fruit trees and shrubs, the only green to abide on the anhydrous landscape, dotted the low, rolling hills whose color had failed.

With the Zephathah River to the left, the host moved eastward, threading through the winding halls of the valley by way of the Great Road, the main artery from west to east, granting passage into the very heart of the strongholds within the Judean Mountains. At times, the deep green of the broad-leafed fig or the muted gray of the olive could be glimpsed amid the withered slopes.

As the day wore on, the summer heat would have been oppressive, save for the north-westerly wind that brought cool air off the Great Sea and through the narrow passages of the Zephathah. The Vale, emerging from the high country, began as deep ravines breaking down from the north at Tappuah. Cutting toward Hebron in the southeast, the gorge passed Mareshah, then turned north to open into a fine broad valley. Upon entering the western plain, the depression swept south of Gath, turning southwest before curving northward to meet the sea just south of Askelon.

Millet fields, once light green, and faded vineyards stretched across the valley floor, as the Ark of the Lord of Israel was borne eastward from Ashdod, a long day's trek through Zephathah, the Vale of the Watchtower, unto Gath.

When the sun stood high above them, the forces stopped to rest midway between Ashdod and Gath. Thirst had left a foul taste upon their tongues. Few trees afforded them shade as the four companions made their way to the river's edge.

"This is foolishness," retorted Lukka. "What do they think they will accomplish?"

"They are visiting calamity upon another city," answered Phicol, "spreading misery and death throughout the land."

Lukka shook his head, the lines in his brow darkening. "We should return the Ark to the Hebrews and be done with this once and for all."

"We do not know," Ekwesh replied, "whether the sickness is truly linked to the Israelite shrine."

Gazing across a wide depression etched into the valley floor, Phicol crouched and scooped a handful of damp gravel, weighing it in his palm, a scowl upon his face. "The stream has failed and the fountains have dried up."

"Aye, and the land is as parched as we are," said Lukka, lifting his eyes toward the bright sky, squinting.

Teresh cast his eyes over the withering meadow that followed the watercourse north beyond the riverbank. "With longing, the land looks for the return of the rain."

Phicol gave a slow nod, fingers sifting the pebbles in his hand.

"Fall in! Fall in!" went up the call.

Dropping the gravel, Phicol stood and wiped his hand across the skirt of his kilt, dusting off the sandy soil from his palm. "Well, it is time we are off."

The four rejoined their cohorts as the contingent drew up in ordered ranks, each man falling into place. Soon, the tread of marching feet marked their advance.

Shadows grew long with the decline of day as the company neared the end of its journey. Passing south of the mountains, a broad plain opened to reveal a city rising stark against the surrounding flatlands. Crescent-shaped was its summit, luminous as the fading light reflected off the white limestone cliffs. High walls encircled the city, which rested on a narrow ridge, beset by precipitous cliffs to the north and west, coupled to the rise by a slender projection that thrust the city into the valley like a mighty bastion.

"There sits Gath, white mound, city of winepresses. My home," spoke Lukka.

"Ah, therein lies the explanation," teased Teresh.

"Explanation for what?" asked Lukka, confused.

"All the drinking!"

Laughing, the four continued on in jovial spirits as they reached their journey's end, for there stood Gath, home of the Gittites, rising near five hundred cubits at the eastern edge of the plain, nestled at the foot of the mountains of Judah.

The largest of the pentapolis, a mighty municipality it was, Gath held fast within the confines of the barren landscape, jutting into the valley like a watchful sentinel. Terebinths crowned the nearby slopes, their broad canopies rising above the cultivated land. Vineyards clung to the terraced hillsides, and olive groves spread like a silver-green carpet across the valley floor.

Situated five miles south of Ekron and fifteen miles inland from the Great Sea, the city commanded a position of strength upon the border between Philistia and the lands of Israel. Gath sat at the crossroads of the southern coastal plain, guarding the juncture of the North-South Pass and the main highway that passed from the Hill Country in the east to Ashdod in the west.

Along the valley floor, water percolated through sand and gravel, forming occasional pools, welcoming to the weary soldiers who paused to refresh themselves before entering the city.

"Look lively, men," commanded Caphtor in his mighty voice. "Let us show these Gittites there is nothing to fear. We come bearing the spoils of victory, let us appear so."

The Ark, held high before the army of Philistia, was paraded through the streets of Gath as drum and timbrel rang out in celebration.

With quickened step, the host bore their burden to the height of the summit, to the temple mount, an acropolis of the mighty deities, to deliver their bane into the keeping of the gods.

Despite the crescent shape of the city, the streets followed the typical Philistine orthogonal design, well-planned blocks dividing the metropolis into distinct quarters, those of the laborers and those of the highborn. Buildings of handsome design, constructed with remarkable skill, lined the thoroughfares, presenting a city of monumental proportions. Shops of keen traders and master craftsmen formed orderly columns within the heart of the city, reflecting the grandeur that was Gath. It stood complete with fortress, markets, palaces, and temples, all enclosed by segmented walls of thick whitewashed mudbrick, a gleaming white city upon a hill.

Once more, the four companions, together with their fellow soldiers, found themselves seated at an enormous feast within the palace court. Before them stood the large and jovial Danuna, reveling in his glory.

"Gentlemen, welcome to Gath! Eat, drink your fill. In this city, you shall find rest and fulfillment after your long ordeal. Within the confines of this glorious city, you shall find peace. Plenty is the bounty within these walls. Fruit of the vine flows freely in this court. Joy is yours for the taking. So eat, drink, and be merry, for this day, we celebrate!"

Taking up a carafe, finely made, glazed white and painted by a skilled artisan, with figures of birds and flowers in black and red; with this carafe, Danuna poured wine through the strainer spout into a beautifully crafted bowl fashioned in the shape of a bird. Grasping it in two hands, he raised the vessel in salute to the men. Those gathered followed his lead, and with uplifted bowls, rendered honor to Danuna. In unison, lord and subject, drank the draft in one great gulp. With a wave of his hand, their ruler sat, and the feast commenced.

Lukka's eyes widened as he beheld the abundance spread before him. "Have you ever seen such an array of meat in all your life?"

With ravaging fervor, they fell upon the feast, for hungry had they been these many months. Music filled the court as the entertainment began, yet none heeded the melody, for the thought of food and drink stopped their ears. For a time, no words were spoken; there was only the filling of stomachs, the quelling of want long endured.

At length, Ekwesh sat back and patted his belly, stretched full with repletion. "Now this is fine. It seems that all has worked out well." Looking across the table at Phicol, he addressed the battle-scarred soldier. "I do not think even you could find cause to complain. All is well, as you see."

"We shall see," answered Phicol. "Naught befell us on our first night in Ashdod. Come morning, we may face a different tale."

"Now, now," interrupted Lukka, "let us not speak of such things whilst we feast. Let us enjoy the goodly food and the fondest of company while we have the opportunity. Tomorrow is not today, and of its ills we do not yet have to bear. Now is good enough company for me."

"Nonetheless, the disquiet of my soul remains," spoke Teresh. "I cannot lightly disregard all that has befallen in the months just passed. Too much has been lost for me to feel not apprehensive. It is as though the storm could break at any moment."

"You must learn, my young friend, to let lie those matters which do not concern you this day. Grasp firmly the joy life offers, for it is true, happiness is hard to hold. Ease your mind with this." Lukka handed Teresh a bowl of wine.

"Forgive me," spoke Danuna, rising, "but I am weary from our travels. I will retire to my bedchamber. Yet you, stay, eat your fill, for this is a celebration. No harm shall befall you in my city."

And so the evening wore on, harmonious and sanguine, until the weariness of the day and the dulling strength of wine lulled the men into torpid sleep. For the time, silent calm settled over the company of soldiers, slumbering where they sat. Lukka rested his head upon the table, his bowl still clutched firmly within his hand.

CHAPTER 17

DARKNESS DESCENDS

Light, triumphant, grew chasing earth's dark night beyond the western sea. As beauty colored the eastern hills, the sun rose crowned in glory, dawning against a pale blue sky to light the celestial dome. The chatter of birds hung on a cool breeze drifting in from the sea. All was still, save the clatter of vessels as servants cleared the remnants of the evening's revelry.

Teresh stirred, awakening to find Lukka gazing down at him, a broad grin alighting his face.

"What has happened?" asked Teresh, still clouded with sleep.

"What, shall this fair morning be dampened by ill thoughts?" replied Lukka. "Let us not respond with dread, for nothing has happened. No cries of woe, no display from the gods, save the comely morning, cloudless and bright. I slept better than I have in months: my belly full, my mind at peace."

"Nothing?"

Rising with outstretched arms, Ekwesh joined in Lukka's mirth. "You see? Nothing befell us in the night. What happened at Ashdod was but a strange turn of chance. No gods meting out vengeance."

"Perhaps you are right," Teresh murmured, though his tone lacked conviction.

"Wake, old man!" called Lukka cheerfully, nudging Phicol with his foot. "There is much I wish to show you this day."

With hearts light and bodies renewed, Ekwesh, Lukka, Phicol, and Teresh walked the streets of Gath, taking in the sights, sampling the local fare, and delighting in the ease of the day. As Lukka revealed to them the city of his birth, childhood memories stirred within him, fresh and vivid.

"It is the time of the grape harvest. The winery will be busy with the making of sweet wine. Come. I will show you," spoke Lukka with enthusiasm.

Guided by Lukka, the four companions strolled care-free toward the central market, where brick cooking hearths and stone wine vats stood within the center of the square. Under the awning of the weaver's shop, many looms sat idle in the morning sun.

"In the off season, fine linen is woven on these looms, but it is the wine for which Gath is known."

Lukka pressed ahead, his pace quickening, a visible bounce in his step as the others followed in his wake.

The winery stood within a vast stone hall, divided into three chambers, each lined with wine presses hewn from the earth. All were fashioned with shallow grape-treading basins, rectangular in shape, one to two cubits deep. The basin stood slightly higher than the adjacent vat so that, once the juice issued through a small opening, the liquid would flow freely down a channel into a deeper collecting tank. The winery platforms, vats, and basins were lined with cobblestones and coated with smooth, shell-tempered plaster of unusually high quality.

"See the men there?" Lukka gestured toward several workers in the shallow basin, pressing grapes underfoot to extract the precious liquid. "They are squeezing the juice from the grapes within the *gath*.

"The juice then flows through a small hole in the low rim of the vat and into a channel, which diverts it into this receptacle. From there, it passes through yet another channel and is deposited into the deeper receiving vat."

Teresh pointed to a small catchment at the corner of the latter vat. "What is that little reservoir over there?"

"This basin drains the water off the wine, leaving a good, strong liquid ready for fermentation. Once the by-products have settled, the clear juice is drawn off and poured into jars where it is left to ripen."

Lukka led the trio into an adjacent room. Lining the walls stood decanting jars, dipper juglets, and fat-bellied amphorae with pointed bases and protruding handles, plenteous in number.

"You see those clay spheres?" Lukka asked, and the others nodded. "A small hole is drilled into the sphere, which is then set neatly over the mouth of the decanter. A wooden stopper may be removed, allowing the vapors from fermentation to escape, preventing the jars from cracking. Just think how much wine this little invention has saved from ruin."

The tour ended at the wine shop, where Lukka carefully poured sweet red wine into bowls through a strainer spout covered with a fine linen cloth.

Handing each his drink, Lukka explained, "Lees settle at the bottom of the jar during fermentation. The strainer spout acts as a sieve, filtering out impurities, even the finest particles unwanted in the wine, giving us a drink both clear and pure."

"This is by far the finest I have tasted," said Phicol, raising his bowl in salute.

"'Tis the sandy soil and temperate climate of this region," Lukka replied. "It yields a heavier wine than that of the coast, a wine bold enough to stand beside the meal, yet sweet and smooth upon the palate."

A flash of brown scampered across the street and vanished into a crevice between stones.

"What was that? Did you see it?" Teresh jolted, eyes wide.

"See what?" Ekwesh laughed. "I think the wine has gone to your head already. You are imagining things."

"No, I saw it also," spoke Phicol. "It was a rat."

"Worry you not," Lukka replied with a shrug. "Every city has its share of rodents. Do not permit fears to overtake you. It is a small matter."

"Let us not drink the dregs and ruin so fine a day," said Ekwesh, clapping Lukka on the shoulder. "Come. What will you show us next?"

"Follow me to the eastern wall. I will show you a most spectacular view of the Hill Country."

"How vast is this city?" asked Teresh, his gaze wandering wide. "Never have I seen one so great. Its grandeur all but blinds my sight."

"Five hundred *dunams*[48] it spans, the largest in all Philistia," answered Lukka. "All routes pass through this city. Many an enterprise doth commence in Gath, and many there be that find their fulfillment."

Upon the eastern wall they stood, while the midday sun gazed down, casting its brilliance upon the land. The Judean Hills stretched across the horizon, ancient and sure beneath the sky's clear flame. Separating the coastal plains of Philistia from the Jordan's Rift Valley, the mountains stood as a natural barrier, running north to south and dividing Philistine from Israelite. Rain shadow, they were called, these heights that shaped the very nature of the land: temperate along the coast, but dry and desolate within the inland desert.

"But a short march eastward lies the border of Israelite territory. And just beyond that outlet, the Valley of Elah." Lukka raised his arm, directing the others' gaze toward the mountains.

"Caverns and grottos, some broad and lofty, with vaulted chambers and towering pillars, are scattered throughout those hills. Hewn from the bare rock by the hand of man, each cavern is lit from above by shafts that pierce the ceiling, appearing as wells to those who walk above. One must tread with care, for the descent into such a hole is long and perilous."

Lukka peered long into the distant mountains, his eyes fixed far beyond the mortal realm.

With a deep sigh, he turned to his companions and spoke, "Giants, men large in stature, dwell among these hills, they say, descendants of the Anakites who once walked these lands. It is they who formed the caverns."

"Surely you are descended from the Anakites, Lukka, for look at the size of you," teased Teresh.

The others laughed with ease, while Lukka turned to Teresh, his eyes wide with quiet wonder. He did not feel as large as a giant, but the thought pleased him well.

Returning to the city proper, the men resumed their post, for it was their time to patrol the streets and guard the township from harm. What remained of the day was quiet and uneventful, the terror of former months all but forgotten. With caution set aside, the city drifted on its daily course. The streets filled with merriment as the

---

[48] dunam ~ 1,000 square meters or ¼ acre.

workday drew to a close. The shops were shuttered for the night, and revelry awakened, for cause there was to celebrate: the Hebrew shrine had come to Gath, a token of her preeminence and might.

It was subtle at first, a whisper upon the wind, but with mounting wings, the sound grew, until the shrieks of distress and terror rose. Wailing ruptured the dead of night. The nightmare resumed, the great procession of the dead. A brown sea surged, rats flooding the streets, slipping into houses, coursing through the city, harbingers of death.

"*Sar,*" Rapha called to Caphtor as he surveyed the scene, "the people are afflicted with tumors. They die in the streets."

Caphtor halted midstep, disbelief upon his face. No words did the dread commander speak as he stood gazing at the frightened soldier before him.

A man, spotted with the marks of Black Death, delirious with fever and wracked with thirst, staggered through the streets, crying out for water. Espying the soldiers, the stricken citizen flung himself at their feet, pleading for aid. In unison, the men recoiled, repulsed by the sight of him.

Teresh alone overcame his fear with pity. Walking over to the well, he dipped the jar into the cool water and calmly stepped toward the one stricken. Those around stood in astonishment. With gentle hands, Teresh slipped his arm beneath the head of the thirsty man, lifted the jar to his lips, and gave him the comforting elixir.

The citizen, undone by fever, a crazed look in his eyes, suddenly sprang to his feet and ran for the well. Without hesitation, he threw himself into the cistern and drowned.

Astounded, the onlookers watched in horror.

"Downward into darkness we descend," spoke Phicol.

Grabbing the jar from Teresh's hand, Ekwesh hissed, "That was a foolish thing to do!"

"It may be so," Teresh answered, "but I will not allow my humanity to be swallowed up by fear. Could you not feel pity for this soul? I could not watch him suffer and do nothing."

"Yah, and little good it did him." Ekwesh turned to go, dread rising in his heart.

But Teresh raised his voice, words rooting him in place.

"Caution comes too late and cannot alter the nature of the thing! Mine eye affects my heart because of all I have seen. Sorrow and death are all around, but we are not consumed, if mercy and compassion fail not!"

Ekwesh wheeled about and stormed over, jabbing a finger but a breath from Teresh's face. "We are covered with wrath and pursued! The gods have slain us and have shown no pity. Fear and a snare are come upon us; desolation and destruction attend us. There is no hope!"

"Come. It is done," urged Phicol, gently taking Ekwesh by the arm. "Much is gained by foresight. Let us leave this loathsome place of death."

CHAPTER 18

THE MASK OF DEATH

Confusion and dismay mounted as the terrors of night endured. Then, as night went down to day, a shock of quiet ruled the masses. The rift of dawn, reddening in the bloody sky, gave rise to a northwesterly wind, the day breeze, coming off the Great Sea. By midday the wind changed to the south, bringing with it an oppressive sultriness that stripped body and mind of all effort, filling each with a great lassitude.

"This is a most disagreeable wind," spoke Phicol as the men began their patrol of the city.

A great dryness choked the air. The atmosphere grew hazy with fine particles of sand and dust, a bluish shroud settling upon the city. Shutters were drawn across windows in a vain attempt to bar the dust, but to no avail, for the powdery granules crept into every crevice of every house.

Ekwesh grew annoyed as the dust and sand penetrated the very folds of his clothing, filling eyes, ears, and nose. Even as he spoke, grit coated his mouth. "Yes, a most disagreeable wind. I cannot see but ten rods before me. The sun is scarcely visible, only a dun and sickly hue, yet the heat of the wind strikes my face as from a burning oven."

"It is the desert waste, carried on the wind from the south," explained Lukka. "Do not fret, it will soon pass. These south winds do not last long. Here, bind this cloth over your mouth and nose. It will ease your discomfort."

A few drops of rain fell, precious rain, yet unwelcome, for it lasted but a moment and served only to smear their garments with mud. Drying, the vegetation withered, feeding the gloom that hung on all within Gath.

After a day, as promised, the winds changed to the west, clearing the atmosphere. Fleecy white plumes came up over the land from the southwest, dotting the sky with tufts of cotton, casting cloud shadows across the brown hills. The heat of the former day eased, tempered by a morning breeze sweeping in from the Great Sea, bringing cooler air in its wake.

The morning meal began as Ekwesh, Lukka, and Phicol sat at a table in the barracks court, eating together in silence.

"It is a fine morning, is it not?" observed Lukka.

"A fine day, save for the putrid stench of death that lingers upon the breeze," muttered Ekwesh.

Frowning, Lukka tore a loaf of bread in his broad hands and handed half to Ekwesh. "Must your eyes always rest upon sorrow? Misery must be your dearest bedfellow."

"Where is Teresh?" Phicol glanced around the court as he spoke.

The others joined in his search, only now noticing the empty seat beside them.

Ekwesh stood alarmed. "I do not know. I have not seen him since—"

Teresh entered the court, walking slowly toward his companions. As he neared his friends, a smile spread across his face, for he realized that their eyes lay upon him. Self-conscious, he sat down in the empty place beside Lukka.

"What has kept you so long from attending the morning meal, my friend?" inquired Phicol. "We had begun to worry for your well-being."

"I am sorry. I had some difficulty rousing this morn. My head aches so." Seeing the look on Ekwesh's face, who yet stood, Teresh added, "But I am better now. Too much celebrating yester-night, I suppose."

Ekwesh, eyeing Teresh with suspicion, slowly lowered himself into his seat.

"We are glad for your company," spoke Lukka as he handed Teresh a portion of bread.

"Your eyes tell a different tale," said Ekwesh, still gazing intently at his young friend. "There is a redness about them, and your face is pale. I do not think that you are fine."

"By all the gods, I tell you I am well—though I am thirsty. Please, Lukka, a drink."

Lukka passed him a bowl of cool water. Teresh seized it and drank deeply, the clear liquid spilling over the rim, trickling down his chin and onto his tunic.

"Really, Ekwesh, you act like my mother," Teresh said with a grin as he handed back the empty bowl, nodding for Lukka to refill it.

"It is time," spoke Phicol.

The soldiers stood and adjusted their uniforms, preparing for duty to patrol the city streets against civil unrest, for the people had grown desperate beneath the weight of the dark sickness. The collection of the dead, those who had passed in the night, had already begun by the time the four reached the heart of the city. The bodies were taken beyond the walls with haste, in an effort to quell panic and lessen the stench of death, which could no longer be masked by the burning of herbs.

Working their way through the streets, the four companions entered the upper city, the neighborhood of the highborn.

"It has not taken long for the noble citizens to flee, for look how deserted the streets be," spoke Phicol.

Hastening toward a large house, a palace it was, Teresh peered in through the door, left ajar.

"Yes, this house is empty. It seems the occupants left in such haste, they neglected the door."

A loud crash resounded from within, and the soldiers started, turning their eyes toward the house.

"Hallo—what was that?" cried Lukka, unsheathing his sword.

"Come, let us investigate this disturbance," spoke Ekwesh. A smile played across his face as he drew his blade and slowly pushed open the door.

The rude shuffle of matter, as the scrape of feet upon the floor, could be heard within the central hall. As the four entered the room, Ekwesh and Lukka took the lead, one on each side of the row of columns that bisected the room. There, two men, bent beneath the weight of plunder, were espied as they heaped yet more treasure upon a mat used as a litter to carry their bounty.

"Halt where you be!" shouted Lukka, his powerful tenor echoing through the chamber.

A fleeting look of terror crossed the bandits' faces as the realization struck, that they had been caught in the very act of looting. With a clamorous din, they dropped their spoils and, with unguided agitation, fled, one to either side of the hall, in a desperate attempt to escape their pursuers.

With ease, Ekwesh and Lukka subdued the first. The second bolted past Teresh, whose limbs were slow to answer the call. At once, Phicol gave chase, darting across the hall after the absconding bandit. Following hard after, Teresh pressed on to close the gap.

After a frenzied pursuit through the upper streets of Gath, Phicol hurled himself upon the thief, bringing him down in a tangled heap. The scoundrel sprawled upon the stones, pinned beneath his captor's weight. Teresh drew up beside them, winded, sweat coursing down his brow. He bent forward, hands upon his knees, struggling to recover his breath.

Ekwesh and Lukka joined the other two, their captive bound and subdued.

"What was that?" cried Ekwesh. "You moved like an old woman."

Still leaning upon his knees, Teresh lifted his gaze to meet him. When Ekwesh beheld his pale and weary face, concern swept over him.

"What is it, Teresh?"

Teresh coughed. "I am not certain. My body weighs upon me, as if forged of iron, and my limbs ache. I must have strained them in the struggle."

Soon moved, Ekwesh spoke, "You are not well. Let us take these vermin in, then we must seek the healer."

"You are overmuch with concern, Ekwesh, for I am well. It is how I have said, celebrating with the three of you has wearied me. I will be fine. Do not fret so over the likes of me."

"Let us be on our way," urged Phicol. "We must deliver our goods to the warder, for I am anxious to be relieved of this burden."

Proceeding to the prison, Teresh hung back, avoiding the searching glances of his companions. Aware that he was scratching his arm, he gaped in wonder as he noted a reddened rash upon it. Glancing up at his comrades a few paces ahead, the young soldier was relieved to find their eyes fixed upon the road ahead.

Ekwesh looked back and met his gaze, his expression grave. Teresh quickly dropped his arm and offered a smile, too swift, too bright. Frowning, Ekwesh turned again to the street.

The sun, in equal plane of sky, rose high within the dome, inflaming the heat of day. Perspiration beaded upon the brow of the soldiers as they returned to their duties among the streets. A disturbance grew, shouts and clamor rising, filling the city with tension and dismay.

"Come, unrest is brewing," motioned Phicol.

Agitation rising, mad nihilism loosed upon the lower city, the people, driven by fear and discontent, erupted in riotous insurrection. With conduct tending to treason, the convulsions of unrest ran rampant. Unrestrained by law, carts were overturned and set ablaze, dwellings broken into and pillaged, bricks and stones flung at the soldiers who attempted to quell the upward warping of murderous rebellion.

"Noisy demagogues of discontent," rebuked Ekwesh.

"It is fear that drives them to these rash deeds," Phicol offered.

A surge of confusion and disorder, the crowd, incited, crashed upon the city like a wave upon the shore. Drawing together, the army of Philistia, shields raised, a wall of stone, pressed into the streets of Gath. Constrained on all sides, the citizens grew still, enfeebled, as the fires of sedition burnt out. The tumult, having lost both spirit and strength to resist, collapsed with the casting down of arms and the scattering of the crowd.

In the scuffle, Teresh, his body in rebellion, stumbled against a wall. There he huddled, arms wrapped around his shaking frame, racked by fits of coughing. His companions found him thus, slumped against the masonry, pale and wan.

Ekwesh knelt beside him and placed a hand upon his brow.

"He is burning with fever."

As they lifted him to his feet, Teresh wavered, unstable, leaning hard upon his friends. Lukka held fast to him as a violent fit of coughing seized his body, racking him with spasms that reddened his face and left him gasping for air. In terror, the men watched as blood splattered from his mouth. The young soldier, with pleading eyes, looked up at Ekwesh. Struck with horror, Ekwesh tore open the tunic at Teresh's neck. It was as he feared: dark patches had formed upon his skin, swollen tumors, beneath his arms and at the nape of his neck. No one spoke of what they all knew, too grieved to give truth voice.

Tenderly, Ekwesh, Lukka, and Phicol lowered Teresh onto a cot in a chamber set apart for the sick. Ekwesh sat quietly upon a stool beside him and placed a cloth of cool water upon his burning brow. As the fever mounted, the youth was thrown into violent rigors, convulsive shudders that stole his strength. Speaking in inaudible syllables, he thrashed against his agitated mind. Teresh's hand shot up and grabbed Ekwesh by the arm, causing him to start.

"He hath bent his bow, and set me as a mark for the arrow,"[49] spoke wide-eyed Teresh. Falling back upon his bed, he returned to his incoherent muttering.

"My soul is removed far off from peace," spoke Ekwesh in his grief.

Far advanced was the decline of day, the long diurnal waning as the hour grew late. Beads of sweat stood upon the brow of the baleful Teresh as the fever, unbearable, bore down upon him. Great pain coursed through his body, stomach cramps intolerable, as he vomited blood in copious amounts. Writhing in anguish, he clutched the hand of Ekwesh, whose strong love held him fast, his loyalty a bias upon his thoughts.

"My hope is perished, and my strength is no more," whispered Teresh. "My end is near. My earthen vessel is moldering away, and this body shall in stillness sleep."

"He hath filled me with bitterness, made me drunk with wormwood, sharp sorrow unencumbered," lamented Ekwesh, deep emotion in his hoarse voice.

Looking up from where Teresh lay, a tear escaped the stalwart soldier's eye and traced a path down his inexorable face, now crumpled in grief.

---

[49] Lamentations 3:12 (KJV)

Bleak darkness filled the room as the last remnant of light faded from the sky. Shadows gathered, hovering about Teresh, delirious with fever. Overwrought by the unsettled dispute, the youth lay restless, agitated in a haze of affliction.

With a final struggle, seizing Ekwesh by the neck of his tunic, Teresh pulled himself up in bed and, with wide eyes, looked into the heavens.

"Forgive me! I did not see!"

Ekwesh soothed the youth, laying him back upon the cot, his strength spent. "You have done nothing wrong. There is nothing to forgive."

Teresh quieted, no more turbulent churning, no more baffling banter, as he slipped into blessed nothingness. The others, Lukka and Phicol, looked on in sallied sorrow, watching the exchange with deep dolor.

"You are at great risk, the longer you remain with him," spoke Phicol with concern.

"I will not leave him 'til it is finished."

"It will not be long now," spoke Phicol with quiet certainty.

"Is there no hope then of recovery?" asked Lukka, his voice low.

"No, my friend," Phicol answered gently. "Only death can bring deliverance from his suffering now."

Lukka dropped his head in brooding stillness, bearing the grief before its time.

In soundless shadows the night followed the path sorrow, ailing, led, until the breaking of the new day. As dawn dissolved the dark, oppressive veil, the rattle of death disturbed the stillness. Teresh, with gasping breath, clung to life, struggling for each moment. Limbs cold and mottled, an algid frost upon his brow, his labored breathing waxed and waned, shallow and rapid. Those attending, sensing the change, gathered close in solemn vigil. Then, with one last gasp, life's breath seeped out in final release. The tension unbraced, Teresh rested, death now delivered.

"He strives no more," Phicol gently spoke as he looked upon the lifeless Teresh.

"It was a battle well fought," murmured Lukka, "but the foe too great. How is it that so much can change in the span of one day?"

"Death's dispatch is quick, doleful in its discourse," Phicol mused.

"This great God," cautioned Ekwesh, "He moves among us, the very hinds discern it. The terror of His name encamps around us. Those lost no longer suffer—but we, left behind, must bear the curse. It is we who are to be pitied, not they."

Thus spoken, a change was wrought in him as the hush reclaimed the room with the sense of something lost.

"Leave us," Ekwesh said at last, his voice heavy with sorrow.

Lukka and Phicol withdrew, leaving Ekwesh to attend his grief. He cleansed the body of Teresh and placed a tunic of white linen upon his lifeless form. When the task was done, he stood over his friend, deprived of breath, and wept bitter tears.

"This was a battle I could not help him fight," lamented Ekwesh. "No way to shield him from the danger he faced. No soldier should die in such a manner, without spear in hand or sword at his side."

Polished and bright, Teresh's armor was laid upon him. Ekwesh set the youth's spear in his right hand and placed the sword by his left.

Stepping back, he looked upon the still image of his young friend. *A soldier worthy of full honor, he is.*

"Sleep the sleep that knows no waking," Ekwesh spoke, his voice no more than a whisper. "Dream no more of waking terror. Go where rest is unbreaking."

Startled out of his sharp sorrow, Ekwesh turned as his companions reentered the chamber. He opened his mouth to chastise them, but the tumult beyond the court stilled his tongue.

"Ekwesh," spoke Lukka, breathless, "they have come to claim the dead. We must surrender Teresh for burial."

"They cannot have him," Ekwesh declared, his voice stern.

"My friend," urged Phicol softly, "he must be buried quickly. The dark sickness spreads, even from the lifeless. We dare not risk another loss. You are already in grave peril. Depart from him in haste and cleanse thyself, lest you be the next to fall."

"I will not see him cast into a common grave," answered Ekwesh, unmoving. "Let us go outside the city and give him a burial worthy of a soldier."

And so it was, that Teresh was gently laid in a clay coffin, encased within a coffer shaped in the likeness of a man. It appeared as a great storage jar, its top third cut away that the body might be laid within and sealed with a fitted lid. Ekwesh took up a figurine, naked, arms raised, and placed it upon Teresh's breast, a guide and protector for the realm beyond. Over the face, a crude likeness of the youth was molded in clay and set upon the lid. Along the sides of the sarcophagus, fluted feathers were carved, echoing the headgear of the Philistine army, a token of valor and stalwart service.

Beyond the gate, upon a lonely mound, a sepulcher was carved, made ready to receive the vanquished, to lie low in the hollow ground. A solemn silence reigned over all as Teresh, staid in his youth, was placed within the tomb. The death-song they raised, a hymn for Teresh, whose valor was unspent.

"A soul is missing among men," Ekwesh began, spoken in lowness of tone, "A soul of the multitudes of the earth. Even now it can be heard, but to what avail? All who are born must come to death."

"'Twas a carol of death, a song of woe sung for the stricken, voiced for the dead," Phicol spoke the doleful incantation.

"O affective grave, a solemn visage be," lamented Ekwesh, giving rise to dubious uncertainty attended with peril.

"I will mourn in blood!"

CHAPTER 19

LEAVE-TAKING

The vault of heaven rose tranquil above the verdure of the fields, ruffled only by the scant, fleecy clouds that held in check the rays of the sun. The herbage of the mead, with vigor lost, cradled but the last of the summer crops. Apart from the foliage of the tree and the vine, the land, dry and tired, gasped in thirst for the early rains. The western breeze, cleaving the oppressive heat of summer, brought cool air that crackled through the leaves of the vine to toy with the ends of Nagad's hair.

With one leg bent, the young conscript rested his forearm upon his knee as he sat astride a half-wall, a low barrier tracing the edge of the garden. Leaning back, he let his weight settle against the wooden beam of the vine-covered arbor. Grapes of deep red hung, fragrant, drooping down from lobed leaves. Long, supple stems, their tendrils fine as thread, clung to the latticework of the shaded bower, twining above his head.

Lounging beneath the shadow of the leafy shelter, he found a reprieve from the summer's heat and sun. Looking upon the fruit, Nagad did not resist temptation, but reached up and plucked a grape, taking it from the vine, and ate of it. The juice ran sweet over his tongue, and he smiled wryly, as a child with a secret vice.

The sharp-pointed head of the spear rested in the open palm of Nagad's right hand, which lay loosely upon his lap. As his thumb traced its fine edge, his thoughts returned to Tiphcar and all that had happened.

Though healing had been impeded by an unhurried pace, the captain had continued to improve as the months passed. Samuel had been a great encourager, ever ready with a hopeful word and a gentle presence.

Nagad's wounds had been deep; however, they were not physical as Tiphcar's, but a marring rooted within the depths of his soul. The prophet had cared for the young conscript with great patience as he mourned and slowly uncoiled from so many battles. Yet, Nagad could not shake the sense that grief and trauma still clung to him. Healing for him would come slowly—if ever.

Samuel's voice drew him from his thoughts. Nagad raised his eyes to meet the prophet, who sat beneath an ash tree upon the great, gnarled roots that reached out from beneath its ancient bark.

Oren, the tree of re-birth, was cultivated for the hardness of its timber. The wood of the ash tree was used as fuel, and to the prophet's sorrow, to carve images of gods, idols of foreign deities, even amongst the Chosen of the One True God.

This aged tree had been on this spot for many generations, far longer than the propagation of the Israelites into Canaan. The Naioth, which was nearly complete, was built around the tree, incorporating it into the courtyard of this house of instruction. Its branches, broad and reaching, provided shade to the prophet as he reasoned with his three pupils, who sat eagerly at his feet.

All were youths, young men called by the Lord to prophetic service, and given by their fathers for sacred training. Much as Samuel himself had once been entrusted to Eli, when but a boy. And so, with these few students, the prophet had begun his instruction in the Naioth.

Leaning forward, resting his arms upon his bent knees, Samuel continued with his lesson.

"There is no other God; Yahweh is the One True God. He is our King. Long ago, the Lord made an oath with our father Abraham—an oath sealed in blood, a pledge that cannot be broken, unless death be the penalty. So we are a holy race to the Lord our God; *El Elyon*, the Lord Most High, has chosen us to be a people for Himself, a special treasure above all who dwell upon the face of the earth.

"It was not for our great numbers that the Lord selected us, for we are the least of all the nations. But He chose us because of His great love for us and because He would keep the oath which He swore to our fathers.

"Yahweh has brought us out with a mighty hand, and redeemed us even from the house of bondage, from the hand of Pharaoh King of Egypt."

Pausing, Samuel picked up a twig from upon the ground and twirled it between his thumb and forefinger. As he did so, he studied it in silence, his thoughts drawn deep within. The prophet, unencumbered by haste, raised his gaze to meet that of his students.

With deliberate and measured speech, he continued, "Therefore know that the Lord your God, He is God, the faithful God, who keeps covenant and mercy for a thousand generations with those who love Him and keep His commandments."

Again, Samuel grew quiet and turned his attention to the twig. Idly, he rotated the scion, severed from its branch, alone within his hands, waiting, as the prophet watched it revolve.

The students, their eyes fixed upon the twig, looked on in anticipation.

Without warning, Samuel snapped the dry twig between his fingers, breaking it with the strength of his hand. Smiling, the prophet cast the broken offshoot aside and lifted his eyes to his pupils.

"Yet also know, that He repays all who hate Him, who go back upon the oath to break it, to destroy them. He will not be slack with any who despise Him. He will repay him to his face.

"Therefore, you shall keep the commandments, the statutes, and the judgments, which I command you this day, to observe them."[50]

Nagad looked down into his open palm, his thumb tracing the edge of the spearhead. Sadness washed over him as he listened to the words of Samuel, and he thought, *How far Israel had fallen from its sacred calling. Could the voice of the prophet break through the hearts of stone that dwell within the Promised Land? Was there still a way back for the Chosen of God? Was there yet time?*

With a shake of his head, Nagad turned his gaze once more to the prophet.

---

[50] Deuteronomy 7:6–11

"In your heart, you may say, 'These nations are greater than we. How then shall we overcome them, seeing they are so much stronger?'

"But I say to you now, you shall not fear them. You must remember well all that the Lord has already done for you.

"Forget not what Yahweh did to Pharaoh and to all Egypt, so great a nation as they were. Remember well the great trials your fathers beheld, the signs and the wonders, the mighty hand and the outstretched arm by which the Lord our God brought us forth. So shall the Lord our God do unto all the peoples of whom you are afraid."[51]

The three young prophets listened intently to all that Samuel spoke, their keen eyes steady upon their teacher, eager to prove themselves in his sight.

Nagad watched the students, their earnest faces alight with conviction, and for a moment, something stirred within him, quiet, unfamiliar, yearning. His hand, unbidden, tightened around the spearhead. He blinked, his thoughts having wandered, and turned once more to the voice of the prophet.

"You shall not be afraid, for the Lord your God, the great and awesome God, is among you. And Yahweh shall drive out those nations before you, little by little. You see, my little ones, the Lord your God will hand them over to you, and bring them low until they are utterly cut off. Their kings He shall give into your hand, and you shall blot out their name from beneath the heavens; none shall stand against you until you have utterly destroyed them.

"And when this comes to pass, you shall burn their carved images with fire. You must not look upon these idols, for they are accursed and shall become a snare to you. Neither shall you bring them into your dwellings, lest you bring destruction upon your house, and upon all Israel."[52]

Nagad found he was only half listening. A restlessness churned within him. Shifting where he sat, he tried to still his thoughts and attend to the prophet's voice.

"Take care, my children, and do as I instruct you, for by your voice, you may yet have a hand in the healing of your people and your land.

---

[51] Deuteronomy 7:17–19
[52] Deuteronomy 7:21–26

Israel has forgotten and bowed down to the idols of the Philistines and the Amorites. But you must teach them the way in which they should go."

No longer able to bear the confinement of the garden walls, Nagad stood and adjusted his armor, for of late he had donned his war-clothes, breastplate and sword, upon rising each day. The peace of the Naioth had been healing, yet something kindled within his soul: a restless energy, an anticipation growing and gaining ground, though he could not name it. He needed to move, to feel the strength of his body in motion—not sit and grow soft.

As he took leave of the garden, the young conscript could hear the voice of the prophet trail off as he warned the students once again to heed all he taught them. Nagad could not help but smile as he thought of the students trapped before the prophet's unhurried counsel.

Though Nagad loved Samuel and often found his words a great comfort, he was glad to be free. He made his way to the inner court, where he found Tiphcar seated at a table, resting in the sun.

He, too, had arrayed himself in armor. It was the first time Nagad had seen his captain so adorned since their arrival in Ramah many months past.

Drawing forth a chair, Nagad sat down heavily and turned his gaze upon the face of Tiphcar. The captain sat with his arms draped along the sides of his chair, his limbs at ease, his breath steady. Gone was the pallor that had long clung to him; color had returned to his cheeks, and with it, the strength of health.

Thus the two soldiers, comrades bound by the forge of war, sat side by side in silence, waiting out the hour together.

Nagad could feel perspiration forming upon his body as he sat beneath the midday sun. A *shapirit*, that is, a dragonfly, landed on his leg, its iridescent double wings pulsing as it drank the moisture from his skin. With quiet interest, he watched as the *shapirit* lingered. A cool breeze brushed over him, soft upon his face, and the dragonfly took to the air. His eyes rose to follow, tracing its swift, darting flight toward the reeds that scratched against the stone walls of the Naioth.

Tiphcar stirred, breaking the silence. "It is time, Nagad—time for us to return to the regiment. Our rest has ended. We must rejoin our men and watch the borders. We must find news of the war."

Nagad wished he had a mind to stay, to learn under the wise instruction of Samuel. But he knew he must return, for he was a soldier, and duty waited. He was not fashioned for confinement. Ever unsettled, waiting plagued him even in repose, for rest chafed his soul. Though he longed for peace and held no love for battle, he hungered for motion, something to break the weary rhythm of each passing day. War had spoiled him. Never again would he be content to settle and live simply. Unrest would always be his bedfellow.

Tiphcar pushed back his chair and stood. "Let us go meet with Samuel. He is waiting for us by the road."

Nagad looked up at his captain, stunned. "You have already spoken with the prophet concerning our leave-taking?"

"Yes, it is all arranged. Come, gather yourself, for we depart ere the sun lowers in the sky."

Nagad rose, sliding his chair back under the table. It seemed all so sudden. His blood quickened with the rising thrill. After months of healing, of waiting, the time had come, and it had come without warning.

Tiphcar lifted his face toward the horizon, a quiet smile spreading across his countenance. "It will be good to be on our way, yet I shall miss the time we have spent here. Peace is a good thing. Is it not the very reason we go to war, to preserve peace for our people?"

Turning to Nagad, he added, "But alas, we are men of action, and cannot be content to rest always."

Laying his arm around Nagad's shoulders, Tiphcar compelled him forward, toward the road that ran before the Naioth.

As promised, the prophet waited, a sack of supplies he held in his hand. Nagad marveled that he had been unaware of the plans Samuel and Tiphcar had made. Clearly the lesson had concluded, and the seer had, in stealth, slipped past him to prepare for their parting.

With heavy hearts, in sweet sorrow, the company looked upon one another. Long had been their fellowship. Now the one who had cared well for the two comrades meant to send them away as a mother bird dispatches her fledglings from the nest.

"So we have come to our parting," spoke Samuel, a smile touching his face. "It is as it has ever been. For a time, we come upon the same path, but soon, we must each take our leave, for the journey is our own, and the way must be walked alone. Each must follow his own road. Each must fulfill his own destiny."

"My friend," returned Tiphcar as he clasped forearms with the prophet. "I cannot speak true of how much you have done for us. We are in your debt. I shall miss our discourse and pray we may yet return to where last we spoke. You have been a comfort to me in this season of trial. I see more clearly, both what has come to pass, and my place within it. The burden, it is less heavy. I can carry it now. For that, I thank you."

The two embraced. And to Nagad, it seemed the men welled with tears at their parting.

Leaving he did not desire, yet staying, this he could not endure. *How do you say goodbye? It always ends with goodbye.* And though he knew the time for detachment had come, still it stung.

Nagad placed a hand upon the prophet's shoulder, searching for a fitting word. But Samuel turned and drew him into his arms, patting him vigorously upon the back.

"Farewell, *Na'ar*," was all he said.

Nagad's breath caught sharply at the name. That was what Orach had called him. The pain of division struck deep, fiercely biting into his soul. He could not speak. Yet he embraced the prophet once more, then quickly released him and took a step back, his face toward the ground. To his dismay, a tear escaped his eye, falling to the earth, leaving a small wet splatter upon the dirt. Embarrassed, Nagad placed his sandaled foot over the mud-splotch.

Tiphcar waved to Samuel, then, with Nagad by his side, walked down the road, leaving the place of healing behind. Samuel stood watching the two companions as they grew small upon the path. At length, the prophet turned from the place of separation and entered into the Naioth. His calling beckoned, even as duty summoned the soldiers from peace.

Nagad and Tiphcar stood on the crest of the hill that overlooked Eben-Ezer. The land lay serene, the sun glinting off the salted waves to the west, the plain resting still before them. A fair wind came adrift from the Great Sea, speaking of the close of the season, flirting with the two soldiers who waited upon the rise as they surveyed the boundary between the Israelite and Philistine nations. After taking their leave of the prophet Samuel, the two had returned to the border to guard the land against the enemy.

"It is far too quiet," spoke Tiphcar as he scanned the horizon.

Looking into the sun, his hand shielding his eye, the captain continued, "Summer wanes, and still no advance from the enemy. What are they waiting for? Why not strike while they hold the advantage? For what cause do they relent now, when they have gained the upper hand? Why not finish us off? Shiloh is destroyed, and they possess the Ark. They have taken the very heart of Israel—yet they do nothing. It would be no great effort for them to press into our lands and crush us. But they wait. Why? Their reasoning eludes me. What stays their hand?"

"It is good they wait," reasoned Nagad. "It gives us time to rebuild our armies."

"I do not complain," returned Tiphcar, turning his gaze to his companion. "For right you are in all you say."

The captain cast his eyes once more upon the land. Before him rose the tower of Aphek, and memory pricked with the sting of defeat.

"But plainly as we stand here, they know we are weak, vulnerable to attack. I do not understand why they delay. But I am thankful for the time. If the Philistines were to strike now, we would surely fall."

Nagad gave a solemn nod. Too well he understood their plight. It would take time to repair their defenses. Most of the conscripts, even some of the seasoned warriors, had returned to their homes to care for their fields and tend their herds. This was a nation of citizen-soldiers, their thoughts ever on home. Men served when they were needed, but as quickly as they could, they abandoned their military obligation for the sake of their own hearth. It was as it had always been, and would remain so, as long as the nation was fractured by tribal clans.

Yet Nagad had no home. The army was his hearth; the men, his kin. He had no crops to tend, no herds to watch over. All he had, his place, his people, was here in the camp. And so, with familial love, he served his people.

Looking south from where he stood, Nagad took note of a green rise upon the field between Aphek and Eben-Ezer, a mound that before had not been there. Curious, he strained his eyes, fixing them upon the place where the earth had been heaped. Slowly, as awareness entered his soul, the young conscript descended from his post and followed a track into the plain below.

Despite himself, his heart thrummed in his chest, racing, pounding, until all his being pulsed in time with its relentless beat. His breath came quick and shallow, suffocating, pressing down upon him. A tremor passed through him, unbidden; his hands would not still. Behind him, he sensed movement. Tiphcar was following, for he too understood where the conscript was bound.

The hillock was the only green upon the face of the field, the place of battle, long past in the hearts of men, but not in his, a common grave where the adversary had inhumed the fallen of Israel, and he knew that Orach was buried there, laid among the many, hidden beneath the mound.

Nagad sank to his knees. With head bowed, he wept bitter tears. He wept for Orach, for the Ark, and for his nation, Israel. The savage sorrow, unpalatable and harsh, spilled over as Nagad released it all, all that had been bridled, all he had buried deep within himself.

At his back stood Tiphcar, in silence, his head lowered, a hand upon the young conscript's shoulder. After a time, he spoke, "For these things I weep; my eye, my eye overflows with water, because the Comforter, who should restore my life, is far from me. My children are desolate, because the enemy has prevailed."[53]

Nagad was spent. He did not move from the spot but knelt there, his shoulders shuddering beneath the weight of grief. He opened his eyes and looked long upon the green verdure of the mound, stroking the grass as though it were the fur of an animal. Small white flowers grew within the turf, delicate sprays of blossoms, clustered like gentle drifts of snow.

Wild carrot, he thought, for set within the center of each tuft, cradled in a fern-like blanket, a single purple floret lay.

The myriad of flowers were as a soft-fluttering spirit burgeoning upon the rise, lifting its face to the sky, opening its arms to heaven.

---

[53] Lamentations 1:16

That alluvial vestment cloaked the fallen in a shroud, a vestige of the endless cycle of life and death. Decay had brought forth new life upon this mound. But the men were all gone, their voices silenced, many cut down in their youth. And though life had returned to the plain, the loss of his companions could not be restored.

He felt Tiphcar's hand upon his shoulder as the captain squeezed his fingers against Nagad's grief.

"It shall be made right," Tiphcar gently spoke. "Yahweh will have His recompense."

At the voicing of these words, Nagad recoiled. The burn of revenge bubbled up gall, wormwood, as bitter herbs to his soul. A smoldering flame, acrid and blistering, scorched his being as he clothed himself in anger.

With his jaw tight and his fists clenched, Nagad thought, *How could this have happened? They will pay for what they have done. This will be answered in blood.*

Reaching down, the young conscript grasped a handful of dirt from the grave mound. Rubbing it between his palms, he allowed the dirt to fall back to the earth, yet his hands bore the stain, as his heart wore the mark of vengeance.

CHAPTER 20

THE FLAME OF DOOM

"So it has been, since the Hebrew Ark was carried to Gath, and placed within her walls, that the hand of this God has been against this city with a very great destruction. He has struck the men of Gath, both great and small, tumors and black-death have consumed them."

Danuna spoke as he paced to and fro upon his dais, wringing his hands in anxious apprehension.

"Therefore, we shall send the Ark of Yahweh up the Valley of Sorek to Ekron. Let them have a go at this God. We shall then know without question if it is He with whom we contend."

"But, *Sar*—" Azuri's voice trembled, yet he dared to speak. "Should we not consult the other lords, to seek their counsel in this matter?"

"Do not question my wishes. It is not their people who suffer. I will be free of this curse that lies upon Gath. I will not wait a moment longer. I am done with this. Get the accursed object out of my city by nightfall! I will have it here no longer."

This Danuna spoke with great agitation, for long had the curse lain heavy upon his shoulders, for he alone bore the guilt of calling this doom upon his people.

"*Sar*—"

"Do as I say! Inform Caphtor of his orders!" A long, shuddering breath escaped him as he wrung the back of his neck.

"Ekwesh, my friend," spoke Phicol, "you cannot continue in this beleaguered state. Please, come with us and take some rest, some sustenance. You must gather your strength. Do not allow yourself to enter into despair."

"Yah, yah!" Ekwesh laughed, a wild gleam in his eyes. "Rest? There can be no rest. Do you not see? I am hell's captive!"

With restless agitation, he paced the tower wall, eyes fixed upon the eastern hills. Overwrought, his mind in disorder, Ekwesh waited, pulse quickened, consumed by a churning desire, as though the enemy might at any moment rise from the field before him. Sweat beaded on his brow. Sword drawn, limbs taut, he held his watch as dread mounted within him.

"You are exhausted, friend," offered Lukka. "And you have taken too much drink. You are not yourself. Come, do as we say, get some sleep."

"It is true—I am not myself. Wounded in my heart, I am. My sword shall not sleep in my hand, my hatred undying. My affections rising, a brother has been stolen away. Innocent of any evil thought he was, yet evil took him. I cannot let this rest, nor let it go unrequited. I must be satisfied. Vengeance will be my recompense."

"You speak madness. How can you contend with a god?" asked Lukka.

"I will take from Him what He cherishes—or I shall die trying!"

"Much is foretold in dark words," spoke Phicol, farseeing.

"Fall in! Fall in!" went up the call, and all obeyed, all save Ekwesh, who yet stood upon the wall, and the two who lingered with him.

"Please, Ekwesh," implored Phicol. "The summons has gone out. We must obey. Come with us, see what is to be."

With reluctance, Ekwesh sheathed his sword and left his post, joining his fellows as they took their place in line.

Before them, the dread commander, arrayed for battle and mounted upon his powerful steed, towered with grim determination.

"We have our orders," Caphtor began. "By command of Danuna himself, we are to bear the Ark of the Hebrew God to Ekron. By nightfall it must be done. Make ready. There is no time to waste."

"You must return this Ark to the Hebrews, before we are all consumed!" cried Ekwesh, his anger aflame.

Phicol and Lukka seized their companion by the arms, lest he lunge at the dread commander before him.

"Stay your speech, soldier, and know thy place," Caphtor answered coldly. "Make ready the Ark, we depart within the hour." He fixed Ekwesh with a hard gaze. "You have your orders."

It was the month of Ethanim, enduring its meaning, the first month of the civil year, when the Philistines lined up in shining array to deliver the Ark unto Ekron. Though their ranks had been diminished by a battle not waged by force of arms, the Philistine contingent remained a daunting edifice of this great war-machine.

The company of soldiers entered the Vale of Elah, northward from Gath, toward Ekron, across the Zephathah River. Cutting through the Shephelah, the southernmost of the great valleys, Elah commenced near Hebron, then descended north until it turned west at Sochoh, running by Gath and on toward Ashdod and the sea.

For the greater part, the valley wound a narrow path amongst rough hills. The vale opened as it entered the region of Sochoh, where several valleys coalesced and widened, becoming a broad plain that leveled into fruitful fields half a mile in breadth. The ridge on either side rose to a great height with steep, uniform slopes, the ideal platform for battle.

The expanse was cleft by two streams that joined to form one watercourse, the River Elah, which lay in the heart of the valley. Though dry in summer, it now stirred to life, a living spring awakened by the autumn rains falling upon the mountains of Judah.

Smooth white pebbles littered the trickling bed as the river carved its way through the vale, etching a slender ravine into the red soil of its fertile floor. Terebinth trees, their twisted trunks bowed with age, lined the banks of this seasonal stream, which breathed life into the patchwork of peach orchards and acacia groves that clothed the land.

An acrid, resinous aroma hung in the air, rising from the copses of lentisk, scrub trees with dark green, leathery leaves, that clung to the surrounding hills. The wind, awakening from the quarter of the rising sun and sweeping across the eastern desert, granted a clear sky, giving rise to a warm day.

"The heavens are unveiled," mused Lukka, resting in the shade of a terebinth tree. "You can see a great distance. The mountains seem close, as though you could walk there within the hour, yet I know they be several days' journey away."

"It will not last long, for look," said Phicol, pointing, "clouds form in the west. Rain comes at last."

"It is a sign of the gods' good favor," declared Lukka. "The parched and thirsty land will soon be revived. Baal, the storm god, is with us. Life will return to this barren land."

Ekwesh, quiet until now, spoke harshly. "There are no gods here who wish to help us. We are alone."

At his words, the others fell silent, for the shadow of loss returned like a hush upon the wind.

A warm rain began to fall as the soldiers bore their burden through the valley and across the plain. The company trudged amidst newly sown barley fields as the fortified city of Libnah, white city of the storax tree, rose on the horizon to their east.

Thunder rolled overhead as lightning streaked across the darkening sky. Rain came down in sheets, driven with great force by the west wind, as the thundercloud burst open. Suddenly violent, the heavens rent, unleashing a mighty storm. The silent expanse of nature, whose bowels ruptured with tumultuous agitation, yielded to the dreadful fury of the tempest amid fitful bursts of wind.

Beneath them, the road gave way, their feet sinking into a rising sea of mud. The Ark lurched, threatening to topple. Soldiers stumbled, struggling to hold their ground, and the line began to unravel. Bludgeoned by sound, the roar of driving wind and rain and the implacable crash of thunder forbade them the exchange of words.

Leaning into the gale, they braced against the storm, yet could make no headway.

"*Sar*, dark is closing in fast, and we are surrounded by the tormented terrain!" Phicol cried aloud. "We will never reach Ekron by nightfall. The way is too difficult."

With sound reverberating through time, notes rising then lost to decay, Caphtor retorted above the thunder's bend with dreadful voice, uttering violent imprecations, oracles severe, as the tempest grew more feral. The internal pressure of nature mounted a crack of thunder as though the fissure of doom rent forth with a terrible fulmination, attended by bursts of flaming light that smote the vault of heaven with violent splendor. Soldiers dropped where they stood, ducking low, arms raised to shield their eyes from the storm-riven pageant.

"*Sar,*" called out Phicol.

"Fall out," bellowed Caphtor. "We go no farther. Make ready camp."

Amidst a thicket of storax trees, the company set to their work with great difficulty. Tents were torn by the terrible tempest, supplies flung in harried havoc, and the battle over the tent-spike raged on into the dark. The rush of the angry wind continued all the night, the sky flying apart, then crashing together in a great explosion that shook the very foundations of the earth.

Looking at the tent now standing tall after the long struggle to raise it, Lukka, with hands on hips and a triumphant grin upon his rain-wet face, spoke, "A good storm is a grand thing!"

With gasping breath and muddied clothes, Ekwesh and Phicol looked upon Lukka with annoyance and dismay.

"'Tis a foolish man who does not know when to get out of the rain!" barked Ekwesh, throwing a wet cloth at Lukka's face.

Laughing, the companions three, for one was missing, huddled wet and weary beneath the shelter of a single tent. Sorrow forgotten for a moment lent a hopeful peace like a message, uninterrupted, that emerges from silence. Yet, when One so great begins to rage, as dire omens spoken, grief bears down unrelenting.

No fire was made to warm the sodden men, for no flame could withstand the torrents of wind and rain, which held the land in thrall for two unyielding days. Confined, the internal tormentor that gnaws and afflicts the mind worked its malevolent will upon the restless nature of the imprisoned.

"One day's travel has turned into three," spoke Ekwesh with the malady of the soul held captive. "Time is fleeing, the hour nearly spent, and our liberty lies in wait."

"There is naught to do but tarry 'til the storm abates," answered Phicol, calm upon his mat.

"Ah, what I would not do for a taste of hot meat charred over a bed of embers," Lukka sighed with longing. "How is a man to live on the likes of stale cakes and dried fish? It is an abomination."

Ignoring Lukka, Ekwesh redressed Phicol, "How can you lie there so at ease? With each moment, our plight grows desperate."

"Sleep, Ekwesh. Rest while you may."

Night invested, the long wakeful hours loomed ahead, meted out by the ebb and flow of the west wind upon the tent's cloth, as waves of rain dashed against the canvas. The fearful howling of the tempest continued, ill-boding portents of evil in great degree, a dreadful chorus echoing through the wooded waste.

"The uproar of the storm is intolerable. Why do the heavens rage?" cried Lukka. "The noise is dire, as maddening wheels of a raging chariot upon the hard earth bearing down upon you. Sleep is not possible!"

"It is a tide of blood that rages," spoke Ekwesh, his throat tight with emotion. "The iniquity that our own offense has wrought."

"Such doctrine, if true, should be fateful to my reasoning," returned Phicol. "When the wind comes from the west, storms rise off the sea. It is how it has ever been."

Pacing, Ekwesh threw wide the tent flap, rain splattering against his furrowed brow.

"Oh! Idols most foul, that quench the soul and drown man's reason!" His wits astonished with sorrow, he spoke with a mournful, artificial strain. "Thou huntest me as a fierce foe, unrelenting, and hidden from my sight."

Sometime in the night of the third day, the storm ceased. Spent by the tempestuous rampage of the day, nature descended into an abysmal and profound slumber, granting rest to the weary soldiers.

The men woke to find their camp shrouded in a dense fog as vapors rose from the earth, gathering in the valleys and low places. Above the mist, hilltops appeared as islands in a sea of white. The wind chopped round to the north, and as the day broke with fine weather, the vapors lifted, clinging to the mountain heights, forming light morning clouds.

The encampment, askew, was littered with the remnants of toppled tents and scattered garments, which had escaped from their owners. Leaves, long and round, torn from the limbs of the storax tree, once firm and waxen, now lay sodden upon the muddy earth, their pale undersides upturned. Grateful to be freed from their mandated confinement, the soldiers walked about, clearing debris and speaking with animation in the fresh air.

With camp broken, the call went out to line up, and the journey commenced. As the contingent passed by Libnah, a great fortress loomed on the horizon, just east of the city.

"There stands the stronghold of Azekah, the gate to the Judean hills and the realm of our enemy," spoke Lukka.

Ekwesh raised his eyes and glared at the shrouded bastion. "The realm of our enemy," he repeated to himself.

"The Hebrew Joshua," Phicol recounted, "defeated the southern coalition of Amorite kings led by Adonizedek of Jebus as the Hebrew God cast hailstones from heaven upon the fleeing armies. Here it was that Joshua commanded the sun and moon to stand still, and so it did."

"If this be true," remarked Lukka, "who is this great God that even the sun obeys?"

"After the battle, the Amorite kings sought refuge in nearby caves at Makkedah, the place of shepherds, it is called," continued Phicol. "Unfortunately, the kings entered into a trap and were captured. All were slain, they and all their people."

"What have we brought upon ourselves?" spoke Lukka. "I tell you, we should not have contended with the gods."

"Too late the warning comes when already evil dwells in our midst," pronounced Phicol.

Too late, thought Ekwesh, *for too well I see the battle which lies before me.*

Several cities were positioned along the length of this well-traveled valley: Azekah, Makkedah, Sochoh, and Adullam among them. Azekah, a strong fortress, held command from its solitary height, rising some two hundred cubits above the valley's western end. From its summit, one could behold the Shephelah and the full stretch of the Valley of Elah.

The watercourse ascended gently eastward for two miles, leading to a break in the ridgeline opposite Sochoh, which itself perched upon a steep hill on the valley's southeastern flank. From there, the stream passed Adullam, a city of refuge set high above the far end of the valley. Here, the east-west route joined the Ridge Road with the Coastal Highway. Further to the southeast, some eleven miles beyond, lay Hebron.

Across the Elah River, the company traveled through fields newly ploughed, prepared for the winter wheat that would soon be sown. The high, rocky hills loomed ahead, distorted and indistinct through the veil, running parallel with the Valley of Elah to the north. Just across this barrier lay the Sorek River Valley, a broad, fertile alluvial plain so named for its perpetual watercourse, a living stream. The route plummeted into the shadowy embrace of boundless olive groves, whose trunks, pierced with gaping holes, gave shelter to a host of nameless creatures.

Grateful were the weary soldiers for the shade beneath the canopy of silvery-green leaves. Each tree, a unique giant, ancient and reputed, its gnarled form hunched and arthritic, told of journeys long since passed.

"You know," began Lukka, "some of these trees are reported to be a thousand years in age, some even two thousand. Each tree is loved as an individual, a living member of the family. Many are given names and celebrated for their singular nature."

"Yes," added Phicol, "to plant an olive tree is to make a promise to posterity, for if you plant one in your youth, it will not bear fruit until you are very old."

"These trees, then," spoke Ekwesh, "are quite old, for see how heavy with fruit they are."

Lukka and Phicol looked intently at him, for these were the first words he had spoken that day. A smile crept across Lukka's face, glad for this quiet sign that his friend was finding his way back.

The sharp cry of a kestrel cut through the silent sky as the contingent broke through the wooden canopy. The well-fortified city of Ekron rose above the fertile plain, planned with precision, as all Philistine municipalities were, with a small upper city and a larger lower city to the south. Thick, mud-covered walls loomed high, encircling the metropolis.

"What is that?" asked Ekwesh.

"It is but the call of a bird," answered Lukka flatly.

"No," spoke Ekwesh, "not the bird. Up ahead, in the clearing."

"Yes, I see," said Phicol. "There appears to be some disturbance before the city gate."

And so it was, that word had spread of the Ark's coming. But these people of Ekron were not so easily taken, for as the Holy Shrine came to their city, the Ekronites cried out, saying: "They have brought the Ark of the God of Israel to us, to kill us and our people!"

Rising en masse to oppose, the inhabitants of Ekron met the army of Philistia on the road outside the gate, refusing to let them enter with the Ark.

"Halt," called out Caphtor, raising his arm to the troops.

Dismounting from his fine steed, he advanced toward the soldiers standing before the crowd.

"What is this foul affront? Move aside and let us pass."

"You are not welcome here. You cannot bring this coffer of doom into our city."

"By whose authority?" Caphtor demanded.

"The lord of Ekron, Nasib himself, has proclaimed it," spoke the soldier, his grip tightening upon the spear, one foot set before him, poised to move.

"Do not take this posture," rebuked Caphtor.

"The fear of your enterprise has moved the crowd to rash deeds."

"Our duty, we will consummate," spoke the dread commander in his stern tenor, "by whatever means necessary."

"Then we are at an impasse."

The men of Ekron stood in solemn array before the city gates, resolved to hinder the task, even should blood be spilled. Unwilling to receive the Ark, they took up stones and the tools of their toil, now turned to instruments of war. Shoulder to shoulder, they stood, steadfast beneath the open sky, and would not yield.

With reluctant tread, Caphtor and his company moved forward, for they were loath to set hand against their own people. Yet the command was given, and under duty's stern hand, they advanced. In bold defiance, the citizens and soldiers held their ground before the host of Philistia, and forbade them passage. As the regiment drew near, a volley of stones was cast from the gathered throng. The soldiers raised their shields above their brows, and withstood the storm that broke upon them.

At the forefront, where the vanguard pressed into the ranks of the steadfast, blades met with fury. Rough-hewn tools, sharpened for toil, turned now to war, and struck out against the armor-clad soldiers of Philistia. And so the clang of arms rose, the din of battle swelling like a storm. At first, the warriors bore the brunt, raising shields to ward off the rain of blows. But soon, as the fire of conflict kindled and blood was drawn, they answered stroke with stroke in grim resolve.

Bravely, the men of Ekron withstood the tide, bound to the cause by bitter dread and ancient pride. It was a trial by sword, and they would not yield. Beneath the hail of iron, they stood fast. Flesh was torn and sinew rent; and in that fell hour, brother turned upon brother, and strife was kindled within Philistia, sundering the unity of her peoples.

Nasib, watching upon the wall, was moved to compassion as he beheld the citizens and soldiers of Ekron strive against the stalwart host of Caphtor's forces. No match were they to the prowess of this seasoned contingent, and many of his people lay in ruin. Seeing the army too well seated to be shaken, the degree of Nasib's passion wavered.

By the sound of the trumpet cutting through the din of arms, a stay in battle was procured. An attendant of Nasib, lord of Ekron, descended from the wall, passed through the city gate, and came forth to meet the dread commander, whom no mortal measure could master.

"My lord, if it please you, our master is at hand and seeks an audience, to speak with you at a distance between our two forces."

"I agree to this assemblage," quoth Caphtor.

With the dispute in cessation and the conflict ranged in just array, the combatants stood to each side. Nasib, lord and master, marched forth from the city gate, his attendants trailing behind him. Caphtor, dismounting once more, strode over to meet him.

"The repute of your skill and valor precedes you, Captain," began Nasib as the dread commander bowed low before the lord of Ekron. "The name of Caphtor alone speaks volumes in our hearts. We know we are not able to stand against you."

Caphtor, greatly strengthened by this speech, dared to redress the insult given him. Rising, he spoke, "My lord, you must restrain the crowd from their open rebellion."

"Commander, you must show pity for our plight. Too well you know of our doom. Do not force this upon our city. Let us not have enmity between us."

"Lord Nasib, you are culpable for this calamity. You have done an injury to one who deserves respect. Lord Danuna has commanded us to bring this Ark of the Hebrew God to Ekron. We must complete this task entrusted to us."

"We cannot allow you entry. My men are prepared to die for their liberty. Let not this slaughter continue."

"Their liberty!" roared Caphtor, his impatience rising as a chill into fever. "You must accept your share in this, as we have endured our own. Do not tempt this force of arms, for we will complete what has been decreed—though all who oppose us be struck down."

Nasib, seeing the evil that poised against his people, relented. "Then we are undone. You bring us to our ruin."

The torment of doom was writ in his voice as he went on, "Well then, in the interest of private men and the public peace, I have but one choice."

"Do not fear. It is a right judgment, my lord," reassured Caphtor.

"There is no more fear of what might be, for there is no more hope."

Turning toward the crowd before him, Nasib, with the voice of woe, uttered the fateful words, "Let them come, lest we all perish by the violence of our brothers' own hand. And let the gods have mercy on us."

Those gathered, though troubled, obeyed their forlorn ruler, and stood back, granting the Ark entrance into the city of Ekron.

Cries of lament rose from the populace as the company of proud soldiers entered the city, the Ark of the Lord before them.

And as kindling to the fire, the flame of doom was ignited upon the city.

CHAPTER 21

A SHARED CURSE

It was a cold wind that blew in from the northwest, steeping the air in chill as frigid as the welcome the troops received from the populace of Ekron. No fine meal awaited them, no celebration marked the prize they had borne. Nasib gave no grand address. No banners flew. No voice was raised in cheer, for the shadow of the curse lay heavy upon them.

"They give us roasted meat only to beat us with the spit," muttered Lukka, disgruntled.

"Judge not too harshly, Lukka," advised Phicol, "for they fear for their people. Forget the injury. We must write kindness in stone and wrongs in the dust, for they deem us the coming of death."

"Death and destruction," Ekwesh broke in, "for foul weather follows in our wake. They fear for their crops as well. If the rains do not cease their deluge, famine shall sweep this land."

The earth in its fitful sleep raged as winter storms, unnatural in fury and number, beset the region, flooding the valley, for the River Elah crested its banks. While the hibernal rains rushed down the rocky slopes, stripping the soil and baring the stone, fear for the newly sown winter wheat and barley grew. A fell dew issued by night, so that even as the rains relented, the ground could not free itself from its sodden berth. Morning's breath gave flight to a frigid day, laden in a lingering frost.

"Water, the great destroyer," quoth Phicol, "who gives life and takes it away: drowning, destroying, killing by its mere existence or its absence. Yes, see how the cisterns overflow. We will suffer come spring."

"Only the divine has power to command water," spoke Lukka. "It cannot be formed, shaped, or tamed by human hands. It is the gods working in our midst."

"Yet," answered Ekwesh, "a drowning man is not troubled by rain."

A hush fell between the companions, for their uneasy thoughts worked inwardly. As the friends strolled through the grand streets of Ekron, the citizens they passed looked upon them with disdain. Lukka grew restless beneath the weight of so many eyes, aflame with scorn.

"Let us find a wine shop," suggested Lukka, "for I could use a drink to wash this malevolent affection down."

With pace quickened, Ekwesh, Lukka, and Phicol took note of the dwellings that flanked the narrow street. As they entered the market district, the avenue broadened. To either side rose buildings of stone, rain-darkened and rough with age. Channels traced the length of the roadway, feeding into a great sewer that ran beneath the main thoroughfare.

"We are but a few lengths from the city's edge, for see, the walls lie before us, and yet we find no wine shops!" cried Lukka, heat rising in his voice.

"Ekron is a vast city," reassured Phicol. "We shall find one, I am sure."

"Yes, maybe we should ask one of these fine and friendly citizens for assistance," muttered Ekwesh, with a bite to his voice.

"Look, up ahead," said Phicol, pointing, "a cluster of buildings near the wall. Perhaps we are close."

Instead of a winery, the companions entered a dense industrial quarter, where rows of buildings stood in uniform alignment along the inner wall of the city. Many were olive oil installations, the lifeblood of Ekron. Each housed three chambers, distinguished only by their use: one for crushing and pressing the fruit, another for separating and storing the oil, and a third, facing the street, served as a textile shop when the time of the olive waned.

The scent of incense drifted on the breeze, for a dozen small altars, set upon platforms, adorned the heart of the oilworks.

"Are there nothing but oil stalls in this place? Have you ever seen so many buildings for the production of oil? Do these people know nothing but tending olives," complained Lukka. "We should have brought wine from Gath."

"It appears they know a bit about textiles," answered Phicol, lifting a length of finely woven cloth from the stall, "for see, there hangs the work of their off-season."

"May I be of assistance, gentlemen?" came the voice of the proprietor.

"This is a fine weave," said Phicol graciously. "You are a skilled artisan."

"I thank you for your kindness, *Sar*. But my especiality is oil. We have excellent olive oil at reasonable prices. See how it glows, golden and clear."

This, the proprietor spoke as he poured a sample into a shallow saucer. "Ah, olive oil, liquid gold it is called, the fountain of wealth and power. Empires rise and fall upon their olive groves. If you would make war on a kingdom, burn its olive trees."

"Indeed, it is a fine example of pure oil," spoke Phicol.

"We use only the finest, unblemished olives. You will find no better oil in all of Philistia."

"I do not doubt this to be true."

"I see you know a bit of the oil trade," declared the proprietor with a pleased grin. "The olive tree has long been a symbol of abundance, glory, and peace. Come—let me show you my press house, where the last of our harvest is being drawn."

Lukka, growing restless, rolled his eyes as Phicol leaned toward him and whispered, "Humor him, and I shall find you your winery."

Reluctantly, the gentle giant entered the shop, stooping as he transgressed the threshold, with Ekwesh in his wake.

"Sun, stone, drought, silence, and solitude," continued the proprietor, "these are what is needed to grow fine olive trees, and this is what we give them.

"Each tree holds the strength of the gods. Harsh winters, burning summers, severe pruning, and yet they thrive, growing proud and strong, reaching toward the sky, bringing forth fruit that nourishes and heals, inspires and amazes."

"Yes, I have heard that the ingestion of olive oil can heal the sick," encouraged Phicol.

Smiling with satisfaction, the olive-master bade the companions attend to the workings of his press house. A great cylindrical stone was in motion, turned by a young lad who gripped a wooden beam affixed to its center. Round and round he walked, circling the stone basin in which the wheel rested, as olives were crushed beneath its grinding weight.

"See here," spoke the proprietor, "first we crush the olives, and from them draw the first and finest oil, collected in these rock-hewn vats. Then the pulp is gathered into these baskets."

Upon a raised platform stood fiber baskets, one stacked upon another, forming a high column. A large slab rested as the capstone to this pillar, its weight borne down by a thick wooden beam, the pressing beam, which jutted from the wall. Its far end hung suspended in the air, burdened by stone weights secured with rope. The proprietor stepped to this beam and laid his full weight upon it, crushing the olives with great force. The yellow-green oil flowed freely into a shallow trough, which poured through a spout and into a waiting vat.

"You see how fine the color is, how clear the liquid stands?" spoke the master, his voice swelling with pride.

Dripping the cherished oil into a jar, he continued, "The oil is permitted to settle further within these jars, allowing any water to sink below, that the pure oil may remain. Come—try some for your health. I guarantee you will be satisfied."

Phicol placed a finger into the jar and tasted the liquid gold. "Yes, it is quite smooth and flavorful. I have tasted no better."

"The secret lies in the heart and soul of the maker. A beautiful oil is born of patient care. It cannot be hurried. Come—you must try some as well."

Phicol nodded at Ekwesh and Lukka as the proprietor extended the jar. With clear reluctance, the two dipped a finger and tasted.

"This is all very fine, but it is wine we wish to purchase," spoke Lukka.

Phicol looked upon him with exasperation.

"My friend is in need of a drink, for he is in a distemper this day. I pray you, excuse his surly behavior, for we have been long in our trials and are sorely in need of rest. We shall purchase a jar of your fine oil."

The purchase made, Phicol looked upon the proprietor. "I thank you for your kind hospitality. May I impose upon you further by asking the way to the nearest winery?"

"Aye, it is but a few lengths beyond this street. Just to the right and down the lane, there toward the heart of the market district. You will have no trouble finding it."

Phicol nodded his appreciation to the proprietor, and the three turned to leave.

"Mind you take care of that mood," called the proprietor after them, "'fore it gets you into trouble. A flower will not grow in salty soil."

Lukka stopped short, shook his head, and with a sharp breath, strode down the lane.

"Mind my mood," he grumbled.

"Let it go, my friend," soothed Phicol. "Come, and we will get you that drink."

As they turned toward the market district, the press of the multitude grew thick about them, and the sound of many voices rose into the air.

"Ah, we are getting close," remarked Phicol.

Passing deeper into the sellers' square, they discovered the city was laid out in a series of levels descending one beneath another, terraces leading downward from the outer reaches toward the core of the city. Its shape formed a hollow, resembling a great basin, wherein water gathered at the center. Amid a tight cluster of buildings, the winery was espied, and the promised vintage bought and consumed.

Renewed by the dulling effects of the wine, Lukka's spirits rose as a ruddy flush spread across his visage. The fellowship, now in an agreeable temper, conversed in jovial merriment as the cares of the day melted away.

The three souls mingled in friendship divine, marked by endless miles and unbounded grief, bringing them to this place of brotherhood, forged by struggle and sealed in loss, which shared their pains and touched their wounds, a bulwark and a treasure found.

Gleams of delight sparked in each eye, as though secretly charged to one another, kindling for the fire that joined them, igniting a flame that crossed the plain and rose as one conflagration. The moment was transcendent, reaching beyond the heavens. A corporeal bond formed, which neither the turning of years nor the breadth of distance could undo, an understanding that brought them together, fettered for all time.

A sudden clap of thunder shattered the fellowship and goodwill as rain poured down in torrents, and with it, cries of despair rose from the city. It had begun. Ekron received its share in the curse as its citizens fell to the death-dealing pestilence. The plague accomplished its work with dreadful haste; the city staggered under the weight of its affliction. Bereft of countless souls, the people panicked as the dark sickness raged through every quarter, spilling beyond the walls into the surrounding countryside.

"The entire city is mounting toward death," spoke Achimiti, attendant to Nasib, lord of Ekron. "Strange black swellings have appeared beneath the arms, or in unspeakable places, oozing of blood and purulence. Foul is its smell."

"We have seen this before, in Ashdod, and in Gath," answered Rapha. "It is the curse, our punishment for taking the shrine of this most powerful God."

"It is the just wrath of the gods, sent down upon mankind," agreed Saph.

Nasib looked upon the soldiers as they reported these happenings with trepidation. It was as he had feared, death had come to Ekron with the arrival of the Ark of the Lord Most High.

"We must call upon Baal-Zebul," commanded Nasib. "For he is our only hope."

Passing along the ridge of the southern slope, the procession of nobles and citizens, accompanied by soldiers, marched toward the center of the city. A broad flagstone pavement led to a monumental entranceway, the gateway to the royal administration buildings, the seat of influence and power, which marked the heart of Ekron's lower quarter.

Standing with prominence among the palatial palaces was the noted sanctuary of Baal-Zebul.

The temple complex consisted of a large, enclosed courtyard, a third of its area covered, and a fine building whose walls were broad. Upon entering, one was received into an elaborate antechamber that led into a great hall. Extending from the central corridor, two rooms lined with pillars supported an upper story. Within the floor of the hall, a circular hearth paved in pebbles rested.

Positioned along the breadth of the walls, several benches and podiums stood awaiting their cultic purpose. At the far end of this vestibule, a narrow room, the inner sanctuary, was entered. Turning right after transgressing the threshold, the approach to the altar, the dais of Baal-Zebul himself, rose beyond a column of stairs and two pillars, his arms extended over an open hearth.

Here the Ark of the Lord waited, biding its time.

It was in spring that the worshipers of Baal and Asherah brought offering to entice the gods to bring fertility back to the land. But spring would wait. Now it was for healing that they came.

And so the priests did all to pacify Baal-Zebul, to turn his face upon them in their distress, with the soothing song of the lyre and the sweet aroma of incense. The meat offering of a heifer and a drink offering of wine was submitted to the gods in recognition of the sovereignty of Baal-Zebul and of his bounty in giving all earthly blessings.

The priest, lifting an infant high above his head, a firstborn son, an oblation to the gods, drew his voice up to heaven and spoke:

"A fearsome God has come to rule us with a hand of iron. He causes us to suffer, and die beneath His reign. We cry unto our mother, Asherah, Lady of the Sea, and to you, Baal-Zebul, prince of the gods, lord deliverer of pestilence and plague. We beseech you: confront this God, intercede on our behalf.

"A life we give for the life of the city, this new life, untouched by evil, passed through fire, a plea for healing, an offering of life.

> *Lord of the heavens,*
> *Prince, lord of earth,*
> *He who rides on the clouds,*
> *King of the gods;*
>
> *A fire—two fires!*
> *He sees a burnished sword!*
>
> *We are thy slave, O Baal!*
> *Dagon's son, we are captive!*
> *We will bring thy tribute like the gods,*
> *Like the deities, thy gift!*[54]

The infant was placed upon the outstretched arms of Baal-Zebul, white with the heat of the fire. The cries of the innocent pierced the quiet, as the babe, tormented with pain, rolled down the arms of the god and passed into the waiting flames. Silence returned as the life consumed ceased its wailing, a propitiation for the populace, trusting their souls in the fire's embrace.

"One feeble of frame shall not vie with Baal," spoke the priest, "nor wield a spear against Dagon's son."

Thus spoken, the priest and the priestess embraced, performing their sacred act of consummation to compel Baal and Asherah to restore fertility to the land, to lift the sentence of death and want that wracked the city. Stirred by these acts, the worshipers soon followed in like manner. Feasting and drinking continued deep into the night, rendering the people insensible to the pain and human sorrow that swelled around them.

Days passed, and from days to months, but Baal-Zebul heard not the cries of his people, and death rained down upon the citizens of Ekron as the winter storms mounted. A great destruction ravaged the city, their heathenish hope diminished, for the hand of God was very heavy there. None would escape; all would be stricken with the dread boils, blackened and foul. And the men who did not perish, their cry went up to heaven.

---

[54] (Khalaf 1996)

The priest stood before Nasib, lord of Ekron, a solitary figure in the narrow throne room, before the raised dais, giving account of the work of the gods, and proclaiming their heavenly decree.

"The gods have lowered their heads upon their knees—yea, even upon the thrones of your lordships," spoke the priest of Baal-Zebul.

> *A knife He takes in the hand*
> *A dagger in the right hand.*
> *To the earth our mighty one falls!*
> *Yea, to dust our strong one!*
> *From his mouth the word had not yet gone forth,*
> *Nor from his lips, his utterance.*

"This Hebrew God, He alone rules over the gods, to command gods and men, yea, to reign over the multitudes of the earth. Lo, His throne is set in the midst of the land.

> *And so we pour ashes of grief on our head*
> *The dust of wallowing on our pate,*
> *For clothing, we are covered with a doubled cloak.*
> *We roam the mountain in mourning,*
> *Yea, through the forest in grief.*
> *Woe to the people of Dagon's son!*
> *Woe to the multitudes of Baal-Zebul!*
> *We shall all go down into the earth.*[55]

"Our hopes now lie in ourselves alone. The gods have abandoned us," thus ended the lament of Baal-Zebul's high priest.

"Lo, the Ark of the Hebrew God hath remained in Philistine hands these seven months," spoke Nasib. "And dark shadows of death have followed its course through our land. Wherever it goes, death follows. The people cry, but no one hears. Pity has moved to terror. It is time. Call together the lords of Philistia. We must act now—or we shall be utterly destroyed."

And so the summons went forth into all the territory of Philistia, to Ashdod and Askelon, to Gaza and Gath, calling upon the five lords to

---

[55] (Khalaf 1996)

assemble at Ekron, to determine what must be done with the Ark of the Most High God. As the inhabitants waited, panic, driven by dread, fell upon the city. Wind and rain raged, storms infernal rising in brutal ambush, while the rabid hands of the plague reached forth to seize the death-price from the people of Ekron.

The disturbed heavens roared, vying against the people, as the violent fury of dark death overran the city, yet still the citizens of Ekron waited. Angrily the skies rushed vehemently as nature broke against the walls, suspending their reprieve, the interval interminable between the death watch and rescue.

"Several weeks have passed since the call went out, and yet not all the lords have arrived. We cannot delay much longer. Where are Lord Sherden and Lord Shekelesh? What hinders them?" spoke Nasib, pacing the length of his great hall.

"My lord," reasoned Achimiti, "winter is in full sway. Word has reached our ears of great storms raging in the south. It is the winter weather, the enemy of all roads, which keeps them. Do not fear. They will come."

"How can I not fear? While we wait, more perish. We are alive only for lack of a shroud!"

CHAPTER 22

REPARATION

Tempests of fate, as the crossing of two iron swords sends sparks into battle, discharged violently over the night sky. The heavens, disturbed by outbursts of tumultuous force, shook as winter storms, drawing their strength from the sea, clashed across the firmament. The rush of wind ruptured the upper veil with the sound of a mighty river hastening down its course. Snowcapped mountains lay to the east, marking the division of ancient foes. And through the curtain of rain stood three, shadows in the dark, set upon the wall of Ekron. Cold and sodden, they watched for the enemy, waiting to cry alarm at the first sign of doom.

"The heavens are agitated, they behave violently," Phicol spoke, his gaze fixed upon the turbulent skies.

"There is no end to this despair." Ekwesh looked upward, resting a hand on Phicol's shoulder. "The skies weep death-qualms, laying waste to all life."

Lukka paced the length of the wall, his steps restless, his voice sharp with frustration.

"They debate while more die. Water sits in the jug, yet they wander with parched lips. There is but one thing to be done. Can they not yet see what must be done?"

As the morning's brightness crept over the eastern hills, the shadows of night retreated into the west, taking with them the convulsive tempest. Stark silence stood in its place. A clear sky broke over the land, reflecting the shimmering latticework of a crystal sea, frozen droplets in a brilliant array of rebounding light, as a field of diamonds scattered across the plain.

The sound of a multitude of marching feet echoed through the valley, unseen beneath the blinding glare of hoarfrost. Trumpets sounded forth, announcing the arrival of the long-awaited lords.

"The gate! Open the gate!" shouted Ekwesh from the wall. "The lords of the south arrive at last."

Heartsore and weary, Lord Nasib approached the gates, his attendants at his side, eager to receive the visitors. At the head of the procession rode the two lords, highborn and grand, arrayed in splendor, mounted on fine steeds. Banner-carriers followed close behind, bearing their colors aloft.

"Welcome to Ekron, my lords," spoke Nasib in a strong voice. "Long have we awaited your arrival."

"Forgive us this late hour," spoke Sherden the Feared, "for long has been our road, and perilous were its passes. The rains fell heavily as the winter months pressed hard upon us. Seventeen days the storm persisted without granting relief. The waters rose, halting our progress. The roads, muddy, deep, and treacherous, have been a great hardship and discomfort."

"Yes, and illness has plagued us at every turn," added Shekelesh, lord of Gaza. "Men dropped where they marched, until we feared none would live to see your gates."

Sherden frowned, casting a sharp glance at Shekelesh, displeased with his words. "Yet by the will of our strength, we have arrived."

"We are most glad for your safe passage," spoke Nasib. "Come—refresh yourselves. Then let us gather in council, for great is our need."

The skies were unsettled; the fair morning gave way to a troubled afternoon as the lords of Philistia gathered within a pillared chamber adjoining Ekron's main court of authority. Hail, mingled with rain, fell upon the earth until a thin mantle of ice lay over the land. Seated upon fine benches about the room, the five lords regarded one another in silence, the hearth fire before them casting a bickering blaze.

"My lords, we are assembled at a grave hour to decide the fate of Philistia. Our very existence hangs by a thread. Choose wrongly, and the thread will snap—and the very fabric of Philistia shall be unmade.

"Therefore, I have called you here to determine our course concerning the Ark of the Most High God, the very shrine that you have thrust upon my city, plunging its people into darkness and despair. I am laid low. Death has become my friend and foe. And so I entreat you, my lords—grant liberty to my people, and to all the people of Philistia."

So spoke Nasib, lord of Ekron, standing before his guests.

"A plague has come upon us by the hand of this God, for the Ark is in our midst," said Seranim, lord of Ashdod. "So we sought relief, sending the Ark from city to city. And yet no relief has been found. Instead, we have been visited by calamity and misfortune at every turn. This Ark brings only trouble. He has set His judgment upon us and upon our gods, Dagon and Baal-Zebul. This God is too mighty, His threat, too great. We must send Him away."

"It is the pestilence that walketh in darkness," lamented Shekelesh. "Once the fire spreads, both the damp and the dry do burn. None are safe."

"It is by our own hand that this has come upon us," said Danuna, lord of Gath, his voice low with grim assent.

"Patience, my lords," spoke Sherden, lord of Askelon. "No lamp burns till morning. Go as far as you can see, and when you come to the end, you will see farther. This dark sickness shall pass. We need not humble ourselves before these Hebrew dogs. Let us hide the Ark away in some secret place, far from our cities, until the plague has passed."

"Yes," Seranim retorted, "you would have us go farther and fare worse."

"Then send it to Askelon—or to Gaza," Danuna snapped. "They were swift enough to send it on to us. Let them now share in our fate."

"We cannot continue as we are," warned Nasib, "else none shall remain in all Philistia."

"This is no longer a matter of politics, my lords," said Shekelesh. "We have entered into the realm of the gods. We must not further provoke this God."

"And many have already paid the last ransom that man can owe," spoke Seranim.

"What then must we do?" asked Nasib.

Unmarked and unseen, a seer was found in their midst; and lifting his arms to the heavens, he spoke thus:

> For this God has plundered the Philistines,
> The remnant of the Isle of Caphtor.[56]
> For Gaza shall be deserted,
> And Askelon shall become a desolation.
>
> Ashdod's people shall be driven out at noon,
> And Ekron shall be uprooted.
> Ah, inhabitants of the seacoast,
> You nation of the Cherethites!
>
> The word of the Lord is against you,
> O Canaan, land of the Philistines;
> And He will destroy you until no inhabitant is left.[57]

At his words, silence claimed the chamber. A hopeless darkness settled upon the room, for the seer's utterance had sealed their doom.

"It is a fearful thing to fall into the hands of this great God,"[58] said Shekelesh, head bowed low. "Beware, we take not the same misstep that Pharaoh of Egypt did. He erred in not letting the Hebrews go. Let us not fall to the same folly. We must let go of this Ark."

"Yes," Danuna murmured, his gaze fixed upon the old seer as he slowly turned and walked from the chamber. "But this God must also be appeased. We have angered Him by taking His shrine from the land of His people."

---

[56] Jeremiah 47:4
[57] Zephaniah 2:4–5 (ESV)
[58] Hebrews 10:31

"Is this the will of all the lords?" asked Nasib. "Do we all agree to return the Ark of this mighty God to those from whom we seized it? Shall we give back our spoil to the vanquished?"

"Send away the Ark of the God of Israel," pronounced Seranim at last. "Let it go back to its own place, that it not destroy us and our people. We have little choice—though it wounds me to bow before these dogs."

"What say you, Sherden?" asked Nasib, his gaze fixed upon the most feared among them. "For your silence speaks of consent."

"I shall yield to the will of the council," Sherden replied, his voice distant, far-seeing. "But know this—we surrender our foothold over these Hebrew. No longer shall we rule this land. You will see. I am right in what I say."

"But how must we do this thing?" asked Shekelesh. "For it is as Danuna says, we must appease this God, that His wrath be turned from our land and from its people."

"Send for the priests," declared Nasib, "and summon the wisest diviners in all the land. Let us hear what they say concerning this matter. We shall return here in two weeks' time."

The barrenness of winter's cold faded as the fetters of frost unraveled and melted away. Hope now forecast, with the coming of spring and the arrival of priests and diviners, as they assembled in Ekron, gathering into one place in answer to the call.

A congregation of witnesses convened within the long hall of the throne room, which stretched between the courtyard and the pillared sanctuary. A short flight of steps approached the dais upon which Nasib, lord of Ekron, sat enthroned. Under a spread of ensigns and banners, the five lords of Philistia sat upon their royal seats, four but temporary thrones, symbols of their shared dominion. Their countenances were firm, their bearing resolute, unified in aim.

Before them stood twelve priests and diviners, complete in their number. One stepped forward, Mitinti, a seer of great age, and raised his voice in lamentation:

"What is this you have done, my lords? A plague you have loosed upon the land! Philistia lies cruelly afflicted, men are dying. And when men are dying in Philistia like this, the plague is in no wise over. As for you, the agony of your heart, the anguish of your soul, you can endure no more. Drive you forth the plague from the land of the Philistines!"

Looking toward the heavens with arms uplifted, the seer cried out: "What is this that you have done, O gods? A plague you have loosed upon the land! The whole of Philistia is dying, so none prepare your sacrificial loaves or pour your libations. The ploughmen who once tilled the fields of the gods are dead; so no one reaps your harvest at all. The grinding women who made your offerings are gone; so they no longer knead the sacred loaves. From the fields where once were chosen sheep and oxen for sacrifice, the cowherds and shepherds lie dead, and the pastures stand empty."[59]

As though on cue from the gods, a thunderclap broke forth. The storm-god Baal gave voice, a terrible rumble that shook the heavens, and fear overtook the assembly. All speech faded as those present bowed low, cowed beneath the tumultuous firmament that transgressed the sky.

Words rose with difficulty as Nasib stood to address the awaiting priests. "It is in darkness that we grope, a curse and a judgment has been laid upon us. Destruction and demise follow this Ark, bringing with it the aroma of death leading to death."[60]

Nasib gripped the arms of his throne as the words caught in his throat. Unable to stand any longer, for the weight of their troubles pressed hard upon him, he sat down, desperation written upon his face.

"What is your need?" spoke the diviner Palastu, an oracle and a soothsayer, one who stood apart from the rest. "Whom have you wronged, my lord?"

"We suffer a great disaster within our land," spoke Nasib soberly. "Even the gods themselves suffer at the hand of this Israelite Deity."

"It is a dreadful trophy which you harbor, my lord," returned Palastu.

"Answer this," spoke Nasib. "What shall we do with the shrine of this God? Who has brought this evil upon us? Is it indeed the Hebrew God who afflicts our people?"

Sherden began speaking boldly. "What must be done to lift the curse, if indeed these disasters are the work of this Israelite God?"

---

[59] (Beyer and Arnold 2002)
[60] 2 Corinthians 2:16

Standing, he lifted his hand toward the assembly. "Why has His hand not turned from us? Speak swiftly—how shall we send it to its place? For time is against us, and death holds us fast."

In deep thought, the soothsayer stood calmly, his hands folded before him. Drawing a slow breath, Palastu addressed the troubled lords. "Only the closed mind offers swift answers. Yet there are signs, omens of things to come, and those who interpret them.

"We shall pry into the future clouds of the world, uncovering things secret. For the lords of Philistia stand at the parting of the road, at the fork of two roads, and so we shall use divination: we shall shake the arrows, we shall consult the images and entrails; we shall look to the heavens."[61]

"Go. Do as you have said," bid Nasib. "But do not tarry over long, for night approaches, and our way is veiled. Go."

And so the priests and diviners, the wisest in the land, forsook the company of the lords and drew apart, deliberating amongst themselves as they sought knowledge of hidden and future things. Each, in solemn silence, consulted oracles and omens, their sight affected, sharpened by divine arousal.

In time, they assembled once more to compare their findings, weighing one another's discernments and debating what should be revealed to the lords of Philistia.

"It is the second question we must answer first," began Palastu. "What shall we send with the Ark to its place? We cannot simply return the Ark of this Most High God, for such a gesture would not suffice to meet the gravity of this offense. The lords have transgressed the honor of this great God."

"We must be cautious," warned Mitinti.

"Be advised," spoke Shekresh, priest of Ashdod, remembering the shame of Dagon. "We must not send this shrine away empty. A guilt offering must accompany it."

"We shall send the Ark with a gift of gold," suggested Mitinti, "gold to appease this God's anger."

"Yes, a guilt offering must be forged and sent, in the image of these afflictions, golden idols, for like addresses like," spoke Palastu, his words falling like a grim decree.

---

[61] Ezekiel 21:21

After a measured pause, he stretched forth his hand as though balancing an unseen scale. "We shall make golden rats and golden tumors, for these are the instruments of this God's wrath."

"How many shall we send?" inquired Shekresh.

"There are five lords and five principal cities within Philistia," answered Palastu, "therefore we must send five golden rats and five golden tumors, to show that all are agreed in this course and submit to the will of this great God."

"Yes," spoke Mitinti, "a fitting reparation for profaning this sacred idol, an offering to placate Yahweh."

"But only if Yahweh is truly the author of this evil," spoke Palastu. "Or is it *miqreh*, fate only, that hath visited these afflictions upon us? We must discern whether this Great God indeed be the cause."

"Yes," replied Shekresh, "that brings us to the first question: what shall we do with the Ark?"

"I have devised a plan," declared Palastu. "One that shall prove true only if the Ark is the root of our suffering, for only a mighty God could override the course of nature."

Once more, the priests and diviners stood in the presence of the five lords of Philistia, bowing low before the high thrones, a plan to tell upon their tongue, to give account of their findings, to declare the message from the gods. And the lords sat in wonder, their hearts turned toward hope, as the divine instruction was proclaimed.

"What is your answer?" inquired Nasib.

So Mitinti answered, saying, "If you send away the Ark of the God of Israel, send it not empty; but by all means, return it to Him with a trespass offering. Then you shall be healed, and it shall be made known to you why His hand is not yet removed from you."

"What is the trespass offering that we shall return to Him?" asked Nasib.

"A golden tribute to the God of Israel, images of the plague in gold: five golden tumors and five golden rats, according to the number of the lords of the Philistines. For the same plague was upon all of you and upon your lords. Therefore, you shall fashion images of your tumors and images of the rats that ravage your cities, and you shall give glory to the God of Israel. Perhaps He will lighten His hand from you, from your gods, and from your land."

Dubious were the looks etched upon the faces of the five lords. In doubt, they gazed upon the priest, hesitant to believe, unsettled in mind as to the truth of his claim.

"This is a great sum that you ask us to surrender to this God. Are we not already forfeiting our honor by returning this shrine, the spoils of war, to these defeated dogs?" Sherden spoke harshly, rising from his seat. "I stand in doubt of your words!"

"Your life shall hang in doubt before thee," replied Palastu. "Why then do you harden your hearts, as Pharaoh and the Egyptians hardened theirs? When He did mighty things among them, did they not let the people go, that they might depart? Let not doubt keep you from believing. We assure you, this offering shall appease this God, and your people shall be healed."

Nasib faltered, his thoughts divided, caught between reason and doubt. "Let us suspend judgment until the whole has been told. Please, Sherden, be seated. Palastu, if you please, what more have you to say? For I see this is not the end of your speech."

"Now therefore," spoke Palastu, "a new cart must be constructed, one reserved from all common use, drawn by fair kine that have not borne the yoke, as is proper for animals of sacrifice. Never struck by staff nor touched with goad, pure and unmarred they must be."

"Yes, and the cart shall be drawn by two kine, milk cows newly calved, still nursing their young," added Mitinti.

"Keep their calves penned apart, within the stall," continued Palastu. "Place the Ark upon the cart, and with it the guilt offering you return to Him, set within a chest at its side. Then let it go, and send it on its way. And watch: if it travels the road to its own land, to Beth Shemesh, then it is He who has brought this great evil upon us. But if not, then we shall know that it is not His hand that struck us, it happened to us by chance."

"This will take some time to prepare," Nasib spoke, his gaze lowered as he weighed the matter.

"In this way we offer homage to this God, and bow before Him, to confess our guilt and plead for His mercy," said Mitinti.

"If this act succeeds in freeing our people from the grip of this fierce God, then we shall know the cause of our great affliction," remarked Palastu.

"But if it is not the work of this God," spoke Mitinti, "then we may yet retain the Ark for ourselves, for surely their nature will compel them to turn back to their calves."

The lords looked upon the soothsayers, uncertain of their meaning.

"If the affliction be from the God of Israel," explained Palastu, "who desires the shrine returned, then the kine will forsake their young and draw the Ark straightway to the land of the Hebrews. Thus shall we know that we have done rightly in returning it. Yet if the kine turn back to their calves, their nature not overcome by divine power, then shall we know that these dark disasters were but *miqreh*, fate only, and we may keep both the Ark and your gold."

"There is wisdom in your counsel," remarked Sherden.

"Let it be done," resolved Nasib, "for your words are well spoken."

As the dregs of winter seeped away and seedlings sprang from the earth, the people of Philistia gathered gold, a levy for their reparation, fashioned into the idols of their judgment. Already all felt the curse easing, as Baal returned, resurrected, riding upon the clouds, bringing gentle rain and new life back to the barren land.

With the gold collected and the images formed, the men of Ekron took two milk cows and yoked them to the cart, and shut up their calves at home. The Ark of the Lord they set upon the cart, and with it the chest that held the golden rats and the images of their tumors.

When all was accomplished, Shekresh the priest lifted his arms and spoke: "They drive up one cow; they drive up two cows. They drive the kine onto the road leading to the enemy, and as they do, we pray—whatever God of the enemy land has sent this plague: see! We have now driven up these cows to pacify thee, O God! As the herd is strong, yet keeps peace with the bull, so do thou, the God who hast caused this plague, keep peace with the land of the Philistines! In favor, turn again toward Philistia!"[62]

And so they sent away the bane of Philistia, Dagon's shame, and let it go. Then the cows went straight along the road to Beth Shemesh. They stayed to the highway, lowing as they went, and turned not aside to the right hand nor to the left. And the lords of the Philistines went after them, following from afar, nine miles up the Sorek Valley to the border of Beth Shemesh, until they beheld the cart and its burden come to rest in Israelite territory.

"It is a hard liberty," spoke Sherden with regret as he watched the spoils of victory restored to the vanquished.

Thus, as in ages past, Philistia, like Egypt before her, the two great powers that had afflicted Israel, bowed their mighty knee to give glory and honor to the God of Israel. The five lords turned and slowly journeyed back to their people, the conquerors now the conquered, just as the seer had foretold.

"It is done then," spoke Phicol. "The Ark is returned, and the curse shall be lifted. We shall see newness of life once more come to our land."

"Ekwesh." Lukka turned to him. "Do you not share in our joy? Why is your countenance so downcast? Do you not see that our doom is past?"

"Too well I see. This is not finished. A heavier fall I must fall," answered Ekwesh. "I know it in my heart, for I have not paid in full the penance that I owe."

---

[62] (DeMaris 2008)

CHAPTER 23

THE THRESHING

Ripples of light and shadow danced over the surface of the wheat field as the morning mist retreated. The wind sang through the long stalks, and the heads, crowned with bristling beards, roared like the sea, a golden tide flowing across the land. Bent beneath the burden of ripened seed, the golden stalks bowed low, as if paying homage to its god.

Qatsiyr reached forth and plucked an ear from the stalk. Between his fingers, he rubbed the seed head, loosening the husk, separating the grain from the chaff.

The color is good, thought Qatsiyr.

Placing the kernels into his mouth, he began to chew. The grain cracked between his teeth, then softened.

"Ah," Qatsiyr murmured, "it is ready for harvest."

He brushed the chaff from his palm, and it caught in the wind as he turned for home.

Beth Shemesh. Thriving was this city, named for the Canaanite sun-goddess, Shemesh, *Har-cherec* it was called, the house of the sun. Situated along the southern edge of the upper Sorek Valley, it lay between the tribes of Judah and Dan, a border town set apart for the Kohanim, Levitical priests descended from the line of Aaron. The city stood as an important frontier, holding the line between the Philistines of the Shephelah and the Israelites dwelling in the Judean Hills.

Built up and fortified, it held firm against Philistine aggression, ever watchful, ever braced for invasion. The village spread across the summit, offering a clear view of the hills beyond and the land below.

Upon this rise stood a great two-storied house, the dwelling of a man of prominence. With quiet pride, it overlooked the northern valley, spacious, glorious, its courts and many rooms paved with smooth river pebbles. Wooden columns, resting upon stone, upheld the high ceilings. Around it, smaller homes gathered, humble, bowing in the shadow of the grand estate.

Looking out across the great Valley of Sorek to the north, beyond its broad swells and rich land, rose the town of Zorah, the birthplace of Samson, whose outward strength was but divinely bestowed, bringing great woe to the enemy.

Life awoke in Beth Shemesh as the citizens assembled themselves together for the harvest. This season of gathering was ever a time of gladness, rich with hope and life, a time of celebration. Now the people were reaping their harvest in the broad, fertile Valley of Sorek. Well-watered, this valley produced an abundance of grain, a soft grassy covering that carpeted the land.

Riyphah bent low, gathering cut wheat into sheaves for the threshing floor. A cool breeze stirred her dark hair. She shuddered. In the distance came the deep bellowing of cattle. The brown-gray flicker of quail, scouring for scattered seed, moved through the golden stalks.

Startled by the flutter of wings, Riyphah looked up as the fowl took flight. Something had stirred them, some unseen presence, urging the feathered migrants to seek a safer banquet.

The lowing of the cattle grew louder.

Strange, thought Riyphah. *Strange that the cattle had not been penned for the harvest. What were they thinking, letting them wander freely through the wheat?*

Yet the sound swelled ever louder. Riyphah stood amid the sea of grain and gazed across the field.

"*Baruch shem Adonai,* blessed is the name of Yahweh," whispered Riyphah in awe.

"*Bat Tziyon,* daughter of Zion, what do you see?" Qatsiyr asked, shading his eyes.

"Look!" cried Riyphah, pointing across the field.

"*Mechiah,*" breathed Qatsiyr, his dark eyes wide.

The people lifted their eyes and beheld a cart drawn by two cows, coming down the road by the fields.

No one drove them, yet the kine went on by themselves, taking the straight road to Beth Shemesh, pulling the cart behind them, veering neither to the right nor to the left, but keeping to the way.

And upon the cart the reapers saw it, the Ark of the Lord Most High, and they rejoiced.

Into the field of Joshua the cart drew, and there it came to rest beside a great stone.

"No man has done this great thing," spoke Qatsiyr. "The Ark of the Lord Most High has come back to Israel. Only God could have brought such a thing to pass. It was not carried back by Philistine, nor by Israelite. It returned by no hand of man, but of its own accord."

"And behold," spoke Qorban, a Kohen of good repute, "an offering the heathen Philistines have sent, golden idols, offensive to the Lord, a bribe to appease His wrath, a vain gift to the Lord Most High."

"Only God's mercy can help them now," mused Qatsiyr, "for great is their trespass."

The Levites, Qorban, and with him Kahan, then took down the Ark of the Lord and the chest beside it, which held the articles of gold. And seeing the great stone, the stone of Abel, that bore witness to the Ark's return, they placed all upon the unhewn altar. There, they split the wood of the cart and sacrificed the cows as a burnt offering to the Lord, upon the stone of Abel, the stone which remains to this day in the field of Joshua in Beth Shemesh. Thus, the Ark of the Lord Most High's journey came to an end. Never more would the Ark wander.

The inhabitants of Beth Shemesh were ecstatic, for it was a great and festive occasion. The Ark of the Covenant of the Lord of hosts, who dwells between the cherubim, had returned.

With music and dance, the people expressed their joy, singing to the rhythm of the lyre, pipe, and tambourine. Parading past the threshing floor and through the city streets, the singers marched, followed by maidens playing timbrels, and last, the minstrels with melodious intonation. Processions of women with hand-drums performed the *Machol*, a round-dance, thrumming their drums for joy as they joined the victorious celebration.

Yet while the people of Beth Shemesh rejoiced, Tiphlah, an Ephraimite, drunk with wine, and several men of the city grew curious. And, as they passed by the field of Joshua, they beheld the form of the Holy Shrine resting upon the stone of Abel. Longing to gaze upon its sacred craftsmanship, the men approached the Ark and reached for the mantle that concealed it.

Together they lifted the covering and peered beneath it. As the sun struck the gleaming surface of pure gold, the veil slipped from their hands, and the Ark stood bare before them. There remained nothing between the men and the sacred coffer of Almighty God.

Beautiful it was, with cherubim upon the covering of the Ark, their faces turned toward one another. With wings outstretched, they formed the throne of God upon the *Kapporeth*, the Mercy Seat, ringed about with a crown of gold.

The precious shrine, measuring two and a half cubits in length, a cubit and a half in breadth and height, held within it the tablets of stone inscribed with the Commandments of God, the rod of Aaron that had budded, and a vessel of manna, tokens of covenant and remembrance.

No eye save the High Priest had ever beheld such holy beauty, the beauty of Israel, the very seat of the Living God.

Many gathered to stare at the sacred object. In wonder, they looked upon the Ark, transfixed by the glory that shone upon the face of the Golden Coffer, unaware that they had been seen.

"What is this you have done?" cried Qatsiyr in horror, shielding his eyes from the temptation to gaze upon the seat of Yahweh. "You have brought condemnation upon us all!"

Startled, Tiphlah turned to face his accuser, arms stretched out in protest. "It is nothing," he said, his voice unsteady. "We looked only—we did not touch. We meant no harm."

"Irreverent and contemptible people!" In anguish, Qatsiyr spoke. "Why do you provoke the Lord? Cover the Ark, lest others look upon it and be ruined! You have profaned that which is holy, misused and violated the sanctity of the Lord's Ark.

"The heavy hand of Yahweh will be upon you all. You will not escape it. His wrath will fall upon all Beth Shemesh because of your great sin."

"Ha!" scoffed Tiphlah. "Do not fret, old man. We will do as you say."

A crooked smile spread across his face as he returned the veil to its place, concealing the Ark from further desecration.

"See, Qatsiyr," with poison he spoke his name, "no harm done!"

"Did not our brethren act likewise," rebuked Qatsiyr, "so that God brought all this calamity upon us? And now you stir yet more wrath against Israel by defiling the Ark of the Most High! Go now—away from here, all of you, and plead for God's mercy. Whatever the Lord of heaven has prescribed, let it be done with diligence."

The morning clouds and the early dew passed away as the people of Beth Shemesh gathered at the *goren*. The harvested stalks were stacked beside the worn stones of the trodden earth, awaiting the time to be buffeted; indeed, some already lay drying upon the floor, for its time had come, and the treading would soon begin.

Yet all that rested upon the threshing floor was not wheat, for all was not grain within those golden sheaves. Even as it lay upon the barren ground, the wheat still clung to the straw that bore it, the husk wrapped about each kernel, each seed hidden within, necessary for a season, but now unneeded.

Dealing sternly with the grain and sparing not its affliction, for well esteemed was the wheat that was gathered, the stalks were scourged with every stroke of the flail to loosen the chaff from the seed. For the wheat must be drawn out of the husk, if it is to be of service.

Standing in the midst of the *goren*, Qorban lifted his hands toward heaven and cried, "The night is far spent, and daylight breaks upon yon hills. O wheat of the Lord's threshing-floor, thou must be bruised and broken, ground beneath so great a weight, or perish as an ineffectual drift!"

With light hearts, the people, renewed by the return of the Ark of God, began their labor, unaware of the shadow that had fallen upon them.

The oxen pulled the heavy wooden sledge across the beaten earth of the *goren*. Its underside studded with jagged flints, the sledge moved in wide circles, cutting the stalks, crushing the husks, tearing out the seed, separating the good from the bad.

The winnowing basket, broad and flat, received the yield of the threshing. Tossed into the air, the chaff flew, carried off by the wind, leaving behind the fine golden grain.

Children ran, twirling in the chaff-rain that fell around them, laughter on the wind, the future of Israel. As the chaff settled to the earth, the children collected the straw into baskets for use in making mud-bricks and pottery, for nothing would be wasted.

The air hung mild and balmy, the face of nature green and pleasant to the eye. The sky stretched serene above the workers, the breeze gentle, the rays of the rising sun filtering through the broad-leafed fig tree.

But the spirits of the Israelites were soon subdued, for the anger of the Lord was kindled against His people, for which there would be but one remedy.

Riyphah, late to the labor, hurried through the passageways of Beth Shemesh, pulling her shawl over her head as she ran. Too often had she been tardy to the work detail. Fearing reprisal from the elders, she hastened toward the threshing floor, set just beyond the walls.

As she turned the corner, her stride faltered, for there before her lay the corpse of Tiphlah, his body marred by the dark blotches of the black death. She shrank back against the wall, recoiling from the horror, pulling her wrap over her mouth and nose. Then she looked, and her eyes beheld the terror all around. The streets were strewn with the dead. With her back pressed hard against the masonry, she slid past the fallen.

Through the narrow lanes she fled, heart pounding, breath ragged, past shuttered homes and silent doors, until, at last, the open fields lay before her. Terrified and short-winded, Riyphah burst onto the threshing floor, crying out in sorrow.

"Tiphlah has fallen, a dark plague set upon him. He is dead, and many others with him, for the wrath of God has come against them and overtaken them."

"So it has begun," spoke Qatsiyr, bowing his head in grief.

Then the citizens of Beth Shemesh lamented, for the Lord had visited upon them a great slaughter. Death, loosed beneath the heavy hand of God, struck down the stoutest among them, choice men, weakened and laid low in a single day. The hour of affliction had come. A great cry rose from the village, each man mourning his own kin, those taken by so grievous a blow, sent forth by the consuming fire of God.

Together, the people gathered upon the threshing floor, waiting for judgment to be meted out against them, as the grain is lashed from the chaff.

In anguish they cried, "What shall we do? Why has God struck down so many?"

"Citizens of Beth Shemesh," spoke Qatsiyr, "drink the wine of the wrath of God, which is poured out full strength into the cup of His indignation.[63] For great is the offense given to *El-Elyon*, our God Most High. These, who were not priests, nor worthy to touch the Ark, have approached and looked upon the Lord's Holy Shrine, to gaze at His glory."

Tearing their clothes, the people cried out in shock and horror, lifting a great wail of grief.

"Your sons have fainted," declared Qorban. "They lie at the head of every street, like antelope caught in a net. They are filled with the anger of the Lord and the rebuke of your God. For because of these things, the wrath of God comes upon the sons of Beth Shemesh.

"The Lord is the true God; He is the living God, the eternal King. When He is angry, the earth trembles; the nations cannot endure His wrath. 'Therefore I have poured out My indignation on them; I have consumed them with the fire of My wrath; and I have recompensed their deeds on their own heads,' says the Lord God.[64]

"Yet what fear has he whose account is clean?"

"If this be the cause, the reason for such a great slaughter," spoke the people as one, "how can the Ark remain among us?"

"Who is able to stand before this Holy God?" asked Yagowr, who stood among them.

"The Ark is an intolerable burden," reasoned Ragaz, a man of Beth Shemesh who ever spoke on weighty matters. "Death follows the

---

[63] Revelation 14:10
[64] Ezekiel 22:31

Ark wherever it roams. It is to us as it was with the Philistines, for we have heard of its dealings among the inhabitants of Philistia. We must send it away, that the fierce wrath of God may turn from us."

"Now, it is in my heart also," said Yagowr. "But to whom shall we send the Ark?"

"Yes, but where can we send it, since Shiloh is destroyed and the Tabernacle with it?" agreed Ragaz.

"To Kirjath-Jearim," answered Qorban. "For there, a high place has been raised to the Lord, and Levites of good repute dwell within the city."

From Beth Shemesh, they sent a messenger to Kirjath-Jearim, the city of the woods. Across the Sorek River, northeast he ran, up the long ascent into the mountains of this wild and rugged land, to the ancient fortress and high place that lay in the hills east of Beth Shemesh, between Zorah and Eshtaol; to the ancient Gibeonite town, the once holy place of Baal, Cloud Rider, now a city of Israel, of the tribe of Judah, a border town between Dan and Benjamin.

The village proper stood on the summit of the main ridge, which rose in the north and tended to the south, then southwest. Noble fig trees and olive orchards adorned the hills. Terraces carved into the mountainside overlooked the wide-spread vineyards that stretched across the valley floor to the south and east.

Leaving the winding vale far below, the runner came to Kirjath-Jearim, past the great cistern south of the city, to the walls and the keeper of the gate, saying, "The Philistines have brought back the Ark of the Lord! You must come down to Beth Shemesh and take it up with you."

No mention was made of the calamity that had befallen Beth Shemesh, for great was the desire to be rid of the dread shrine. And so, like the Philistines before them, the people of Beth Shemesh sought to send away the Ark of Yahweh, hoping to turn the heavy hand of God.

BANISHED

As spring revived, the west wind from the Great Sea brought with it rumors of unrest. Fear grew in the hearts of the people, for with the season of war came the ever-present threat of battle. The long, wet winter had slowed their recovery from the wounds inflicted by the enemy's sword, and the Hebrew cities, unprepared for open conflict, stood in need of strengthening. In answer, Tiphcar and Nagad set out to visit the border garrisons and villages, offering guidance where it was most needed. They inspected the troops and surveyed each defense, only to find but a handful of soldiers stationed at every outpost. Most often, it was the citizens themselves who manned the watch, a living rampart for their towns, standing guard against the foe.

Strategically placed, the garrisons held vigilant watch over the approaches into the Judean hills, established to hinder the enemy from making war against the villages. With Nagad's assistance, Tiphcar set up staging points to reinforce the troops, supplying arms and stores to fortify the defenses. Emboldened by this added support, with provisions furnished for endurance and resistance, a stern bulwark took shape.

Skirting the uplands of Ephraim just east of the Philistine border, Tiphcar, and Nagad with him, traversed the mountains southeast to Zeredah, where they paused by the spring of *Ein Seridah*. After a time of repose, they journeyed to Beth-Horon, a city built upon a slope, like so many in the Hill Country. On they trod, past the Canaanite city of Gezer, through olive groves and wildflowers, until they came upon the town of Eshtaol. From there, they pressed on beyond the place where Samson was laid to rest, to Zorah, then crossed the Sorek River to Beth Shemesh.

"Look, *Sar*," spoke Nagad as he pointed toward a mound outside the city gates. "So many newly sealed tombs. Something terrible has happened here."

"Aye," answered Tiphcar. "You can feel the mourning in the air. Perhaps we have come too late."

"I see no signs of battle," said Nagad as he scanned the area. "No fire. No battered walls. What could this mean?"

With care, the two passed through the gates. The streets were deserted, hushed. As they advanced into the heart of the village, voices rose to meet them.

"Over there," observed Tiphcar. "Beyond the southern wall."

Nagad gave a silent nod and followed his captain beyond the gate. In the field, the people gathered, a crowd arrayed in sackcloth. He stood transfixed by the scene until at last he found his voice.

"*Sar*—look. Upon the rock!"

"I see it," Tiphcar answered, his voice low and restrained. "It is the Ark."

"But how? How can this be?" whispered Nagad.

Tiphcar shook his head but spoke nothing. The two stalwart soldiers approached the crowd, parting the sea of people as they entered their midst. Faces, ashen and gaunt, turned to behold the battle-arrayed men, bewildered by the sight of soldiers. Nagad gazed upon them, ill at ease.

Around the great stone upon which the Ark of the Lord rested stood a gathering of priests, five there were in all.

Tiphcar made to approach, but one from the crowd came forward, staying his advance.

"What is it that has brought two men of war among us?"

He looked calmly on the man, yet Tiphcar's hand rested upon the hilt of his sword.

"What has happened here to cause such loss of life? Tell me—how is it that you possess the Ark of the Lord Most High? It was lost. We saw it in the hands of the enemy. How came you to retrieve the Golden Coffer from so great a foe? Speak, we must know."

Seeing the pain in the captain's face, the citizen of Beth Shemesh softened.

"I am Qatsiyr, elder of this city. This is Qorban, our priest, and these are the priests of Kirjath-Jearim, come to receive the Ark from our hands, for the Lord's wrath has been heavy upon us."

Within the space of two days, the men of Kirjath-Jearim had arrived at Beth Shemesh, eager to recover the Ark of the Lord Most High. Four men there were who had come: Laqach, Qabal, and Kuwl, and Eleazar the son of Abinadab with them, all Levites of good repute. And so they had assembled but moments before in the field, by the stone of Abel, to question Qorban and Qatsiyr, seeking the account of the Ark's return.

Tiphcar surveyed the priests, perplexity still written upon his face. "And the Ark, how came you by it?"

"The Ark—it came to us of its own accord," spoke Qatsiyr. "We had not a hand in bringing it back. The Philistines, too, have felt the heavy hand of God upon them and have sent the Holy Seat of God back to His people."

Now Eleazar, hearing all that had occurred, how the Ark of God had been restored to Israel, spoke, "Yahweh went freely into exile, and now freely He has returned to us."

Yet a shadow lay upon the people and, though none had spoken openly of the devastation, the sorrow within the land could not be concealed.

Hearing the cries of the people and seeing the calamity that had befallen those of Beth Shemesh, Eleazar spoke again, beseechingly, "What is this that you have done, to bring the indignation of God upon you?"

With reservation, Qatsiyr answered, "Some of this city have treated the Ark without reverence, and death has entered into our midst. Now we send the coffer away, lest we all perish for their disobedience."

"The Lord Most High has struck the men of Beth Shemesh," said Qorban with quiet grief, "because they have looked upon the Ark of God. The people languish, for the Lord has struck them with a great slaughter."

"They weep and lament," voiced Qatsiyr, his head bowed low. "A baleful song they have raised to God, sorrowing over the sins of their brethren. And though we deplore this hostile act, still we mourn with them in their loss, for their pitiful cries can be heard throughout the city."

Qorban picked up the thread, his arms lifted toward heaven. "A song of elegy echoes across the land, and the terror of the Lord moves through the streets, causing the people to quake in fear. How can we stand the presence of this God among us?"

He turned again to the priests before him, extending his hand toward them. "So we called out to you of Kirjath-Jearim, to come and take the Ark from our midst, that we might hide our faces from God."

Astonished, Nagad looked again upon the crowd. One there was who captured his gaze. A girl, some years his junior, stood between the shoulders of the men, her countenance striking in its quiet beauty. Long dark hair, hair that was meant to be veiled, spilled from beneath a scarf that had slipped from her crown, catching the light with its rich, silken sheen. Her eyes were large and questioning, and in their depths lay sorrow. Yet something else stirred there, quiet and unspoiled, a gentleness untouched by grief.

A flush of heat coursed through him; his pulse quickened. He could not take his eyes off that face. She met his gaze and smiled, shy, fleeting, then lowered her eyes, uneasy beneath the strength of his stare.

Nagad turned back, reluctantly, as the priest began to speak.

"My sons," Eleazar counseled with grief rising, "give glory to the Lord, the God of Israel, and give Him the praise. Tell Him what you have done; do not hide from *El Roi*, God all-seeing."

"Even so," spoke Qorban, "we cannot abide the presence of the Lord. Take the Ark from us, for it is too great a burden for us to bear."

Nagad looked again toward the crowd, to the place where he had seen the girl, but she had vanished. Scanning the faces before him, he could not find the one he sought. With a quiet breath, he tucked the image into his mind and held it there, longing for one more glimpse.

After a stretch of silence, Laqach spoke. "We must retrieve the Ark and bring it to our city, else we too may suffer the fate of Beth Shemesh."

In agreement, the priests of Kirjath-Jearim prepared the Ark of God, taking it down from its place upon the rock. The people looked on in guarded sorrow as the men lifted the Ark upon their shoulders. The burden of the coffer rested heavily upon the priests, yet its weight was not more than they could bear. In solemn procession, the Ark of the Lord was carried through the streets of Beth Shemesh toward the outer gate of the city.

The people followed in one accord as they sent the Ark away. Nagad and Tiphcar took up the rear, their charge to accompany the Holy Shrine to its resting place. For having lost it once before, they would not turn aside until they beheld it safely bestowed, harbored in a place secure.

As the procession entered the main thoroughfare that led to the tower gate, Nagad caught sight of the countenance he had longed to see. Slipping through the press behind her, he reached out, and as his hand closed around her arm, she reeled about. Eyes wide, she found herself a breath's space from his intense stare, and without thinking, she pulled against his hold.

Easing his grip, he offered her a gentle smile.

"Do not be frightened. Only, tell me your name."

Her scent was of lavender in bloom, as if spring clung to her even now. Nagad breathed her in, eyes closed for but a moment, lost in the quiet wonder of it.

The steadiness of his touch, though firm, bore no threat. She let her shoulders soften, and her lips curved into a faint smile.

"Riyphah."

Cool and clear, her voice flowed like water through a shaded glen, soothing as summer rain upon parched earth. Something bright and sudden moved in him, and his heart leapt.

"Riyphah," he whispered, tasting the name as it lingered on his tongue like honey.

When he gave breath to her name, a thrill passed through her, soft and unexpected, like wind through unseen leaves. She marveled at it, though she knew not why.

"I am Nagad."

She met his gaze and could not turn away. The world narrowed to the space between them, and her breath caught, as if a wind had left her. A strange weakness stirred in her limbs, yet she did not move. For a time, they stood thus, held in the stillness of a glance that asked nothing, yet said all.

Forever that face remained with him. From that moment on, it became his lifeline through many difficult days. As for now, it would have to wait. Remembering his duty, Nagad looked to the column, which was already passing through the gate and out onto the road.

"I wish we had more time." He tilted his head toward hers, his breath brushing against her cheek. "I must go. But I will return. Do not forget me. Nagad—remember. I will come for you as soon as I can. You must wait for me."

Riyphah stood amazed, blinking as though to clear her vision. Unthinking, she gave a slight nod and reached for his hand. Leaning forward, he pressed his lips against the palm of her hand, then laid it against his sparsely bearded cheek.

With one final glance, he stepped aside and made his way back to the procession, hastening to catch up to Tiphcar. She remained where she stood, bewildered, yet her heart was alight with a strange joy.

What am I thinking? I do not even know who he is. He will forget me.

She shook her head. Yet in her heart, she knew something profound had just passed between them. The young conscript slipped away into the throng, but just before the distance could take him, he paused, and looked back. He smiled broadly, and waved. Unbidden, her hand lifted in reply. At her own boldness she marveled, and though she scarce knew it, her face was lit with gladness.

Long she stood there, watching, until he was but a speck upon the road.

Nagad's heart sang. His step was light, a buoyant rhythm beneath him. Tiphcar regarded his companion and smiled. It gladdened him to see the boy joyful, for it had been long indeed since such lightness had touched Nagad's countenance. In truth, he could not recall ever seeing him so unburdened. The captain reached out his hand and clapped him upon the back. Side by side they walked, journeying with the Ark, bearing the Golden Coffer in its banishment. Though their task was solemn, joy was felt even in the midst of sorrow.

North-east they traveled, conveying the Ark of God from Beth Shemesh at the root of the mountain, ascending the road to the summit, and following the ridge to the ancient town of Kirjath-Jearim. The walls of the city rose in layers, newly mortared stones joined with ancient, rude blocks, a remnant of the old Canaanite town. The wounded side of the northern slope, slashed by the fracturing earth, bore traces of the devastation in the hollow and roughly wrought caves it had carved into the face of the steep cliffs. And beyond them, away to the west, the ancient camp of Dan lay within the lush Sorek Valley.

Through dwarfed oak and hawthorn, and carob groves, upon a carpet of thyme and sage that crept between the crags of flagstone, their fragrance divine, rising about them as the aromatic plants were trodden under the feet of the Ark bearers, east they passed beyond the gates of Kirjath-Jearim, across the summit beyond the fine rock-cut winepress. Turning south, along a bold spur that jutted from the slope, the sacred procession advanced toward a raised platform, marked by a line of olive trees enclosed within the confines of a stone wall.

Amid the chants of priests and the shouts of the populace praising God for the Holy Coffer's safe return, high in the coarse hills, to Gibeah they came, to the secluded retreat above the city of Kirjath-Jearim, to the house of Abinadab. Apart from the confusion and impurities of the city proper, atop the lofty mount, within the venerable ascent of uncut woods, the Ark of the Lord, who sits between the Cherubim, came to rest. And to this quiet nook, long secluded, the Sacred Chest was safely guarded.

As Tiphcar and Nagad watched the Ark put away, a sense of unease stirred within them, something was lacking, something was not quite right. Pierced with dread, the two soldiers looked on in silent vigil as the shrine of God was discarded and shunned under the pretense of its safe-keeping. Cast forth from the sight of the people, partitioned from the populace, the Ark was to suffer expulsion, its destiny withheld for a time. Though absent from the hearts of men, quietly set aside, Yahweh had found a resting place for His Holy Coffer. For even as some had thrust it away, there were those who would take it in.

And so, upon the hill, beneath the vault of heaven, the Ark of the Lord waited, keeping watch over Israel.

Eleazar, son of Abinadab, father of nobleness, was ordained its keeper, set apart to care for the Ark in its exile. With Shiloh destroyed, the priesthood collapsed, the Ark neglected, and the people's confidence in its divine protection shattered, the Sacred Chest was put away and left, banished from the territory of Beth Shemesh. And though the Ark returned to Israel, Israel had not returned to Yahweh's favor.

"Well, it is done," spoke Tiphcar as he turned away from the place of banishment, his hands resting on his sheath-belt.

"Yes," Nagad sighed, dipping his head.

"We must go to Samuel, for he will desire word of the Ark's return," spoke Tiphcar solemnly.

With haste, the two soldiers set upon the road. Straightway they journeyed north, until they came to Ramah to seek the counsel of the priest, Samuel, who had been their friend.

As the account reached the prophet's ears, he stood unmoved, his arms folded about his chest, his hand upon his chin. His face, ever still, gave no sign, so that Nagad could not read his thoughts.

When the telling was complete, the three men abode together in silence, waiting. Nagad watched as Samuel considered all, still and unresponsive.

Samuel lifted his face, dropping his hand from his chin. He looked upon the two before him, his countenance marked by disapproval.

"The Ark has been hidden away, to be unused and forgotten."

He turned and nodded his head several times as he walked slowly away. Tiphcar and Nagad did not move, their eyes following the prophet. After a moment, Samuel turned again and came back to where they stood.

"We Israelites find ourselves in a situation much like that which the Philistines faced, with one exception."

He paused, inhaling thoughtfully.

"The Ark does not belong in Philistia. It belongs to Israel. Yet we find that God is no more easily at home in Israel than He is in Philistia."

Nagad, stirred with emotion, stepped forward, his hand upon the hilt of his sword.

"Then we shall go to Kirjath-Jearim, for the time has come for retribution, to heal our land of this pestilence that has so long plagued our people. The Philistines must pay for this dishonor they have done to the Lord and His Chosen Ones."

Samuel lowered his head, shaking it from side to side.

"I cannot go, for it is not yet time."

The prophet looked again at his companions.

Seeing Nagad's face downcast, Samuel placed a hand upon his shoulder and spoke gently.

"*Al Tid'ag*, do not worry. The Ark of the Lord Most High shall remain safe, in the care of Eleazar, for the Lord has found favor with the son of Abinadab.

"Until the hearts of men turn inward, to their own sin, and upward to the holiness of God, we cannot act. Israel has placed her trust in the Ark of God instead of the Lord. She must now trust in Yahweh Himself."

"My *adon*—"

Shaking his head, Samuel raised a hand to stop him. "A stone thrown at the right time is better than gold given at the wrong time. Come. We have work to do."

CHAPTER 25

RIYPHAH

As the weeks passed, tidings of the Ark's return spread throughout all the territories of Israel. Celebration replaced the spirit of fear and sorrow that had brooded over the people. Yahweh heard them in their despair, and had answered. He came back to Israel. Swift revenge Yahweh exacted on the adversary, His hand heavy upon them. And all Israel rejoiced at the enemy's affliction.

Yet as it has always been, soon the burden of daily life overshadowed the feeling of unity. The flame of revival that had been ignited quickly burned out. The trivial cares of the world replaced the spiritual concerns that should have been harbored in the hearts of men.

Trusting not to the peace that lingered between the two nations, Nagad returned with his captain to the border, keeping watch over the outer reaches of Philistia.

Tiphcar understood that this peace, born of the enemy's affliction, would not endure, for when their strength returned, they would rise again to trouble Israel. So the boundary was kept with vigilance, eyes ever westward, hearts braced for the hour when the adversary would once more press into the land.

Nagad, through the long weeks of watching and waiting, remained faithful at his captain's side. The time grew stale as the pool of action turned stagnant. To ease the restless inactivity, as time and circumstance allowed, Nagad joined Samuel at the Naioth, and under his tutelage, learned much concerning the things of God. Together they carried the message into the surrounding villages, teaching the people and urging them to return to the ways of the Lord. At least with the prophet, there was something to do, something to pass the slow advance of time.

In the hours of inoccupation, Nagad's thoughts often wandered to a face in the crowd, the image of one he longed to see again.

Having been with his company for many weeks, Nagad sought out his captain. He found him standing upon the ridge, eyes westward, surveying the hills that marked the land of the Philistines. The young conscript approached.

"*Sar* Tiphcar," spoke Nagad with quiet resolve. "I must request a time of leave."

"Leave, you say?" the captain echoed.

"Yes, *Sar*. I must go south. I have a promise I intend to keep."

Tiphcar turned, one brow arched in wonder as a grin touched his bearded face.

"Oh?" he said.

"If you please, *Sar*—will you grant it?"

Tiphcar laid a hand upon his shoulder and gave a firm nod.

"My son, I would not dream of keeping you from this fulfillment. Go in peace. Collect some happiness while you may."

"*Todah*, thank you, *Sar*."

Taking leave from his captain, Nagad journeyed south, returning to the region of Beth Shemesh. Across the heights of the Ridge Road, past the grove of pine trees, their scent thick and heady in the afternoon warmth, he traveled, unceasing, until he reached his destination. His heart was light, his step quick, a quiet canter rising within as he entered into the gates of the city.

He knew not where to go, for though he had asked her name, he had not learned where she dwelt. For a time, he wandered the streets, searching every face he passed, seeking the one for whom he longed.

Then he saw her.

She stood upon the stone-hewn half-wall of a garden beside a modest, flat-roofed house of sunbaked clay. In Nagad's eye, she stood in radiance, the beauty of the fair land outstripped, as waves of fabric billowed in rhythm to her movement.

In her hand, she held a woven mat, waving it frantically as she called out, "*Yatsa*! Go! Shoo, you nasty beast—shoo!"

Nagad bore witness to the scene, arms folded across his chest as he leaned against the bole of a nearby tree.

Riyphah's face was flushed. Clearly, she was agitated, for within her garden stood a goat, its coat black as pitch, merrily munching the tender green delicacies.

The beast looked up at her, its lower jaw making a pronounced sideways movement as its teeth ground the herbage within, the ends of the plant protruding out of the corners of its mouth. The goat's affect was flat as it watched her wave the mat. Then, unbothered by the antics of the crazed human before him, it lowered its head and resumed the wanton consumption of early vegetation.

Under the shadow of the leafy canopy, Nagad laughed quietly. Riyphah fumed with indignation, unaware of the audience in attendance. Her hair caught the breeze, escaping from her scarf, dark and rich, the shimmering ends fluttered, taken by the current of air that circled about beauty's face, a river of light cascading from the stray strands as honey dripping from the ends of a honeycomb.

Attempting to draw nearer to the animal, Riyphah took a step forward.

But the stones beneath her feet gave way. She teetered briefly upon the loose surface, then lost the struggle to regain her footing.

A sharp breath escaped her as she felt the balance slip. Backward she fell, vanquished by the forces of the earth below. The mat flew from her grasp, flung to the ground as she groped the air for a handhold to arrest her descent.

Yet ere she met the garden loam, her course was swiftly stayed. For it was in the moment her footing failed that Nagad had emerged from the mottled shadow of the leafy canopy, reaching out to take hold the prize he meant to claim.

She gasped, bewildered, and lifted her gaze to the face of her rescuer. Her eyes went wide as she cried, "You!"

A quiet laugh escaped him as he looked upon her startled countenance. "I told you I would come back."

He held her far longer than need required, keeping her close to his heart. He breathed her in, the urge to press his lips upon hers growing fierce within him.

But ere desire overcame restraint, Riyphah set her hands against his chest and said, "Release me. Put me down."

Obedient, yet reluctant, he let go his hold, lowering her gently to the earth.

She regarded him with a soft smile. "*Todah*, thank you," she said, brushing out the folds of her garment.

"It was my pleasure, *sarah*," Nagad answered, bowing low before her. "Now then, shall we go and fetch that goat from your garden?"

With confidence in his stride, Nagad stepped into the enclosure, taking care not to trod upon the tender shoots that rose from each furrow. Cautiously he approached the animal, which grazed, untroubled by the stir about it. Just as his hand reached for the goat's horn, it backed away, slipping from his grasp.

He rose to his full height and looked toward Riyphah, who now stood as he had, arms crossed, watching him. He smiled, adjusted his sword belt, and once more advanced upon the creature. Yet again it stepped back, and he stumbled slightly forward.

Determination set in as Nagad, now with renewed purpose, lunged forward, seeking to encircle the goat's neck with his arms. But at the very moment his momentum left no hope of retreat, the beast sidestepped.

Nagad flew through the air and landed hard upon his stomach. His body struck the earth, flattening the plants beneath him, while a cloud of butterflies, startled from their foraging, took wing in flurried flight.

Dazed, he shook his head, then sprang to his feet, seething as he brushed the dirt from his leather breastplate.

Regaining himself, Nagad stomped toward the goat and muttered, "Why, you ornery, good-for-nothing, garden-grubbing little beast!"

Then the sound of sweet laughter reached his ear. He halted mid-stride and looked toward Riyphah. She was doubled over, laughter spilling from her lips, joy glinting in her dark eyes.

Nagad chuckled despite himself, caught by the warmth of her delight.

Turning back to the horned menace, he said in a low voice so Riyphah would not hear, "Now, goat, help me out here. You do not want to embarrass me in front of the lovely lady, now, do you?"

The goat stopped chewing and regarded him, as though considering what the young soldier had said. Nagad met its gaze with an imploring eye as he slowly reached for the beast's horn.

Yet again, with the same stubbornness that Israel bore, whose heart had turned to stone, the goat sidestepped, and Nagad missed his mark.

"Con-founded creature!"

"Perhaps, if we were to work together?" suggested Riyphah, her warm eyes gently nudging Nagad's.

For a moment, he forgot the cause of his trials. Transfixed, he stood, unable to comprehend the words she spoke. She tilted her head, gesturing with an outstretched hand.

"Shall we give it a go?"

"What—?" stammered Nagad. "Oh—yes. Let us try again."

From opposite sides, they advanced, closing in upon the goat's position. The horned beast skittered to one side, thinking to best the young conscript once more. But its design was foiled, for as it veered toward Riyphah, seeking to elude capture, she seized hold of its right horn.

A look of surprise passed over the creature's face, yet it relented, allowing her to lead it from the garden and into its pen, bleating its complaint as they went.

Riyphah latched the gate, then brushed her hands together as she turned to face her pursuer. He stepped forward and caught her gently, drawing her hands into his. Lifting them to his face, Nagad pressed his lips to each in turn, his kiss deep and lingering upon her soft flesh.

Heat rushed into her cheeks as she looked down at her hands, cradled within his. She perceived the weight of his gaze. Slowly, she raised her face to meet his eyes.

There she was undone, impaled by the longing in his stare.

"I have come for you, Riyphah, as I promised."

His words were soft, yet laden with an intensity that stole her breath. And in the boldness that youth affords, overtaken by the fire within, Nagad gave voice to the desire of his heart.

"Marry me."

Riyphah let out a gentle chuckle and stepped back.

"Why, Nagad, you know nothing about me. How is it that you say, 'Marry me'?"

But Nagad placed his hands upon her shoulders and drew her near once more.

"I know all I need know. You have seized me so that I will not rest until you are mine. We have the whole of our lives, that you might teach me of who you are. *Ha'im tinas'i li?* Marry me, Riyphah, for it is the only way to mend the wound you have inflicted upon my heart. Marry me."

A shuddered breath escaped her as tears welled in her eyes.

"What excess of vapors has captured and ensnared my heart, that I should yet consider an act so rash as this? Why, I know naught of you—yet I am enthralled, subjugated into this kingdom of bliss, bound to serve in fealty its master. So then, I am yours, to do as you command."

"Woohoo!"

Nagad swept Riyphah into his arms and spun her about. And in the aftertaste of joy, overcome by temptation, he pressed a kiss upon her lips, deep, unguarded, and full of promise.

He had no earthly possessions, no kin to lay forth a dowry. The bride-price would be his love alone.

And fidelity was all she required, vows taken and held in sacred trust, even as Yahweh had taken to Himself a nation and pledged Himself a faithful husband.

The people entered into covenant with God, yet soon forgot His works and the wonders He had wrought.[65] It was not in Israel's heart to obey. Creased and marred, the contract was cast off.

As the Chosen of God, now broken and scattered, were crushed and trodden underfoot by their own disobedience, Nagad and Riyphah were joined, the two made one in marriage.

In the depths of the sorrow of his life, Nagad found a respite from his grief in Riyphah his wife.

Yet Yahweh waited, for His bride had left the marriage bed. Her spirit was not steadfast; she spurned her first love and gave herself to

---

[65] Psalm 78:10–11

foreign deities. And though the people cared not to return to the Lord, Yahweh would raise a fused people, melded from the fragments that yet remained.

245

PART THE THIRD

He gives power to the weak, and to those who
have no might He increases strength. Even the
youths shall faint and be weary, and the young
men shall utterly fall, but those who wait on
the Lord

Shall renew their strength;
They shall mount up with wings like eagles,
They shall run and not be weary,
They shall walk and not faint.

ISAIAH 40:29–31

CHAPTER 26

BLOODLUST

Time grew long. Weeks turned into months, months turned into years, and the hearts of men grew cold. And what should have been remembered was soon forgotten.

For twenty years, the Ark of the Lord remained at Kirjath-Jearim, banished from the hearts of men. Though all Israel lamented after the Lord, Dagon destroyed, the Ark restored to their care, the people still turned their faces toward the Ashtaroth and the Baals of the nations.

The Lord remained quiet, absent from among His people, waiting, as He had done so many times before, for them to return.

And so from Ramah, Samuel had begun to fulfill his destiny, his influence going forth on every side, to unite all Israel beneath the rule of the One True God. Loved and respected, his unwearied zeal grew among the people, drawing them toward Yahweh, awakening them, becoming not only their judge and prophet, but their father also.

The war-torn and ragged tribes, once divided and estranged, now drew near to one another, clinging to the hope that they might yet become a unified people.

From the border, the Israelites watched, feeling the shadow of fear growing. For even as they drew together, rumors of unrest rose from the west. Tension mounted as the Hebrew people listened for whispers of Philistine aggression. Time had healed the wounds the adversary had sustained, and with renewed strength, the enemy was about to make its move. With breaths held in check, the Chosen of God went about their daily lives: rising with the dawn, tending their fields, shepherding their flocks.

As the first blush of morning yawned over the hills surrounding Beth Shemesh, Riyphah lay watching her husband sleep. At first, his image was merely a silhouette; then slowly, as the light grew, his features gently emerged.

She ran her fingers along the contours of his face, brushing strands of hair from his brow. He rested so peacefully, the turbulent internal storm well hidden under the veil of his slumber. A soft smile touched her lips as she traced the tiny lines that had begun to form at the corners of his eyes. His beard, once sparse, now sat full upon his chin.

The years were showing, a quiet record of their life together.

He stirred slightly, then settled again in his repose. She was glad he was there. So often had his restless nature kept them apart, for long he could not stay before the call of duty pulled him away. Much of his time was spent with his captain and his men, ever watching the border, defending the towns that lay in the Philistines' path. Even as Samuel maintained a circuit of influence, so too did Nagad hold a sphere of obligation, his time always divided between his regiment, his wife, and the prophet. And so Riyphah looked upon her husband, treasuring the time she had, knowing that soon he would leave her once more.

The rays of the sun came on full, illuminating Nagad's face in warmth's glow. Slowly, he opened his eyes. Seeing his wife gazing upon him, he smiled. Reaching up, he drew her into his embrace and kissed her tenderly. She held him close, loath as always to let him go.

A shriek pierced the morning. It was guttural, panic-driven, shattering to the nerves. Nagad sprang from his bed and threw on his tunic.

"Quick, Riyphah—my sword!"

Riyphah ran to where the blade rested against the wall. Its weight pulling at her strength, she bore it to its master. Nagad laced up his sandals, then claimed his weapon from her hand, drawing it from its sheath.

Husband and wife burst from the house into the open air. Chaos engulfed all. People ran this way and that. Screams echoed through the narrow streets. The thunder of hooves resounded, galloping steeds tearing through the city, trampling all in their path.

Then he saw them—the red feathers of the Philistine hordes, sweeping in fury, wreaking havoc, raiding crops, pillaging homes. Smoke rose above rooftops. Bodies lay in the dust. Beside him, Riyphah stood frozen in horror.

"Stay here!" Nagad shouted as he pushed Riyphah down into the shadows. With his sword gripped tight in hand, he ran headlong into the fray.

Riyphah hid near a stack of baskets, watching in fear as Nagad fought his way through a knot of Philistine soldiers. Terror gripped her as swords sliced the air, each one seeking to take the man she loved. Battle had come for him, and she was witness to the trial. Riyphah stood transfixed, struck by the fierce grace of her husband's form. She ought to have looked away, but she could not. The sight was terrible—and beautiful. He moved like one born to the blade, the enemy falling all about him as his sword bandied with ease, gliding freely from one foe to the next. Deftly, he parted flesh from soul.

Feeling exposed, Riyphah backed farther into the shadows, her eyes wide with fear. Too far had she retreated, for as she moved, her body struck the stack of baskets. Down the wicker tower collapsed, crashing to the ground in a clattering ruckus. She leapt from her hiding place, startled by her own clumsiness. From behind, a hand seized her arm—then a second wrapped about her waist, lifting her from her feet.

"Aaaah!" she screamed, kicking and clawing at the arms that held her. "Let me go! Take your hands off me!"

It was enough, for even as the din of battle raged, the sound of her cry pierced the air and entered into the hearing of Nagad.

"Riyphah!"

His feet were swift. He flew toward the sound of her cry. His sword reached out and claimed the life of any who barred his path. All who hindered his advance paid the final price. As he rounded a corner in the narrow street, Nagad beheld the Philistine who had taken hold of his wife, his love. With malicious intent, the enemy had her fast, meaning to bear her away.

Memory flashed. Mother and sister lost to such hands. A flood of terror surged down his spine. Then the fire rose.

"Not this time."

With a roar, Nagad lunged and flung himself at the enemy. He thrust Riyphah aside, too roughly, and she fell hard, a cry escaping as she struck the earth. Stunned, she looked into the face of her rescuer, and though she knew him, a stranger stared out from behind his eyes. Unbridled rage, raw and unrestrained, burned in his gaze, like a flame unloosed. Ravaged by revenge, his bloodlust poured out in a savage fury that showed no mercy.

Tears welled in Riyphah's eyes to behold him thus, consumed by torment.

When at last the frenzy ceased, the alley ran red. Crimson soaked the stones, the path awash with lifeblood spent, an offering laid upon the altar of his wrath.

Shaking, Nagad stood over the carnage of his frenzy, stricken by the savagery of his own aggression. Riyphah sat, frozen to the place she had fallen, silent as the flame went out.

He bowed his head. After wiping his sword on the enemy's kilt, he came to his wife and extended his hand.

As she reached for his bloodied palm, her eyes searched the hollow of his. He would not meet her gaze as he lifted her to her feet.

"Nagad," she whispered, her heart aching for him.

"Come, let us leave the city. It is overrun and I must keep you safe." His voice was flat and hard, as though his soul was empty. "Keep close. We are not out of this yet."

"My love," Riyphah spoke gently, clinging to his arm.

Then he broke. Tears escaped his sorrowful eyes as he took her in his arms, kissing her face, bloodying her visage with the touch of his hands.

"I could have lost you." The words were raw and raspy.

"But you saved me."

"I am so sorry," he groaned in his anguish. "I never wanted you to see me like that. You must hate what I am."

She kissed him tenderly upon the cheek.

"I love you, Nagad. Nothing can change that. You did what needed to be done. Do not think on it again. Leave it in the alley."

He laid his forehead against hers. Looking into her dark eyes, he spoke gently, "We need to go."

Together they went, she grasping his strong hand, he gripping his sword, ready to defend. Troops of robbers bearing weapons stained with blood hurried through the streets. They came to plunder and to despoil.

In haste, Nagad led Riyphah down the winding way, past homes and shops once dear to her. The places of fond memory, the city of her childhood, now lay ruined and scarred. She looked upon the destruction and despaired. Her husband, pulling her forward, kept her close, unwilling to risk separation.

Through the meandering passageways of Beth Shemesh they fled, but at every turn, at each crossing, enemies barred their path. Again and again, Nagad was forced to fight. Weariness crept over them as they pressed toward the city's edge.

Rounding a corner, they drew up short, nearly colliding with the poised blade of a Philistine soldier. Even as they faltered, the foe's sword was already in motion, sweeping toward the side of Riyphah's neck.

In an instant, Nagad let go her hand and shoved her head down, ducking her out of reach as he brought his sword up to meet the blow.

Metal shrieked against metal. The blades scraped close, sliding just beyond the hollow of Riyphah's ear. She cringed at the sound, eyes clenched shut, as though darkness alone could shield her.

With his strong arm, Nagad took up his wife and pressed her against the wall, even as he held the warrior at bay. Assault and slaughter were the foe's intent: thrusting, striking, cleaving, the argument set forth by the sharp-edged sword. The bitter quarrel engaged to mete out punitive justice by the flashing of the unsheathed sword.

Defiant, Nagad stood unclad, yet still he yielded not. In his haste, he had taken nothing but his sword. No shield to guard his frame, no helm to crown his head, only the edge he wielded came between him and the stone-cold grip of fate. No sheath he wore, nor scabbard hung to take the weapon he bore. His hand alone upheld the blade: no rest, no pause, no peace. The cost was great, the danger nigh, so on he fought.

The clash resumed. Iron against bronze. Nagad met each stroke, deflecting and driving, pressed hard beneath the weight of wrath. The enemy blade swept for his neck—he ducked low, slipping beneath its deadly arc.

"Stand firm, dog," growled the Philistine, "and receive the judgment of my blade."

Nagad drew back, winded, his chest heaving. He watched the warrior, bracing for the coming blow.

"Put up again thy sword, Hebrew," mocked the Philistine, "that you might die with honor."

With sudden fury, the foe descended, his onslaught brutal, unyielding. The slanderous tongue of his blade lashed out with implacable malice.

Nagad quailed under the unwavering assault of the enemy. Riyphah, watching, felt her breath catch, terror rising within her as her husband faltered beneath the storm.

The Philistine bore down with the strength of his mighty arm, driving him to one knee, their blades locked in bitter strife.

"Nagad!" Riyphah cried out, her voice torn with terror.

He felt the strength in his limbs beginning to fail. A tremor passed through his sword arm. The enemy pressed harder upon the locked blades, inching the sharp edge ever closer to his face. He caught the glint of metal, cold and near, as the blades strained in their deadly embrace. Veins rose upon his brow beneath the weight of effort. His back bent under the pressure. He knew he was losing the fight.

Gathering all the strength that yet remained, that final adamant held in reserve, drawn forth only when summoned by the need of last resort, Nagad gritted his teeth. With a mighty groan, he planted his foot, the one that still held ground, and strove upward, rising upon unsteady legs.

His breath hissed between clenched teeth, sweat streaming from his brow as he bore down upon the blades, forcing them into the face of his adversary.

Seizing his chance, he drove his left fist to the man's jaw, delivering such a blow that the Philistine staggered back.

The blades wrenched free.

An opening came.

And Nagad struck, the point of his sword finding its mark, and smote his enemy.

With the strength of the foe broken, Nagad's vengeance was sated by the outpouring of his life-blood.

Standing over the ruined body of the Philistine, his own life now redeemed from death, ransomed for a time by the crimson dower of the adversary.

He was breathless, his face streaked with dirt and blood, his hands trembling as he reached for hers. Riyphah saw the toll—saw the weariness in his eyes, the ache beneath his strength. Yet his voice came low and steady, as though nothing had passed.

"Come."

Numb and weak, she took his hand. He guided her through the winding, narrow streets to the edge of town, his bearing unshaken, his steps sure beneath his silence.

She followed blindly, stunned at what she had almost lost. His peril had left her bereft of will, yet she followed as a child guided by a parent, under the shelter of his dispensation.

Slowly, as though a fog lifted from her mind, she came to herself. "Where are we going?"

"I am taking you to Samuel. I cannot protect you here. In the Naioth, you will be safe."

CHAPTER 27

MIZPAH

"This is not the first," spoke Samuel. "I have heard of other cities that have fared as Beth Shemesh. Even now, as the hearts of Israel are kindled once more for the Lord, they are sorely oppressed by their enemies, the Philistines. It is the adversary's desire to rule over the Hebrew people, to seize their cities and possess their fields."

"We cannot allow this," said Nagad, his voice weighted with resolve. "The time for waiting has ended. Shall we sit idle while our cities fall and our people are struck down by the sword? Samuel, we must act."

"Nagad," the prophet answered, "I have foreseen that the time of renewal has come. The Chosen of God have done well to put away their foreign gods. At the very hour you entered into the Naioth, I summoned the people to gather at Mizpah, for I have perceived that the time of deliverance is upon us. It is to Mizpah we must go. The people are waiting."

Nagad smiled as his hand rested upon the hilt of the sword sheathed at his side.

Mizpah, the watchtower of Benjamin, the most poignant peak in the Judean range, has ever been a place of gathering in times of national crisis. From this pedestal, a temporal vision exalted in beauty wrapt the soul in hues of paradise, girding the rostrum with delicate apparitions. Terraces heavy with fruit trees, vineyards, and olive groves rose in gentle tiers, their edges traced by green lanes that wound upward through the cultivated heights to the summit, whose crown commanded a far-reaching survey of the land.

From this elevation, the major highways could be discerned, each approach visible beneath the gaze. The land beyond the mount lay bleak and fruitless. Roughhewn gorges isolated the hill, an island in a sea of brown. Yet within the folds of deep ravines, wisps of color washed across the sterile gray rock, wildflowers abloom in glory, crisp in the morning mist.

Away to the west, beyond the mountains, lay the Vale of Aijalon; farther still, the Plain of Sharon; and beyond them all, the Great Sea, a distant haze of deep blue against the pale azure sky. The cities of Benjamin and Ephraim, each in its place, could be seen from these lofty heights. Behind the rocky backbone, east of the Judean hills, the vast trench of the Jordan Valley could be traced north and south, shrouded in a drifting brume that issued forth until halted by the faint glint of the Salt Sea.

Hither it was that Samuel called upon all the houses of Israel to meet, to offer sacrifice before Yahweh, and to judge the people. Beyond the two springs, enduring waters that flowed ever on, one to the north and one to the east, springs that in days to come would bear the names of Samuel and of Hannah, an oath was to be taken upon the altar of Mizpah, which sat atop the high hill.

There stood Nagad, with Tiphcar, his captain, and Riyphah, his wife, each by his side, a buttress against the foul weather of the world, strengthening and upholding him as the travails of life gathered and heaped against him. Together, they looked on while Samuel waited for the people to assemble. A smile broke upon the prophet's face as he beheld the crowd pressing forward. Nagad gazed upon the familiar visage of his friend, his stomach churning with anticipation.

This is the defining moment, thought Nagad. *This is what the years of labor have been for. But will the people listen? Will they heed the call?*

The past, the present, and the future of Israel seemed to converge in Samuel, unbending and true, a dauntless bulwark, looked to for guidance since the failure of the old ways.

Here he had come to stir the house of Israel with new courage, to forge a change, which had already begun.

Taking up a position beside the prophet, Tiphcar stood, confidently poised, his old wound forgotten, as he observed the deference the people gave to Samuel.

His voice rang out strong with enthusiasm as he addressed the prophet, "Look upon these thousands whom you have called. See how they cling to your presence, eager to mend their fettle and fortune."

Samuel leaned forward, inclining his head toward the captain, and spoke, his eyes still fixed upon the approaching crowd, "Something new is about to happen, the like of which has not been seen since the days of Joshua. A light arises in the dark."

Then, with the upward call of his arms, the congregation grew quiet, and Samuel began to speak to all the house of Israel, saying:

"Hear me, O priests! Take heed to my words, O men of Israel! Give ear! Listen to me, you stubborn-hearted, who are far from righteousness. I have come to bear a message, for the Lord your God has spoken.

"Too long have you put your trust in foreign gods. Too long have you bowed before false idols. Because of your harlotry, you have borne the yoke of the Philistines these many years. But I tell you, a greater enemy holds sway over you, a double bondage you suffer. For the wrath of the One True God presses hard upon you, to crush your hearts, and this yoke is the heavier.

"O Israel, return to the Lord your God, for you have stumbled because of your iniquity. You have transgressed against the Lord your God, and have scattered your fealty to alien deities under every green tree, and you have not obeyed the voice of the Lord."

All the congregation stood astounded at the prophet's words. Mute they were in their defense, shocked by his bold speech. Samuel searched their faces, discerning their thoughts.

Shaking his head, he withdrew his gaze and looked to the ground, grieved at heart. A hush lay heavy upon them. Sighing deeply, he lifted his eyes to the people.

Spreading his arms before the onlookers, Samuel spoke harshly, "Why do you gape at what I tell you? Your error is no different from that of the Philistines, who regarded the Ark of the Lord of Hosts as a common thing.

"Lightly they looked upon it, for they did not apprehend the holiness of God. Reaching out, they seized the Sacred Coffer of Yahweh, thinking it no more than a graven image of the Hebrew God.

"But you, my brothers, are no better. Usurpers you are. It was you who bore the Ark into battle as the portal of God, seeking to harness Yahweh, to compel His mighty hand against your foes. But the Lord did not fight for you that day, for you placed your trust in the effigy of God's presence rather than trusting in the Lord Himself and obeyed not His commands."

Samuel, with his hands clasped behind his back, fixed his gaze upon the face of the people as he paced, first to the left, then to the right, his steps the steady cadence of a war-drum, beating out the rhythm of judgment. Halting in his measured march, he lifted his eyes to the heavens, noting the feathery wisps of white clouds drifting across the brilliant sky. A faint breeze stirred the crowd, caressing the assembly with the fresh scent of spring, of earth and grass wafting lightly, awakening the senses with the promise of rebirth.

The prophet stretched out his hand toward the multitude.

"Who shall ascend the hill of the Lord? And who shall stand in His holy place?"[66]

Lowering his arm, Samuel turned his gaze aside, pausing in his oration. Then, lifting his chin as his voice rose, he declared, his hands shaping the air.

"He who has clean hands and a pure heart, who has not lifted up his soul to an idol, nor sworn deceitfully.[67] The Lord watches between you and me; nothing is hidden from His sight. He shall be your Judge."

The people shuddered at the words of Samuel, for his tone was grim and his words rang true. Sorrow descended, pressing upon their hearts. Many dared not meet the eyes of this man of God, for they began to understand their guilt, the magnitude of their disobedience.

---

[66] Psalm 24:3

[67] Psalm 24:4

How utterly different, how vastly superior was the One True God, and how unworthy they stood before Him.

In their despair, the people cried out, "Who then can stand before this mighty God? What must we do?"

Nagad felt the sting of the prophet's reproach, ensnared by his own guilt. He hung his head, eyes falling to the ground at Samuel's feet. A deep sigh escaped him. His chest tightened beneath the familiar weight, his thoughts bearing heavily against his soul.

Sensing his discomfort, Riyphah glanced up into the face of her husband. She tightened her grip on his hand, lending silent strength, hoping to ease his burden.

Then she saw it, a tear escaping his eye, tracing the line of his cheek until it vanished in the forest of his beard. Moved, she leaned into his side, unknowing the full fury of the storm that raged within him.

Nagad swallowed hard and set his jaw, retreating into himself, his thoughts drawn inward, pressed hard behind the door of his mind, as though to lock the matter from view.

Samuel looked upon the crowd, their faces downcast with guilt, stricken by the sorrow of his rebuke. Pity stirred his heart. The prophet softened his bearing and smiled, speaking now with gentle tenor, for he loved the people.

"Do not look for help from these foreign gods. The time has come to lay aside your faithless wanderings. The Lord will not always chide, nor will His anger burn forever, for He is merciful.[68]

"Lift your eyes to the Lord, from whence your help comes. Trust in God alone—not in the work of men's hands. Return to the Lord with all your hearts. Let not your hope rest in created things, but in the Creator Himself.

"Put away the foreign gods and the Ashtoreths from among you. Prepare your hearts for the Lord and serve Him only, for He alone is your salvation and rest from all your struggles.

"Pour out your hearts like water before the presence of the Lord, O people. Cleanse your hands, and purify your hearts, you double-minded. Humble yourselves in the sight of the Lord, and God

---

[68] Jeremiah 3:12; Psalm 103:9

will be a refuge for you. He will lift you up, and He will deliver you from the hand of the Philistines.[69]

"For by strength no man shall prevail. Yet the righteous shall hold to his way, and he who has clean hands shall be stronger and stronger. And who is he that shall harm you, if you be followers of that which is good?[70]

"If you are willing and obedient, you shall eat the good of the land. But—if you refuse and rebel, you shall be devoured by the sword for the mouth of the Lord has spoken."[71]

Then the sons of Israel cried out to the Lord, saying, "We have sinned against You, for we have forsaken our God and served the Baals. Yet now we return to You, for You alone are the Lord our God."

So Yahweh's Chosen, resolved to cast off the Baals and the Ashtoreths, renounced every rival and served the Lord alone. Not since the days of Moses had so many bowed in true repentance before the Lord.

Tiphcar stood tall, bearing himself with renewed purpose, for the prophet's charge had emboldened him. A quiet smile rose to his face. His hour of redemption had come, and he would not let it pass unanswered.

Samuel drew water from the spring, living water for the Lord.

"Who is like You among the gods, O Lord?"

The prophet poured out the pure offering before the Lord, a libation, like tears shed for the hearts of Israel.

"Yet hear me now, O Israel, whom God has chosen. Thus says the Lord, who made you, who will help you:

> I am the First and I am the Last;
> Besides Me there is no God.
> And who can proclaim as I do?
>
> Do not fear, nor be afraid;
> Have I not told you from that time, and declared it?
> You are My witnesses.

---

[69] Lamentations 2:19; James 4:8
[70] Job 17:9 / 1 Peter 3:13
[71] Isaiah 1:19–20

Is there a God besides Me?
Indeed, there is no other Rock;
I know not one."[72]

As Samuel poured out the last of the water upon the earth, he declared, "Thus says the Lord, the King of Israel, and the Redeemer, Lord of hosts:

Remember, O Israel, you will not be forgotten by Me!
I have blotted out, like a thick cloud,
Your transgressions;
And like a cloud, your sins.
Return to Me, for I have redeemed you.[73]

Fear not, for I will pour water on him who is thirsty,
And floods on the dry ground;
I will pour My Spirit on you."[74]

A free flood of repentance flowed forth from Israel. In humbleness and sorrow, they came before the Lord. As Samuel lifted up an intercessory prayer for the washing away of past offenses, the sons of Israel, through fasting and prayer, laid bare their emptiness and need. And as the sun went down in the west, so ended the wandering of the Chosen of God, for Yahweh had returned to the hearts of the people.

---

[72] Isaiah 44:6–8
[73] Isaiah 44:21–22
[74] Isaiah 44:2-3

CHAPTER 28

SHATTERED

"What do you see?" whispered Lukka.

Ekwesh peered out over the ridge that concealed him.

Before him rose the gleaming white ascent of Mizpah, a lone platform set high above the land. Struck silent by disbelief, he could not at once speak.

"What is it?" ventured Lukka, louder this time.

"I—I cannot believe what lies before me," stammered Ekwesh. "All of Israel has gathered. It is a mighty host."

Crouching low, Lukka clambered up beside him. He raised his head above the crest. There the multitude gathered near the high place, and his mouth parted in awe. "What is it? Why are they gathered there?"

Ekwesh did not answer. He watched the swelling throng, straining to grasp its meaning.

Lukka shifted beside him. "Surely, they do not assemble to rise against us."

Still, Ekwesh gave no reply. Hatred churned within him as gall rises in the throat, searing the unhealed wound.

I have not forgotten. My sword yet yearns for blood. Soon I will have my retribution.

"They appear to be praying. See how they bow before that man upon the hill," observed Lukka. "It does not look to me like a war party. These are no soldiers. Look—women and children are among them."

"Do not be deceived, my friend," Ekwesh muttered, his gaze narrowing. "See, some bear arms. It may be a ruse. Come. We must inform Caphtor."

With the decline of day, as the radiant orb sank beyond the western horizon, the Philistine spies descended the ridge and returned to their camp. Caphtor stood in the entrance of his tent, hands upon his hips, gazing eastward.

Ekwesh and Lukka hastened to bring report.

"*Sar*, we bear news." Ekwesh bowed.

"Come." Caphtor turned and entered the tent. The two spies followed behind him.

"My lord," said Ekwesh and Lukka in unison, bowing low to the ground. For there upon a carved throne sat Seranim, lord of Ashdod.

"You bring us word," spoke Seranim, his voice euphonic. "Rise and speak."

"*Sar*," began Ekwesh as he straightened, "we have seen a great assembly of Hebrews upon the heights of Mizpah."

"And the purpose of this gathering?" queried Seranim.

"Many thousands amass there," replied Ekwesh. "Yet their purpose I could not discern. Some bear arms, but women and children are among them."

Seranim looked to Caphtor. "What do you make of this, Commander?"

"*Sar*, this mustering of tribes may be the first stirring of rebellion. We must root out this vermin from the land—once and for all."

"Lord Seranim," spoke Lukka, tentatively, "if I may."

"Speak your mind, soldier."

"It appeared to me that this assembly is of a religious nature. The people bowed in prayer and lifted up offerings to their God. Though some were armed, many more were not. I do not believe this gathering is to wage war on us."

Seranim sat in thought for several moments, drawing the back of his hand over his clean-shaven chin as a furrow formed between his eyes.

"It has been long indeed since these Hebrews mounted any major resistance to our rule. I wish to anticipate their movements. What is the meaning of this gathering? You say they pray to their God. Or perhaps they gather in preparation for war."

"Either way, my lord," spoke Caphtor, "it is an opportunity. If we act now, we may cut them off before they are arrayed—strike while they are unready. Mizpah is well-situated for defense. We cannot allow them the advantage. If we forfeit surprise, they will be more difficult to dislodge. Their humility before their God will be their weakness."

"My lord," ventured Ekwesh, "do not forget what their God has done to us. These Hebrew dogs still owe us recompense. Their blood is all that will satisfy. I plead with you—do not let this chance for requital pass."

Gathering his robes, Seranim rose from his throne. His voice was melodious, his words as fine linen to the ear:

> Gold to grasp,
> Meat to eat,
> And blood to stain your blade.

"If it is the blood of Israel you thirst for, then it is the blood of Israel you shall have."

Pointing a ringed finger at Caphtor, he declared, "We shall answer this call, this new complaint. Send forth runners. With all speed, summon the lords of Philistia. Let them call up their armies. We march in full strength against Israel, to crush these dogs wholly, for all time."

Fearing an uprising, the Philistines rallied in answer to the Hebrew gathering, the sting of past shame yet sharp in their hearts. From the south came the host of the Seren, swelling their ranks; Askelon and Gaza soon moved to join them, their forces mustered with haste. And so, as prayers rose on the heights, an army rose in the valley. Philistia drawn up behind the mountain of Shen, a throng bent on war.

Nagad stood, looking west, over the dark horizon. Shadows grew long across the open plain below as the gathering dawn began to illuminate the sky beyond the distant hills to the east, chasing the stars away. A slight breeze rose and caressed his face, lapping at his hair, causing it to dance upon his shoulders.

Closing his eyes, he drew in a slow breath.

So much has happened. All these years of labor have not been in vain. At last. The people finally see their sin and are offering amends. They have done well to make manifest their repentance, their desire to serve God alone and to cast off the foreign gods.

Yet his own guilt weighed heavily upon him. Slipping a hand beneath his tunic, Nagad drew out the spearhead and looked at it in silence. Long had he carried this token, as long as he had carried the loss of his family. He ran his fingers upon the keen edge. With each passing year, his thirst for vengeance had grown sharper. Even now, he felt its searing heat rise within him.

And yet, there was something casting doubt over his resolve, an inner voice crying out against the reprisal for which he had long sought.

Have I laid aside my own idols? Have I truly yielded to serve the One True God?

Clasping his hand tightly over the spearhead, Nagad stood with his fists clenched at his side. He closed his eyes once more, bowing his head, listening. His chest was heavy, his frame drawn taut. Half expecting to hear the voice of God, he remained still for a long while. Yet nothing did he hear, save the brush of the wind across the land. His mind ran to Samuel. He had learned much from this wise man of God.

A quiet warmth welled within him as the prophet's words came to mind. *Let go. Be free of the curse of hate.*

Opening his eyes, Nagad spoke aloud, though none stood by to hear. "With Samuel is wisdom and strength. He gives good counsel and sound understanding.[75] His words are surely inspired."

Looking again across the open plain that lay between the high place of Mizpah and the cliffs of Shen, Nagad noticed that the prominent hill cast a shadow that resembled a tooth upon the field. He lifted his gaze to the mount of Shen and gave a quiet chuckle, for indeed, the crag jutted forth in the shape of a tooth.

In the waning darkness, a horn sounded to the west, sharp and sudden, cleaving the air. Nagad's eyes flew wide, though he could see

---

[75] Job 12:13

nothing in the plain below. A chill of dread crept over him as the hairs along his neck rose. Then came the sound—thousands of footfalls echoing off the barren hills.

No! Not now!

Over a rise in the land came the mighty army of Philistia.

"Sound the ram's horn! War is upon us!" cried Nagad as he ran down the embankment toward camp.

At the sight of that great host, the people cried out in fear, "The Philistines have come to kill us!"

Roused by the uproar, Samuel stepped from his tent. Nagad rushed to him, breath short. Tiphcar joined them, tightening his sheath-belt about his waist.

"The hour has come," spoke Tiphcar, running a finger along the edge of his blade. He thrust it into its sheath. "We must cast off the yoke of the Philistines."

"We are not prepared for war," Nagad said, each word dragged from the hollow of his chest. Realizing that he still clasped the spearhead, he shoved it roughly into the pocket within his tunic. "We cannot hope to stand against so mighty a foe, scantly armed as we are." And the women, the children—they have no time to flee."

"No," came Tiphcar's reply. "But this time—we do not fight alone."

Samuel smiled, placing a hand upon his shoulder. "It appears that the Philistines have yet to learn their lesson from the heavy hand of God."

Turning toward the crowd, Samuel lifted his voice. "You have no more understanding than the Philistines. Where is your faith? Do not fear, for their foot shall slide in due time.[76] You should have more confidence in the Lord. Do you not yet see? A little faith in the true and living God is mightier than the strongest belief in a lie. Fear nothing of this world, for no foe can contend with the God who created all things."

The children of Israel pleaded with Samuel, saying, "Do not cease to cry out on our behalf. We dare not look upon the face of the Lord our God, for we are fearful and greatly ashamed by our great depravity shown to us this day. As Moses once interceded for his generation,

---

[76] Deuteronomy 32:35

so now pray for us, that God may deliver us from the hand of the Philistines."

As light broke over the eastern range, Samuel offered up a suckling lamb, eight days old, an offering consecrated to God. The yearling was laid upon the stone table, its life forfeit: a shadow of good things to come, of that which is purchased upon the altar. The sacrifice was wholly burnt, consumed by fire, to restore favor with Yahweh and make atonement for the people.

Facing the altar with arms uplifted to heaven, Samuel cried out unto the Lord for help, beseeching Him to deliver Israel.

He turned to the crowd. Samuel, the one who prays, lifted his voice before the people and said,

"Though you come up against my people Israel like a cloud to cover the land, yet I tell you, O Philistines, you shall perish. For those who love the Lord God Jehovah shall be as the sun when it rises in its strength. The loftiness of man shall be bowed down, and the haughtiness of men shall be brought low. He will reduce to nothing all the gods of the earth. The Lord alone will be exalted this day. Thus let all Your enemies perish, O Lord!"[77]

As the advancing army drew near, the raw wound of double defeat, though distant in time, remained fresh in the memory of God's chosen race. Yet the people prepared themselves for a great war against the Philistines, trusting in the counsel of the prophet to guide them, and in their God, to deliver them. Even as fear and dread of the coming invasion pressed sore upon them, God answered Samuel's prayer. And though the battle had not yet been fought, the victory had already been won.

The dawn rose red in the east as a heavy mist lay upon the ground. In the field west of Mizpah, beyond the rolling hills, in the Valley of Aijalon, the battle would be waged. With the clash of spear against shield, the Philistines arrayed themselves for battle. Across the plain, the mighty menace stood with strength and power.

It was a ragged rabble of soldiers, ill-clad and wary, that stood facing this magnificent wonder of warfare. Intimidation spread through the Hebrew ranks as they beheld the host before them with troubled awe.

---

[77] Isaiah 2:17 / Judges 5:31

With the tension of a storm not yet broken, the two forces stood in sullied stillness, each opposing the other across the great divide.

"They are here!" called Tiphcar. "It is time!"

Drawing his sword, Nagad spoke through clenched teeth, "Long have I waited to avenge Orach's death, and the slaughter of my family."

The prophet looked upon Nagad and reached out to him, placing a steady hand on his shoulder. "Vengeance belongs to the Lord, for the day of their calamity is at hand, and the things to come hasten upon them."

Long had Samuel discerned the sorrow that shadowed Nagad's heart, for often they had spoken at the Naioth. "My friend," he said, "He will not spare in the day of retribution. But we—we do not fight because we hate what is wrong, but because we love what is right."

Nagad bowed his head, unable to hold the strong yet gentle gaze of the prophet. Still, the wound within him, newly awakened, would not be soothed. *I know Samuel is right, but it is hard to forget. I wish Orach were once more beside me, to fight with me as once he did.*

Dominating the landscape across the undulating ground, Nagad beheld various shades of yellow and crimson, short-lived flowers of summer, fluttering in the soft morning breeze. The scent of spring, of uncertain glory, hung in the air, a variant wave of freshness, faintly perceived, borne on the wind with the distant sweetness of apples rising from the golden blooms of the crown daisy. He breathed in the fragrance of the field.

The green lap of the vernal season beckoned from sleep and issued forth a flood of memories of youth and peaceful times, of white linen robes and love's first kiss, and the soft laughter of a virgin.

Transfixed by the flowery field, by the scarlet crowfoot growing low to the ground, each with a single stem bearing one ruby flower, and the gilded display of the crown daisy rising high above the crimson carpet, Nagad thought: *How like a flower we are. We come forth, and then we are cut down and fade; as a shadow we flee, lost in the dark of night, and continue not. Of neither do we make much account, for neither can bear our confidence, for all wither and are gone.*

"At the end of day, we shall be lifted up," Nagad spoke under his breath as he raised his sword before his face. "Though the way be long and hard, we will endure."

Tiphcar, displaying his blade before the readied troops, cried aloud, "New is the dawn before us! Now is the hour that the Lord will be glorified! If God be for us, who can stand against us!"[78]

And there, between Mizpah and Shen, the Philistines came rushing toward them in great number, hastening unto their own fate. The vision of the heavily armored and highly trained Philistines advancing in tight formation sent fear into the hearts of the Hebrew lines. Yet, through the knee-high stems of the crown daisy, trudging through the bushy display of golden heads, the Israelites marched, increasing their pace until at last they burst forth in swiftness of speed.

Across the expanse they sprang, as lodestones drawn by an unseen hand. Colliding, the opposing lines recoiled, the violent concussion of the impact sending men back a step in a carom of clashing colors. Trampled underfoot by the myriad of sandaled feet, by the forward thrust of the rushing troops, the scarlet flowers were soon crushed and covered in the crimson stream of life's hemal nectar. As a wave strikes a vessel amidships, the soldiers dashed against each other, dealing deadly blow upon deadly blow. In contention, they strove to take what the other possessed, but which only one could hold.

Tiphcar moved ahead of the pack with frenzied fury, as one possessed by a power not his own, heedless of the peril that swelled within the fray. Calmly he met the foe, unwavering in his resolve to gain the upper hand. Nagad drove through the clash, cutting down a soldier who barred his path, until he reached his captain amid the melee. Together they fought as they had before, side by side, striking in unison against the common enemy.

One soldier rushed upon Nagad, arm raised to strike a mortal blow. With a sweeping arc, Nagad hewed the man's right arm above the elbow, painting the edge of his blade in blood. The enemy fell, writhing and clutching the ruined limb. The score so made, he pressed forward, blade flashing as he lunged to strike the next who came against him.

Crouching like a beast poised to spring, Nagad spoke through clenched teeth, "Awake, O sword! I will whet my glittering blade upon those who hate my people."

In one fluid motion, he swept his sword in a wide horizontal slash, laying open the belly of his adversary. Dropping to one knee,

---

[78] Romans 8:31

his foe now above him, Nagad drove his blade upward beneath the man's chin and into the skull, spraying himself with the blood of his opponent.

As he rose from his knee, Nagad sensed movement behind him. Spinning to his left as he made to stand, he took a powerful clout to the jaw from the pommel of a sword, dealt by a surly Philistine who had sought to slit his throat. The metallic tang of blood surged over his tongue and spilled onto his bearded chin.

Spitting the warm rush from his mouth, Nagad turned swiftly to his defense. He caught the next blow on the edge of his sword, notching the blade, yet his guard held.

With his fist closed tightly over the grip of his weapon, Nagad struck the enemy a powerful punch to the face. The skin over his knuckles split, but the stunned foe was forced to take a few steps back. Grasping his sword firm in hand, he took the momentary stay in the Philistine's onslaught and dealt the deadly blow, his enemy falling to the earth with a thud.

Fury mounted as the iron swords of the Philistines sliced through the Hebrew lines, splitting them as water over rough rocks. The full measure of the Philistine force heaved forward, hacking men down in their wake. There Tiphcar stood against the barrage of a whole host of foes, as a tree well-rooted withstands a storm.

"Do not falter! Stand fast! Be brave. Be strong!" Tiphcar cried, his voice clothed in deliberate valor, perceiving the weakening resolve of his men. "Spend the arrows! Release the missiles!"

Yet even with the arrows loosed, the onslaught faltered but little. Quickly recovering, the Philistine force struck forth sternly into the ragged rabble of weary troops. And though outmatched, the Hebrews ran forward into the heart of the fray, meeting the enemy headlong.

The din of battle echoed off the distant hills proclaiming war, the malady of brutes, as two clouds do fight when storms arise in the heavens. Sparks rained down as blade struck blade, kindling dry patches of rye-grass into flame. Smoke clouds curled low upon the ground, swirling through the ranks and lending an otherworldly cast to the battle raging over the plain.

Sweeping back across the crimson-stained field, deflecting many a thrust, Nagad strove to glimpse Tiphcar through the smoldering haze.

Unforeseen, a heavy stroke fell upon his helm, casting it from his head and sounding a myriad of bells within his pate, plundering his senses. The rebuke came sudden and fierce. He staggered, his quaking limbs recoiling at the insult. His shield slipped from his arm. Blood trickled down his brow and into the corner of his eye, stinging, blurring his sight.

He shook his head to shed the veil. Movement stirred, jolting his senses awake.

Agitation flared. Straightway, he turned aside, just beyond the reach of the strike. For several moments they sparred, sword ringing bright, neither prevailing over the other.

Holding back his stroke, Nagad gave no sign—then at the last breath, he drove his sword forward. The point struck home, yet the armor caught the force, blunting the blade's advance. Still, the blow jarred him, halted his stroke—and in that breath, Nagad seized his chance.

Raising his sword in both hands, he brought it down in a wrathful arc, cleaving the foe's shoulder.

The man gasped, gaping at the Hebrew before him, and with a downward sweep, Nagad struck again and severed his head.

Controlling his breath, he moved forward across the field, his strength yet undiminished. Shrouded in a thick cloud of smoke, the rumbling thunder of horse-hooves could be heard ploughing through the Hebrew lines. The sound came from a distance behind him.

He turned and scanned the field, but the gray veil cloaked his sight. Figures moved through the haze, yet none he knew. He stumbled over bloodied flesh and shattered arms, searching for his men, but none were near. Nagad fought alone.

From the gloom came a whistling cry, slipping through smoke and tore the air. The iron point drove deep into Nagad's left thigh, tearing muscle as it burst through the far side, the shaft lodged fast in flesh. Pain seared down his leg.

He staggered back to find his balance, but a blade swept in from the side, slashing for his neck. Nagad winged right and flung back his head to evade the fatal stroke.

The sword missed its mark but glanced off his left cheek, laying open his flesh. His footing lost, he fell hard. The earth took him with brutal force, pain rippling through his battered frame.

Stunned, he came to rest on his right side—then, with quiet dread, he lifted his eyes.

Above him loomed a towering Philistine, sword poised to plunge into his unguarded side.

Between them passed a look, fraught with fire and the weight of old hatred. The enemy's voice dropped low, hoarse and steeped in scorn.

"You are broken."

His senses slowed. Sound fell away, until all that remained was the wild beating of his heart and the ragged drag of his breath.

With effort, he raised his arm to shield against the fatal stroke.

He had no fear, for all hope had failed him.

It comes to this.

Noticing the red gleam of the Philistine's sword in the late afternoon sun, he watched motionless as the blade descended toward his body.

Slowly, it moved downward, yet he knew in truth the stroke came swift, for the strain upon the soldier's face betrayed the force behind it.

He surveyed beads of sweat dripping off the brow of the man standing over him, his gaze fixed, intent on quitting his life.

The slayer's focus faltered, and there came a strange awe upon his countenance. His unwilling eyes, drawn wide, flickered and dropped to his chest, taking Nagad's with them.

A silence lay heavy between them, as together they beheld the sharp point of a spear breaking forth from his breast.

He pitched forward and fell beside the Hebrew.

Nagad watched, unmoving, as the last breath slipped from his lips.

The world returned in pieces. Smoke. Pain. The weight of his own limbs. Nagad lifted himself onto one elbow, seeking the cause of his reprieve. Out of the veil of smoke came a shadowy figure, familiar to his eye.

"Orach," he breathed, the name catching in his throat. "Orach," he spoke again, his voice steadier.

The soldier drew near and offered his hand. Nagad grasped it, peering deep into the eyes of his rescuer as he was pulled to his feet. A sharp pain shot through his leg, and he winced, then looked again, confusion stirring.

The eyes were Orach's—but too young.

"Orach?" he murmured once more. No, but like Orach.

With a familiar laugh, the soldier caught him gently and held him steady.

"I know you not, but of my father you do speak. I am Helek ben Orach. Orach was my father."

Still gazing in wonder, warmed by the likeness, Nagad stood as one caught between two moments in time.

"Come now," said Helek, "we cannot have you carrying this about, can we?"

He watched in silence as Helek took hold of the spear yet lodged within his thigh. With one great tug, it gave way. Nagad groaned as pain coursed through him, and he nearly collapsed.

"Now, that will do you better."

Helek drew a cloth from his pouch and bound it tightly about Nagad's leg, drawing a sharp breath from him as the wound flared anew.

Nagad reached out, placing a hand upon Helek's shoulder, if only to touch him, and know that this son of Orach stood truly before him.

"So much you favor your father." His voice was thick with emotion. "My thanks to you."

Before Helek could reply, movement beside them drew the warriors back into the fray. He stooped and retrieved his spear from the fallen foe. Swinging it from side to side, he met the enemy's charge and drove the point forward. The man recoiled beneath the sudden force, barely escaping its sharp edge. Then came four swift, arcing strokes, each more pressing than the last, until, with a final, piercing blow, he brought the Philistine down.

And so the battle raged; with bandied swords the Philistines held sway, driving back the Hebrew ranks with unabated violence. Unable to withstand the onslaught, the tribal troops were splintered. Piercing the flank of the Israelite line, the mighty host carved out and severed the band of warriors. The furious intensity of the Philistine storm dealt a heavy stroke, laying open what was obvious: fatally overwhelmed, the Chosen of God had but to capitulate—or die.

"Look at these men. There is no ground to hope, yet in faith they fight," spoke Nagad with pride.

"Ah, yes." Helek's voice brimmed with relish, so much like his father. "The overwhelming odds make the victory that much sweeter!

I shall render to them interest upon their own desires. It was to this glory I was created."

"Victory?" Nagad was stunned by the thought.

A voice rose above the din of battle. Samuel stood upon the height of Mizpah. With arms uplifted, he spoke, "The Lord shatters His adversaries; against them in the heavens He thunders!"[79]

---

[79] 1 Samuel 2:10

CHAPTER 29

RETRIBUTION

The sun stood centered above the clearing, casting down its warm rays upon the raging battle, clothing the field in veils of lambent air. Streams of light broke into fractured angles, bounding off smoke clouds as the radiant columns filtered through the haze of the smoldering plain. Where the beams pierced the brume, they glanced off sword-blades, flashing brilliant beacons through fine motes of suspended matter that drifted in the murk. Fires smoldered across the ground, branding the earth with blackened wounds. Here and there, fresh blazes breathed to life, kindled by the husks of the fallen as the fire fed upon the dead.

Intoxicated by battle, Ekwesh cried in fevered distemper, "My spear shall be drunk with blood, and my sword shall devour flesh, with the blood of the slain, from the heads of the chiefs of the enemy!"[80]

Phicol turned toward the battle-worn Ekwesh, whose face bore the heavy reckoning of revenge. His spear he clasped, set firm within his hand, crouching low, bracing for the coming charge.

"We shall make good work of it," spoke Lukka, towering by his side.

"Aye," agreed Phicol, readying for the next advance. "The one whom the gods favor shall sing this night by the warmth of the fire."

"Sound the charge!" called Caphtor, his voice ringing through the lines.

---

[80] Deuteronomy 32:42

With swift release, the Philistines fell upon the foe. Blades swung and spears struck; they drove forward with savage purpose, hewing their way into the Hebrew line. The throes of battle writhed with ruinous convulsions, waxing strong through a sweep of brutality that lay death open upon the field. The smoke and noise of war bore down amid the onslaught, reaching out with clasping hands to bruise the adversary.

Ekwesh broke upon the enemy with unbridled wrath. He suffused the contest with his indictment, demanding the price for the hurt that was done him. The deep wound burst forth, reopened by the violent strain of his tortured soul. So great was his distress that he yearned to destroy those he deemed the cause of his torment. Each thrust released a flood of pain that flowed from himself to the wreckage of his foe, as though, by fighting Yahweh's Chosen, he could strike vengeance upon the God who had wrought all his suffering. Long he had waited to exact the penalty for the wrong committed unto him.

Desperate for revenge, Ekwesh tore through the enemy ranks, meting out justice, slaughtering without number, marking his path with the leverage of destruction. He swept his spear in a ruinous arc and struck the warrior square. The man before him crumpled, flung to the ground as though struck by a god. With his strong hand, Ekwesh raised the dread shaft above his fallen foe, who, shielding his face with upturned hands, looked into the wild eyes of retribution.

Ekwesh spoke to the stricken Israelite at his feet. "I have come to inflict great misery upon you. I am the touch-stone of justice. Your life is forfeit."

So spoken, he thrust the spear-point into the man's belly, the iron tip cleaving the thin leather breastplate, rending his life from him.

"Aye!" called Lukka. "Mind the arrows!"

Looking up, Ekwesh dropped to a knee and raised his shield—just as the sky gave answer. A thousand feathered shafts hissed through the air, scorching the veil of heaven and earth. Shields lifted in unison, a wall of iron and wood braced for the coming storm. The missiles struck like hail, drumming against them before falling broken at their feet. But few found flesh—cries rose where guard was not raised.

Quickly recovering, Ekwesh, Lukka, and Phicol, driving forward, struck for glory and in so striking, hastened toward their doom. Without mercy, the three companions hewed a savage line, laying low all who dared to stand. Many who beheld their advance gave way, fleeing the fury of their blows in fear and disgrace.

With fluid grace, the three whirled their spears aloft, surged forth, stabbing, drawing back, and striking again, each motion woven into a grim ballet of slaughter. None withstood their might; they cut a swath through the melee, leaving naught behind but blood and dust.

As the onslaught issued forth, the trio were drawn apart into the chaos of the fray, severed from one another's side, each cast into his own contest. Standing apart, yet not unbound, they fought on, resisting the violent tide that sought to rend them asunder.

Lukka drove his spear into the Hebrew's side, striking where flesh met bone. The young soldier, brave enough to stand against the towering giant, staggered as the shaft lodged within his body. Wrenching hard, Lukka sought to free the weapon, but the deep-seated point snapped off, remaining fixed within the Hebrew's hip.

Seizing the shaft with both hands, Lukka twisted low, bracing his weight on his heels. With the shattered ends of his spear, he parried the flurry of sword-blows that followed. Pivoting to avoid the edge, he struck back, driving the jagged butt into the warrior's side.

Releasing one hand, he grasped the Hebrew by the throat. Fingers clenched, he held fast until the fight was ended, not by blade, but by the crushing strength of his grip.

And though Lukka's adversary fell, the war had not yet spent its wrath.

Into the tumult pressed Phicol, and with a mighty thrust he pierced his foe's side, rending a wound deep and wide across the belly, his life fleeing, for once wounded such, he had no choice but to die.

Wheeling about, Phicol beheld Ekwesh poised, his spear drawn back and ready to strike. He took a stride and lunged, but the Hebrew twisted aside, and the point passed harmless.

The warrior recovered swiftly and answered with a sharp barrage, which Ekwesh caught on his shield. Driving forward with his shield arm, he stabbed with the weapon, leaning in to add his weight. Pivoting clear of the counterstroke, he swept his back foot wide and sent the point home. The blow landed true. The Hebrew staggered, then fell, life spilling at the edge of the Philistine's spear.

Ekwesh marked the Hebrew lines advancing, and cast his weapon into the charging throng. His shaft flew straight, his point cleaving the throat of a young conscript, death darkening his eyes as he fell heavy upon the ground. As the ranks closed about him, Ekwesh drew his sword and crouched low, bracing for the onslaught.

Scowling at the Chosen of God, he spoke, "With my blade I do make mine enemy's edge blunt, and though he strikes with sword or spear, he shall not bite."

Swiftly he struck, turning each mighty blow aside with the strong edge of his blade.

Ekwesh slammed the pommel of his sword into the face of his foe, sending the man staggering back. Close he followed, with one stroke of his blade, to claim the upper hand.

Stunned by a sharp blow to the back of the head, he fell hard, his shield torn from his grasp. Rolling beyond reach, he sprang to his feet, wild fury alight in his eyes.

The Hebrew closed in, weapon poised to strike. Ekwesh feigned high, drawing up the man's shield, then swiftly reversed his stroke, dropping low to carve an upward line behind the enemy's leg. His blade found flesh, slashing deep into the back of the thigh.

Blood gushed from the wound.

Reeling, the warrior pivoted on his sound leg to guard against a downward stroke, but Ekwesh was already upon him. With force enough to take down a beast, he drove the pommel of his sword beneath the man's ear, shattering bone.

From his slackened jaw blood spilled as he staggered back and fell hard upon the ground.

The Hebrew sprang to his feet and lunged, fierce and unthinking. In that over-hasty ardor, he gave the Philistine the opening he needed. Ekwesh seized the uplifted sword arm, halting the fatal stroke.

Locked in struggle, the two wrestled for dominance, but the wounded son of Israel could not break free.

Ekwesh met his eyes with a scowl, his voice low and strained. "You try my patience."

With his free hand, he plunged the blade into the man's belly, quitting his life with a single thrust. He tore his weapon free and shoved the body aside, turning once more to the fray.

A flicker in the air caught his eye, a spear, whistling through the din. He sheathed his sword in a single sweep, seized the shaft mid-flight, turned its point, and hurled it back with deadly aim. The missile found its mark, striking the chest of the one who had loosed it, and laid him low.

And so the battle raged until the sun, wearied of the day, bowed down upon its downward path. Though bravely fought, the valiant assay to forestall the mighty horde of the Philistine host availed them naught. None could stand before the swords and ardent wrath of the ironclad Peleset. The Hebrew ranks staggered and gave ground, hewn down by the blade of the terrible machine that was Philistia.

"The victory shall be decisive," spoke Seranim, seated high upon his magnificent steed, watching from a rise, his gaze east over the field.

"Yes, my lord," answered Seren, mounted beside his liege. "Against you, *Sar*, no man can prevail."

Seranim smiled and gave the command, "It is time, Captain. Let the horsemen ride—release the charioteers. Let us end this ere the sun is fled."

"As you say, my lord, so shall it be done."

With the sound of a mighty rushing wind, the cavalry and charioteers were loosed upon the throngs. Flanking the enemy, Seren charged at the head of his mounted soldiers, his heavy chariots thundering close behind. Moving in a rack, the fast four-beat gait of war-trained steeds played out their warning, each iron-shod foot striking the earth with judgment, trampling the foe beneath hoof and wheel.

Swiftly, the Hebrew forces were hemmed in, clenched in a death grip. And yet with hope spent, the Chosen of God refused to yield to the power of Philistia.

In the midst of the encircled host, one stood apart. A mighty captain fought on, as though the victory were already won. Amid the upheaval, the three Philistine companions paused, unable to look away, their spirits stilled by awe. Light from above broke through the haze, striking his armor until it gleamed, as if some greater power bore him up. The exhortation inspired dread, melting those who beheld the sublimity and might of this Hebrew captain. Before him, courage faltered, and the hearts of men grew faint.

Restrained by solemn wonder, the Philistines came to themselves as a mighty voice rose above the clash of the battle.

"The Lord shatters His adversaries; against them in the heavens He thunders!"[81]

Lukka tapped Ekwesh with his sword arm, nodding toward a man with uplifted arms upon the height of Mizpah.

"It is he, the one we saw before, the man to whom the Hebrews bowed."

And to Ekwesh, it did seem that the voice came from him.

"He has cursed us," cried Lukka.

"Never mind," Ekwesh snapped. "What can these few Hebrew do against the might of all Philistia? The battle is ours. Come—let us be done with them."

---

[81] 1 Samuel 2:10

CHAPTER 30

REQUITED

Through the raging sea of men they fought, Ekwesh, Lukka, and Phicol, side by side. From behind the lines emerged two figures, one with a limp from a wound to the thigh, the other young and broad.

Ekwesh fixed his gaze upon the blood-streaked face of the injured Hebrew. Determination sat deep in the eyes of this armed adversary, and for a fleeting breath, Ekwesh faltered. But the moment passed—his enemy was upon him.

Iron clashed with bronze as Ekwesh locked arms with the Hebrew, swords caught mid-course, each straining for the upper hand.

The contest seethed with emulous might, blades crossed, muscles taut, neither yielding ground.

Using his left arm, by dint of great force, the Hebrew, Nagad, he was, broke the grip that bound him and cast his foe back. Two paces fell between them.

So loosed, Nagad pressed the advantage. His blade swept in a swift arc and found its mark. Flesh gave way beneath the blow, blood flowed in rivulets from the rent about the left shoulder.

Ekwesh did not wait for the next attempt, but drove up the fist of his opponent with the heart of his blade. Though turned aside, the edge yet grazed his neck, leaving but a shallow bite.

Anger festered, and in his rage he threw himself at his enemy, forcing him back a step. This he followed with a long stroke, one

Nagad evaded in a bounding leap. The effort tore fire through his injured limb, and he staggered.

Holding his ground, Ekwesh waited. As the Hebrew charged forward, he moved to meet him. The thrust was met and held, stayed by the forte of Nagad's sword.

Long had it held—but the blade was notched. And when he brought it down hard against the Philistine's iron, it shattered in his hand. For a breath he stood, staring at his sudden ruin.

A flicker of motion caught his eye. Danger stirred within. Dropping to the ground, he rolled to his right and sprang to his feet in one fluid motion, barely avoiding the downward arc of the enemy's sharp edge. Pain lanced through his leg, sending a surge of fire through his frame, quickening his limbs with the will of battle.

Drawing his knife from his girdle, Nagad crouched low, ready to face the glaring Philistine. He knew he had no chance against so mighty a foe, armed as he was. Yet bent on following after ruin, he would not shrink from the fight while strength remained.

He lunged—but the effort was swept aside by the enemy's blade. Iron found his left flank and cut deep, and he reeled from the might of it. The Hebrew labored beneath his wound, aware of the choking groans of death that heaved forth around him.

Staggering upright, Nagad drew a shuddering breath, his eyes wide with pain as he turned toward the foe.

Ekwesh stood at ease, a smirk playing upon his lips.

"You are undone, my friend. Where is thy sword?" he taunted.

"You speak truth, yet there is One more powerful than the sword."

"There is none who can stand against me whilst I am so armed," spoke Ekwesh as he crouched, preparing for attack.

Tempting him forward with feigned strokes, Ekwesh brought down his blade, striking Nagad across the face with the hilt of his sword, laying open anew the wound upon his left cheek. The blow drove him back, his breath escaping in quick gasps. He squeezed his eyes shut and gave his head a sharp shake, endeavoring to still the pulsing in his pate.

"What—wearied already? Shall I grant thee pause?" Ekwesh mocked.

With a growl, Nagad dipped his head and hurled himself at the Philistine, catching him in the belly with his shoulder. Laughing, Ekwesh cast him aside with ease.

The bloodied Hebrew stumbled back, struggling to keep his feet.

"You cannot win this fight," spoke Ekwesh.

Nagad coughed, blood threading from the corner of his mouth. His words came thick, his tongue heavy with iron. "That may be so, but I do not fight alone. It is your ruin that stands before me."

"Ah, but I am already doomed. What more can you do to me? Yet there is a price that must be paid, and I am come to see it rendered in full."

The protracted controversy continued, each striving, grappling with the other in slow ordeal. Loss of blood and long conflict strained Nagad into a lassitude of weary movements that only his strong will made possible to prevail. The air became stifling. His armor grew heavy; his tortured limbs cried out with fatigue.

Threatened by despair, his mind grew thick with an overwhelming desire to yield in defeat—yet still he persisted, unwilling to surrender the last shred of hope he yet held.

Taking a deep breath, Nagad gathered his strength and began circling as a lion sizing up its prey. A guttural growl rose in his throat as he glared, eyes locked upon his foe. Ekwesh gave ground, drawing the circle wide, amused, smiling with malice, as his battered pursuer advanced, still loath to fall.

Nagad lunged in pretense, then drew back.

Ekwesh came on, but checked his advance, a cruel laugh breaking loose at the deceit.

"Do you not yet yield to my blade?"

"I will not give up the fight, though you may cut my life asunder," Nagad replied between short breaths. "I will not yield while yet my breath remains within me."

"Why do you persist? Yield to me, and I will quit your life in one fell stroke. Is it not better to die all at once than to have your life carved from you piece by piece?"

Ekwesh cast a glance to either side, spying Lukka grappling with the young Hebrew soldier. The waste of battle reached out to them, grasping the hem of death upon their heels.

"Look around you," Ekwesh cried, spreading both arms wide. "Behold—the end has come. Can you not see? Fate is against you. All is lost. The battle is already decided, and even now your life's blood flows from you."

"It is as it has always been," Nagad answered, "when times become most desperate, that we are taken to the edge of the cliff, and just as our footing is about to fail, God stretches forth His hand and draws us to safety. I tell you—even now, our salvation is at hand."

"Fool! Nothing can save you now!"

Ekwesh raised his sword and made to take off the Hebrew's head.

Nagad ducked at the last moment, rolled to his right, and sprang to his feet. As he rose, he stabbed out with his knife, catching the Philistine in the side, just beneath the breastplate.

Stunned, Ekwesh pressed a hand to the wound and drew it back bloodied, staring at it with awe.

"You fight well," he spoke, a sideward smirk on his lips, the rush of battle still thrumming through his veins. "I will not dishonor you with a slow death. Only come—and I will end your suffering swiftly, so that your name may be renowned forever."

"I care not for renown," Nagad answered as the vision of his purpose became clear in his mind, the veil of shadow drawn back to expose the light of a clear day. "But for the will of the Lord my God.

"I am but a passing thought in the deeps of time. My actions are a little thing in the cause of God, yet the effect of our obedience combined will wreck a mighty conclusion as a drop of water coupled with many issues forth a mighty flood that covers all the land."

"Your stubbornness will only bring ruin upon you!" Ekwesh tightened his grasp upon the sword "Prepare yourself, for death comes for you this day!"

"In the end, we all must arrive at the same conclusion," spoke Nagad, a calm settling upon him like a mantle.

If death be the price, then I shall pay it.

"None may escape the grave—but I may yet choose the manner in which I meet it. I do not fear death, only the wrath of Yahweh."

"On with it then!" Ekwesh snarled, his fury held in check behind clenched teeth. "No more words—your doom is upon you!"

With unrestrained violence, Ekwesh unleashed a torrent of fierce wrath against Nagad. Unable to withstand the madness of his assault, Nagad gave ground, stepping back, ducking under a blow.

Slipping, he fell; his weight, pitching backward, cast him hard upon his back. Ensnared by Ekwesh's rage, he rose, only to be struck across the head by the hilt of his enemy's sword, which sent him sprawling to the ground.

His fingers closed around a stone. Waiting for the right moment, he hurled it with all the strength that remained. The stone found its mark, striking the Philistine upon the brow and tearing the flesh.

Stumbling back, Ekwesh put his hand upon his wound, then drew it down to his face and looked again upon the bloodied palm.

"You are full of surprises, dog. But sticks and stones will not save you."

Ekwesh, with distemper foul, advanced upon the Hebrew, hatred burning in his eyes. He raised his sword with both hands, prepared to cleave the life from Nagad, when a deep rumbling halted him.

Nagad spied a branch from a dead tree. Grasping it firm, he sprang to his feet and swung with force, the crude club crashing against the Philistine's temple.

He lurched, then staggered, reeling to his right beneath the violent blow.

The earth groaned, a deep and dreadful sound rising from the dust, followed by a crack like the splitting of stone. And though the day stood clear, thunder rolled, low and brooding, as though the heavens did rage against them.

A rushing wind rose like a cry from the deep, sweeping through the ranks with a fury more ancient than storm. The sky rent from end to end; the air recoiled. The fissure of heaven ruptured; a long, resounding boom struck against the firmament, shaking the very foundation of the world.

Ekwesh lifted his gaze, yet the sky bore no cloud.

"How can this be?"

Remembering the conflict, he turned to seek his foe.

Confusion surged on every side—yet the Hebrew was gone.

The peal of thunder broke, awful and consuming, filling the plain with oracles severe. With startling utterance, His dreadful voice of denunciation rang upon the Philistines. So terrible was the sound that they were overcome before Israel.

Charioteers fought to steady their steeds, but the horses reared and fled the field, panic seizing them as they trampled their own men, dashing and rumbling below. Those not crushed beneath the wheels were sprayed with blood, flecked with the gore of the dead.

Bewilderment clouded their eyes until they could no longer discern friend from foe. In fear and dismay, they struck out, raging wildly against an enemy unseen.

Nagad leapt back as horses bolted through the ranks, severing him from the Philistine who but moments before had been poised to take his life. Through the chaos, Helek came upon him as he sank to one knee, clutching his wounded side. The young Hebrew rushed forward, grasping him by the shoulders to lend support. Nagad winced in pain.

"A shadow has fallen over me," spoke Nagad through clenched breath.

"Shadows are but a passing thing," replied Helek, patting his arm. "Look—see how they fly."

Before his eyes, Nagad beheld the ruin of Philistia. "I need a sword."

Rising with effort, he took up the blade of a fallen soldier.

"We will teach you to fear the Lord," declared Nagad as resolve gave him strength.

Thunder resounded once more as the heavens quaked and the earth shook with the sounds of confused battle, proclaiming that Yahweh was a refuge for His people. No one—no, not one—could stand against this God, who spoke with the voice of power, reigning upon His throne in the heavens.

"Who is like the Lord our God,"[82] cried a Hebrew soldier in awe, as the truth became clear: the Chosen, forfeited as they were, had now been purchased.

Rising beyond the wreck of battle, Tiphcar, the glorious captain, yet aflame with the eternal fire, lifted his voice above the din.

"To me! Reform the line!"

The Chosen of God, with renewed purpose, gathered to their captain, falling into ordered ranks of ardent men. Tiphcar looked with favor at the eager host.

---

[82] Psalm 113:5

Raising his sword into the thunderous sky, he cried aloud, "Awaken, sword and spear, for now is the time! By the might of God, after me!"

The Hebrews rushed forward into the bewildered Philistine forces, running upon them, casting themselves against their foe anew, and smote them with the edge of the sword. Into the fray charged Nagad. With his new-claimed blade, he felled two men in a single sweep.

Beneath the troubled sky, the ruin of Philistia raged, borne downward by the hand of judgment.

"Rise up! Stand firm—or be forever lost!" cried Seren, raising his sword atop his majestic steed, making one final, desperate effort to rouse his men to battle.

Aware of the new onslaught, Ekwesh surged forth and cast his weapon into the path of a soldier who barred his way.

Then his eyes were opened.

Pale and dreadful was the scene before him.

There stood Phicol, clutching the end of Ekwesh's blade, the point buried deep within his gut. Blood welled and spilled from his mouth. Their eyes met—and in that moment, horror struck a heavy blow. Ekwesh looked upon his friend, and for a breathless pause, all noise fell away. His trembling hands grasped the hilt that had wrought his friend's doom. He neither cried out nor turned away, for the weight of that stroke was beyond all reckoning. And in that silence, his fate was sealed.

"No!" breathed Ekwesh in a whisper.

Phicol seized his arm, his chest heaving with the struggle to speak. "Do not fret, my brother, for even the best of friends must part."

"No!" cried Ekwesh, clinging to him as he lowered him to the ground.

Then Lukka was at his side, placing his great hand upon Phicol's brow. "Go now, my brother. Enter into peace and rest upon your bed."

Ekwesh grasped Phicol with both hands. "I will not let you go! I will not lose you!"

Phicol reached for the last of his breath. "My dear Ekwesh—I am already lost."

Gasping, Phicol's body shuddered and drew taut as his eyes looked long into his smitten companion who had delivered him up to death. As Ekwesh strove to hold him, the struggle fell away. Strength left his frame, and his eyes emptied. Cradled within Ekwesh's arms, he breathed his last.

"Ekwesh, there is no time. The tide has turned against us. Come—we must flee," spoke Lukka, lifting him from Phicol's side. "We are not safe. Confusion reigns, and death closes in on every side."

Like a man riven from his own soul, he stood, torn from the side of his fallen companion. He did not move, though Lukka urged him. From the hollow of his chest, a cry broke forth. "Am I to suffer this? Does not death release me from the icy grip of despair?"

He cared not for his life. Shock washed over him, numbing limb and will. His soul was dredged from him, ripped from his being, banished. And so he tarried there, blind to the chaos about him, of the soldiers falling at the hands of the Israelites.

"Come," spoke Lukka, drawing Ekwesh with force, compelling him bodily from the field of battle.

With great strain, he caused his legs to move, resistance unavailing against Lukka's great mass. Retreating with weary effort, Ekwesh trudged as one beneath the sea, grief a dragnet about his feet. Together they passed in sorrow from the trampled plain to a refuge beyond the fray.

"I am hemmed in and undone," spoke Ekwesh in anguish, "yet death has abandoned me."

"The hour is evil. The loss, regrettable," spoke Lukka thoughtfully. "But much is lost in war."

Ekwesh lifted his gaze to the heavens, his eyes hollow and dark. "I am pierced through with many sorrows. I have suffered the loss of all things. My strength fails, wasted by grief, and I slip away as an evening shadow."

Falling into depths innumerable, the loss irreparable, Ekwesh shuddered and dropped to his knees. He bowed his head, clenching his eyes shut, then loosed a long and broken breath.

At length, he raised his head and looked into Lukka's eyes. "I am ruined, for I have looked into the eyes of the One True God, and He has slain me!"

The toil of battle continued till the day broke, and the shadows fled the field. It was a frightful thing to behold, as the army of Philistia turned upon itself, stricken with panic. As fear took hold of them, the war machine disintegrated into a wild mass of fugitives fleeing from the face of the enemy.

From Mizpah, the men of Israel went forth in pursuit, driving back the Philistines and smiting them beneath the broad meadows of Beth-car, the House of the Lamb.

The sun sank in naked majesty over the western hills. Reforged, the people of Israel stood upon the brink of a new order. His wounds having drained him of strength, Nagad halted to rest upon the crest of a hill, with Helek ever by his side. There, he watched the triumphant Chosen of God pursue the remnant of Philistia's army as they fled toward the mountains in the west. Samuel approached the weary soldiers and took his place upon the rise, looking out across the field of victory with a quiet confidence in his gaze.

Nagad glanced toward the prophet and spoke, "The Lord has fought for Israel this day."

Samuel raised an eyebrow as he took in Nagad's battered and bloodied form. "Indeed, He has delivered us from dire distress."

As the wounded warrior moved to descend and join his brethren in pursuit of the Philistines, the prophet's hand came to rest upon his shoulder, staying his step.

"It is enough," he spoke. "Let them go, for justice must also be tempered with mercy. They have had enough; they shall trouble us no more."

Seren looked upon the ruin of his army and swore, "O! Idols foul!"

Rearing in his saddle, he turned and rode swiftly away. When he reached camp, he quickly dismounted and entered Seranim's tent. There he found his lord seated upon his throne, his head low, cradled in his hand. As Seren approached, his sovereign raised his head, dragging his hand down his face.

"What fell words do you bring me?" bade Seranim.

"It is over," replied Seren. "All is lost."

"As we have heard, so we have seen," quoth Seranim. "Ah, my soul is quenched within me."

He rose and walked over to a basin of water and washed his hands. Gazing at his reflection, Seranim lamented, "I have lived too long. It is Time's tragedy that I should live to see the fall of Philistia."

Pausing, he drew a deep breath and turned to face Seren. "I have been cursed with long life, for death is a gift from the gods."

CHAPTER 31

THE STONE OF EBENEZER

"Who is this who follows you so mindfully?" Tiphcar's voice came to Nagad from afar, though he could not find him.

Turning, Nagad made to answer, but the sight of Orach, smiling back at him, stilled his tongue.

"Have you ever been north, *Na'ar*? Have you ever seen the beauty of the land about the Sea of Chinnereth? You must go there."

"Orach?"

Orach placed a hand upon Nagad's shoulder. Still smiling, he spoke again, "Kings came, they fought; the kings of Canaan fought. By the waters of Megiddo thundered the horses' hoofs."

"I do not understand," spoke Nagad, as one lost in a mist. He closed his eyes and shook his head, striving to lift the veil that hung upon his mind.

Casting his gaze toward Orach, he found he had faded from view. Reeling about in desperation, he searched the emptiness.

"Orach?"

"Aye."

A hand reached from behind and laid firm upon his shoulder. Nagad looked back and beheld Orach once more.

"Are we fighting for the right reasons, Orach?"

"*Na'ar*, do you still walk in the shadows? Come—enter into the light, and doubt no longer."

Light shone brightly, blinding Nagad for a moment. As his sight returned, he found himself alone in an empty field. A low mist lay heavy upon the ground, swirling about his feet.

"Orach! Leave me not alone!"

"Do not fret, *Na'ar*," came Orach's voice, soft within his ear. "I will walk with you."

The vision dimmed, and Nagad became aware of the bed's warmth. Enrapt in the cover's quiet hold, he lingered, content to remain as he was. Yet rest fled from him, his thoughts troubled by what had passed.

Was it but a dream?

Yet the message tarried, feeling no less real for its strangeness.

A faint light filtered through the high lattice of the window, falling in pale bands across the chamber floor. All was quiet, peaceful after the thunder of war.

"Nagad."

Orach's voice came to him once more. Slowly, he opened his eyes and saw the blurred image of one leaning over him.

The line between dream and waking is not easily marked.

Then it came to him. Helek it was before him.

"You have caused us great worry for a time," spoke Helek, in his familiar jovial manner. "It is good to see you awake, my friend."

Attempting to sit, Nagad winced at the discomfort that gripped his whole frame. Every limb, every sinew ached from the strain of battle.

"Easy now." Helek rose to his feet. He placed an arm about Nagad's back and slid a cushion behind him, easing him down with care. When he saw that Nagad rested well, propped as he was, Helek returned to his seat.

Nagad sat in silence, studying the face of his friend, lost in memory. Though the wounds of war had begun to be covered over, re-clothed, the scars would not so easily mend. They would linger long after the battle had passed.

"Why do you gaze so fixedly upon my face?" Helek tilted his head slightly, a faint crease forming between his brows. "What is it you see?"

"You remind me much of your father."

"I never knew my father," said Helek thoughtfully. "He is but a faint memory from my childhood."

"He was a good man," Nagad replied, "and my friend."

How often his thoughts had turned to Orach of late. Each man sat in silence, lost in his own reflections.

Nagad looked about the room. There, resting upon a mat near the wall, lay his armor. Someone had cleaned and polished it, though the marks of battle remained, forever evident upon its surface.

"So, son, it seems this time it is you who lies upon the bed."

He lifted his gaze to meet the voice. Tiphcar it was who spoke as he entered the room. Beside him came Riyphah, her face alight with relief. She came to Nagad and slipped her hand into his, kissing his brow with tenderness. Then she settled upon the edge of the bed beside her husband. Nagad squeezed her hand tightly, forgetting his damaged knuckles.

Tiphcar walked over and patted Helek's shoulder, then allowed his hand to rest there. "Well done. You have executed the battle with skill and efficiency. We have been delivered out of our troubles, for the Lord has heard the cry of the righteous. The Lord is good, a stronghold in the day of trouble. He knows those who trust in Him."[83]

"So it is over, and all is well." Memory stirred as the shadow lifted from his mind.

Tiphcar nodded his head, *"Ken, Hodu Adonai Ki Tov!* The Lord is good."

He stepped to the bed and took Nagad by the arm. "But now, Samuel has summoned us all to meet with him outside upon the plain."

Nagad swung his legs over the side of his cot.

"Nagad, you are not well enough to go," Helek urged, concern in his voice.

"I have lain here long enough," came Nagad's quiet reply. "I will go where I am summoned."

Rising from his bed with no small pain, Nagad winced at the discomfort, yet hoisted himself up, Tiphcar supporting one arm and Riyphah, his wife, taking the other. Stiffly, he gathered his armor and, with their help, placed it upon his war-wracked frame. Lastly, he fastened his borrowed-blade about his girth and limped from the chamber, Tiphcar and Riyphah by his side. Helek followed close behind as they departed the place of healing and stepped out onto the field.

---

[83] Nahum 1:7

Mist rose from the dew-laden grass as the new light of morn washed over the empty plain. Once littered with the carcasses of the dead, now only the scars of battle remained disfiguring the field, gouged and charred, a lasting tale told of trouble. In silence, Riyphah slipped into the gathering that waited upon the high place of Mizpah.

Samuel stood smiling as the three soldiers joined him. He dipped his head, then turned and walked out across the plain, with all Israel following after, until he reached the center of the field. There, in the midst of the field of battle, between the lookout of Mizpah and the crag of Shen, a great standing stone had been set. Facing the people, Samuel lifted his hands to quiet the crowd.

> Come near, *Am Yisrael,*
> To hear and heed, O people of Israel!
>
> Once you walked in darkness,
> In the shadows you dwelt.
> New has the day arisen,
> And behold, the light you now see.
>
> Death ruled the region,
> But its dominion has passed away.
> For the dawn has come to the people,
> And the night has fled from the land.
>
> The sword of the Lord is filled with blood,
> For this is the day of His vengeance.
> It is He who has utterly destroyed them;
> He has given our foes to the slaughter.

"For forty years, the Philistines have oppressed our people. But now the invisible has been made visible. This battle was won by the Lord, not by Israel. Therefore, let him who thinks he stands take heed, lest he fall.[84]

"And so that all Israel will not forget that the Lord has fought for them, I place this memorial stone: a stone uncut by human effort,

---

[84] 1 Corinthians 10:12

a rude, unpolished stone, enduring, fashioned by the hand of God. A sure foundation, set upon the very scene of this victory, upon the heights down which the Philistines were hurled in their defeat. I name it *Ebenezer*, that is, the Stone of Help, for thus far the Lord has helped us."

With reverence, the people waited as the prophet of God spoke his heart. Then Samuel gestured with his outstretched hand toward the standing stone.

"When generations look upon this memorial stone, it shall stand as a dreadful reminder of what befell us when disobedience clouded the judgment of Israel, of the terrible defeat at Eben-Ezer, and the loss of the Ark.

"Then we will remember that without God, we can do nothing.

"We shall be reminded that when we turned back to Yahweh, He fought for us. We shall remember the victory wrought upon this very place. How, when all seemed lost, God intervened, routed the enemy from among us, and utterly destroyed them."

Thus spoken, Samuel passed among the people, sharing in their joyous return.

They exulted in the victory, made glad by their piety. And so Israel responded with renewed faith, seeking to walk in fealty to the Lord Most High.

Slowly, the people made their way back to Mizpah to celebrate the occasion of their restoration. Following after Samuel, they departed the field and entered into the city.

Yet Nagad lingered, unable to leave the place. Something stirred in his heart that caused him to pause. So he remained behind.

Tiphcar and Helek, seeing where he stood, turned back and came to his side, concern etched upon their faces.

"Come, Nagad," spoke Helek as he placed a hand upon his friend's shoulder.

"Yes, my son," agreed Tiphcar. "Return to your bed, for you are not yet wholly mended."

Shaking his head, Nagad smiled at his companions. "Leave me. I will come shortly. There is something I need to do."

"I will stay with you," offered Helek.

"No," returned Nagad gently, "please understand. This is something I must do alone."

Reluctantly, the two men left Nagad to tend to his task. Much had they shared together, and loath were they to part. Yet the two stalwart soldiers knew the heart of their friend, so with quiet compassion, they took their leave.

Nagad knelt down upon the cool earth, beneath the stone of Ebenezer, and he began to dig. The earth was cool upon his flesh. The musty smell of damp soil rose and filled his mind with memory.

With care, he drew the spearhead from his tunic. He looked upon it, touched the smooth surface, caressed it, and traced his thumb along the sharp edge. He heard the sound of a young girl's laughter, the joyful glee of her tender heart. A voice, bold and familiar, called out, *"Na'ar."* He saw father and mother embracing a small boy with chestnut hair, welcoming him home.

Home. He was home.

A tear tracked a path down his battle-scarred cheek. He brought the spearhead to his mouth and placed his dry lips upon its smooth surface and kissed it. Then, gently, he lowered it into the ground.

With slow deliberation, he swept the dirt over the spear-filled impression and buried his burden. He was free, free from the bondage that had long racked him. The heavy weight of vengeance ceased to have a hold on his heart. He let it go.

"Vengeance is the Lord's," he spoke softly.

Rising with difficulty, he brushed the soil from his hands. He looked to the heavens. Breathing deep, he took in the full measure of peace.

Renewed, Nagad turned and limped from the field, rejoining his brothers, glad to have the company of such good friends.

The storm within was stilled.

A wife awaited his unencumbered heart. Now he could give it fully, for he had opened himself to the future. The past he had left under a stone called Ebenezer.

And so the advancing tide of Philistine incursions was stemmed, and they came no more into the territory of Israel, for the hand of the Lord was against them.

The cities that had been taken by the Philistines were restored, from Ekron even to Gath; and Israel recovered its regions from the hand of the adversary.

Moreover, the Amorites withdrew their alliance with the Philistines, and there was peace, for a time, between Israel and the Amorites.

Yet a threat loomed, quickening to life, even at the birth of the new age, growing in the shadows, a silent murmur in the east. As the Chosen of God returned to their lives, as they passed by the Stone of Ebenezer, their memories grew short, and the lessons learned soon became dim.

Though but a vision through the fog, the threat enlarged over the distant hills, echoing off the mountains, trailing through the valleys, intercepting the light to cast a shadow, indistinct, upon the hearts and minds of Israel. And as it has always been with men, their thoughts soon forgot that which should have been recalled, for fear creeps into the hearts of men and distorts memory.

APPENDIX A – GLOSSARY

Altar of Incense – As a symbol of prayers offered up to Yahweh, incense was burned by the priest twice daily upon this golden altar. Its horns were also sprinkled with the blood of the sin offering.

Ark of the Covenant – Sacred chest where the Hebrews kept the two tablets containing the Ten Commandments; the symbol of God's presence; the throne of God on earth. Also called: Ark of God, Ark of the Testimony.

Balm of Gilead (*bam ov gil'-e-ad*) – A healing compound made from the resinous gum of a small evergreen tree, Commiphora gileadensis, of the family Burseraceae, known for its medicinal properties.

Conquest, the – The Israelites' migration into the land promised to Abraham by Yahweh and the conquest of the people of Canaan.

Day of Atonement – The holiest day for the Hebrew people and the only day on which the High Priest may enter the Holy of Holies. A day set aside annually for fasting and the atonement of the sins of the people. It was kept on the tenth day of the month Tisri, five days before the Feast of Tabernacles.

Dunam (*dûnăm*) – A unit of land area; forty standard paces in length and breadth; the amount of land that can be ploughed in a day; approximately 1,000 square meters.

Ebenezer (*eh'-ben haw-e'-zer*) – A memorial stone placed by Samuel near Mizpah after the battle to commemorate the divine assistance given to Israel in their great battle against the Philistines.

Ephod (*ay-fode'*) – Sacred vestment worn by the High Priest, resembling an apron, made of fine linen twined of gold, blue, purple, and scarlet, intricately embroidered in two parts fastened together at each shoulder by a large onyx clasp.

Holy of Holies – The innermost room of the Tabernacle where the Ark of the Covenant was kept.

Kalathos (*kal-a-thos*) – A shallow bowl with flat horizontal handles.

Kapporeth (*kap-po'-reth*) – The place of atonement; the mercy seat; the throne of Yahweh upon the lid of the Ark of the Covenant.

Kesitah (*ke-se'-ta*) – Pieces of money.

Mitre (*mi'-ter*) – Headdress most often worn for religious purposes.

Ostraca (*os'-tra-ka*) – Potsherds used as ballots when casting a vote.

Rhyton (*rhy-ton*) – An ancient drinking vessel in the shape of a horn, made of pottery or metal, with a base fashioned in the form of an animal.

Sledge – A threshing instrument embedded with sharp flints, used to separate grain from chaff. In The Stone of Ebenezer, it appears symbolically as an image of judgment, severing the holy from the profane.

Standing Stone – A vertical stone erected as a memorial to mark divine aid or covenant. In Israelite tradition, such stones bore witness to the acts of Yahweh. (See also: Ebenezer.)

Tent of Meeting – A sacred tent, a portable and provisional sanctuary where God met His people; resting place of the Ark of the Covenant prior to its capture by the Philistines. (See also: Tabernacle; Sanctuary.)

Urim and Thummim (*yū'rĭm, thŭm'ĭm*) – Sacred stones carried inside the breastplate of the High Priest of ancient Israel and used as an oracle to divine the will of God.

Yn 'dm (*yeen ah-dawm*) – A term found inscribed upon an ostracon outside a wine shop at an archaeological dig in Askelon, probably meaning *red wine*.

APPENDIX B – HEBREW TERMS

Abba *(ab-bah')* – Father.

Adon *(aw-done')* – Master, lord.

Al Tid'ag *(ahl tid-ahg')* – Do not worry.

Am Yisrael *(ahm' yis-raw-ale')* – People of Israel.

Attah *(at-taw')* – Now.

Avi *(ah-vee')* – My father.

Baruch shem Adonai *(bah-rookh' shehm ah-doh-nigh')* – Blessed is the name of Yahweh.

Barukh ata Adonai Eloheinu melekh ha'olam, Dayan ha'emet *(bah-rooch ah-tah ah-doh-noye eh-loh-hay-noo meh-lehch hah-oh-lahm – dai'-yahn ha-e'-met)* – Blessed are You, Lord, our God, King of the universe, the True Judge.

Bat Tziyon *(bat tsee-yone')* – Daughter of Zion.

Boker tov *(boh-kehr tohv)* – Good morning.

Calach *(saw-lakh')* – Forgive.

Ethanim *(ay-thaw-neem')* – Enduring; first month of the civil new year, corresponding to modern September–October.

Goren *(go'-ren)* – Threshing floor.

Ha'im tinas'i li *(ha-im' ti-nas-I li)* – Will you marry me?

Iyyar *(ee-yahr)* – The eighth month of the civil year, falling within April and May.

Ken, Hodu Adonai Ki Tov *(ken hoh-duh ah-doh-nigh' kee tohv)* – Give thanks to the Lord, for He is good.

Kohen *(ko-hayn)* – Priest.

Kohen Gadol *(ko-hayn gah-dohl')* – The high priest, or chief of the Kohanim; he alone may enter the Holy of Holies.

Laylah Tov *(lie'-lah tove)* – Good night.

Machol *(maw-khole')* – A round-dance.

Mechiah *(me-khee-ah)* – A great feeling.

Me'il Techelet *(meh-eel' te-khe'-let)* – Blue robe of the High Priest, worn beneath the ephod. Upon the hem were fastened, in alternating order, golden bells and pomegranates.

Miqreh *(mik-reh')* – Fate.

Na'ar *(nah'-ar)* – Lad.

Oren *(o'-ren)* – The tree of rebirth; ash or pine.

Refu'ah *(ref-oo-ah')* – To heal, make healthful; healing.

Reggah *(reh'-gah)* – Wait; in a moment.

Rofe *(roh-feh')* – Physician, doctor; one who heals.

Sar *(sar)* – Sir, captain, ruler.

Sarah (*saw-raw'*) – Noble lady.
Shapirit (*shah-pee-reet'*) – Dragonfly.
Shofet (*shoh-fet*) – Judge.
Todah (*to-daw'*) – Thank you.
Yatsa' (*yaw-tsaw'*) – Come out.
Y'hi ratzon mil'fanekha Adonai Eloheinu vei'lohei avoteinu (*yee-hee' raht-tsohn' meel-fah-neh'-khah ah-doe-nai' eh-loh-hay'-noo veh-eh-loh-hay' ah-voh-tay'noo*)– May it be Your will, Lord, our God and God of our ancestors.

APPENDIX C – PEOPLE

Aaron (*air-uhn*) – Light bringer; the first High Priest of the Israelites; a Levite who was the older brother of Moses and a prophet of God. (Exodus 4:14)

Abdon (*ab-dohn'*) – The tenth judge of Israel; son of Hillel the Pirathonite, buried in Pirathon in the land of Ephraim. (Judges 12:13)

Abimelech (*ab-ee-mel'-ek*) – Father of a king; son of the judge Gideon by his Shechemite concubine. He murdered his brothers to become king. His rule lasted three years, during which the city of Shechem was destroyed. Mortally wounded by a millstone dropped by a woman from a wall, he ordered his armor-bearer to kill him to avoid the shame of death at a woman's hand. (Judges 8:22–9:57)

Abinadab (*ab-ee-naw-dawb'*) – Father of nobleness; a Levite of Kirjath-Jearim, in whose house the Ark of the Covenant was placed after its return by the Philistines; father of Eleazar. (1 Samuel 7:1)

Abraham (*ab-raw-hawm'*) – Father of a great multitude; son of Terah and founder of the Israelites. After hearing the voice of God, he left Ur of Sumer and traveled to Canaan, where he entered into a covenant with Yahweh. (Genesis 12)

Achimiti (*ahkh-em-ee-tee*) – A brother is sent; attendant to Nasib, lord of Ekron.

Adonizedek (*ad'-oh-ni-zee-dehk*) – Zedek is Lord; King of Jebus who led a coalition of Canaanite kings against Joshua during the Conquest. He and all who followed him were utterly defeated by the Israelites. (Joshua 10)

Amalekite (*a-mal'-e-kīt*) – A semi-nomadic people descended from Amalek, the grandson of Esau. They inhabited southern Canaan and were frequent enemies of Israel. (Genesis 36:12)

Ammonites (*am-mone'-nahytz*) – A people descended from the incestuous union between Lot and his younger daughter. The Ammonites dwelt east of the Jordan River and were frequent adversaries of Israel throughout biblical history. (Genesis 19:36–38)

Amorites (*am'-o-rīts*) – Highlanders or hill men; one of the principal Canaanite nations. The Amorites east of the Jordan River are sometimes confused with the people of Ammon. (Numbers 13:29)

Amun (*ah-mūn*) – The hidden one; patron god of Thebes and Egyptian god of air and breath. *Amon.*

Anakites (*a-nah-kahytz*) – Descendants of Anak who dwelt in the south of Canaan near Hebron; said to be a mixed race of giant people. (Deuteronomy 9:2)

Asher (*aw-share'*) – Happy; the eighth son of Jacob and ancestor of one of the twelve tribes of Israel.

Asherah (*ash-ay-raw'*) – Groves; Canaanite fertility goddess and cohort of Baal, called "she who walks on the sea." *Ashdoda; Anoth.*

Azuri (*azh-er-ee*) – Attendant to Danuna, Philistine lord of Gath.

Azzuzath (*ah-zoo-zahth'*) – A soldier in the Philistine army who was at Ashdod.

Baal (*bey-uhl*) – Lord; Canaanite storm god, son of Dagon, cohort of Asherah; called "Rider of the Clouds," god of thunder, storms, and fertility. *Aliyan Baal, Baal Hadad, Athar-Baal, Baal-Zebul.*

Barak (*baw-rak'*) – Military commander who, with the prophetess Deborah, defeated the Canaanite army under Sisera. (Judges 4)

Benjamin (*ben-juh-muhn*) – Son of the right hand; youngest son of Jacob and Rachel, brother of Joseph (Genesis 35:18), and founder of one of the twelve tribes of ancient Israel.

Benjaminite (*ben'-ja-meen'it*) – People from the tribe of Benjamin.

Caphtor (*kaf-tore'*) – Captain; crown. Captain of the army of Philistia. Also the original homeland of the Philistines, believed to be in Asia Minor or Crete.

Cherethites (*ker-ay-thahyts'*) – Executioners; either Cretans or proto-Philistines.

Dagon (*daw-gohn'*) – A fish; Philistine god of agriculture and the earth, represented as half man and half fish. National god of the Philistines.

Dan (*dawn*) – A judge; fifth son of Jacob and founder of one of the twelve tribes of Israel.

Danuna (*dahn-oo-nuh*) – Lord of Gath and one of the Philistine pentapolis.

Deborah (*deb-o-raw'*) – Bee; a prophetess and judge of Israel who led the people to victory over the Canaanites. (Judges 4–5)

Denyen (*den-yen*) – One of the groups comprising the Sea Peoples; believed to be of Indo-European origin.

Ebed (*eh'-bed*) – Servant; servant to the priests Hophni and Phinehas.

Ekwesh (*ek'-wesh*) – A soldier in the Philistine army; one of the four companions who carried the Ark to Ashdod. A group of Bronze Age Greeks.

El (*'el*) – Deity; strength; Canaanite supreme god, considered father of all.

Eleazar (*el-aw-zawr'*) – God has helped.
    1. Son of Aaron and High Priest. (Exodus 6:23)
    2. Son of Abinadab, keeper of the Ark of God during its banishment. (1 Samuel 7:1)

El-Elohim (*'el e-loh-him*) – The name of God as eternal Creator and Judge of the universe.

El-Elyon (*'el 'elyon*) – The Most High God.

Eli (*ee-lahy*) – Ascension; descendant of Aaron through Ithamar; High Priest and Judge of Israel; guardian of Samuel. (1 Samuel 3)

Elkanah (*el-kaw-naw'*) – God has possessed; father of Samuel. (1 Samuel 1:1)

Elpaal (*el-pah'-al*) – God is maker; father of Shemed, a Benjamite. (1 Chronicles 8:12)

El Roi (*el ro-ee'*) – God who sees.

El-Shaddai (*el shad-dah'-ee*) – The Lord Almighty.

Ephraim (*ef-rah'-yim*) – Double ash-heap; "I shall be doubly fruitful." Second son of Joseph and founder of one of the twelve tribes of Israel.

Ephraimite (*ef-rah'-yim-ahyt*) – A person from the tribe of Ephraim.

Esha (*e'-shuh*) – Wife; the wife of Phinehas, son of Eli, who died in childbirth after the Ark of the Covenant was taken. (1 Samuel 4:19–22)

Etsah (*ay-tsaw'*) – Counsel, advice; the wise. An elder of Shiloh who has seen many days.

Gad (*gawd*) – Troop; seventh son of Jacob; founder of one of the twelve tribes of Israel.

Gadowl (*gaw-dole'*) – Elder; haughty. A member of the council of elders present during the battle of Aphek, in which the Ark of the Covenant was lost.

Gibeonite (*gib'-e-un-īt*) – Little hill; an inhabitant of Gibeon.

Gideon (*gid'-e-un*) – Hewer; youngest son of Joash from the Abiezrite clan, tribe of Manasseh. Fifth judge of Israel. Led the Israelites against the Midianites. *Jerubbaal*. (Judges 6–8)

Haddabar (*had-daw-bawr'*) – Counselor, minister; elder of Israel who spoke out against Gadowl after the Ark was taken by the Philistines.

Hannah (*han-naw'*) – Grace; mother of Samuel, wife of Elkanah. (1 Samuel 1:2)

Helek (*hay'-lek*) – Traveler; Hebrew soldier, son of Orach, who befriends Nagad during the battle of Mizpah.

Hophni (*hof-nee'*) – Fighter; pugilist; one of the two sons of Eli, the High Priest. By their scandalous conduct, he and his brother brought down a curse upon their father's house. (1 Samuel 1:3)

Israelites (*iz'-ra-el-ītz*) – Name given to the Hebrew people, comprising twelve tribes descended from the line of Jacob. Also called: Children of Israel; *Hebrews; Chosen of God.*

Issachar (*yis-saw-kawr'*) – There is recompense; ninth son of Jacob; founder of one of the twelve tribes of ancient Israel.

Jabin (*yaw-bene'*) – Whom God observes; king of Hazor, whose general Sisera was defeated by Barak. (Judges 4:2)

Jacob (*ja'-kub*) – Supplanter; son of Isaac, grandson of Abraham, and father of the twelve patriarchs of Israel. (Genesis 25)

Jael (*ja'-el*) – Mountain goat; wife of Heber the Kenite. She killed Sisera by driving a tent peg through his temple as he lay sleeping. (Judges 4–5)

Jehovah (*je-ho'-va*) – The personal name of God.

Jeshurun (*yesh-oo-roon'*) – Upright one; a symbolic name for Israel representing her ideal character.

Joshua (*jeh-ho-shoo'-ah*) – God is salvation; leader of the Israelites during the Conquest and settlement of Canaan. He led the covenant renewal at Mount Ebal and Mount Gerizim. (Joshua 1)

Judah (*joo'-da*) – Praised; fourth son of Jacob; founder of one of the twelve tribes of ancient Israel.

Kahan (*kaw-han'*) – To act as a priest, or minister in the priest's office; priests at Beth Shemesh.

Kamar (*kaw-mawr'*) – Priest; to yearn, be kindled; a priest at Shiloh who carried the Ark to Eben-Ezer.

Kohanim (*ko-han-eem*) – Priests descended from the line of Aaron.

Kohath (*keh-hawth'*) – Assembly; the second of Levi's three sons and progenitor of a family within the tribe of Levi.

Kuwl (*kool*) – To seize, sustain, endure; one of the priests who traveled from Kirjath-Jearim to retrieve the Ark at Beth Shemesh.

Laqach (*law-kakh'*) – To take and carry along; one of the priests who traveled from Kirjath-Jearim to retrieve the Ark at Beth Shemesh.

Levi (*le'-vi*) – Joined to; third son of Jacob; ancestor of the priestly tribe of Levi.

Levite (*le'-vit*) – Of the tribe of Levi; set apart by God for His service.

Lilith (*lee-leeth'*) – Night hag; a female demon said to dwell in desolate places, attacking children.

Lukka (*look-ah*) – A soldier in the Philistine army; one of the four companions who carried the Ark to Ashdod. Also a region in western Anatolia.

Manasseh (*men-ash-sheh'*) – Causing to forget; eldest son of Joseph; founder of one of the twelve tribes of ancient Israel.

Maryannu (*mahr-yuhn-noo*) – Chariot; term used in ancient texts for chariot-using warriors.

Merneptah (*mer-ne-ptah*) – Pharaoh of Egypt (1225–1215 BC); son of Ramses II.

Mitinti (*me-ten-ee*) – A Philistine diviner who joined the coalition to determine the fate of the Ark.

Moloch (*mo'-lok*) – Mountain devil; soldier in the Philistine army who fought at the battle of Aphek. Also a Canaanite god said to require child sacrifice.

Mot (*mawat*) – Canaanite god of death and infertility; Baal's rival.

Nagad (*naw-gad'*) – Messenger; a Hebrew soldier who brought word to Eli of the loss of the Ark following the battle of Aphek (*Eben-Ezer*). (1 Samuel 4:12)

Naphtali (*naf-taw-lee'*) – Wrestling; my struggle; fifth son of Jacob and founder of one of the twelve tribes of ancient Israel.

Nasib (*nah-sib*) – Lord of Ekron and one of the Philistine pentapolis.

Nine Bows – An ancient Egyptian term representing the enemies of Egypt.

Orach (*o'-rakh*) – Way, path; traveler, wayfarer. Hebrew soldier of the tribe of Naphtali who befriends Nagad the Benjaminite; father of Helek.

Palastu (*pal-es-too*) – People of Philistia; a Philistine diviner who met with the coalition to decide the fate of the Ark.

Peleset (*pe-lé-set*) – See Philistines; part of the Sea Peoples.

Phicol (*fahy-kol*) – Great, strong; soldier in the Philistine army and one of the four companions who carried the Ark to Ashdod.

Philistines (*fil'-is-tēnz*) – Aegean people who settled ancient Philistia around the 12th century B.C., and waged war against the Israelites. *Peleset; Sea People.*

Phinehas (*pee-nekh-aws'*) – Mouth of brass.

    1. One of Eli's sons, slain in the battle of Aphek for contempt of sacred matters. (1 Samuel 1:3)

    2. Son of Eleazar and grandson of Aaron, who earned an everlasting priesthood for his zeal. (Exodus 6:25)

Pidray (*pid-rey*) – Girl of light; Canaanite goddess of light and mist, daughter of Baal.

Polchan (*pol-khawn'*) – Service, worship; priest at Shiloh who carried the Ark to Eben-Ezer.

Ptah (*ptah*) – Egyptian god of craftsmen and architects, worshipped at Memphis.

Qabal (*kaw-bal'*) – To take, receive, accept; priest who traveled from Kirjath-Jearim to retrieve the Ark at Beth Shemesh.

Qatan (*kaw-tawn'*) – A priest at Shiloh who carried the Ark to Eben-Ezer.

Qatsiyr (*kaw-tseer'*) – Harvest, harvesting; man of Beth Shemesh.

Qorban (*kor-bawn'*) – Offering, oblation; priest of Levi, a Kohen of Beth Shemesh.

Ragaz (*raw-gaz'*) – Tremble, quake, rage, quiver; a man of Beth Shemesh.

Rapha (*raw-faw'*) – High, tall, heroic; called "the tall," a conscript in the Philistine army.

Reuben (*reh-oo-bane'*) – Behold a son; eldest son of Jacob; founder of one of the twelve tribes of Israel.

Riyphah (*ree-faw'*) – A grain or fruit (for grinding); daughter of Beth Shemesh who witnessed the Ark's return. Wife of Nagad the Benjaminite.

Samson (*sam'-sun*) – Like the sun; Nazarite from the tribe of Dan whose strength was legendary. Betrayed by Delilah; judged Israel for twenty years. (Judges 13-16)

Samuel (*sam'-u-el*) – God has heard; last judge of Israel and a prophet of Yahweh. (1 Samuel)

Saph (*saf*) – Tall; soldier in the Philistine army.

Seranim (*ser-uh-nihm*) – Lord; lord of Ashdod, within the Philistine pentapolis.

Seren (*ser-uhn*) – Captain; captain of the Philistine army who led the siege against Shiloh.

Sharath (*shaw-rath'*) – To minister, serve; priest at Shiloh who carried the Ark to Eben-Ezer.

Shekelesh (*shek-uhl-esh*) – Lord of Gaza within the Philistine pentapolis. In history, part of the combined force of Libyans and Sea Peoples that attacked Egypt.

Shekresh (*shek-resh*) – Priest of Ashdod.

Shemed (*shee-med*) – Son of Elpaal who built Lod. (1 Chronicles 8:12)

Shemesh (*sheh'-mesh*) – Canaanite sun-goddess.

Sherden (*shur-dehn*) – Lord of Askelon within the Philistine pentapolis; part of the confederation of Sea Peoples.

Simeon (*sim'-ē-on*) – Heard; second son of Jacob; founder of one of the twelve tribes of ancient Israel.

Sisera (*sis-er-uh*) – Battle array; general of Jabin, slain by Jael. (Judges 4–5)

Tallay (*tal-ley*) – Dewy; girl of rain; daughter of showers; Canaanite goddess of dew.

Teresh (*teh'-resh*) – Firm, solid; soldier in the Philistine army; one of the four companions who carried the Ark to Ashdod. Part of the confederation of Sea Peoples from the Anatolian coast.

Tiglath (*tig-lath'*) – Adviser to Seranim, lord of Ashdod.

Tiphcar (*tif-sar'*) – Captain; officer in the Hebrew army during the battle of Aphek. Rescued from Shiloh by Nagad.

Tiphlah (*tif-law'*) – Folly, silly, foolish; an Ephraimite in Beth Shemesh who, drunk with wine, violated the Ark.

Tjeker (*che'-ker*) – One of the Sea Peoples.

Weshesh (*weh'-shesh*) – One of the Sea Peoples.

Yagowr (*yaw-gore'*) – Fearful; a citizen of Beth Shemesh.

Yahweh (*yah-way*) – YHVH; the name of God; "I Am."

Yam (*yawm*) – Sea; Canaanite sea god, jealous of Baal's power.

Zaqen (*zaw-kane'*) – Elder; Hebrew elder present at the council of Eben-Ezer. Opposed the use of the Ark in battle.

Zebulun (*zeb'-u-lun*) – Exalted; tenth son of Jacob; founder of one of the twelve tribes of ancient Israel.

APPENDIX D – PLACE NAMES

Adullam (*ad-ool-lawm'*) – Justice of the people; a royal Canaanite city in the Valley of Elah.

Aijalon River (*a'-ja-lon riv-er*) – The river that flows through the Aijalon Valley from the central hills of Judah to the Great Sea.

Aijalon Valley (*a'-ja-lon val-ee*) – Field of deer; the northernmost valley of the Shephelah, just south of the Plain of Sharon. Though appointed to the tribe of Dan, but under frequent pressure by Philistine invasion, they surrendered the valley. Here, Joshua commanded the sun and moon to stand still; *Valley of Aijalon; Vale of Aijalon.*

Amurru (*ah-moor-roo*) – Amorite kingdom located in the region of Lebanon, north of Israel.

Aphek (*ay-fehk*) – Strength; a rapid torrent; a stronghold near the source of the Yarkon River in the Sharon Plain, northeast of Joppa. The Philistine armies encamped here during the battle in which they captured the Ark of the Covenant.

Arumah (*ar-oo-maw'*) – I shall be exalted; lofty. A place south of Shechem, home of Abimelech.

Arzawa (*ahrz-uh-wah*) – A region and federation of local powers in western Anatolia.

Ashdod (*ash'-dod*) – Powerful; a major Philistine city between Gaza and Joppa, about three miles from the Great Sea. It was a center of worship for Dagon and one of the capital cities of the Philistine pentapolis.

Ashdod-Yam (*ash'-dod yawm*) – Ashdod-on-the-Sea; the harbor near Ashdod on the Great Sea.

Askelon (*ash-kel-one'*) – The fire of infamy; I shall be weighed. A coastal city on the Great Sea between Joppa and Gaza; a capital of the Philistine pentapolis.

Azekah (*az-ay-kaw'*) – Dug over; a town in the Elah Valley west of Gath, where Joshua defeated the coalition of Amorite kings led by Adonizedek.

Beth-car (*bayth kar*) – House of the ram; place of the lamb; southwest of Mizpah.

Beth Horon (*bayth kho-rone'*) – House of hollowness; Upper and Lower Beth Horon, two towns in the hills of Ephraim built by Sheerah, daughter of Beriah.

Beth Shemesh (*bayth sheh'-mesh*) – House of the sun; named for the Canaanite sun-goddess Shemesh. A Levitical town on the border of Judah and Dan, located on the south side of the upper Sorek Valley. The Ark of God returned here after being taken by the Philistines; *Har-cherec.*

Canaan (*key-nuhn*) – Lowland; the land between the Jordan River, the Salt Sea, and the Great Sea, promised to Abraham by Yahweh and conquered by the Israelites under Joshua; *Promised Land.*

Carchemish (*kar-kem-eesh'*) – Fortress of Chemosh; a Hittite capital northeast of Israel, on the Euphrates River.

Djahi (*da'-hey*) – The Egyptian term for southern Retenu (Canaan), stretching from Askelon to Lebanon and inland as far as Gennesaret.

Eben-Ezer (*ehb'-ehn-ee'-zehr*) – Stone of help; the place where the Israelites camped before the battle of Aphek, in which the Ark of the Covenant was captured.

Ebenezer (*ehb'-ehn-ee'-zehr*) – The stone of help; the memorial stone set by Samuel near Mizpah to commemorate Yahweh's aid in Israel's victory against the Philistines.

Ein Seilun (*ah'-yin sey-ley-oon*) – A spring located outside the city of Shiloh.

Ein Seridah (*ah'-yin seer-ee-dah*) – A spring located outside the city of Zeredah.

Ekron (*ek-rone'*) – Torn up by the roots; the northernmost of the Philistine capital cities, located in the lowlands of Judah. It was home to the famed sanctuary of Baal-Zebul.

Elah River (*ay-law' riv-er*) – An oak; the river that flows through the Elah Valley. In later history, David selected stones here before facing Goliath.

Elah Valley (*ay-law' val-ee*) – Valley of the oak; a triangular plain on the western edge of the Judean hills, near Socoh and Azekah. It was within this valley that David slew Goliath; *Valley of Elah; Vale of Elah.*

Ephraim (*ef-rah'-yim*) – Double ash-heap; doubly fruitful. A mountainous territory in central Canaan, west of the Jordan and between Manasseh and Benjamin.

Eshtaol (*esh-taw-ole'*) – Entreaty; a town in the Shephelah north of Beth Shemesh. Childhood home of Samson.

Field of Joshua – A field in Beth Shemesh where the Ark came to rest after being returned by the Philistines. (1 Samuel 6:14)

Gath (*gath*) – Winepress; one of the five royal Philistine cities, situated near Israelite territory at the end of the Elah Valley.

Gaza (*gah-zuh*) – The strong; the southernmost of the five Philistine cities, situated on the Great Sea; *Azzah.*

Gennesaret (*ghen-nay-sar-et'*) – A garden of riches; a town of Naphtali near the Sea of Chinnereth, famed for beauty; *Chinnereth.*

Gezer (*gheh'-zer*) – Portion; a Canaanite city between lower Beth Horon and the sea, located on Ephraim's border.

Gibeah (*gheh'-bah*) – Hill, height; a city in Benjamin overlooking Kirjath-Jearim. The Ark was brought here upon its return from Philistia.

Gibeon (*gib-ee-uhn*) – Hill-city; a Levitical city in the tribal territory of Benjamin.

Great Sea – The inland sea west of the Philistine coast and north of Egypt. Later known as the Mediterranean Sea; *Western Sea.*

Har-cherec (*har-kheh'-res*) – The house of the sun; another name for Beth Shemesh.

Hatti (*hat-ee*) – The land of the Hittites.

Hebron (*he'-brun*) – A community; alliance; Levitical city south of Jebus.

Heshbon (*hesh-buhn*) – Intelligence; a Levitical city east of the Jordan, on the border of Gad and Reuben.

Hormah (*hor-maw'*) – Devoted to destruction; broken rock. A city also known as "the city of palms," located in the Valley of Zephathah; *Zephath.*

Isle of Caphtor (*kaf-tore'*) – The ancestral homeland of the Philistines, believed to be the island of Crete.

Jabneel (*yab-neh-ale'*) – God builds; a coastal town eleven miles south of Joppa.

Jabneh-Yam (*yab-neh'yawm*) – Harbor of Jabneel, located on the Great Sea near Askelon.

Jebus (*jee-buhs*) – Threshing place; Canaanite city later renamed Jerusalem.

Jericho (*jer'-i-ko*) – Its moon; city north of the Salt Sea. The first city conquered by the Israelites during the Conquest; *City of Palms*.

Joppa (*jop'-a*) – Beautiful; chief seaport of Judea, located on the Great Sea and held by the Philistines.

Jordan River (*jawr-dn riv-er*) – Descender; river in northern Canaan flowing south through the Sea of Chinnereth to the Salt Sea.

Jordan Valley (*jawr-dn val-ee*) – The low-lying land along the Jordan River forming part of the Great Rift Valley; stretches from the Sea of Chinnereth to the Salt Sea.

Judean Mountains (*joo-dee-uhn moun-tnz*) – North-south mountain range extending west and east of Jebus (Jerusalem). These hills divide the coastal plains from the Jordan Valley and contribute to regional climate variation; *Judean Hills*.

Kanah Ravine (*kaw-naw' ruh-veen*) – Reed; narrow, steep-sided valley formed by the erosion of the Kanah River, which flows from Tappuah into the Great Sea. It marks the boundary between Ephraim and Manasseh.

Kirjath-Jearim (*keer-yath' yeh-aw-reem'*) – City of woods; Gibeonite town on the border of Benjamin, northeast of Beth Shemesh. The Ark of the Covenant was brought here and placed under the care of Abinadab the Levite.

Kishon River (*kee-shone' riv-er*) – Winding; a seasonal stream beginning at Mount Tabor and flowing through the Jezreel Valley to the Great Sea. Site of Sisera's defeat.

Lebanon (*leb-aw-nohn'*) – Whiteness; majestic mountains north of Canaan, famous for cedar forests and snow-covered peaks. A symbol of beauty and strength in Scripture.

Lebonah (*leb-o-naw'*) – Frankincense; a town in the territory of Ephraim, northwest of Shiloh.

Libnah (*lib-naw'*) – White; associated with the storax tree. A Levitical city in Judah on the eastern edge of the Elah Valley, bordering Philistia.

Lod (*lode*) – Travail; a city southeast of Joppa in the Plain of Sharon, founded by Shemed, son of Elpaal, a Benjamite.

Makkedah (*mak-kay-daw'*) – Place of shepherds; Canaanite city captured by Joshua and assigned to Judah. Near the cave where Joshua executed five enemy kings.

Mareshah (*mar-ay-shaw'*) – Crest of a hill; a fortified city in the Shephelah of Judah, near the Zephathah River, south of Beth Shemesh.

Megiddo (*me-gid'-o*) – Place of troops; strategically located along the Way of the Sea, guarding the pass through the Carmel Ridge overlooking the Jezreel Valley.

Mizpah (*miz'-pa*) – Watchtower; a sacred site in Benjamin near the Valley of Aijalon. Here Samuel led the people in a national repentance. After routing the Philistines, he set a memorial stone called Ebenezer near Mizpah.

Mountain of Kenkeny (*ken'-kuh-nee*) – An unknown location within the Baal Cycle.

Mountain of Shen (shane) – Tooth; crag; a tooth-shaped projection across the plain from Mizpah.

Mount Ebal (mont ay-bawl) – Stony; one of the twin mountains flanking the valley of Shechem, forming the northern side. One of the highest peaks in Canaan.

Mount Gerizim (mont gher-ee-zeem') – Cuttings off; the southern counterpart to Mount Ebal, enclosing Shechem Valley. One of the highest peaks in Canaan.

Mount Tabor (mont taw-bore') – An isolated peak in northern Canaan, at the eastern edge of the Jezreel Valley. Barak defeated Sisera's army here.

Naioth (na'-yoth) – House of instruction; located in Ramah, the school of the prophets established by Samuel.

Philistia (fi-lis'-tē-a) – Land of sojourners; coastal region in southwestern Canaan, home of the Philistines.

Pirathon (pir-aw-thone') – Princely; a city in Ephraim, home of Abdon, the tenth judge of Israel.

Plain of Sharon (pleyn ov shaw-rone') – Fertile coastal plain north of Joppa and west of the central mountains, renowned for beauty.

Promised Land – See Canaan.

Qode (kohd) – An area in Syria or Asia Minor known for trade with Egypt.

Ramah (raw-maw') – Height, high place; also called Ramathaim-Zophim. Birthplace of Samuel, located in the Benjamite Plain opposite Gibeon.

Saphon (suh–fuhn) – The holy mountain where the goddess Anath built a temple to Baal.

Sea of Chinnereth (kin-ner-oth') – Harp-shaped; early name for the Sea of Galilee; *Lake of Gennesaret; Sea of Tiberias.*

Shechem (shek-em') – Shoulder; city located in a narrow valley between Mount Ebal and Mount Gerizim. Abraham received Yahweh's covenant here; Joshua later renewed Israel's covenant.

Shechem Valley (shek-uhm val-ee) – Valley lying between Mount Ebal and Mount Gerizim; *Vale of Shechem.*

Sheol (sheh-ole') – The underworld, the abode of the dead.

Shephelah (shef-ay-law') – Low place; the rolling foothills between the Judean highlands and the coastal plain. This borderland marked the contested zone between Israel and Philistia.

Shiloh (shī-lō) – Tranquil, secure; a meeting place and sanctuary for the Israelites, and the site of the Tabernacle where the Ark of the Covenant was kept until its capture by the Philistines. Both city and sanctuary were destroyed following the battle of Aphek.

Shiloh Valley (shī'-lō val-ee) – The valley surrounding the ancient city of Shiloh, where the men of Benjamin lay in wait for the daughters of Shiloh, seizing them to be their wives; *Valley of Shiloh; Vale of Shiloh.*

Socoh (so-ko') – Bushy; a town in the Shephelah, situated between Adullam and Azekah.

Sorek River (*so'-rek riv-er*) – Choice vines; a river within the Sorek Valley, forming part of the border between the Philistines and the territory of the Hebrew tribe of Dan.

Sorek Valley (*so'-rek val-ee*) – Nachal Soreq; the valley of the choice vine, a crescent-shaped valley in the Shephelah between Zorah and Ekron; *Valley of Sorek; Sorek River Valley.*

Stone of Abel (*stohn ov aw-bale'*) —— Meadow; the name given to the great stone in Joshua's field at Beth Shemesh, upon which the Ark of the Covenant was set when it was returned from the Philistines (1 Samuel 6:18).

Syria (*sir'-i-a*) —— The land lying to the northeast of Phoenicia.

Taanach (*tah-an-awk'*) – Sandy; a city in northern Canaan, four miles south of Megiddo. It is mentioned in the song of Deborah (Judges 5:19).

Tappuah (*tap-poo'-akh*) – Apples; a town in the hill country of the tribe of Judah, northwest of Shiloh.

Two Rivers – The Tigris and Euphrates.

Way of the Sea – The main road running north–south through the coastal plain; later called the Via Maris, and also known as the Way of the Philistines.

Yarkon River (*yahr-guhn*) – A swampy river supplied from the hill country of Ephraim and flowing into the Great Sea. Its headwaters are at the fortress city of Aphek.

Zephath (*ze'-fath*) – Watchtower; a Canaanite city in the Valley of Zephathah, renamed Hormah by the Israelites.

Zephathah River (*zef'-a-tha riv-er*) – Watchtower; a river flowing through the Valley of Zephathah, north of Mareshah.

Zephathah Valley (*zef'-a-tha val-ee*) – A valley in western Judah near Mareshah; *Valley of Zephathah; Vale of Zephathah.*

Zeredah (*zehr'-ih-duh*) – Ambush; change of dominion; a city in the hill country of Ephraim, north of Beth-Horon.

Zorah (*tsor-aw'*) – Hornet; birthplace of Samson; a town on the crest of a hill overlooking the Valley of Sorek in the low country of Judah, allotted to the tribe of Dan.

Zuph (*zuhf*) – Honeycomb; a district in Benjamin, northwest of Jebus.

REFERENCES

Appendix A

"Day of Atonement." *Easton's Bible Dictionary.* 1897. Accessed February 6, 2015. http://dictionary.reference.com/browse/day%20of%20atonement.

"Dunam." *WordSense.eu Dictionary.* Accessed February 6, 2015. http://www.wordsense.eu/dunam/.

Brown, Driver, Briggs, Gesenius Hebrew Lexicon. Keyed to the *Theological Word Book of the Old Testament.* Public domain. Accessed February 6, 2015. http://www.biblestudytools.com/lexicons/hebrew.

Easton, M. G. *Illustrated Bible Dictionary.* 3rd ed. New York: Thomas Nelson, 1897. Public domain. http://www.biblestudytools.com/dictionary.

Orr, James, ed. *International Standard Bible Encyclopedia.* 1915. Public domain. http://www.biblestudytools.com/encyclopedias.

— "Balm."

— "Gilead (1)."

— "Mitre."

— "Ostraca."

"Yn 'dm." *Jewish Magazine,* March Purim 2001 Edition. Accessed February 6, 2015. http://www.jewishmag.com/41mag/ashkelon/ashkelon.htm.

Appendix B

Chayim, Orach. "Jewish Phrases." *Headcoverings by Devorah.* 2003–2013. Accessed February 12, 2015. http://www.headcoverings-by-devorah.com/Hebrew_Phrases.htm.

Brown, Driver, Briggs, Gesenius Hebrew Lexicon. Keyed to the *Theological Word Book of the Old Testament.* Public domain. Accessed February 12, 2015. http://www.biblestudytools.com/lexicons/hebrew.

Orr, James, ed. *International Standard Bible Encyclopedia.* 1915. Public domain. http://www.biblestudytools.com/encyclopedias.

— "Iyyar."

"Jewish Blessings." *JewishYellow.com.* Accessed February 12, 2015. http://jewishyellow.com/jewish_blessings.html.

Appendix C

Brown, Driver, Briggs, Gesenius Hebrew Lexicon. Keyed to the *Theological Word Book of the Old Testament.* Public domain. Accessed February 12, 2015. http://www.biblestudytools.com/lexicons/hebrew.

Easton, M. G. *Illustrated Bible Dictionary.* 3rd ed. New York: Thomas Nelson, 1897. Public domain. http://www.biblestudytools.com/dictionary.

Orr, James, ed. *International Standard Bible Encyclopedia.* 1915. Public domain. http://www.biblestudytools.com/encyclopedias.

— "Philistines."
— "Philistia."
— "Adonibezek."
— "Amalek; Amalekite."
— "Amorites."
— "Dan (1); Dan, Tribe of."
— "Elohim."
— "Elyon."
— "El Roi."
— "El Shaddai."
— "Ephraimite."
— "Gibeonites."
— "Gideon."
— "Children of Israel."
— "Jacob (1)."
— "Jael."
— "Jehovah."
— "Judah (1)."
— "Levi (1)."
— "Levites."
— "Moloch."
— "Samson."
— "Samuel."
— "Shemed."
— "Simeon (2)."
— "Zebulun."

Appendix D

Brown, Driver, Briggs, Gesenius Hebrew Lexicon. Keyed to the *Theological Word Book of the Old Testament.* Public domain. Accessed February 12, 2015. http://www.biblestudytools.com/lexicons/hebrew.

Orr, James, ed. *International Standard Bible Encyclopedia.* 1915. Public domain. http://www.biblestudytools.com/encyclopedias.

— "Aijalon."
— "Aphek."

— "Ashdod."
— "Beth-Shemesh."
— "Caphtor; Caphtorim."
— "Eben-Ezer."
— "Gibeah."
— "Hebron (1)."
— "Jericho."
— "Joppa."
— "Megiddo; Megiddon."
— "Naioth."
— "Philistia."
— "Shiloh (1)."
— "Sorek, Valley of."
— "Syria (1)."

BIBLIOGRAPHY

Anderson, Robert. 2011. "Egypt: Who Were the Sea People." *Tour Egypt*, June 9. Accessed on or before 2011. http://www.touregypt.net/featurestories/seapeople.htm.

Baldwin, Joyce G. 1988. *The Tyndale Old Testament Commentaries: I & II Samuel.* Bristol: Inter-Varsity Press.

Barkat, Amiram. 2005. "Dig Backs Biblical Account of Philistine City of Gat." Haaretz, August 9. http://www.haaretz.com/culture/arts-leisure/dig-backs-biblical-account-of-philistine-city-of-gat-1.166315.

Benner, Jeff A. 1999–2012. "Numbers 6:24–27." *Ancient Hebrew Research Center.* http://www.ancient-hebrew.org/40_numbers1.html.

———. 1999–2012. "The Aaronic Blessing." *Ancient Hebrew Research Center.* http://www.ancient-hebrew.org/12_blessing.html.

Beyer, Bryan, and Bill T. Arnold. 2002. *Readings from the Ancient Near East: Primary Sources for Old Testament Study.* Grand Rapids, MI: Baker Academic.

Breasted, James Henry. 2001. *Ancient Records of Egypt: The Twentieth Through the Twenty-Sixth Dynasties.* Vol. 4. Chicago: University of Illinois Press.

Bunimovitz, Shlomo, and Zvi Lederman. n.d. "Beth-Shemesh: A Biblical Border City between Judah and Philistia." *Tel Aviv University.* Accessed 2010. http://www.tau.ac.il/humanities/archaeology/projects/proj_bethshemesh.html.

Campbell, Antony F. 2003. *Forms of Old Testament Literature: 1 Samuel.* Vol. VII. Grand Rapids: Wm. B. Eerdmans Publishing.

Campbell, Lee. n.d. "Idolatry in the Ancient Near East." *Xenos Christian Fellowship.* Accessed 2008. http://www.xenos.org/classes/papers/aneidola.htm.

Clarke, Adam. 2002. *Commentary on 1 Samuel.* Concord, NC: Wesleyan Heritage Publications.

David M. Howard Jr. n.d. "Philistines." http://people.bethel.edu/~dhoward/articles/articles2/PhilistinesPOTW.htm.

de Geus, C. H. J. 2003. *Towns in Ancient Israel and in the Southern Levant.* Bondgenotenlaan, Leuven: Peeters.

Deffinbaugh, Bob. 1995–2012. "The Fellowship Offering." *Bible.org.* http://bible.org/seriespage/fellowship-offering-leviticus-31-17-711-34-195-8-2229-30.

———. 1995–2012. "The Hands of Dagon and the Hand of God (1 Samuel 5:1–7:17)." *Bible.org.* Accessed 2008. http://bible.org/seriespage/hands-dagon-and-hand-god-1-samuel-51-717.

DeMaris, Richard E. 2008. *The New Testament in Its Ritual World.* New York: Taylor & Francis.

Dothan, Trude, and Seymour Gitin. 2012. *Tel Miqne–Ekron: Summary of Fourteen Seasons of Excavation 1981–1996 and Bibliography 1982–2012*. Jerusalem: W. F. Albright Institute of Archaeological Research and Hebrew University.

Dowling, Mike. 2011. "The Black Death." *Mr. Dowling.com*, August 8. http://www.mrdowling.com/703-plague.html.

Easton, Matthew George. 2008. "Samuel." In *Easton's Bible Dictionary* (1897). Wikisource. Accessed 2009. http://en.wikisource.org/wiki/Easton's_Bible_Dictionary_(1897)/Samuel.

"Ekron: A Philistine City." 2012. *Jewish Virtual Library*. http://www.jewishvirtuallibrary.org/jsource/Archaeology/Ekron.html.

Geikie, Cunningham. 1888. *The Holy Land and the Bible: A Book of Scripture Illustrations Gathered in Palestine*. Vol. II. New York: James Pott & Co.

Guzik, David. 2004–2010. "David Guzik's Commentary on 1 Samuel." *Enduring Word Media*. http://www.enduringword.com/commentaries/09.htm.

Henry, Matthew. 1838. *An Exposition of the Old Testament*. Vol. II. Philadelphia: Haswell, Barrington, and Haswell.

———. 1997. *Matthew Henry's Concise Commentary on the Whole Bible*. Nashville: Thomas Nelson Publishers.

Heyhoe, Kate. 1994–2012. "Olive Oil History." *The Global Gourmet*. Accessed 2009. http://www.globalgourmet.com/food/egg/egg0397/oohistory.html.

Josephus. 1930. *Jewish Antiquities, Volume I: Books 1–3*. Cambridge: Harvard University Press.

Khalaf, Salim George. 1996. "The Baal Cycle." *Ethnic Origin, Language and Literature of the Phoenicians*, September. http://www.phoenicia.org/ethnlang.html.

Kitto, John. 1859. *Daily Bible Illustrations: Being Original Readings for a Year, on Subjects from Sacred History, Biography, Geography, Antiquities, and Theology*. New York: Robert Carter & Brothers.

Knapp, Christopher. 2006. *Life and Times of Samuel the Prophet*. Believers Bookshelf, Incorporated.

Mills, Watson E. 1997. *Mercer Dictionary of the Bible*. Macon: Mercer University Press.

Orr, James. 1915. *The International Standard Bible Encyclopaedia*. Vol. II. Chicago: The Howard-Severance Company.

Reilly, Jim. 2000. "Chapter 6: Sea Peoples & Natural Disasters." *Displaced Dynasties*. Accessed 2008. http://www.displaceddynasties.com/volume-3.html.

Rich, Tracey R. 2006. "Sukkot Blessings." *Judaism 101*. http://www.jewfaq.org/prayer/sukkot.htm.

Robinson, Edward. 1865. *Physical Geography of the Holy Land*. London: John Murray.

"Shechem." 2002–2011. *JewishEncyclopedia.com*. http://www.jewishencyclopedia.com/articles/13522-shechem.

"Shechem." 2012. *BiblePlaces.com*, October 3. http://www.bibleplaces.com/shechem.htm.

Smart, Anthony E. 1999. "El." *Encyclopedia Mythica*, December 26. http://www.pantheon.org/articles/e/el.html.

Souvay, Charles. 1908. "Dagon." In *The Catholic Encyclopedia*. Vol. 4. Edited by Kevin Knight. New York: Robert Appleton Company. Accessed December 4, 2012. http://www.newadvent.org/cathen/04602c.htm.

Stewart, Robert Laird. 1899. *The Land of Israel*. New York: Fleming H. Revell Company.

"The Black Death, 1348." 2001. *EyeWitness to History*. http://www.eyewitnesstohistory.com/plague.htm.

"The Black Death: Bubonic Plague." 2011. *TheMiddleAges.net*. http://www.themiddleages.net/plague.html.

Thomas, Kelly Cheyne, and John Sutherland Black. 1901. *Encyclopædia Biblica: A Dictionary of the Bible*. 2 vols. London: Adam and Charles Black.

ABOUT THE AUTHOR

Susan Van Volkenburgh is an award-winning author of Christian fiction and nonfiction, celebrated for her lyrical style and immersive reimaginings of biblical history. Her *Trilogy of Kings Saga* brings ancient Scripture to life with depth and spiritual resonance; the first edition of the opening volume, *The Stone of Ebenezer*, received the Grand Prize in the New Look Writing Contest sponsored by WestBow Press and HarperCollins.

Shaped by personal loss, Susan began her literary journey after the death of her father in the September 11, 2001 attacks. Her experience of grief and faith is poignantly explored in *Silent Resolve and the God Who Let Me Down (A 9/11 Story)*.

With experience as an oncology nurse, homeschool educator, and member of the gospel music group *The Van Martins*, Susan draws from a well of empathy and understanding, crafting stories that resonate with emotional and spiritual truth. She formerly owned *Savannah's Meadow*, a treehouse bed and breakfast that embodied her love of beauty, wonder, and rest—a spirit that continues to shape her storytelling. Now living in Northeast Texas, she and her husband raise Texas Longhorns, embracing a life rooted in tradition, perseverance, and grace.

Through every page, Susan invites readers into timeless narratives of hope and transformation—stories where the broken find purpose, and the past speaks into the present with eternal significance.

Susan would love to hear from you. Visit her online.
www.susanvanvolkenburgh.com

OTHER BOOKS BY
SUSAN VAN VOLKENBURGH

SILENT RESOLVE AND THE GOD WHO LET ME DOWN
(A 9/11 STORY)

TRILOGY OF KINGS SAGA
BOOK I: THE STONE OF EBENEZER
BOOK II: THE ANOINTED ONE
BOOK III: BY THE WATERS OF EN GEDI

www.ingramcontent.com/pod-product-compliance
Lightning Source LLC
Chambersburg PA
CBHW021228060726
47590CB00005B/1677